INHERITANCE
of
LION HALL

ALSO BY CORINA BOMANN

Butterfly Island

The Moonlit Garden

Storm Rose

The

INHERITANCE

of

LION HALL

CORINA BOMANN

TRANSLATED BY MICHAEL MEIGS

AMAZON **CROSSING**

Text copyright © 2018 by Ullstein Buchverlage GmbH, Berlin
Translation copyright © 2021 by Michael Meigs
All rights reserved.

Previously published as *Agnetas Erbe* by Ullstein Buchverlage GmbH in Germany in 2018. Translated from German by Michael Meigs. First published in English by Amazon Crossing in 2021.

Published by Amazon Crossing, Seattle

www.apub.com

Amazon, the Amazon logo, and Amazon Crossing are trademarks of Amazon.com, Inc., or its affiliates.

ISBN-13: 9781542016841
ISBN-10: 1542016843

Cover design by Shasti O'Leary Soudant

Printed in the United States of America

INHERITANCE

of

LION HALL

PART I

1913

1

A dazzling brilliance filled the room. I opened my eyes, thinking for a moment I was in my old room at Lion Hall, but the vision that greeted me in that first groggy moment wasn't elegant plaster molding. It was a long crack across a water-stained ceiling. The darker stains were already there when I'd moved in two years earlier; the lighter ones were recent, added by flooding in the apartment upstairs. Walls in Stockholm's university district were like sponges.

That was why students paid such modest rents. My mother would have pronounced the place shabby and far beneath my status, but here, I was free to live my own life. I was taking art classes, even though the upper crust disdained such studies. What did I care about a few stains on the ceiling?

A chilly breeze caressed my face. I looked around and saw the newspaper had peeled away from the damaged window. Again. The bottom panes had been broken long before by a boy whose antics in the street below had included flinging a rock. My landlord hadn't bothered to repair it. And I couldn't, because I'd have had to ask my father for money. He and I'd had another furious argument during the Christmas holiday. I hadn't been back to Lion Hall since. I hadn't written home either.

I knew full well that my parents disapproved of my lifestyle. Two years earlier, I'd petitioned the court to be declared independent and free of their guardianship, and they took it as an affront. They'd been expecting me to marry before I turned twenty-five. I didn't. Instead, I took charge of my own life and made it perfectly clear that I had no intention of following the path they'd set out for me.

I wouldn't inherit the estate anyway. It would go to the first-born male heir, my brother, Hendrik, the model child. Count Thure Lejongård, my father, never tired of holding him up to me as an example. Hendrik was older and I wasn't male, so I had the right to live my life as I pleased. My women friends and I were firmly of that opinion, in any case, and we expressed it at every opportunity.

One feature of the room I'd chosen for my new life was the sharp, persistent odor of turpentine. Its penetrating smell dominated the milder aromas of varnish and oil paint. Those smells never dissipated entirely, even when I wasn't painting. I had no idea who the previous tenant of this room had been, but the next would know her predecessor had been a painter.

Michael stirred at my side. His mass of reddish-blond hair came into sight between the pillows, followed by his squinting face. He opened one eye and then the other, then shut them tight to block out the sunshine. "Why are you up so early?"

Laughter swirled through me like bubbles through sparkling water.

I reached for that tangle of hair. It was thick and as soft as a kitten's fur. I loved to plunge my fingers into it, especially when he buried his head between my thighs.

"Past nine," I said. "We really should have been up a long time ago."

He looked at me and held out both arms. "Says who?"

Some suffragettes were man-haters who'd have been repulsed by a man's attempt to embrace them. But not me; I liked it. I realized my potential when we frolicked in bed. Michael had been my only lover for the past year, and I couldn't imagine life without him. We'd probably get married once he finished his law studies. Perhaps it was odd that I'd fought for my independence and now was considering marriage, but the idea warmed my heart. I was sure Michael wouldn't object to my painting. After all, he'd had no misgivings about falling in love with a campaigner for women's rights.

"I grew up in a proper home. The order of the day was discipline and good conduct!"

"Oh really?" Michael reached out to caress my neck and then slowly slid his hand down to explore my body. His lingering kiss drove my parents' admonitions out of my mind.

The throbbing between my thighs was irresistible. I adored making love first thing in the morning. The ecstasy of our embraces gave me strength for the day ahead.

A hammering at the door interrupted us. I tensed, and Michael stopped what he was doing. He glanced at the door and turned to me with a puzzled expression. "Are you expecting someone?"

His face was flushed with passion, and I'd have preferred to keep at it, but I couldn't imagine who might be pounding on my door so early in the day.

"Miss Lejongård? Are you there?" The knocking resumed, even more insistent. "I have a telegram for you. It's urgent!"

A telegram?

"Just a moment! I'm coming!" I gave Michael an apologetic look.

"Must you?" he murmured. He pulled me close and kissed my throat. I wanted so much to nestle in his arms under the warm blanket, but I rolled away and climbed out of bed. The cold bite of March air woke me instantly; unfortunately, it quenched my passion as well. I grabbed my robe, pulled it on, and belted it. I went to the door.

A uniformed postman met my eyes a little sheepishly. "Good morning! Excuse the intrusion, but I was told to deliver this as soon as possible."

I accepted the slim envelope and signaled the postman to wait. I went to the chest of drawers where I always kept a few coins, then returned to press ten cents into his palm, and shut the door. The flimsy envelope felt terribly heavy in my hand.

"So what is it?" Michael was sitting up, bare-chested and leaning back against the pillows. Posed like this, his skin shimmering in the golden sunlight, he looked like an artist's model. Many local artists would have loved to paint him.

"We are about to find out." I slipped a finger under the flap and opened the envelope.

Whatever could Mother want? I unfolded the telegram and gasped in alarm.

FATHER AND HENDRIK IN ACCIDENT
+STOP+ COME HOME IMMEDIATELY
+STOP+ MOTHER +STOP+

An accident?

I stood petrified. My pulse surged, and for a moment I told myself this had to be a trick to force me to return home.

But Stella Lejongård was always deadly serious when it came to family matters.

Michael got up. "Tell me!"

I couldn't say a word. I was immobile, my eyes fastened on that cryptic text. The transcribed words blazed on the page.

Only when he put his arm around my shoulder did I awake from my trance.

"My . . . my father," I stammered. "He and my brother . . . There has been an accident."

"Where? How?"

"No idea. Maybe something with the horses . . ."

My head was spinning. Father and Hendrik were excellent horsemen. It seemed impossible for both to have been injured in a riding accident. How badly were they hurt? It must be serious; otherwise, Mother would never summon me. The sheet of paper slipped from my fingers. Michael bent and picked it up.

"I have to go home," I whispered.

"Good God!" Michael muttered. He took my hand, a hand so numb it seemed to belong to someone else. "Can I do anything? Should I go with you?"

"No," I said as I tried to get my thoughts together. "I . . . I have to take a train. Or a coach."

"A coach would take too long. But there is probably a train for Kristianstad today."

I nodded. I had to hurry, but I was paralyzed. More than anything, I wanted to crawl back under the covers and pretend the telegram hadn't come.

But I had no choice, none at all.

Finally, I managed to take a step.

"Can I help you?" Michael asked.

I shook my head. This was something I had to face alone. As for taking him to meet Mother—God forbid!

My numbness turned into violent trembling as I pulled open the warped wardrobe door and tried to pick my clothes. Anything would do. I didn't care what Mother would say. I'd left my best clothing at Lion Hall, and she'd disapprove of whatever I wore. I grabbed a black blouse and then flung it down. I couldn't take my eyes off it. A wave of fear washed over me. *No black*, I told myself. *Black is for mourning.* Taking something black would be bad luck, so I pushed the blouse into the back corner of the wardrobe. *An accident*, I said to myself. *It was just an accident. They were injured, but they're still alive. Mother would have told me if one of them was dead.*

I dressed feverishly. The fabric rubbed unpleasantly against my skin. The winter coat hung heavily over my shoulders. I packed a valise, my hands still shaking.

I shut the bag and turned to Michael, who was watching me, wrapped in his robe. He spread out his arms. "Come here." He pulled me close and buried his face in my hair. "I am at your side, you hear?" he whispered in my ear. "No matter what you must face, I am with you. I will be sending thoughts your way."

"You're a dear," I replied. "Thanks."

His pledge deserved a better response, but I couldn't find the words. Despite all that Michael meant to me, the telegram had turned me back into the Lejongård girl required to remain chaste until her parents chose an acceptable husband. That broke my heart. I disengaged reluctantly and turned to pick up my bag.

"Agneta," I heard him say behind me, "will you come back?"

I stopped. I'd heard Michael's inevitable query whenever I left for Lion Hall. I'd always tossed it off with a carefree "Yes!" but this time my mind was elsewhere. Of course I'd come back, but I had no way of knowing when.

"As soon as I can. I promise!" I blew him a kiss as I left the apartment.

I was greeted by the fresh smells of spring—for once not polluted by the stink of urine from the nearby doorways where men relieved themselves after leaving the taverns. The temperance unions were having little apparent success.

I strode quickly down the street. On that Monday morning, the Norrmalm neighborhood of wide streets and classic architecture was full of activity. Workers and travelers headed for the central train station pushed past the many students on their way to class.

That Monday, I was supposed to attend a seminar in the Royal Academy of Fine Arts, but now my daily routine had become irrelevant, and I groped my way through a mental fog. I was aware only of the weight of my valise and the uneasy feeling in my belly. When would the train be departing? Would I have time to send Mother a telegram?

Fate alters one's life in astonishing ways. I hadn't had a single thought of my parents' estate the day before. Now I could think of nothing else. Suddenly Lion Hall haunted me with its sounds and scents, its sunny days and bitter arguments, and all the vivid images I couldn't get out of my mind.

"Agneta!"

I stopped and turned.

Marit rushed up to me. She'd lifted the hem of her green skirt to run, and I caught a flash of her long underwear. Her brown, perpetually battered little boots were splashed with mud. A knit scarf was wound around her neck. "My dear, are you deaf?" she gasped. "I've been running after you forever!"

As usual, Marit was exaggerating. We were only a couple of hundred yards from the front door of my building.

I dropped my bag to hug her. "Sorry! I was distracted. I'm going to the train station. A family matter."

"So you won't be with us outside the dean's office?" Marit looked disappointed. She organized our demonstrations with single-minded zeal, procuring material for banners and marshaling supporters. That day, we were supposed to protest proposals to limit the number of women enrolled at the university. "I thought you weren't on very good terms with your family."

"I'm not, but something has happened to my father and my brother. Mother sent a wire summoning me home immediately."

Marit put a hand to her mouth. "That's horrible! Did she say what happened?"

"No. But she wouldn't have contacted me unless it was serious."

"Oh, I'm so sorry." She threw her arms around me. "Can I do anything?"

"I don't think so, but thanks. I'll contact you as soon as I know more."

"Yes, please. I'll pray for your father and your brother."

Marit almost never attended church because the institution was doing nothing to secure equal rights for women. This made her offer of prayers even more meaningful. I wished I could take her with me for support.

"Say hello to the others for me." I released her from my embrace. "Tell them I'll keep my fingers crossed for the dean's decision."

"Don't worry about that now," Marit responded. "It's family before anything else. Though I have to admit we'll miss you. When I remember the hard time you gave Professor Svensson . . ."

"Thanks." I hugged her again, pressing her to my heart, then grabbed my bag. It seemed even heavier than before.

Marit waved. "All the best, and take care of yourself!"

I walked past the beautiful home of the Royal Opera. On other days I often stopped to admire it, but today I was intent on getting to the station as quickly as possible.

Clouds of smoke hung heavy over Stockholm. A blast from a steamer resounded in the harbor, followed by the whistle of a locomotive. Sweden had prospered over the many decades since it had embraced political neutrality. Even the condition of women had improved slightly. At the age of twenty-five, we were allowed to petition the courts for independence—if we were unmarried. And only a few years earlier, the Riksdag, our national parliament, had changed the law to allow women to retain inherited property rather than ceding it to their husbands. Those were important victories, but we still hadn't achieved our greatest goal, the right to vote, which Finland had granted its female population a full seven years earlier. Norway was likewise making progress. But not Sweden. Politicians pretended to be deaf, but they were aware of us. Our fight would continue.

The movement had already had some success with the Royal Academy of Fine Arts. Anna Nordlander had been admitted in 1866 as one of the first woman students. Granted, the efforts of some students and artists to establish an "Opposition Union" in favor of more sweeping reform hadn't succeeded, but increasing numbers of women were allowed into the academy. Some conflict was inevitable, but every initiative advanced our struggle for freedom.

My face and back were soaked with perspiration by the time I finally reached the station. Even so, I was glad I'd taken my heavy coat. The hint of spring in the March air was deceptive.

A turbulent mass of people surged in all directions before the classic white facade. Here and there, a hat or a cream-colored suit jacket stood out from the crowd. Horse-drawn carriages rolled forward in a queue to deliver more passengers. I wondered for a moment how all these people managed not to trample one another.

My painting of the train station the previous year had earned me a blistering reprimand from my professor. I knew Andersen worshipped Van Gogh, and I'd sought to imitate the Dutch painter's style. That had been a mistake. The professor had rounded my easel, the eyes of all my classmates upon him as he tilted his head from one side to the other. He scratched his chin, narrowed his eyes, and addressed me. "A fine job!"

I was stupid enough to think he was actually about to praise me.

"Really fine . . . for a copyist!" His expression went so dark, I felt as if the sun had disappeared. "However, I do not believe it is the mission of this university to train students to produce forgeries. If that is your ambition, I will insist you be expelled immediately."

Andersen's roar echoed through the studio. My classmates' mocking looks pierced me. Few of them sympathized. Andersen's seminar was attended mostly by men, and almost all of them shared the professor's view that the kitchen, bedroom, and nursery were the only appropriate places for women.

The professor read my thoughts.

"And before you lecture me with the opinions of your precious little suffragette friends," he went on, now really in a rage, "I can assure you that, were you a man, I would have physically thrown you out of this room. When I want to see a Van Gogh, I travel to Paris. In this studio, I want to see who *you* are! And whether you have enough talent to be my student!"

I stared at the professor, realizing the enormity of my earlier mistake. Why had I talked back to Andersen last time? What had I been thinking?

I felt tears coming, but I didn't want them to see me blubbering. The male students would certainly have howled with laughter. I considered what my mother would have said and done in such a situation, and instantly my self-pity turned to scorn.

Andersen was probably expecting tears. Instead, he got the most furious glare I was capable of.

Pushing that memory out of my mind, I went into the station's waiting room and caught sight of the huge clock. Only an hour had passed since I'd received the telegram. A long queue stood before the ticket window. I had no choice but to join it. My head ached. Crowd noises echoed against the vaulted ceiling, blending in an incomprehensible, thundering roar. There'd been a time when I'd found this urban rush of sound invigorating, especially compared to the silence that prevailed on my family's estate. This was the noise of the world, and it represented freedom. But today I found it disturbing, almost unbearable.

The shrill whistle of an arriving train distracted me. More people streamed into the waiting room. Some were wearing coats of loden wool, like mine, while others were wrapped in expensive furs. A woman with an enormous feather hat caught my eye. My mother had dozens of hats like that. I didn't care much for pomp, and I liked even less that style of head covering. Those hats, heavy and expensive, served mainly to conceal the person beneath.

"Miss?"

I spun around. The queue had moved forward, and it was my turn.

"Yes, hello. I wish to purchase a ticket to Kristianstad. When is the next train?"

"Half an hour," he replied. "One way?"

I agreed without thinking it over. I'd promised Michael I'd come back as soon as possible. But when would that be? I knew I couldn't return until everything was sorted out. And just then I couldn't afford to spend money on a return ticket I might not use.

The ticket agent gave me an odd look and quoted the price. I pushed the money across the counter, picked up the ticket, and walked away. There was just enough time to send Mother a telegram.

2

I gazed moodily out the train window and recalled a time years before when I'd feared for my parents' lives. I was only twelve. They'd traveled to France, but their announced return date came and went. Two days later we'd still heard nothing. The estate was in an uproar.

Miss Rosendahl, now our housekeeper, was Mother's chambermaid back then. She was a stolid, placid, self-contained person, but that day she broke down and wept for her mistress.

I was worried too, though not as distraught as Miss Rosendahl. My brother, Hendrik, was quite composed, telling me they'd probably stopped off somewhere for a visit. If they'd sent a telegram, he said, it had simply been misrouted. He shrugged and walked away.

I tried to distract myself by spending time at the foals' pen and wandering the pastures, but Miss Rosendahl's tears were a clear sign. Hendrik and I were orphans. Some stranger would be appointed to oversee our upbringing.

Back in my room, I stared out the window, imagining every possible catastrophe—until a coach came up the drive. My parents' coach! My heart almost burst. I saw them climb out and felt relief such as I'd never experienced.

They were back at last, the royal couple of my childhood kingdom. I always did my best to win an expression of my mother's love, but I always failed. She saw me as a sort of doll to play dress-up with. She expected me to keep quiet, and that was hard. In contrast, my father was generous with his affection—while I was still a child, at least, ignorant of his grown-up problems. We would go riding together, and at home, he often carried me on his shoulders. He made up bedtime stories of knights and bandits for me.

Relations with my parents took a turn for the worse as soon as I graduated from the Östermalm Secondary School for Girls in Stockholm. My parents expected me to marry as soon as possible and furnish them with grandchildren. But no acceptable suitors appeared, not even after my debut at court. My mother was quite dissatisfied with all the candidates, and my father foresaw a dismal future for me. Neither was remotely aware I wanted a life quite different from the one they'd imagined. I wanted to study, to see something of the world, to frequent art exhibitions. I wanted a wider perspective, I wanted to fill my mind with knowledge, and above all I wanted to experience new things. And I was determined I would choose my own husband. The rupture was inevitable, so I wasn't too concerned when it came. After all, my brother was there to inherit Lion Hall. My parents had assumed I would give up my freedom, surrender my name, and leave for some other manor.

And now . . .

I silently cursed my mother. She could at least have given me some notion of what had happened and how the two of them were doing. Alone in my compartment, I tried concentrating on the scenery. Stray sunbeams filtered through the dense canopy of trees along the railway line. Forests had always excited my imagination. I'd dreamed of elves and trolls, of a magic world dotted with enchanted clearings.

The train emerged from the forest and rolled past immense fields where dirty snow still lingered. Within weeks, the rounded hills would be carpeted in green and gold. In Skåne province, the breadbasket of Sweden, the estates were as famous as the landscape. Some of the landowners were counts, while others were landed gentry. But all were important for Sweden, and they were united in most of their demands: when they'd wanted trains, they'd gotten them. I could imagine how my grandfather must have campaigned for this very line long before I was born.

The horizon glowed red with the setting sun as the train pulled into Kristianstad. Not many passengers got off. I pulled my valise down from the luggage rack and disembarked from the train. An icy wind stung my cheeks. Winter hadn't given up yet.

I looked around and found no one waiting for me on the platform. Had my telegram not arrived?

I huddled inside the station until I finally got impatient and made my way to the exit, where the ticket booth was still lit. I carried my valise down the stairs. When I emerged, I heard the clip-clop of approaching horses. Our familiar dark-red coach jolted down the street, a lantern dangling next to the coachman. Mother had sent someone after all.

Old August the coachman pulled on the brake and climbed down. He doffed his cap. "Ah, there ye are, gracious miss." His thick white hair was tousled. "Such a long time it's been!"

"Only three months!"

"An eternity for an old man." He took my valise. "Where is the rest of yer baggage?"

"In Stockholm, of course!" Alarmed by his question, I tried to smile.

"Ah! If ye wish, I can arrange for it to be picked up and sent here."

What had my mother told this poor man? That I was moving home? She couldn't be serious!

"How are my father and my brother?" I asked. The horses' warm breath condensed into swirling clouds.

"I cannot tell ye, gracious miss. Sorry!"

I frowned. "You can't tell me because you don't know, or . . ."

"Yer mother says I mustn't discuss it." August wore a grave expression. "She wants to inform ye in person."

"Are things that bad?"

The coachman pressed his lips together. He didn't need to say anything. I saw it in his face.

"Can you at least tell me what kind of accident it was? Were they riding?"

"Ye will see in good time," August said dispiritedly. He opened the door for me.

The coach set off, swaying and jolting as it went.

My stomach cramped and my head ached. What if the worst had come to pass? Why hadn't Mother at least come to the station to tell me? I couldn't imagine her playing the ministering angel at the bedsides of my father or my brother. Stella Lejongård was content to leave the care of the sick to physicians and nurses.

After an hour's drive, the manor house appeared ahead of us. The sun was down, leaving a red glow along the horizon that was enough for me to make out the heavy stone walls around the manor. The huge, elegant iron gate with the lion's head had served in earlier times to keep out thieves and revolutionaries. Now it stood wide open.

The coach continued along a drive lined by bare linden trees. In summer, their crowns would grace the drive with the shade of a leafy ceiling. Bees would hum, and the scent of honey would fill the air. But now there was none of that. A flock of crows perched in the bare branches. A strange odor tainted the air. I couldn't identify it. That unnerved me.

The white walls of the manor gleamed in the gathering dusk. Every window in the lower floors glowed.

The sight aroused a strange sensation in me. On one hand, I was still tormented by fear and uncertainty; on the other, those windows radiated peace and warmth. It wasn't the estate itself that had driven me away. Its lush meadows and towering forests, horse barns and stalls, and even the white manor house had always comforted me. They hadn't judged me.

I'd learned every corner of that ancient mansion as I hid both from my governess and from my mother. When we were little, Hendrik and I used to huddle together, making up stories. Perhaps that was when I decided to devote myself to art, to painting or perhaps to writing.

I suddenly recognized the strange odor, and the knowledge struck me like a blow. It was the acrid odor of burned wood. One of the hay barns had burned when I was little, and the wind had carried the smoke to the manor. A foul smell had lingered for days, even though the maids set out sachets of lavender everywhere.

Had there been a fire? I saw no sign of one from the coach. The lights of the manor dominated the evening.

August finally rounded the circle to the front door. I didn't wait for the coach to come fully to a stop. I tore the door open and leaped down as soon as August called "Ho!" to the horses. I tripped and nearly fell but caught myself and ran up the steps. The door was locked at night, so I rang the bell.

After a moment, Father's majordomo, Arno Bruns, appeared. He was in his late fifties. His hair, once black, was now almost entirely silver. His face was square, his eyes were as brown as coffee beans, and his eyebrows were bushy. As a child, I'd been afraid of him. He and Miss Rosendahl headed up the staff and zealously saw to the welfare of our family.

He greeted me with a slight bow. "Good evening, gracious miss. I am pleased you have arrived safely."

"Thank you, Bruns," I replied. "Where is my mother?"

"In the gracious master's bedroom. I will escort you."

I'd have preferred otherwise, but everything in this house was done according to the rules, even upon the return of the prodigal daughter.

We climbed the thickly carpeted stairs in silence. Given that it hadn't done any good to ask August, I expected no information from Bruns. His face was completely blank. He'd lived in England as a young man, training to be a butler. He never tired of reminding the staff of "the English way of doing things."

Distraught about my father and Hendrik, I paid scant attention to the elegance of our entry hall. It was lit by an enormous crystal chandelier. Here hung a hunting scene, there hung a vast landscape with a glowing sky, and between were imposing portraits of various deserving ancestors. The most famous was Axel Lejongård, who had supported the Bernadotte appointment as crown prince and had later served as the king's confidant. Axel loomed over visitors with his sideburns, brilliant blue eyes, and starched uniform, self-confident and doubtless irresistible to the ladies of his day.

I glanced absently at my famous ancestor and followed Bruns, who proceeded as ceremoniously as if conducting me to a ballroom.

We stopped before the door to Father's bedroom. Mother had had her own bedroom as long as I could remember. The actual matrimonial bed stood in a connecting room, and they almost never used it. I recalled being four or five years old and crawling into that bed with my parents, but they soon put a stop to that. Only later did I realize I wasn't allowed into the master bedroom because they didn't sleep together anymore.

Bruns knocked. There was no answer, but he opened the door anyway. That was odd, but perhaps Father was already asleep. I probably hadn't heard Mother's voice.

I took one step into the room, then stood rooted to the spot. Mother wasn't there. All I saw was my father, dressed in his best tuxedo and lying on the bed. His face was so pale, it looked as if someone had covered it with white cream. It reminded me, horribly, of the makeup on a circus clown.

I recoiled. I couldn't breathe. My father's chest was motionless. His hands were folded, heavy and lifeless, across it.

"Gracious miss, please sit," Bruns said as he placed an upholstered stool behind me.

Instead, I spun around and stared at Bruns in confusion. "Bruns," I gasped, "what is the meaning of this? Why did you fail to warn me?"

Ferocious anger filled me. My father was dead, and no one had told me. No one had tried to break the news gently. The butler's face flushed deep red, then went deathly pale and then red again.

"Forgive me, gracious miss. I thought—"

"Do not lie to me!" I snarled. "Why did you not say my father was dead?"

The butler gaped at me in confusion, unable to meet my eyes.

"That was my decision," said a voice from behind him. I saw her in the doorway, dressed in unadorned black. Her face was chalk white.

I shook uncontrollably. Tears flooded my eyes.

"I was not aware you had arrived, so I absented myself for a moment." Her voice was completely emotionless.

My vision narrowed and my pulse thundered. How could Mother be so cruel? I wanted to flee the room, but my legs refused. Bruns placed his gloved hands on my shoulders and gently maneuvered me to the footstool. As soon as I was seated, I swatted his hands away. Bruns stepped back in surprise.

"You may go, Bruns," I snapped. He bowed and retreated.

I sat there like a broken doll, my eyes fixed on my father, an empty shell now but once so proud and strong. I burned with hatred for my mother and anger at the majordomo who hadn't had the courage to defy the strict instructions of his mistress. Raging emotions left me weak.

"As I informed you, there was an accident. The main horse barn caught fire. Your father and brother were trying to evacuate the horses when the roof collapsed."

I didn't budge. My mother's words were ice-cold drops boiling away on my feverish skin: they caused nothing but pain.

More than anything, I wanted to scream and ask what I'd done to deserve such humiliation. Why hadn't she met me to tell me of my father's death? She hadn't comforted me or given me time to master my emotions before having me presented with Father's rigid, formally prepared corpse—the worst moment of my life. This was more wickedness than I'd ever seen from her.

"Your brother is still in the hospital. The doctors are tending to him," she went on, still without a trace of emotion. As if Hendrik weren't her own son. Had my father's death deprived her of all reason?

My brother was alive. That was something, but I was too numb and shocked to react.

I stared at Father. He lay there, lifeless. Dead! That word exploded into my consciousness, and something deep within me gave way. But I was determined to yield to the pain only when I was alone.

The tears in my eyes now were not those of grief.

I sprang up and glared at my mother. Even in my youngest childhood, she'd been an ice queen, a person from whom it was impossible to wrest any affection. Now she'd become an evil witch. I wished she had run into the barn after them.

My eyes burned with scorn.

"How could you not tell me?" I cried. "Why did you bring me up here without warning?"

Stella Lejongård's expression didn't change. My mother had always been cool and in control, but in this moment of catastrophic loss, I understood her less than ever.

"I would not have been able to reach you during your trip," she replied as if discussing a shopping list. "Your father was still alive when I sent the telegram."

"You should have told me," I shot back. "At least you could have let August or Bruns say something."

I saw the world through a sudden mist of tears. The furious burning in my chest was unbearable. My father was dead. Killed by fire.

"You should have met me downstairs!" I repeated. "You should have told me before I saw him! What kind of mother are you?"

She didn't flinch; the rebuke just bounced off her icy calm. She stood there, as if carefully formulating a response.

"And what kind of daughter are you? You have not cared about this family for a very long time. You were stubborn and intent on doing just what you desired."

"You're saying this is my fault?" I stabbed a finger toward my father's corpse, and my voice rose to a shriek. I'm sure even the maids upstairs in the servants' quarters heard it. "Because I wanted to take charge of my own life? This is the twentieth century, Mother, not the Middle Ages. Barns do not go up in flames because a daughter fails to live up to her parents' expectations!"

Why was she bringing all that up again? Why hit me with the same old refrain now, in the face of disaster?

"Your father hoped you would come to your senses! He was asking for you on his deathbed, wanting to know when you would get here."

I stared at Mother. How could she? That cruel claim shocked me as much as my first glimpse of Father's body. I was buffeted by a wave of nausea. My hands and knees shook.

"I set out as soon as I got your telegram!" I stammered.

I saw now what she was up to, why she'd deliberately hidden my father's death from me: she was punishing me for my independence.

"If you had not been in Stockholm, you could have been with him." Her voice was steely. Father's death was her opportunity to put me through hell.

I wanted to smash something in frustration, but my arms were limp, and my heart ached.

I stormed out of the room, exactly as I'd done so many times before. Bruns hovered just outside the door, but I didn't care that he'd overheard. I ran the length of the corridor and turned into the wing with the children's rooms. Long ago, I'd always sought shelter with Hendrik. He hadn't understood why I would want to be independent, but at least he offered me support.

But now he wasn't there. I flung myself into my old room, collapsed onto my bed, and wept like a baby.

3

I awoke the next morning with the feeling I'd had a bad dream, the sort that's so vivid you think it's true. I had such dreams from time to time. Michael said I brought them on by brooding too much. He'd advised me to devote myself to my art so as to cleanse them from my mind.

Art. How could I possibly paint after my father's death?

That's when I realized I hadn't been dreaming at all. This was real. I wasn't in my drafty apartment in Stockholm. Here, the windows were tall, and the sunlight streaming through their spotless panes warmed my face. Hints of lavender and rose hung in the air instead of the stink of turpentine and varnish. I was back in the place from which I'd fled.

I lay on my childhood bed, still in my travel clothes. Michael wasn't with me. How I'd have loved to take him into my arms. When I sat up, I saw no easels or covered canvases. Instead, I saw the antique painting over a cold hearth, the wardrobe of forgotten ball gowns, and heavy curtains left open the night before. The clammy blanket beneath me smelled musty. No one had made my room ready. Never mind; I wouldn't be staying any longer than was necessary.

I moved my stiff limbs and groaned. Sleeping on my stomach always gave me terrible back pain.

I'd just let down my tangled hair when a knock at the door startled me. I remembered that no one was ever really alone in this house.

"Come in!"

First to appear was the maid I'd met on my most recent visit. Susanna's blonde hair was plaited into a crown, the style I'd so envied in the past. It was all the rage among the village girls. She was quite pretty. My mother and Hendrik had probably been hard put to keep her from being swept away by a suitor. I didn't know the maid who followed her, a pale, skinny, long-limbed thing. Her brindle-brown hair and dark, darting eyes made her look like a sparrow ready to fly out the window at any moment. She was fourteen or fifteen at the most.

"Good morning, gracious miss. Excuse our intrusion. The gracious mistress wishes to know if you will come downstairs or take breakfast in your room."

The gracious mistress . . . I almost laughed. My mother didn't care whether I ate breakfast. But she had to preserve a certain decorum in front of the servants.

"I will come down." There was no way to avoid facing my mother. I preferred to do so courageously.

"As you wish, gracious miss." Susanna looked a bit relieved. The maids were always reluctant to tidy in the presence of a room's inhabitant.

Susanna nodded toward her companion, somewhat embarrassed. "This is Lena Tyske. The gracious mistress has told her to attend to you personally."

I must have looked puzzled, for Susanna added, "Lena has been at Lion Hall for three days now, and she's still learning. But she's eager, and I'll do my best to show her what to do."

So that's how the wind is blowing! I thought grimly. My mother had assigned me the least-experienced serving girl, knowing she wouldn't be missed elsewhere.

But that wasn't this little sparrow's fault. "Thank you very much, Susanna. That is very kind of you. Lena, I am sure you will do a good job."

"Shall we help you dress?" Susanna still sounded a bit apprehensive, for it was getting late. I'd have to hurry if I wanted to breakfast downstairs. My mother was certainly waiting for me as custom prescribed, and the servants would suffer for every passing minute.

"No, that is not necessary. Just set out clean clothing. I intend to visit my brother."

"You'd prefer dark clothing?"

I looked blankly at Susanna. Dark clothing? Yes, of course. The colors of mourning—everything I'd decided not to pack in Stockholm. The undertaker would be putting my father into his coffin. A funeral had to be organized. The daughter of the house would be called to help with those duties. But did that mean putting off the visit to my injured brother?

"Dark clothing. Of course." I reflected for a moment. "I did not pack anything dark. If you cannot locate anything appropriate in my wardrobe, please ask Linda if my mother will lend me something."

The maids exchanged a look that spoke volumes. My mother's personal maid embraced the preferences and dislikes of her mistress so profoundly that she despised me just as much as Mother did.

"Oh well," I added. "If there's nothing appropriate in black, then pick out something in dark blue."

Susanna allowed herself a shy smile. "We'll see what we can find."

"I am very grateful." I indicated that they could leave.

For breakfast, I picked out a dark-gray blouse and dark checkered skirt. Neither was mourning garb, strictly speaking, and I wouldn't be permitted to wear them outside the manor. But they would do for now. My clothing would have no impact on my mother's opinion of me.

The breakfast table was as meticulously set as if Father and Hendrik had just come back from their morning ride. Mother sat at her usual place.

"Good morning, Mother," I said and took my seat. I'd half expected to find my place set with chipped or mismatched pieces to remind me I no longer belonged at Lion Hall. But there weren't any such dishes in our cupboards.

Marie, the serving girl, appeared with a pot of coffee. I felt as if Father or Hendrik were about to walk in, but the pouring of coffee was the signal breakfast had begun. Meals in this house never started until all available family members were seated.

I wasn't hungry. The smell of oatmeal porridge, a dish I usually enjoyed, almost made me gag. I couldn't stand the sight of the breakfast pastries, the dots of red marmalade like open wounds. But I welcomed the coffee. It would give me the strength to get through this day.

All was still. For a time, the only sound was the ticktock of the grandfather clock and the muted clacking of Marie's heels. My mother spooned up the porridge from her bowl with a hearty appetite. She wore black, a very plain dress, and I reflected on how much she had to do: instruct the undertaker, make arrangements concerning the family vault, and send the death announcement to the newspapers.

I wrapped my hand around the coffee cup, appreciating its warmth, and took a sip. Black coffee, unsweetened, just the way I liked it. Michael always said I drank a man's coffee. Most women preferred cream and sugar; some even added spices. I'd never been like that.

I looked up the table at my father's empty place. The untouched morning paper was beside his plate. Hendrik's place had also been set, certainly at my mother's instructions. The sight sent a shiver up my spine.

"Did you sleep well?" My mother's words interrupted my thoughts.

I almost choked on my coffee. I looked up to see her gazing at me. Not with an affectionate, questioning expression, nor with any sign of grief. Her eyes were flat black pearls in her blank face.

"Not particularly well." My emotions had subsided. I was still sad, but now it was a muted ache in my heart. I knew the pain would come back in waves and rise to a torrent, but for the moment my sea was calm.

My mother regarded me for a moment with those beady eyes of hers, then turned her attention back to breakfast. I should have given her a fuller answer. But after the horrid events of the previous night, I couldn't.

"I am going to visit Hendrik," I said at last. "Is he in the hospital in Kristianstad?"

"Yes." Mother lifted her cup to her mouth as a pretext for not saying more.

I decided not to disturb her further. My decision to move to Stockholm had definitively cut the umbilical cord. She'd made that much clear.

I wanted to say farewell to my father before going back to my room. Sleep had overwhelmed me the night before, but now I needed to see him one last time before the wooden coffin lid closed.

The door to his death chamber intimidated me more than any nightmare monster. Father could no longer harangue me, reprimand, or make demands. I'd have humbly accepted any reproach if he'd only been able to deliver it.

"Gracious miss?"

I looked around and saw Arno Bruns step forward from the shadowed corner of the hall.

"Good morning, Bruns," I said coolly.

"I . . . I wanted to apologize for yesterday evening," the majordomo said, hanging his head. "I should have warned you. I should have given you an idea of it. I . . ."

His crestfallen demeanor touched me. "You obeyed my mother's instructions. You are not to blame for them."

"Doubtless that is so, but I have known you since you were a small child. I should at a minimum have told you to prepare for very bad news." He fell silent a moment. "I am very sorry. If I had been in your place, I certainly would have collapsed when confronted with the sight."

And I had—but later, all alone in my room. A Lejongård never betrays emotion in public.

"Quite all right, really," I said as if reassuring a small child. "I do not take offense."

The majordomo nodded but hardly seemed comforted. Others might say I'd forgiven him, but he knew that the words of a master or gracious mistress might conceal entirely different sentiments.

"I wish to see my father again. And after that, I will visit my brother. Would you be so good as to notify August I need the coach?"

"As you wish, gracious miss." He bowed.

I turned back to the door, took a deep breath, and turned the handle.

The curtains were half drawn, as if someone were concerned the sleeper might wake. A narrow beam of light from outside fell across my father's face, like a spotlight illuminating a theatrical tableau.

I took the chair by the bed and did my best to ignore his burns and the pungent smell of embalming fluid. I was afraid to look at him directly or examine his terrible injuries. I contented myself with being in his presence, glimpsing him from the corner of my eye. A lump rose in my throat. Gone was the shock and panic; it was replaced by a full, rounded grief. It was palpable, but it was bearable.

"I am so sorry, Father." My low voice echoed dully. "I am sorry I made you angry so often. I am sorry I was selfish. And that I was not here for you. I thought you would live as long as Methuselah, and nothing would ever change. Forgive me my mistakes. I was not prepared for this."

There was no reply.

"I did not want to complicate your lives. Not then, and not now. But I have only one life to live. This is a new century, and everything is changing so fast. We should not stand still. Especially not those of us whose lives are not yet decided. You surely rebelled against your mother, in your own way."

My father's mother had been a dark, mysterious old woman dressed in black who rarely spoke more than she had to. The Bible was the only book that mattered to her, and she'd enforced God's laws with demented severity. There was never any expression of joy from her; she'd reserved all happiness for Paradise. I didn't know if it was possible to rebel against such a force.

"Or perhaps not. Perhaps you were always dutiful. But I want you to know I am very sorry. I cannot promise to become the person you wanted me to be, but I guarantee you I will do my best to find my own happiness. Somehow."

A rustling behind me made me stop. I looked back at the door, which seemed slightly ajar. Was it Bruns? My mother? I couldn't tell.

The person who'd started to enter had apparently decided against it. Quiet footsteps retreated down the hall.

I gathered my courage and looked directly into Father's face. "I promise to be here for Hendrik and for Lion Hall. But I will do it in my own way."

That pledge was of no use to him now, but it was important to me. I felt calmer, and the pain in my heart was less acute.

4

The coach trip to Kristianstad was just as bone-jarring as my return to Lion Hall had been, even though August was obviously doing his best to avoid the potholes left by the winter weather. For a moment, I wished our family had one of those motorcars I'd seen so often in Stockholm. But my father had been adamant in his insistence that a horse-drawn vehicle was the best mode of private transportation.

I was glad to get out and stretch my legs when we reached the hospital. "I'll be inside for about an hour," I told August as he helped me down. "Take a rest and look around a bit."

He gave me an astonished look. I knew my mother never let him go off duty while she was running errands. She might need August to carry her heavy packages.

"As you wish, gracious miss."

I nodded and clutched my purse to my chest as I walked toward the tall redbrick hospital with its wide windows.

The building had two entrances. The one in front was for visitors and patients who could walk in. The one in back was for those patients who couldn't. I'd visited often with my parents, who were advocates of medical progress and felt a special bond with the institution and its director, Professor Lindström. He often attended our evening receptions. The Lejongårds were major donors, and Lindström frequently conferred with my father in private concerning use of the funds.

When our parents brought us here on their visits, Hendrik and I liked to slip away to watch as a pair of orderlies lifted patients on stretchers from wagons and horse-drawn ambulances. Often, the new arrivals groaned in pain. Others were completely inert. Some were injured, some flushed, and others white as chalk. Despite our limited knowledge, we made a game of guessing what was wrong with them. Those with visible injuries we assumed had come from accidents at construction sites, the ones with red faces had scarlet fever, and the pale ones needed appendectomies. I shuddered to think of the orderlies receiving Hendrik.

The nurse at reception checked the registry and said my brother was in room 17. There was a note. Professor Lindström wanted to speak with me first.

No one answered when I knocked on the director's office door. The chairs in his waiting room were empty. I sat and looked out the window. A number of patients were strolling around the lush grounds, some accompanied by nurses. I wanted to see Hendrik down there, healthy enough to enjoy the sunshine and make light of his injuries.

Footsteps broke into my fantasy. I turned.

Professor Lindström was a tall, haggard man who'd always reminded me of King Gustav. The physical resemblance was further enhanced by the professor cultivating a full beard that turned up at the end, just like the king's. Lindström had a stack of folders tucked under one arm. A stethoscope protruded from his lab coat pocket. He'd obviously just completed his rounds and was startled to see me.

"Miss Lejongård!" he exclaimed. He regained his composure and held out his hand. "You managed to get back from Stockholm quickly."

"Yes, I took the first train. How is my brother?"

He gave me a grave look, his lips pressed into a tight line. "We should have this discussion in the privacy of my office. Is your lady mother here?"

"She is arranging my father's funeral."

"In that case, please follow me."

I was twenty-seven years old and legally independent, so there was no need for my mother to be present. And I could marry whomever I chose. Those matters were uncontested now—legally. The sands of time ran at a different pace in aristocratic families, though, where offspring were still expected to seek parental permission for everything.

The professor's office was vast and imposing. The tall windows gave it the atmosphere of a church. The stained glass had symmetrical patterns of small brilliant flowers alternating with expanses of yellow and white. The sun threw the vivid patches of color across the shining parquet floor, making it look like a thin but elegant carpet. In contrast, the bookshelves laden with thick volumes and file boxes were dark and sinister. I hadn't been here often, but each time I felt vaguely threatened by the skeleton displayed on a stand by the far window. Was it there to remind the guest that Death was a regular visitor in this institution? Or was it a memento mori, a reminder of our mortality?

"You may already know that your brother was brought to us yesterday at about half past nine in the morning. He had second- and third-degree burns, as well as serious injuries caused by falling debris. He was suffering from smoke inhalation, which was the easiest of his afflictions to treat."

My stomach turned over. How the coach must have raced along that terrible road! And my nausea intensified at the mention of burns, of my dashing, handsome brother disfigured by horrible flames!

"We supplied him with oxygen to counteract the inhaled fumes. There was some improvement. His burns are of greater concern. We applied ointments and bandages as best we could."

I had a wild urge to flee. A horrible weight pressed upon my chest, my mouth filled with saliva, and my guts heaved. Cold sweat covered my forehead. I clutched the arm of the chair and fought against my sudden malaise. I needed to see Hendrik!

Professor Lindström saw my reaction and gave me a moment.

I regained control. "How is he now? Is he conscious? May I see him?"

"Yes, he is awake, but he should not see you in your present state of dress."

My eyebrows rose in astonishment. "My state of dress?" I looked down at myself. Susanna and Lena had located a black skirt in acceptable condition and a black frilled blouse. I wore a short black jacket with bulky sleeves. It was my mother's, and I'd been surprised Linda had allowed my maids to take it.

"You are in mourning," Lindström explained.

"My father passed away yesterday."

The professor nodded. "My deepest sympathies. Your appearance is, of course, understandable and appropriate, but . . . in these circumstances, your brother—well, I believe it unwise to let him know your father died."

"Oh!" I leaned back hard in the chair.

"Your mother insists that, whatever may happen, we must ensure he remains unaware of his father's fate until he has begun to recuperate. Frankly, given the extent of the burns, I was amazed he lived through the night. Informing him at this time of the terrible truth might fatally hinder the healing process."

"What is the extent of his burns?" I remembered a fire in our Stockholm neighborhood shortly after my move there. Witnesses told me the woman carried from the building had burns over half her body. She hadn't survived.

"Roughly thirty-five percent of his body was affected." The doctor took a deep breath. "As I said, it is a miracle he made it through the night. Perhaps his survival is due to the fact that he was found curled up in a fetal position. His torso suffered only minor burns because your father had thrown himself across Hendrik."

Father had tried to protect him. The doctor's words echoed in my mind. I saw Father's body again, his face ghastly white with undertaker's putty. I hadn't seen any injuries to his hands, but the putty was proof his face had been destroyed. I fought against the image, refusing to succumb to tears.

"I brought no other clothing with me because I was not informed of the seriousness of my brother's condition." I hoped my annoyance with Mother wouldn't register with Lindström. "But I wish to visit him now. It will comfort him to see me."

I saw the doctor hesitate and had a flash of inspiration. "Might you be able to find a nurse's uniform for me?" I asked. "A skirt and blouse, at least? We could tell my brother you wished to avoid contaminating his room with dirt from the road."

The doctor's eyebrows went up. He nodded. "That is a good thought, Miss Lejongård. Just a moment, and I will arrange everything." He quickly left the room, apparently relieved to get away from me. In any case, a nurse soon appeared with the uniform.

What followed felt unreal. Behind a screen in the professor's office, I transformed myself into a different person, an angel in white for my brother. I'd never thought much about what work I'd have done if I'd come from different circumstances. The daughters of the gentry and aristocracy didn't work; they waited for a man to marry them and provide for them in exchange for children and a life of housekeeping. But Swedish women from other classes worked as nurses, as well as midwives, serving girls, seamstresses, secretaries, and teachers.

I examined myself in the mirror. I was dressed as a working woman for the first time in my life. I had no intention of becoming a nurse, but the image pleased me. My only misgiving was the deceit. If I'd been badly injured and close to death, wouldn't I have wanted to know the truth? As children, Hendrik and I had always hated it when our parents refused to discuss something or misrepresented it to us; we found out the truth often enough, even if we had to eavesdrop to get it. But the professor believed Hendrik would be further endangered if he learned of our father's death, so I resolved to play the role as best I could. The only difference in dress between me and the nurse who escorted me to Hendrik's room was that I wore neither an apron nor a starched cap.

They'd given my brother a private room, as befitted his status.

"Please do not be alarmed," the nurse said to me. "His appearance may be shocking at first. If you feel faint, just ring, and one of us will help you immediately."

Ring? Hendrik had a buzzer in his room, like those at the manor? Or a little bell at his bedside?

The nurse took something from her apron pocket. "This is China-Gel. In case you find the odor overwhelming."

Her words terrified me. She seemed to be struggling to maintain her own composure, though surely she was used to seeing injured patients. I nodded, took a deep breath, and gripped the little bottle with the odd label depicting a cheerful Chinese man.

I opened the door. The only furniture was a metal cabinet, a chair, and the large iron-framed bed. A boring seascape hung on the wall behind the bed. There wasn't even a flower to grace the top of the low medicine cabinet by the bed.

The nurse hadn't exaggerated. The smell in the room was unspeakably bad, even though the window was ajar. I was used to urine on the Stockholm streets, but I'd never known a stomach-churning odor like this. I opened the bottle of gel. Its mint perfume was strong but not quite pungent enough to cover the reek of festering injuries and burned flesh. I dabbed a generous amount beneath my nostrils.

My brother's condition was horrifying but not more than I could bear. After the clumsily reconstructed face of my father's corpse, the sight of my brother breathing was a revelation, despite the blood and other fluids that had soaked his gauze bandages. He was alive, though scarcely visible under all the wrappings. They'd secured his arms and legs to keep him from thrashing and dislodging the dressings. He seemed to hover above the sheets. That position must have been terribly uncomfortable, but it was surely intended to help his injuries and burned flesh heal.

Hendrik's face, at least, was almost untouched, other than a bandage on his forehead and a gash on one cheek. His eyes were closed.

"Hendrik?" I grazed his cheek with my fingertips. It radiated heat, as if the fire had buried itself within him.

After what seemed an eternity, his eyelids flickered. The lashes were gummed together, and at first he was only half aware of his surroundings. Then he saw me.

"Hello, brother." I smiled despite my urge to weep.

He fixed his eyes on me. "Neta?" His voice was barely audible.

"Yes, it's me. I'm here."

Hendrik tried to smile but failed. "How long have you been here?"

"I arrived last night," I answered.

My heart nearly burst. I so desperately wanted to tell him what Mother had done and how much I hated her. But then he would know Father was dead.

"Mother sent a telegram, and I took the first train. You know how long it takes to get here from Stockholm. The train stops at every little crossroads."

"That's true." Hendrik tried to laugh but almost choked. He twisted his mouth into a crooked smile instead. "How is Father?"

I didn't know what to say. "Well, he—"

"They said he is here," Hendrik added. "In another part of the hospital."

An icy shiver went down my spine. Father hadn't even made it to the hospital.

"He . . ." For a moment, I couldn't find the words. But Hendrik would suspect something was wrong if I hesitated any longer. "Father's doing better. He . . . he is not in pain."

I froze, thinking I'd given everything away. That's what people always say about the dead; they console themselves with the thought that their loved ones no longer feel pain.

My brother seemed relieved. "Good. I guess he must not have been hurt as badly as I was."

"Perhaps the medicine is helping him." Now that Hendrik had swallowed the lie, I felt compelled to keep going. "His injuries are just as serious as yours because he was trying to protect you. At least that's what the doctor told me."

Hendrik pursed his lips hesitantly. Maybe I shouldn't overdo it with the details.

"The fire broke out so suddenly," he said. "Father had just returned from his morning ride. He tried to put it out, but it spread too fast. We got the horses out." Hendrik paused to catch his breath. "I shouted at him to get out of the barn. He should have listened. We could have given up on the last couple of horses, but now we are in a terrible fix. Neither he nor I can take care of the estate. And we have caused you and Mother such terrible grief."

Drops of perspiration appeared at his temples. The effort to talk was sapping his energy terribly. I brushed his cheek, not daring to touch him anywhere else for fear of causing pain. He trembled beneath my touch.

"Shh," I whispered. "Calm yourself, please. Everything will turn out well. Mother and I will take care of it. Father had to protect you. You are his son!"

Hendrik sank back against the pillow. I was surprised to find myself almost believing my own words. Everything was going to be fine. My brother gathered his strength, then turned his head ever so slightly to see me better.

He was confused to see me dressed in white, but I forestalled his question. "The professor asked me to change. Because of the road dust. They don't want any dirt in here."

Hendrik gave me the shadow of a smile. "Sounds like Miss Bloomquist. You remember that time I scalded myself?"

I nodded and fought back tears. Getting scalded had seemed like a catastrophe in those days. Life plays cruel tricks by serving up disasters that make previous troubles pale in comparison.

Hendrik's eyes dwelt on me in silence and then turned to the window, where the dark trunks of linden trees swayed in the wind. "Mother and Father must see now they are no match for you."

"Really? You think so?" Oddly, discussing their opinion of me no longer hurt.

A few months earlier, I'd sworn that I would never again attend any of my parents' events. At Christmastime, my mother once again invited prospective suitors and their parents. I'd long had to put up with such public showcasing, but I'd always managed to elude her traps.

Daniel Oglund was one of the prospects. His father, Pelle Oglund, a parliamentary official, was tactless enough that, soon after arriving, he began to expound on his thesis that women were unqualified for government service. Given their immaturity and spiritual shortcomings, he said, there was no reason to grant them any rights at all. His scorn wasn't just for suffragettes; it was for any woman with a mind of her own. I could have ignored his provocations—I had in the past—but something in me snapped. I angrily called out his patronizing male arrogance and his ignorance of gifted women's achievements.

"Take Marie Curie, for instance!" I exclaimed. "Do you think she was feebleminded? Or Professor Kowalewskaja, who held the Stockholm University chair in mathematics? If so, you are in fine company with the late August Strindberg, who called her an abomination. Assuming, that is, you know who Strindberg was." My face was a furious scarlet.

I might've had a bit too much to drink, but the man in his ill-fitting formal wear infuriated me.

"I do not consider anyone an abomination." He gave Father an awkward, appealing glance, as if seeking confirmation that I was out of line. "I simply said that women are not capable of fulfilling the demands of high office." And with that, he just poured oil on the fire.

"You stand there and pride yourself on appointment to an office you got only because one of your friends pulled some strings!"

I'd gone too far, but I was spoiling for a fight. I wanted to show this callow boy and his family whom they were dealing with.

"There are probably hundreds of women all over Sweden vastly better qualified than you! They are never considered, because in your men's clubs, you constantly assure each other we women are lesser beings! Are we just as insignificant when you and your despicable friends climb atop your wives and mistresses?"

That was the last straw for Father, who ordered me to my room, as if I were a naughty child.

I shrieked, "If that's what you want, go ahead and adopt Daniel Oglund. You are obviously trying to recruit him to tame your useless daughter!"

Tomato-red with rage, Father seized my arm and fiercely walked me out of the ballroom. "What has gotten into you?" he reprimanded me. "The Oglunds are our guests! Has Stockholm made you entirely forget your manners? You talk like a guttersnipe now, is that it?"

"Surely you heard him, Father!" I protested. "He called women immature and feebleminded. He insulted your daughter! How can you tolerate that? And to top it off, now you accuse me of being a prostitute?"

"Oglund is right!" Father snapped back. "A woman's place is not at the university or in any public office. God created women for one purpose only. And a woman needs a man, otherwise she is little more than a—"

"A whore? You think that is what I am? And I should abandon any talent I have for a desolate life of breeding in some man's manor house, where by the age of forty I will be old and worn-out, drowning my miseries in drink?"

"You forget you were born in exactly such a manor house!"

"I have not forgotten that in the least," I hissed, trembling all over. "But when my own father believes me incapable of taking my life into my own hands, when he considers me a prostitute because I want to make something of myself, then I wish I had never been born in this house." I turned and ran upstairs.

I was secretly hoping he would come after me and apologize. Or that Mother would come to console me. But nothing of the kind occurred. I was left to myself.

On the second day of the holiday, the atmosphere in the house was so cold I left without saying goodbye. The only person I stayed in contact with was Hendrik. He wrote and described the consequences of the scandal I'd caused.

"Mother and Father knew you wanted to break all ties." Hendrik's whispered comment interrupted my brooding. "You are legally independent and subject to no one. But now that you are here, you must see it was a mistake to flee without reconciling." After a pause, he said plaintively, "I want to hold your hand so badly, but I have no sensation in my limbs." He made another effort to smile. It was an even greater failure than before.

"They're all still there," I reassured him, looking nervously away. "And soon you will be back on your feet, hard at work."

"I'm so tired." His eyelids fluttered. "Will you come back to see me? Or are you off to Stockholm again?"

"I will stay until the first of the month, and of course I will come back." I did my best to hide the shudder I felt as I made that promise. I couldn't return to Stockholm now, even though I desperately wanted to. I had to stay for our father's funeral.

Hendrik knew nothing of that.

"That is fine." He looked pleased at the prospect of another visit. "Then you will have to tell me about your adventures at the university. And if you have an admirer."

I'd said nothing about Michael on previous visits, not even to Hendrik. I hadn't wanted to make things even worse by revealing I had a lover.

"My professors are demanding, you know. Not much time for romance. I am sure Father has kept you just as busy."

Hendrik began to drowse off. "Yes. That is . . . he certainly has."

"Rest. Tomorrow I will tell you everything you want to know." I bent to kiss the uninjured part of his forehead and then turned to go.

"Neta?" he murmured behind me.

I stopped, panic bathing my neck in sweat. I composed myself and turned back.

"Yes?" I leaned close, for I saw he was struggling to speak.

"If I do not make it—"

I wanted to clap my hand over his mouth. "Please don't say that!" I begged in a low voice.

"Neta," he said, swallowing hard. "Please, just listen."

I nodded, even though I wanted to flee. My marvelous brother couldn't die!

"If I don't make it, you must take my place in the family. I know you would rather cut off your right arm, but you would be the last of the Lejongårds. You inherit from me."

"You are not going to die, do you hear?" I insisted through my tears. "You cannot leave me all alone!"

He swallowed again. "Not planning to. But if that happens, you will inherit everything. I know you have . . . other plans. You want to paint. But this is where you belong. You are part of us. Please do not abandon Lion Hall. Will you promise me that?"

He looked up with such anguish, it nearly broke my heart in two.

"I would do anything for you," I said. I pressed my cheek to his bandaged hand. "You know that. But—"

"No 'but,' Neta. Please!" He was fading fast. "Promise me you will continue your painting but take care of Lion Hall too, the manor and the estate. And our parents. You know how important that is to me."

"Am I important to you too?"

"Darling sister, I love you more than anything. That is why I beg you to come back home."

I didn't want to make a promise I couldn't keep. But I didn't want to upset Hendrik either.

"With one condition," I said finally.

"What?"

"That you get well," I replied. "If you should ever die, I will take your place immediately. But not yet. You are still young, you have so many years ahead of you. I refuse to shoulder your responsibilities just so you can run off somewhere."

A smile flickered across his face. "So that means yes."

"Not at all. However, I solemnly promise I will make sure the estate is well managed. But I won't have to, because that is your job."

"And Father's as well." Hendrik stopped struggling and closed his eyes.

His words knocked the breath out of me, but I couldn't let it show.

"Sleep now," I whispered and ruffled the curls not covered by dressings. "We can discuss this tomorrow."

"You mean we can quarrel about it some more." Another drowsy smile, this time with the hint of a challenge.

"Until tomorrow, Hendrik," I said softly and left the room.

5

I somehow maintained my composure as I left the room, but my knees buckled a few steps from the nurses' station. I knelt on the floor and wailed, loud and desolate.

Two nurses got me to my feet and eventually back to the professor's office. Lindström sprang up from his desk as we entered. "What happened?"

"She simply collapsed in the corridor," one of the nurses said.

"No, it's nothing. I'm fine," I gasped through my sobs. "It's just—my brother! I feel so terribly sorry for him."

"You may go," Lindström told the nurses. "Check the patient."

Lindström squatted down and regarded me closely. "Believe me, we are doing everything in our power to bring him back. You have been very courageous."

"I lied to him," I sobbed. "I pretended Father was still alive. He asked me . . ."

"It was for the best, believe me. Hendrik is still in critical condition. We must take no risks."

"And when he gets better? Are you going to tell him our father died here in the hospital? But Father never got this far, did he?"

Professor Lindström bowed his head. "No, he did not. Your family physician, Dr. Bengtsen, found his injuries too severe. More than fifty percent of your father's body had been burned, and he was severely affected by smoke inhalation." The professor paused to take a deep breath. "We could not have helped him, given the extent of his burns."

His words were a cold shower of reality. Dr. Bengtsen had decided not to take Father to the hospital—but certainly after consulting my mother. Had she known Father was going to die? Their separate bedchambers were surely only one symptom of a failed marriage.

"We will of course tell your brother the truth as soon as he regains some strength. He is not likely to take it well. No one likes being deceived."

Hendrik least of all, I thought.

"But he will probably understand we had no other choice. He would make the same choice for his own son."

I was suddenly too exhausted to argue. "Thank you for letting me visit him." I got to my feet. My legs were still shaky, but the pain in my heart had subsided to a level I could bear. "I would like to change back into my own clothes, if you don't mind. I will visit again tomorrow."

Professor Lindström rose with me. "But of course, Miss Lejongård. Take your time." He left the office.

I stepped behind the screen. For a moment, I toyed with the thought of rifling through the folders on Lindström's desk to locate his notes about Hendrik. My mother could have demanded that the doctor lie to me as well.

I decided against it because I really didn't want to know. I didn't want to find it was hopeless, to discover Hendrik wouldn't recover and release me from a pledge I'd never be able to fulfill.

On the return trip, I leaned against the window frame of the coach, heedless of the heaving and jostling. I was drained and completely at a loss.

Hendrik's injuries were far worse than I'd imagined. I was grateful that at least Mother had not been standing there, requiring me to hide my emotions. There inside the coach I could abandon myself to my fear and misery, at least for a time. Questions and doubts assailed me. Most had to do with the contradictions between the two lives I was leading.

I'd assured Michael I'd return soon, but could I do so while my brother's life was in peril? With my father dead? Could I find some way to reconcile with my parents? Of course, Father and I would never have the chance. As for Mother, she'd continue treating me with cold disdain.

Maybe a couple of days would be long enough for Hendrik to start to get better. He'd always been quick to heal. And once his recovery was assured, I'd be free.

We arrived at Lion Hall, and I went directly to my room, avoiding Mother. The promise I'd made to Hendrik sat uneasy with me, and I was trying to figure out what to write to Michael.

I sank onto my bed with a sigh and stared up at the plaster medallion above the chandelier. I'd felt nostalgic for it all the time I was in Stockholm. And now, I found myself wishing for those familiar water stains.

Images flashed through my mind: the day I left Lion Hall; the first day in my newly leased apartment, when I was wondering if I hadn't made a huge mistake. My first experiences in the Royal Academy of Fine Arts, white canvases on easels, and the sharp smell of turpentine. Michael's face.

I'd met him on a Sunday, in a café in Old Town. I'd been with Marit and some other friends. He was with some rather rowdy boys. I caught Michael's eye, he stared back, and that was that.

We took our time getting acquainted but eventually gave in to our passions. That first wild night made me realize I wanted to spend the rest of my life with him. He began to attend our demonstrations for women's rights, and once he even stood between us and a group of angry men threatening to thrash us. That did it for me; I let him into my heart. I'd already enjoyed other men, but with Michael, I knew we were in love. But now . . .

At last I rose. Brooding was getting me nowhere. I had to write to Michael. He'd certainly reply immediately and relieve me of my doubts.

Despite my ardent support for women's rights, I still dreamed of an old-fashioned marriage. I was looking for a man to get on one knee and offer me a ring, be it gold, silver, or steel. Would Michael ask that special question someday? Should I perhaps broach the subject myself? He knew very well I needed him and wanted him at my side . . .

I went to my private desk, now carefully dusted, polished, and arranged by Lena and Susanna, and opened the drawer where I stored stationery and my old fountain pen. I filled it with ink I'd carefully preserved in a screw-top glass container. I started to write.

Dearest Michael,

I'm writing to say that you've been constantly in my thoughts. I've just been remembering that winter day in Old Town when you were sitting in the tiny café across from me and my friends. What would have happened if we'd chanced to go elsewhere that day? Would we ever have met? I feel enormously grateful that fate brought us together.

You remember that terrible telegram? Things have gotten far worse. My father passed away even before I caught my train, and my mother arranged for me to be brought to his body without the slightest warning. Can you imagine anything more ghastly? I was horribly shocked! My brother escaped with his life, but he is gravely injured. I was just at the hospital, and I am still beside myself.

Hendrik has made me promise that, should he die, I will take over management of the family estate. I could not refuse my brother; even though I ardently hope he will recover, he remains in critical condition. The doctor is so concerned that he has forbidden me to tell Hendrik of our father's death. If Hendrik were to die, I would be the last descendant of my centuries-old family and obliged to take on responsibilities I never desired.

I am consoled, in any case, by thoughts of seeing you. My future no longer seems so bleak when I imagine that someday both of us may live together here on the estate.

I heard footsteps in the hall and paused with my pen hovering over the paper. Was that Mother? Or just one of the maids? No, for the servants kept their steps as quiet as possible. Those footsteps were assertive. Stella was surely out there, about to demand a report on Hendrik's condition.

I hastily finished the letter.

Be assured my heart belongs fully and unreservedly to you. After the funeral, we two will have time to speak of the future. I know we have put that discussion off for a long time, but now it has caught up with us. We have one another, and nothing in the world can change that.

May all go well with you! Assuring you of my eternal love,

Your Agneta

I'd already blotted the letter when the knock came. I quickly folded my note, hands trembling, and slipped it into an envelope. "Come in!"

The menacing figure of my mother appeared. "Might you have a moment?" she asked in her chilly voice. "I would like to discuss your visit to the hospital."

Her expression and her words were like a bucket of cold water dumped on the feverish passion I'd felt while writing. A future with Michael . . . What would Mother say to that? He would enjoy a certain status as an attorney, but he wasn't from a noble family . . .

I pushed these thoughts from my mind. Hendrik was alive. He'd recover soon, and then I could go back to Stockholm.

6

I breakfasted quickly in my room the next morning and then went to walk around the grounds. I took my time, impressed as always by the massive majesty of Lion Hall's white stone walls, ever proof against the ravages of time.

Stockholm had many elegant buildings, some even larger than the Lejongård family manor. But my parents' home had always had a forbidding quality that I found unmatched elsewhere. My gaze swept across the tall windows that reflected the clouds. The facade had been altered over the many generations as each Count Lejongård left his mark. The foundations were laid by the first of our family line, Axel Lejongård, who'd been granted the estate by King Charles XI as a reward for loyalty during the Scanian War that Sweden fought to retain formerly Danish provinces. Axel had the lands cleared and planted, began the practice of breeding horses, and helped establish Swedish dominion over the lands his king had occupied.

Bullet holes in the rear walls of the manor had been left untouched as a reminder of attacks by Danish partisans.

The most extensive modifications were undertaken by my great-grandfather, a good friend and fervent supporter of the founder of the

Bernadotte royal line. He converted the old Renaissance structure, passionately hated by many of Danish ancestry as a symbol of unjust occupation, into an elegant, classical manor celebrated by contemporary writers and admired by travelers. The descendants of families who'd opposed Sweden eventually accepted us, the zeal of their ancestors having faded.

The last count to make significant modifications was my grandfather. To emphasize the family name, he commissioned small sculpted lion heads, each with a different expression, to be installed above all the windows.

Hendrik and I had named them and made up stories about them. We imagined the lions speaking to one another, making naughty comments about us or our parents, and getting irritated every time a storm broke.

An involuntary smile crossed my face when I looked up at Grumpy, the lion peering down from a window of the great ballroom. He'd been my favorite, and I'd made him a grumbler of valiant character. Brother, the lion next to him, was Hendrik's favorite because he was inquisitive and clever. We'd always imagined the two of them trading tales of the magnificent balls they hadn't been permitted to attend.

Maybe I should take Hendrik some news from Brother and Grumpy. Would he remember our game? Had he thought of the lions in recent years, as he strode past the windows, absorbed in estate business?

Warmed by those thoughts, I turned toward the pastures where Hendrik and I had often played. Mother told us it was unseemly for us to ramble about there, but my father always maintained that the children of a landed family should be well acquainted with their future inheritance. *"They must be familiar with every aspect of their land and the region, and they must never fear nature!"*

The path to the pastures ran past the stables. The spectacle of the charred remains of our largest outbuilding made me gasp. Fires had occurred from time to time, usually out in the fields or in some part of the forest. Flames had never touched any essential building of the estate before.

My affectionate memories of the lion heads faded before that ugly reality. I tried to recall better, more beautiful times and envision a brighter future. But it was no use. A dark void consumed everything else.

I broke out in a cold sweat, and my hands began trembling again. Why hadn't anyone tried to clean up this damned mess?

I spun around and ran as fast as I could, for as long as I could. The gravel path beneath me gave way to grass that snatched at the hems of my coat and skirt. I stumbled on uneven ground and kicked aside tall weeds left from the previous year. I stopped, breathless, and looked around, finding myself surrounded by trees. I gradually calmed down, and the pain eased. The only hint of disaster here was the faint, bitter smell of blackened ruins, wafted by the wind.

I'd instinctively found the same place where I used to flee as a fourteen-year-old whenever I'd once again failed to live up to my parents' demands. The small clearing wasn't far from the pasture. It was like a room walled with trees, sheltered from the perpetual chill and foreboding of the manor house.

I plucked the seed-filled heads of tall June grass and rolled them in my hands. Once upon a time Hendrik and I had played Hen and Rooster. One of us pushed the seed heads up the stem into a tight bunch while the other tried to guess the result. "Hen" was a stem without any protruding seed heads, while the "rooster" had a "little tail." It was a game of pure chance, even when Hendrik tried to cheat, as he often did. We'd play for hours until at last we had to go back inside.

The memory made me laugh. I lingered there awhile before returning to the pasture, which was lined with oaks and tall linden trees. The fence must have been replaced recently, for the posts looked quite new. I walked until I saw the horses. Racehorses were stabled at night for safekeeping, while working horses spent almost all of spring and summer in the pasture.

One of the horses broke away from the others. At first I thought it was Edwina, my father's favorite, but as she came nearer, I recognized Talla, the mare I used to ride. She was a palomino, like Edwina; they'd had the same mother. Because Talla was older and much calmer, Father had given her to me.

Talla trotted over and stuck her enormous head across the fence. Her warm smell of horsehair and hay moved me to tears.

"Hello, Talla." I stifled a sob as I gently rubbed her neck. She pushed her head closer so she could snuffle at my hair. Our old, familiar greeting. I'd forgotten how lovely she was. She snorted and held her head against mine, as if we'd been together just the day before.

Talla was old and not particularly valuable anymore, but it looked as if she was still stabled inside. I found a wound on her flank, a sign that she must have barely escaped the fire.

I gently rubbed her snout. "So, my girl, how are you?" She nibbled at my hand, and I wished I'd thought to pocket a carrot. "That fire gave you a scare, didn't it?"

Talla snorted again. She gathered herself a bit, raised her head, and looked over my shoulder.

"Ah, our gracious miss!" a voice behind me exclaimed.

The blond man in heavy boots, riding pants, and a checkered shirt was Sören Langeholm, the stable manager, an acknowledged expert in horse breeding. We owed it to him that our stallions had for years been at the very top of the country's stud list.

"Mr. Langeholm." I offered him my hand. "So pleased to see you."

Talla nudged my shoulder, her usual sign of farewell. She trotted back to the other horses.

"The pleasure is entirely mine," Langeholm replied. "Even though I would have preferred other circumstances for your visit. Your father's death has hit us all very hard. I'm very sorry for your loss."

"That is very kind of you." His firm, strong grip did me good.

"Your father and brother fought heroically to save the horses. We freed all but one before the roof collapsed."

I knew how important the horses were, both to Father and to Hendrik. If only they hadn't risked their lives for them . . .

"How could this happen?" I asked, hoping I might get something useful out of Langeholm.

"The truth is, we're all mystified. The police were here not long after the fire died down. The officers rummaged around in the ruins, but they shared nothing with us. Maybe it was a discarded cigarette. Or something else—hot straw can ignite spontaneously, for example."

I'd never heard of straw catching fire by itself in March, but I supposed it might be possible.

"Were there other men in the stalls?"

"Yes, two of the lads, Lasse and Sven. Your father ordered them out when the smoke thickened. Your brother tried to get your father to leave as well, but he wouldn't hear of it. Then suddenly the roof caved in. Your father was trying to save the last horse, a breeding mare he particularly valued."

I closed my eyes. Langeholm's description of the events sent a shudder through me. "Which mare did we lose?" I asked in a strangled voice.

"Sigursdottir," Langeholm replied. "We did get her out of the ruins alive, but she was so badly injured we had to put her down."

I knew that name well. We'd bought Sigursdottir from a Norwegian breeder, and she had given birth to several excellent foals.

"If only Father and Hendrik had left sooner. You can replace a horse, but . . ." I gritted my teeth, furious.

"True. No one can replace your father."

I nodded. We shared a long moment of silence. Then I spoke. "You said the police were here. Can you tell me more about that?"

"Well, since the fire broke out so suddenly, they say they can't exclude arson. That's nonsense as far as I'm concerned, but the detectives still want to question the staff over the next few days."

I marveled at how much Mother had kept from me. "That will make people uneasy," I said. "No one would want to be suspected of causing the death of the lord of the estate."

We were interrupted by the rustle of dry grass. Lasse Broderson, one of the stable boys, came running up the path. My heart stopped. Had something happened with my brother?

"It's happening!" the boy exclaimed. "It's started! Red Dawn is giving birth!"

Langeholm looked at me. "Well, gracious miss, it seems you might think about a name. Horses give birth pretty quickly, and Red Dawn isn't foaling for the first time."

Our custom was the same as that of the royal family; naming a horse was the privilege of the owner of the estate.

"Shouldn't Hendrik choose? He is the master now."

"I fear your brother will be in the hospital for a while longer. So the honor passes to you . . ."

I wanted to suggest that we delay the christening until my brother recovered. But tradition dictated naming foals immediately after birth. In olden times, people thought the practice fended off evil spirits. The custom was still observed, even though few believed in evil spirits anymore.

We rushed to the stall. The stable boys were gathered there, along with old Linus, our "horse wizard." He sat in the straw next to Red Dawn, gently stroking her neck and muttering in an ancient dialect. The words sounded like incantations.

I checked the stall window and spotted little shards of a mirror strewn along the ledge to keep away malevolent spirits. I'd always found this a senseless, even dangerous, practice. Pieces of broken mirror could be knocked off, potentially into the feed boxes. To be sure, horses could use their lips to find a needle in a haystack, but the practice seemed entirely too risky to me.

Father hadn't been comfortable with it either, but Linus, who firmly believed in trolls and phantoms, refused to be dissuaded.

"Ah, it's Miss Agneta," the old man said. "Lovely to see ye again."

"Thank you, Linus," I replied. "I am pleased to see you doing well."

"Hmm, well, let's see . . . me bones ache, and none of the rest is getting any younger. But as long as God lets me open me eyes to the morning, I'm just fine."

Old Linus's ministrations weren't limited to horses. Villagers went to him for relief from minor aches and pains. Our family had begun funding the village clinic 120 years earlier and had kept it staffed with a competent physician ever since. But the elderly healer, by now at least eighty years old, perhaps ninety, knew everyone in the village, and they were devoted to him.

"How long will it take?" I asked, leaning against the stall door.

"No more than another hour. Probably less. This girl's familiar with foaling."

The mare had now stretched her head out on the ground. She snorted. Her flanks quivered convulsively. I didn't need to be a horse wizard to see she was in pain.

Langeholm now joined the old man. He'd pulled on long gloves. Newfangled nonsense, Linus certainly thought, judging from his expression. The two viewed one another as rivals. Langeholm was an educated man with plenty of experience, while Linus's knowledge had been handed down from his forefathers. They'd had sharp disagreements initially, but Langeholm eventually acknowledged Linus might have something to contribute: knowledge not taught at the university but derived from centuries of experience. And Linus must have realized that many of his techniques had been surpassed.

Since then, they'd respected one another, if reluctantly at times. If a case was simple, Langeholm left it to Linus, whom my father held in great esteem. He would never have failed to include Linus. Nor, I was sure, would Hendrik.

"Come on now, my girl. You can do this!" The old man encouraged the mare, stroking her neck. He got to his feet and turned to us. "We'd best stand back. I believe she's about to get up and start pushing."

Mesmerized, I watched the horse. I'd witnessed this countless times over the years. As children, Hendrik and I had often slipped into the stables to watch mares giving birth, even though Father wasn't pleased to see us there.

If only Hendrik could see this! I thought. It was such a beautiful assurance that life goes on.

Red Dawn stamped her forelegs, and her whole body quivered as she pushed into the pain. She sank down, only to right herself moments later for another push. At last she got all the way up and staggered around the stall. The old wizard kept whispering magic spells, or at least that's what his toothless mumbling sounded like to me.

Finally, the foal's first leg appeared, black as night. That told us little. Even horses that later turned white were born black, and the father of this little one was a gray.

Once the foal had emerged halfway, the mare knelt again. The caul was off the head now, and the little one was already twitching. Its exhausted mother snorted and lay there with the foal's front legs on the ground.

"Ah, look there, a little stallion," Linus said, earning himself a look of incredulity from Langeholm.

"What tells you that?"

"I just know," the old man answered. "I see it in the head, as certain a sign as anything ye'll see beneath."

My heart pounded with excitement. I'd nearly forgotten the exhilaration of seeing a horse being born—and the joy when the little one was hale and hearty. I didn't care if it was a stallion or mare. The sweet ache at seeing the adorable little thing drove the grief from my heart for a moment.

In the end, there it was: four neat little legs, each with a white spot at the knee, a white blaze on the forehead, a tiny damp tail plastered to its hindquarters, a black hide gleaming wet as if varnished, and dark eyes that shimmered like glass beads. My eyes filled with tears, and this time they were tears of happiness.

The foal tried to rise, but Red Dawn was in the way. She remained on the ground for a while longer, the heaving of her flanks gradually subsiding. When she did get up, her motion peeled the remaining birth tissue almost completely off the creature. She started licking the foal with her rough, dry tongue.

"Good girl!" Linus turned to Langeholm. "Ye can take yer gloves off now. The mother knows what needs doing."

The stall master smiled wryly but kept his gloves on.

It took a while, but once Red Dawn had licked her little one almost entirely dry, the foal rose and regarded us.

"Well, then, what'll we name this fella?" Linus asked. Not only did he serve as midwife to the horses, he also performed the christenings. For that purpose, instead of filling his flask with homemade brandy as usual, he'd brought real holy water directly from the church. Or so he claimed. Linus wasn't the most zealous churchgoer, and he and the local priest were somewhat at odds.

"How about Evening Star?" I suggested.

"Why?"

"Well, a red dawn starts the day and the evening star ends it. What's more, the name is good for either a mare or a stallion."

"Ye don't believe me about the sex, gracious miss?" Linus asked, sounding aggrieved.

I quickly shook my head. "No, Linus. I don't mean to imply any such thing. I was just speaking in general." I looked to Langeholm for support and saw he was trying to hide a smile.

Linus considered my suggestion, then nodded. "Not a particularly original name, but it's pretty, and the meaning is good. Most folk are afraid of the night; they imagine everything is ending. But night prepares us for the new day, after all. Ye can't separate one from the other. Fine, then." He unplugged the flask and anointed the foal's forehead. The little one pulled back in surprise as Linus declared, "I christen thee 'Evening Star.'"

I left the barn with straw stuck to the hem of my skirt and a smile on my face I couldn't quite explain. At that moment I caught sight of my mother, a small black shape on the front steps, looking like a crow gone astray. Had she been searching for me? At least she wouldn't be able to accuse me of neglecting the business of the estate—after all, I'd helped bring a new foal into the world!

"Red Dawn has foaled," I called to her. "We have a new stallion!"

Mother showed no emotion. Why should she, faced with a daughter showing no sign of mourning? The new foal had briefly driven misery from my mind and made me forget my deep rancor against Stella Lejongård. Now her expression seemed chiseled in stone. "I must speak with you."

"Let me take a moment to change my clothes." I tried to step past her, but she grabbed my arm and forced me to meet her eyes.

I stiffened instantly. My elation vanished like mist in the morning sun.

"Hendrik is dead," she said. "A messenger from the hospital just arrived. He died an hour ago."

"That's not possible!" I cried. "I saw him yesterday!" A wild quiver of panic shook my insides.

I remembered his eyelids fluttering. I again heard him ask about my life in Stockholm and complain that he couldn't feel his hands.

My mother's lips tightened into a sharp line. "Did you tell him about your father?"

I shook my head. "No, the professor would not allow it. And I—I told him that Father was doing well . . ."

Oh! No, Mother. You're not going to blame me for Hendrik's death! I thought, rejecting this cruel twist of the knife. My brother was gone. I pressed my clenched fist to my mouth. Tears streaked my cheeks, and I didn't try to hide them. I rushed into the house.

Inside, my legs gave out again. I sank down by the stairs. The pain and hurt ripped through me. They robbed me of my breath; they exploded in my mind. For a moment, the world was reduced to the thunder in my ears, and I couldn't feel my own limbs. I was deaf to my own cries of grief.

7

My night was mostly sleepless, haunted by the irrational fear that Hendrik would appear in my dreams to rebuke me for not telling him of Father's death. If there was a heaven, I tried to convince myself, Hendrik would be happily reunited with Father there.

Toward morning I dropped off and dreamed the two lion heads were scolding me savagely. I awoke with a start and resisted closing my eyes again for fear Grumpy and Brother would shout at me.

I couldn't stay there any longer. The blanket weighed upon me, stifling. The dark circles under my eyes would testify to my lack of rest, whether I stayed in bed or not.

I got up to put on a morning robe and slippers, then left my room. I heard murmured conversations between the servants downstairs as they began their usual morning routine.

When I was little, I often slipped away from my room, usually to visit Hendrik and tease him. Or to hide in his room. Often the two of us would race outside, barefoot in the dew-covered grass, especially on early mornings in high summer before the heat became unbearable.

I found my way to Hendrik's room that morning as well. I raised a hand to the door, ran it across the wooden surface, and sought some sign of Hendrik's presence. Something, anything, he'd left behind. I closed my eyes and tears welled up. This time I gave in and just let them flow. Pain rose from deep inside and coalesced in my chest, choking me.

In my mind's eye, I saw my brother during our childhood, a boy with golden-blond hair and more freckles than I could count. I saw his eyes and his smile and felt his hand reach out to help me up when I'd fallen. He'd always been my shining hero. He comforted me when I was afraid. When I doubted, he showed me I could trust him. We learned to keep each other's secrets.

Why had God torn us apart? Why couldn't God have spared him? I became dimly aware of a strange noise. The flood of memories dimmed, and my tears dried up. I quickly wiped my eyes and strained to identify the sound. I heard a low whimpering. But whose?

Was my mother sitting in Hendrik's room, lamenting, hiding from prying eyes? Had she at last given in to the need to mourn her son? The thought disconcerted me. How long I'd waited for my mother to show some sign of emotion, some proof she had human feeling! I knew I should knock, but Mother would instantly put her mask back in place if warned. I carefully turned the handle.

My brother's room had been decorated in quite a somber fashion. Beautifully executed portraits of horses hung on the dark-paneled walls. The morning light streaming through a narrow opening between the cream-colored curtains fell across the shape of a disconsolate figure huddled on the edge of the bed. She blew her nose, wiped her eyes, and looked up. At the sight of me, she bolted to her feet.

"Susanna?"

"Forgive me, gracious miss, I was about to air the room, and then it hit me again . . ." Her tears began to flow once more.

"Of course, Susanna," I said and stepped through the doorway. "We are all terribly sad about the loss of my brother."

Susanna pressed a handkerchief to her mouth. "I'll leave now. Forgive me."

"Of course."

I watched her go and felt a pang in my heart. Hendrik's bed was untouched and would remain so forever. The sight of the bedcovers was suddenly too much for me. I sobbed all the way back to my room, threw on a dress, went downstairs, and put on a coat and shawl. I needed to get my thoughts in order.

The glow of the March morning resisted my gloom. The sun was rising behind the wood. Mist steamed from the treetops. The estate had a special charm at this early morning hour. It was a fairy tale, and I was the princess of an enchanted castle whose mission was to lift the spell cast upon the prince. We'd had a French governess who read us fairy tales from her country. *Beauty and the Beast* had always been my favorite. The reddish-gold light touched my face and penetrated the wool of my coat. Warmth filled me.

In that moment, I ached for Michael, who would surely appreciate the silent beauty. My head swam at the thought of giving up Stockholm and my education. I was an independent woman, exercising the rights for which my friends and I fought. I'd wanted for as long as I could remember to become an artist and live as I chose. Surely I couldn't turn my back on that.

But I'd made a vow. And returning to Stockholm would mean burning all my bridges, destroying all ties to Mother and to Lion Hall. Why did Hendrik have to die?

I walked toward the flower garden, which was still somewhat bare in the March chill. My mother had ordered most of the gardens planted in the English style, but we also had some rose beds and formal plantings of colorful perennials, including lilies of the valley, narcissus, and summertime poppies. Mother hated wildflowers, but Father had always insisted on setting aside a nature preserve on the estate, an area where the grass was cut, but everything else was left wild.

I'd have loved to sit on the ground, but the grass was soaked with dew. I squatted to pick one of the snowdrops sprouting up like weeds and held it to my nose. How simple life had seemed when I was a child!

Now everything was endangered, and I would have to determine what future lay ahead for me and for Lion Hall.

Michael came to my mind again. I didn't know if country life would please him, but surely he would accept it for my sake. And why shouldn't we wed? True, other aristocratic families would turn up their noses because Michael wasn't of noble blood, but we were living in modern times, weren't we?

If I were to quit Lion Hall, there were two possibilities: either Mother would run the estate or it would be put up for sale. Hendrik had known that when he'd pressed me to take his place. He had pinned his hopes on me as he lay dying. I had no choice; I could not fail him.

The enchanted quiet of the outdoors vanished when I returned to the manor house. The kitchen hummed with activity, and maids hurried through the corridors. Most of the rooms had already been aired, and the chimneys were smoking.

I went down to the kitchen. Our cook, Mrs. Bloomquist, had always slipped me a treat and poured me some milk when I visited her. I desperately desired that solace after the grim night behind me and the dark hours ahead.

"Good morning," I said as I came down the stairs. As I'd expected, Svea, the kitchen maid who dreamed of someday becoming chief cook, was already lighting the stove. Marie, who'd worked here for many years, was pumping water into a dented enamel pail.

The two looked up in confusion. "Good morning, gracious miss," Svea finally managed to answer. "Can we do something for you? Should we call Mrs. Bloomquist or Miss Rosendahl?"

I shook my head and went to the long table where the servants had their meals.

"No, thank you. I just want to sit here for a while the way I used to when I was little." I placed myself at the center of the bench. Whose place was this now? One of the maids or perhaps the majordomo? I knew a strict hierarchy determined one's assigned place at the common table.

The maids stared, uncertain what to do. After a moment, they returned to their daily tasks and their motions became less self-conscious. Not wanting to be perceived as inspecting their work, I stood up and gazed out the window. From here one had a good view of the stables—and, unfortunately, of the charred remains of the barn.

Mrs. Bloomquist arrived and interrupted my musings. "Gracious miss, is everything as it should be?"

"Good morning, Mrs. Bloomquist. Yes, thank you." I knew my expression belied my words. Nothing was as it should be, nor would it ever be again. But family members were required to exude confidence to the servants, even when times were at their darkest. "I was just wondering if you might make me some oat porridge with lingonberries, the way you used to do."

Our cook's face glowed briefly with gentle amusement, remembering how much I used to love that dish. My mother insisted the family always eat together, but Mrs. Bloomquist, who had no children of her own, could never refuse me—even though she risked Mother's wrath.

"Of course. But I should remind you that the gracious mistress will not be pleased if you have no appetite at breakfast."

I gave a short laugh. "My mother will not be pleased regardless."

The cook nodded, then picked up a kitchen towel and tucked it into her apron before she went to work.

A few minutes later, the smell of sweet oat porridge filled the kitchen, a scent that evoked childhood and carefree days. How much I wished those hours could return. Back then I'd had everything and didn't know it, didn't know about loss. But now . . .

"Here you are, gracious miss." Mrs. Bloomquist placed the bowl before me. The porridge was fragrant with milk and sugar and topped with a generous spoonful of the lingonberry jam I loved so much. "Enjoy. There's plenty more if you want it."

"Thank you, Mrs. Bloomquist," I replied and allowed myself to sink for one moment more into memories of my childhood.

8

I regretted my double breakfast on the way to Kristianstad. My stomach was as heavy as lead.

Mother sat across from me in the coach. She wore her hair artfully gathered in a low bun. Linda was an expert hairdresser and could have put to shame even Stockholm's most skillful coiffeurs. I'd often wondered why she showed no ambition to make anything more of herself than my mother's personal maid.

But for all her talent, Linda obviously could do nothing to keep my mother's black dress from hanging loose upon her frame. I hadn't noticed it the previous day, but now it was obvious Stella Lejongård had lost weight. Nonetheless, she still held herself with grace and a posture many younger women couldn't emulate.

The corset under my own dress kept me almost equally upright. I never wore a corset in Stockholm and was used to sprawling entirely at my ease. Now it felt as if I'd been shoved into a wooden barrel. But my mother would have noticed instantly if I hadn't been wearing one, and I didn't dare quarrel with her, considering the occasion.

It was well past noon when we arrived in Kristianstad. Church bells were tolling—whether for a funeral or a wedding, I couldn't say.

The odor of carbolic acid at the hospital was overpowering. Mother pulled a handkerchief from her sleeve and held it to her nostrils. Her face remained expressionless. Perhaps she'd wept that morning, but now she was absolutely in control, the way people like us were trained to be. In contrast, I had no idea how long I'd be able to hold back the tears.

Professor Lindström received us in his office. The sun had disappeared behind thick banks of clouds looming beyond the broad windows.

"My most sincere condolences," the physician said, bowing his head to Mother and me. "I am very pained we were unable to do more for your son. You are aware I feared complications. And those indeed occurred—"

My mother silenced him with a gesture. "You did everything in your power. I am well aware his injuries were severe. It was God's will."

God's will. I thought of the arguments I'd had in Stockholm with clergymen who asserted God's will was that women should stay in the kitchen and have children.

"Do you wish to view the deceased a last time before we deliver the body to the undertaker?"

"Yes, we would," Mother replied.

I gave her a startled glance, for I'd have preferred to remember Hendrik as he was in life. But what was my most recent memory of him? A brother swathed in bandages! That last horrific sight overshadowed my memories of a Hendrik bursting with health, running across the meadows, and swinging himself effortlessly up into the saddle.

And what spectacle awaited us now? Had they smeared him with the same stark putty they'd used on Father? My stomach cramped with dread. Cold sweat trickled down my back, and a roaring filled my ears.

"Please excuse me for a moment," I blurted and rushed out of the room without waiting for a reply.

Pressing one hand against my corset, I dragged myself down the hallway to an open window and shut my eyes. The fresh air eased my nausea and helped relieve my feeling of suffocation. I concentrated on breathing deeply and regularly until at last the roaring subsided, and

I heard birds twittering. I slowly opened my eyes. The door opened behind me.

"Miss Lejongård?" The physician's voice was grave and concerned.

My mother had not followed him. Of course.

"I'm better now. You will understand that this is all a bit too much for me right now."

The professor nodded.

"Perhaps she should take a moment to rest," my mother said in the distance. She'd come out after all. I looked past the professor and caught her expression of censure.

"No, I am quite all right now." I had no desire to give Mother more grounds for recrimination. "I am ready."

Professor Lindström looked doubtful. "Are you quite sure?"

His expression infuriated me. He'd promised to save my brother, and now all he could propose was to show us Hendrik's corpse.

"I am entirely certain," I replied sharply.

Lindström stepped back and pretended not to notice my tone. "Good, then. Please follow me."

I smoothed my dress and fell into step behind my mother.

The staff had moved Hendrik to the hospital morgue. The incandescent light of the basement merely intensified the deathly cold. I'd have preferred candles, for the harsh illumination would reveal every wound, every indication of decay, everything. They'd wrapped Hendrik in a tight white sheet. Professor Lindström advanced and turned the drape back just enough for us to see my brother's face.

"The funeral director's wagon is parked in the inner court," the physician told us. "You may take as much time as you wish."

"Thank you, Professor. You are very kind." My mother was unlikely to stay more than a couple of minutes, enough to fulfill social expectations.

He pointed to a bell pull by the door. "Simply ring when you are ready."

My mother lowered herself onto a chair. Her gaze remained fixed on Hendrik's face. The pitiless light made her look even more pallid than usual, and the circles under her eyes stood out deep and dark. No tears glistened in her eyes. She looked as if she'd been sculpted in ice.

The sight of Hendrik rent my heart in two. I gave a low involuntary whimper, seeing him still swathed in gauze. Why hadn't they removed those bandages? Were the wounds beneath them that hideous?

The image of my brother blurred as tears gushed onto my dress and dripped to the floor. The pulse thundering in my ears nearly drowned out my mother's cutting admonition to control my emotions.

I mastered my tears somehow, but a deep-seated shudder possessed me. I longed in vain for some sign of comfort from my mother, but she merely rose, crossed the room with great dignity, and tugged the bell pull. She returned to her chair, refusing to meet my grief-stricken gaze.

A young physician escorted us back upstairs and out the back entrance to where the coach from the funeral home was waiting. We stood by as the stretcher was delivered to the hearse. Services for my father and brother would take place in Kristianstad, after which they would be transported to the family mausoleum in the village cemetery.

"We should tell the priest we wish the service for Hendrik to be held at the same time this Saturday," my mother said.

I stared at my mother in disbelief. We'd just now watched as her son, my brother, was carried to the horse-drawn hearse, and she was already discussing practicalities. Shouldn't we be embracing and comforting one another?

Her voice interrupted my thoughts. "Do you agree, or do you have objections?"

I was bewildered. "Excuse me?"

"The burial services for your father and brother. Do you have any objection to my asking the priest to hold a joint ceremony on Saturday?"

"To placate the superstitious locals, you mean?" I asked. My tone was more sarcastic than I'd intended. "Those yokels who fear the two of them will drag more folks into the grave if we do not put them in their tomb right away?"

My mother looked horrified. "How can you say such a thing? Can it be that you simply do not care?"

I shook my head. Were my ears deceiving me? Was my mother accusing *me* of indifference?

"I am not in the least indifferent!" I insisted, not even trying to hide my tears this time.

"Mind your tone!" Mother hissed.

"My tone?" My voice was shrill, and I didn't care whether the undertaker's employees heard us. Let them! "Which of us is the indifferent one? I, who do not know what to say when my mother wants to get the funerals over and done with, or my mother, who seems completely unmoved by the fact that she just saw her son for the last time?"

My words rang through the courtyard, but I scarcely noticed, for my heart was pounding as if it were about to burst.

Shaking like a leaf, I realized that once again I'd done exactly as Mother expected. I'd reacted thoughtlessly, stupidly. Couldn't I have just agreed? Why was it impossible for me to keep my mouth shut?

For just a moment I saw a flicker of feeling in her face, but she did not rise to my challenge. She turned and stared at the hearse that had swallowed up Hendrik's body.

I wiped the tears from my cheeks. *Any other woman would have defended herself,* I thought. Stella Lejongård behaved as if the confrontation hadn't occurred.

Instead, she stalked toward the undertaker's employees and conferred briefly with them. I stood there, like a piece of discarded furniture. My anger had turned into numb disappointment. On the way back to Lindström's office, Mother had acted as if I weren't there. If I hadn't followed, she probably would have left me behind. She expressed her thanks to the professor, who then said farewell to both of us. Not another word passed between us until we were seated in the coach.

"One moment!" she called to August, who was waiting for her sign to get underway.

At last she turned to me. Her eyes were cold, her lips quivered, and her voice was low. "I am not in the least indifferent. Perhaps you have forgotten, but a family of our standing has certain responsibilities. We maintain our reserve. That means we do not give in to emotions, above all not in public." She paused as if expecting an objection. "Your behavior was that of a cheap prostitute. Thure should never have allowed you to go to Stockholm, where you forgot every vestige of your upbringing. Hendrik would never have behaved in such a despicable way. But you insisted on unpacking your heart! Contrary to what you may believe, I deeply regret that Hendrik fell victim to the fire. He was the ideal son!"

She gave me a long, hard look, then rapped on the door of the coach. I stared at her in shock. She didn't deign even to look at me after that.

Her rebuke tormented me during the entire return journey. If I'd dared, I would have asked straight-out if she wished I'd died instead. But I was afraid of what she'd say.

I did not go down to dinner that evening. I wandered aimlessly around the horse barns, wishing I were far away from all this. I wanted to be back in Stockholm with Michael. The thought of him was no longer a consolation, though, for I had the feeling something enormous and terrifying was bearing down on me.

I was the only one left now, Thure Lejongård's last heir. The heir to Lion Hall.

I crossed my arms and clutched my shoulders. Was there no way for me to escape these responsibilities?

The rising wind blew my hair and ruffled my clothes. I looked up. Dark clouds loomed. I lifted my skirt and ran.

The storm burst just as I reached the manor. I hurried up to the front door and then to my room, peeling off my wet clothing. I found a clean blouse in a drawer, put it on, and wrapped myself in an old morning robe. I felt heavy and sad. All I wanted to do was sleep, until the break of a new day.

9

Mother excluded me from funeral preparations, so I had to find some way to pass the time.

I was expecting news from Michael, but none came.

I told myself the post was often slow. Perhaps my letter had been delayed. So I wrote a shorter one to tell him of Hendrik's death. That made me feel no better. The pledge I'd made to Hendrik hung over me, as menacing as a thundercloud, and I was desperate for comforting words from Michael. I needed his promise of support. I needed him to say he loved me.

More than once my eyes fell on my old easel, but I couldn't find the energy to touch it. I'd used it often as a child, painting picture after picture. At first they were naive and amateurish, but later efforts were more sophisticated. Now my fingers felt numb and useless. My mind was devoid of images, filled instead with grief, confusion, and gloom. A true painter with a heavy heart is still capable of creating art, but pain and grief had left me inert.

If I'd been given something to do, I wouldn't have brooded so much over how Father and Hendrik must have felt as they ran into the burning barn or when the roof fell on them. I couldn't put those obsessive thoughts out of my mind.

I spent the afternoons in the manor library, even though I never actually brought myself to start a book. I would pick up a volume and glance through it, then return it to the shelf and go through the same distracted ritual with the next.

On Friday, I decided to walk to the family vault. I had no idea what was drawing me there. My grandmother was the only one interred in the mausoleum whom I'd known personally, and I hadn't been at all close to her. Hendrik and I had never visited the family mausoleum while growing up. It stood in the village graveyard and was no place for high-spirited children.

But that day I morbidly wanted to pay homage to the remains of my ancestors, those men and women who'd lived their whole lives on the estate and dedicated themselves to the Swedish royal family. Father and Hendrik were now of their number.

The mausoleum stood on a low hill by the church. When I arrived, the undertaker's men had already begun preparations for the next day's burials.

They'd dug a grave and covered it with turf. It wasn't for the Lejongårds, who weren't put in the ground. Lejongårds slumbered in stone niches as they awaited Judgment Day. The bronze statue of a weeping woman dominated the mausoleum entrance, her arm stretched over the grilled gate. An angel bent over her, one comforting hand upon her shoulder and the other raised toward heaven, reassuring us all that Paradise awaits us on the far side. The statue must have gleamed like gold when new, but now it was covered in a green patina. A pool half-covered with lily pads reflected the passing clouds. You might imagine this was the entrance to a magic kingdom if you didn't know that generations of Lejongårds were walled up inside.

I went to the entrance and peered at the line of engraved markers visible in the shadows. Later, the men sweeping the path would go inside, open two empty niches, and set up candles and floral displays. Funeral guests would not enter, but my mother and I would.

I nodded to the workers and pushed open the gate. Mother normally kept it locked, but she'd probably lent the key to the undertaker's men. There was nothing to steal anyhow. Our family custom was to inter our dead without valuables or jewelry. The bodies were laid out in plain clothes or simple nightgowns. My ancestors wished not to be weighed down with worldly possessions when they appeared before Saint Peter.

Inside, there was a musty odor of dust and damp. I took a match from my shoulder bag and lit the lantern that stood on a pedestal in the antechamber. With lamp in hand, I moved deeper inside.

Entombment in this place was reserved for the principal line of Lejongårds, families of the firstborn sons. Each couple was united forever inside a deep niche closed off with a stone slab. Fate had been kind to our family. Children had died young in earlier times, but there had always been a son who lived long enough to carry on the family line. That was now at an end. Thure's son had died without an heir.

The inscribed markers did not much move me. It isn't the name that makes a family; it's the love they share. And the only family love I felt was for Father and Hendrik.

A noise at the entrance brought me out of my meditations. I expected to see one of the workers, but my mother appeared instead, an inky shadow with a pale face.

"You, here?" She must have taken me for an apparition.

"Yes."

My mother shook her head in disbelief but made no comment. She strode to the section of empty chambers instead. The niche next to Thure's was vacant, awaiting her. Hendrik's untimely death had interrupted the planned order, for he was no longer a child to be entombed with the deceased young. There would be neither a wife at his side nor any child. Only me.

"Why will you not let me help with the funerals?" I asked. My voice echoed faintly in the vault. This was no place for conversation and certainly not one for argument. But it afforded my mother no opportunity to withdraw into her usual unreachable hauteur.

"You have been busy with your Stockholm existence, and you have been absent for some time," she answered, her gaze still fixed on the empty niche. "Your life is elsewhere. As mistress of this estate, I am responsible for the funerals."

"And that prevents you from accepting my help?"

Mother did not reply, so I continued. "I am very sorry I lost control of myself at the hospital. I . . . I was horribly anguished when I thought how they got up that morning full of hope and then had to suffer so. I know I would not be here now if the fire had not occurred. But believe me, I am not indifferent to the suffering of my family. I am still one of you, even as I struggle to live my own life." I bowed my head. "I wish more than anything that you could understand."

My mother stood motionless, looking away. I heard her panting quietly, as if struggling against tears.

"There is not much more to do," she said and turned toward me at last. Real tears glistened in her eyes, but she blinked them away. "I got started on Monday. Dr. Bengtsen examined your father and told me there was no hope. Bengtsen told me to stay with him and make his last hours as comfortable as possible. The doctor gave your father opium, so he could at least pass away without any pain." She stopped for a second, bowed her head, and then looked up again. "Things did not look much better for Hendrik, but Bengtsen thought perhaps his youth and strength gave him a chance. That is why he was transported to Kristianstad. But I knew, deep in my heart, he would never be whole again."

"And he was not allowed to know of Father's death."

"Yes. I wanted his last hours to be as easy as possible. He needed to believe his father would survive. Or were you cruel enough to tell him the truth?"

"I already told you! I lied. But I was expecting his condition to improve. Professor Lindström did say it was serious, but he did not tell me Hendrik was likely to die." I paused, wondering what other truths I could learn.

"Why weren't you there to receive me and say Father had died?" I asked in as low and controlled a voice as I could. "Why did Bruns conduct me to his deathbed without informing me what I was about to see?"

Mother pressed her lips together. "I . . . I was so full of grief. And anger. You should have been here! You belong here. But you were in Stockholm, living your frivolous life—"

"There is nothing frivolous about education, Mother." I tried to remain calm. "I do my best, and my teachers are satisfied with my progress. And believe me, there's nothing easy about the life I lead. I simply refused to remain under anyone's control."

Mother said nothing. Why was she so adamant?

She straightened herself, the tears gone. "Well, there is nothing more to be done here, in any case. You are free to leave for good."

I nearly gasped aloud. "If I intended to stay, would I be allowed to help with the arrangements?"

"No. The funeral is set. It was finalized even before your father died. But if you come back, you can oversee Lion Hall. And the family inheritance."

Was she expecting me to swear to that in the presence of my deceased ancestors? I would not, and she seemed to know it.

"I have instructions to give the workers," she said. "You may stay if you wish, but your presence is not required." She left.

I looked after her, my heart aching. For one short moment, I'd thought she would thaw, open up, perhaps even apologize for her heartless behavior. I couldn't have been more wrong. Her tone was calmer, but she obviously didn't regret taking her anger out on me. That made me terribly sad.

I waited until she'd left the vault, then followed. As she spoke with the burial crew, I set out for the estate, as abject and miserable as a whipped dog.

I shut myself away in my room the whole evening and tried to forget.

Saturday morning, someone shook my shoulder, startling me awake. I looked up, confused, and saw the maid. I couldn't for the life of me remember her name.

Ah. Lena. Yes, that's it: Lena.

"Are you ailing, gracious miss?" Lena asked, as alarmed as someone noticing a black eye. Only then did I realize that I was stretched out on the floor with a book under me. I must have fallen asleep while reading.

I struggled to sit up. When I was a child, I could sleep anywhere, but obviously that was a thing of the past. My back was stiff, and I had a pain in my neck as if I'd been painting for hours on end.

When I at last managed to get to my feet, I felt as ancient and creaky as a grandmother.

"Are you ill?" Lena nervously shifted her weight from one foot to the other. "Should I inform your mother?"

"No, I am fine," I replied. "I was reading by the fireplace."

The girl nodded but didn't look entirely convinced. I wasn't so sure either. Why on earth had I been prostrate in front of the hearth? I'd probably been overpowered by grief and exhausted from weeping.

"Very well, then. Let us start our day."

"I've brought hot water for your bath."

My mother was obviously of the opinion that I needed to wash away my sins before going to church. A futile effort; ordinary household soap wouldn't do the job.

"Good. Please proceed."

Lena curtsied and disappeared into the little side room that housed the bathtub with green enameled claw feet.

I examined my image in the mirror above the bureau. Good Lord, I was a wreck! I had dark circles under my eyes, my cheeks were ashen, and my lips were chapped. Michael would have packed me off to bed and called a doctor.

I didn't feel ill, except for the strange numbness in my chest. Grief had wrapped my heart in an impenetrable cocoon.

People would expect no more from me at the funeral than proper manners, and I didn't care about my appearance. I would hide all day long behind a black veil, a shield against hypocritical condolences.

Father's and Hendrik's deaths had shocked many, especially among the villagers. Those people knew them from the hunts and summer festivals my male relatives had always joined, paying no heed to Mother's objections. Father had devoted special attention to the villagers in recent years, making sure they saw Hendrik as the future lord and master. He'd succeeded; many were devastated by my brother's death.

Others would cheer our catastrophe, especially those few landowners who'd always envied us and wished us ill. Some were formidable business competitors who hoped to profit from our misfortune. I could imagine all too well their glee when they heard a woman was taking over management of the estate. The thought made me sick.

I resolved to put it out of my mind.

"You come from the village, I think?" I asked Lena as she poured steaming hot water into the tub.

"Yes, gracious miss."

I studied her in the mirror. She was wiry yet muscular. Like many peasant girls, she'd started work very young.

"Tyske," I commented. She stopped instantly and looked up. "Is that your family name? Or does my memory fail me?"

She gave me a wary look. "That's our name."

"You are Björn Tyske's daughter? The farmer who married the German woman?"

I knew of Björn Tyske only by hearsay, and Father had once mentioned him to the stable master. "Tyske" is the Swedish word for "German." That a man with that surname should take a German wife was one of the curious ironies of fate.

Lena's face was tense. "That's right. I hope it's not a problem for you."

Her reply surprised me. "Problem? Why would it be a problem?"

"It was a problem for most in the village. Foreigners and all. It still is."

Now I understood. "Nothing to worry about, Lena. In this household, one's parents' background isn't important. What counts is ability and dedication. I see no reason to reproach you."

Lena smiled uncertainly. I wished I could read her mind. She'd been here for only a short time, and already she'd been a witness to disaster. Presumably there was all sorts of talk in the servants' quarters on the top floor. Might they be worried we would let some of them go?

I undid my hair. It had become so tangled that the task took some time. "How have your first days here been?"

"Good," Lena answered. "Well, of course, I still don't know very much, but I really do like the house."

"Do you get along with the other girls?"

She nodded. "Yes. I mean, I don't know them well yet. I've been here only since the day . . ."

I looked at her for a moment, then realized what she had hesitated to say. "The day of the fire?"

Lena nodded again.

"Were you there?" I asked as nonchalantly as I could.

"Yes. We all were. We tried to put it out."

She was clearly ill at ease. What a fright it must have been to see the horse barn go up in flames! But I couldn't resist pressing her. "Can you tell me what it was like? How it started and how my father . . ." Without thinking, I reached out and clutched the girl's arm. She gave me a frightened look.

I released her. "Please forgive me. That was not appropriate. But I need to understand what happened. Did you see it? Or did people describe it to you?"

"Your father and your brother . . ." Lena struggled to find words. "They took their morning ride. We fixed breakfast and brought it up, and the gracious master made a little joke to Miss Rosendahl. A few minutes later, we heard a stable lad shouting 'Fire!' Your father and brother ran to the barn to get the horses out, the pregnant mares and your father's favorite."

"Edwina." I started to get choked up.

"Yes, Edwina. They were able to drive most of the horses out of the barn, and the rest of us were trying to put out the fire. Someone even brought a pump from the village."

The pump—Father's donation so the villagers could set up their own fire brigade.

"But it was no use. It was terrible. The fire spread, and suddenly . . ." Lena couldn't go on. She seemed to be seeing those frightful events once again.

"Thank you, Lena." I put my hand on her arm, gently this time. "I know the rest already."

Lena hesitated and then picked up the bucket. The water had cooled considerably. She poured it into the bath, however, straightened up, and looked at me. "Gracious miss, may I ask you something? Something personal?" She bit her lip and appeared to regret her presumption. "Please forgive me. I don't want to step out of line. Miss Rosendahl told me not to ask, but . . ."

"Please do," I said. I knew the strict household rules all too well, but this was a day to make exceptions. I was enormously grateful that she'd shared her experiences.

"That thing over there. Susanna called it an easel?"

My eyebrows shot up at her interest. Most people saw it as merely a collection of long sticks smeared with paint. Mother thought it should have been chopped up and fed into the fireplace long ago. I'd been surprised to find it still in my room.

"Yes, an easel. For resting canvases on while I paint. What about it?"

"Why did you leave it here?"

Again my eyebrows rose in surprise. Of course she'd heard that the "gracious miss" had refused to languish at home, awaiting the attentions of aristocratic suitors. "This is an old easel, the one I used while growing up. It is far too small for my work in Stockholm."

"Stockholm must be beautiful," she said with a dreamy expression.

"You've never been there?" I responded and immediately wanted to bite my tongue. Of course she hadn't. Peasant children rarely left their villages. They were put to work at a tender age. As soon as they grew up, they married and established their own families, rooting themselves forever.

"No, gracious miss," she replied. "But I'd so like to see the city. Especially the palace, the theatres, and the shops." Her eyes shone. "Oh, and the harbor and all those sailing ships that go out to foreign lands."

I was reminded of how fortunate I was. Of course Father hadn't been pleased when I left for Stockholm, but at least I'd been able to go.

"You're very kind, gracious miss!" Lena curtsied and ran to fetch more water.

10

When I'd finished dressing, I inspected myself in the mirror. The dress my mother had lent me was tight and stiff. Although Mother was slim, she always insisted her clothes be sewn one size smaller, so a corset was required. I found this feeling of being stuffed into a dress absolutely unbearable. It seemed to stifle me even more now than on the day we'd gone to the hospital for Hendrik's body.

But I had no time to change. August was waiting out front with the coach, and Mother would brook no delay. I stood while Lena adjusted the veil around the hat that completely covered my hair. I took one last look in the tall mirror. I was a younger version of my grim grandmother, but Stella wouldn't fault my appearance.

She waited for me in the downstairs hall. She'd somehow managed to cinch her waist even smaller than usual. Or had she lost more weight?

Her veil didn't hide her sharp gaze. She inspected me from head to foot, then approved with an almost imperceptible nod.

"We must hurry," she said. "It has rained, and we do not know the state of the roads."

"But most roads have been graded, Mother. Around Kristianstad, they are even paved. We'll be there on time."

"Come now."

I had no desire to quarrel over trivialities. We had greater burdens to bear.

August held the door for us. He wore his best livery, and a shining black top hat perched upon his white mane. I hadn't seen him in that hat since my grandmother was buried.

My mother immediately gave the signal to start.

At Holy Trinity Church in Kristianstad, I looked out at the vast crowd of black-clad mourners that filled the square. Many faces were obscured by veils like mine. My mourning dress was hot, and I wished I could tear off all this garb along with the pain and grief. But that was impossible.

More people streamed into the church. Everyone rose when we entered the nave. I saw landowners from throughout the region, all of them business associates or friends of my father. The crown prince himself was present. Mother hadn't told me he would be coming, but I wasn't surprised, considering our close relations with the royal family. I settled into the front pew, feeling numb and trying to ignore the eyes fixed on my back.

The coffins of my father and brother stood before the altar and were covered with enormous floral arrangements in yellow and red, our heraldic colors. I loved roses, but today the heavy perfume of those hothouse blooms was nauseating.

The tall doors closed, and the murmur of mourners quieted, replaced by an oppressive silence. The organ played a prelude. The priest came out, bowed to the cross and then to the coffins, and climbed the steps to the pulpit to begin his sermon.

My eyes remained fixed upon the caskets. I imagined my father and brother lying inside upon the white satin lining, but those images faded as I was flooded with memories. Something strange happened: as the priest droned on, I was transported to the distant past, to a moment when I'd been thrilled by my father's approval.

It was the day I first learned to ride. I was only five or six. For months I'd been envious of my brother, who was three years older and had been riding for what seemed an eternity. I was always told I was too little. My mother would have found it entirely inappropriate for me to get onto a saddle, but my father lectured her: "She is a Lejongård! My daughter must be just as knowledgeable about horses as her brother!"

"But that will be of no use to her," Mother countered. "Someday she will move to another house, and it will not matter whether she can ride or not."

Back then I wasn't yet aware that she was aiming to marry me into some distant branch of the royal family.

"A lady must be comfortable in the saddle," my father declared. "And she will learn to ride, starting today. I will hear no more about the matter!"

And that was that. Father led me to the pen with our horses. A pony awaited me there. It was brown and shaggy with a long, bright mane and tail. I was thrilled by the sight of the tidy little saddle. This was really going to happen! I was going to learn to ride!

My father stood by the horse and told me to climb into the saddle. Hendrik assumed I wouldn't be able to get up without help—after all, I was quite small. But before he could come to my aid, I scrambled over the fence and ran to the pony. My brother, who'd been trained on the same little horse, had told me its name was Happy. I'd sometimes been allowed to feed Happy sugar cubes.

"Neta, wait!" my brother called, but I was already next to the pony. I'd watched Hendrik climb up into the saddle so often. Why shouldn't I be able to do the same?

I put one foot in the stirrup and tried to haul myself up, but I wasn't strong enough. Instants later, Hendrik was behind me and gave me a boost. I managed to grab the saddle horn. With a bit more assistance, I got up into the saddle.

"Very good, Agneta!" Father called and applauded. He could have placed me in the saddle himself, but I already knew my father was particularly pleased whenever someone took the initiative.

I sat on Happy, proud as a queen on a throne, and it didn't matter a bit that the horse probably wouldn't have budged even if a shot had been fired next to him.

My father taught me how to tell the pony to move and how to stop him. He put Happy on a lead and walked him around a circuit. The swaying frightened me a little, and I clutched Happy's mane. No one seemed to notice my nervousness. One of the men watching outside the fence called, "The little lass wouldn't be scared even of the devil!"

"She's a real Lejongård," my father shouted back. He beamed with pride and satisfaction. He almost never looked at me that way again, even though I tried so often to please him . . .

Organ music brought me back to the present. I was startled to find that the priest had already finished his sermon. Pallbearers approached the coffins. After a moment, we rose, and to my surprise, I found myself smiling. My memories were so strong and vivid that they broke through the grief of the recent horrible days. I gathered those memories and tucked them away in my heart, thankful that the veil hid the smile on my face.

We drove in a long cortege to the cemetery. People lined the way to the mausoleum, and this time most of them were village folk. My mother and I took our place at the very front, before the gate to the vault.

The priest resumed with a blessing and the Lord's Prayer. His words echoed hollowly from the stone walls. Someone was sobbing, deeply moved by the ceremony.

My mother stood there like a statue, and I myself was unable to weep. I would cry later, sheltered from inquisitive eyes, curling up to lament where no one could accuse me of weakness or judge me in any other way.

"Forever, amen!" The priest's closing words rang out over the crowd.

The pallbearers lifted the caskets and carried them into the mausoleum. My eyes followed. The image of my father and brother confined forever in those cramped niches weighed upon my heart like an immense stone. Hendrik had always loved being outside in the fields or on the shore of the little lake bordering our property. He loved the sun but now would dwell in eternal night. We'd never discussed funerals or his wishes for his own. It had all seemed such a distant prospect. We'd felt immortal. Now I wondered if Hendrik wouldn't have preferred a grave under the open sky, perhaps by a linden tree, with the stars twinkling overhead.

I took a shuddering breath, swaying dizzily. How I longed for an arm to lean upon! Michael's arm or perhaps Marit's. She'd have hugged me and consoled me, even though she didn't think much of my family. But neither was there, and my mother didn't even extend her hand. I felt more alone than I had in a very long time.

When the undertaker's men emerged, I felt a deep desire simply to enter the vault, sink down, and abandon myself to slumber. But that was against protocol. I wasn't given even a moment to stand alone and unmolested before their resting places. My mother gripped my arm in a gesture that looked like support but was really a warning to comply.

I was tempted to resist but didn't. I let her march me back to the coach.

11

Back at the manor house, we arrived to find the entire staff of servants and employees assembled on the front steps as if for a formal photograph. Those who didn't have a complete outfit in black at least wore a black mourning band. The women stood with their hands folded before them; the men were bare-headed, caps in hand. Bruns, bent with grief, was in the front row, next to Miss Rosendahl, whose eyes were red from weeping. All the way to the left, I saw Susanna, Marie, and Lena. On the right were my mother's chambermaid, Linda; Svea, the assistant cook; and Mrs. Bloomquist. The stable boys huddled behind. All faces were somber.

The coach stopped. August opened the door and helped us down. A long procession of carriages followed, the first one belonging to the crown prince. At the church he'd briefly expressed his condolences, but I hoped that now we'd have the opportunity to speak with His Highness at greater length.

I liked Gustav Adolf and his young wife, Margaret. The English princess had brought a bit of color back to a Swedish court that had become increasingly dull after King Gustav V's accession. The king disliked ceremony. I remembered how furious my mother was at my debut at court. For once I wasn't the target of her wrath. She was offended by the ceremony's lack of glamor. She wanted elegance. The presentation and the ball that followed were quite spartan, and the king took an early leave. The queen stayed until the ball was over, but everyone had the impression she'd have preferred to be elsewhere. She'd been in poor health since the birth of her last son—that was an open secret—and the Swedish climate was hard on her. She'd had a Mediterranean villa constructed and lived there most of the time, attended by her personal physician. She appeared at court only when obliged to do so.

It's odd, but my mother's annoyance was all I really remembered of that evening. I didn't recall the banquet or my dance partners. I cared as little about the debutante party as the king did. I already knew I wouldn't be leading that life.

The funeral reception took place in the great ballroom, Lion Hall's most beautiful space. We'd held many brilliant parties here: our traditional hunt ball, the midsummer festival, and more. Today, for the first time since my grandmother died, the space was used to receive condolences. I'd been very young then, but I had vague memories of long lines of subdued visitors similar to those now lining up.

My mother received the guests, and servants provided the refreshments. The crown prince approached us after the reception line closed.

"Your Majesty!" I curtsied, but Gustav Adolf extended his hand.

"Let us not be so formal. Today is not about the crown but rather about your tragic loss. My father was devastated when we heard of it. As was I."

"Thank you very much. That is extremely kind of you."

I looked into the prince's face. He was about the same age as Hendrik, though already married and blessed with children. It was sad that Hendrik hadn't established a family, but just then I was relieved he hadn't left behind a grieving widow and children. On the other hand, if he'd been married, perhaps he wouldn't have rushed into a burning barn.

The crown prince turned to my mother, and the princess gave me a shy look. I hardly knew her. We'd chatted a bit the last time they were with us. The royal pair occasionally visited Lion Hall for a couple of weeks in the summer. Margaret, the granddaughter of Queen Victoria, often seemed overly stiff and a bit ill at ease. Even my mother thought so. But the princess wasn't unsympathetic, and she surprised me by spontaneously reaching out to press my hand.

"I am so sorry," she said, her English accent less pronounced than I remembered. "Your father and brother were close friends of our family. I hope we may continue the same with you and your mother."

"You will, Your Majesty."

A shy smile flickered across her lovely face. She pressed my hand once more, and I had the fleeting impression she wanted to take me aside for a private conversation.

Her husband turned his attention to us again. "If you need any assistance, do not hesitate to write. Your family has always been loyal supporters of the royal family, and we would be honored to return the favor."

"That is very kind of you, Your Majesty. Thank you very much." I knew we would never take the prince up on his offer. The Lejongårds made it their duty to support the crown and never to turn to the royal family for help. We had not appealed to a king for assistance at any time since we were granted this estate shortly after Skåne province was reincorporated into the kingdom of Sweden.

I felt the touch of my mother's hand on my arm after the royal pair turned away. It startled me. "I see you remembered your manners in the presence of the crown prince."

I didn't know what to say.

"I am going to retire for a time," she continued. "Please take care of our guests and make excuses for me if anyone notes my absence."

My mother wanted to withdraw? She did look exhausted, but this was quite unlike her.

"Yes, Mother." I watched as she vanished through the crowd of guests.

I felt completely at sea. The visitors were entertaining one another, and most would surely want to chat about Father and Hendrik, then go on to talk business. I looked away.

Samuel Jensen, our family solicitor, approached me. He wore a dark suit, as always. Mr. Jensen didn't care for bright colors, which he considered inappropriate for a man of his responsibilities. "My office is no place for frippery," he liked to say. "It is a sanctum of competence and serious counsel." He underlined that message with his ever-impeccable appearance. He had white hair and an impressive gray beard.

"My dear Miss Agneta, I am very sorry you and your lady mother must face such bitter loss. One could speak of God's will, as the priest did, but you know I do not share his opinion."

Jensen was always frank, never one to condescend. That punctilious attitude had become more marked with age. His condolences were surely the sincerest I received that day.

"Thank you, Mr. Jensen. You are very kind."

The solicitor nodded. "I do not know if your lady mother has already informed you: in consideration of the fact that yours is one of the largest and wealthiest estates in the land, I would be pleased to communicate to you the contents of the wills of your father and your brother the day after tomorrow."

"My brother left a will?" Hendrik had never mentioned such a thing. And why would he? He was so young and couldn't have had any premonition of disaster.

"Yes, he did. He was, after all, heir to the estate. Surviving your father by two days, he became the owner, so his directives are definitive. Now you are the heiress, so you yourself should consider making out a will."

I shuddered. "Must I?"

"It is always wise to make arrangements," the solicitor replied. "Especially if one wishes to make any specific provisions."

Did I have any such wishes? Whom might I designate to inherit Lion Hall? I had no children yet. And I had no idea who should succeed me. None of my Stockholm friends would want anything to do with the estate. Michael, perhaps? After all, as soon as we married, he would be entitled to inherit.

Jensen noted my confusion. "I understand you have other matters on your mind at the present moment. I simply want to assure you I will be in my office from ten o'clock on Monday to break the seals on the wills. We can discuss afterward what is to be done with the estate."

"Many thanks." I'd been saying that all day long to everyone who addressed me, so the expression was beginning to sound trite. "We will be punctual. If you wish to speak with my mother—"

"Oh no, that is not necessary. I have already spoken with your lady mother, and she is aware of the situation. But I did not know whether she had informed you."

My mother's usual practice was to share information only at the last moment and imply my ignorance was my own fault. But I didn't tell Mr. Jensen that. I merely nodded blandly to hide the bitterness welling up within. "Please accept my sincere thanks, Mr. Jensen."

My courage and resolution were beginning to fail. I needed room to breathe and a moment to myself. I stepped outside onto the front steps, where the air was fresh and fragrant with greenery. I pushed back the veil and filled my lungs. I studied the bare linden trees along the drive, and for a time I contemplated the spectacle of immense clouds gathering in the blue sky. Still, the murmur of the guests was just behind me. They were too near. I hurried down the steps and around the corner of the manor.

Many carriages were stationed in the inner court. Some were light and simple; others were large and portentous. The royal buggy at the fore looked humble and flimsy. I doubted that Gustav and Margaret had traveled all the way from Stockholm in it. They'd probably taken the train to Kristianstad. I assumed they would stay with us, unless the crown prince was called to attend to state business.

I walked through the garden, toward the small pavilion that stood at its southern edge. My parents had taken their marriage vows here but left it to sag and deteriorate in later years. To my great surprise, I saw someone on its platform.

I approached and made out features I knew well: Lennard Ekberg, an old family friend I hadn't seen for at least three years. I hadn't noticed him come through the reception line.

Lennard's father, a count, had inherited and maintained a family fortune accumulated by grain dealing. The family lived a day's ride from us, and Hendrik and I had frequently played with Lennard during our childhood. Now the old count was ill, so his son had taken responsibility for most of the estate's business. The past three years had transformed a young, uncertain, pale young man into an impressive masculine figure any woman would find attractive.

Lennard's blond hair was thick and lustrous. His face, now tanned, bore creases and wrinkles that made it even more interesting than his down-covered cheeks of yesteryear. He wore no beard. Fortunately, his thin lips went well with his long face and narrow nose.

"Lennard, whatever are you doing out here?"

"I might ask you the same!" He came down the steps, beaming, and hugged me. "You are incredibly beautiful. Did you know that?"

"Oh really?" I sighed and gently freed myself from his embrace. "You should see me on a good day."

Lennard thrust his hands deep into his trouser pockets. "I am sure you are tired of hearing this, but it pains me greatly Thure and Hendrik have left us."

"It all depends on whether the speaker is sincere. At least your words come from the heart."

Lennard's sad smile widened. The intensity of his gaze surprised and confused me. Had I really forgotten the friendly candor of those blue eyes?

We'd been friends since primary school, which meant we'd known one another for more than twenty years. Hendrik and I had always been happy when the Ekbergs brought Lennard and his sister, Lisbeth, to visit. He'd been pallid and quite thin, but his face always radiated vigor. Lennard had a boundless imagination. He told us family legends of how they were descended from a race of feisty Norsemen, and while Lisbeth stayed with her parents, the three of us scampered across the estate, waving wooden swords and engaging in pretend duels. I was always terribly sad when they left, even when the Viking sagas were forgotten amid the trials of growing up.

"Your father was an uncle to me," he said after staring up into the clouds for a time. "But you know that, of course. My father took news of his death particularly hard."

"How is he, then? Has he come to the funeral?"

Lennard shook his head. "No, he was forced to stay home. The news of Thure's death was a terrible blow. I should mention that to your mother."

"She is not feeling well just now. She went to lie down."

"I understand." Lennard paused. "Father has had health problems for years now, but I have the feeling they are getting worse. Even though the doctors claim his condition is stable."

I knew that Gustav Ekberg had suffered from gastrointestinal problems in the past, and he scarcely left the manor anymore.

"I do hope he recovers from the shock and you suffer no additional adversity. You will say hello to him for me?"

Lennard nodded. "I will indeed. Thanks. But we do have good news. Lisbeth is expecting her first child!"

"Really?"

That was marvelous news, for I knew Lisbeth had always dreamed of having babies. She'd made a good choice of husband; he owned a small estate in Småland. Their finances were assured, and, better, they were very much in love—not always the case in our circles.

"Yes, she is over the moon!" Lennard said. "You should come visit. It has been too long since all of us have been together."

"Let me see what I can manage. Just now, with no master for the estate, things will certainly be changing. For me, for my family . . ."

"You will be a magnificent head of the family."

"Perhaps. But maybe you had not heard I have found a different calling."

"Oh dear. Indeed I have!" Lennard exclaimed. "And you are notorious for it."

"Really? Notorious?"

"Certainly. Mrs. von Löfven blushes furiously when my mother mentions you are studying art in Stockholm."

I had to grin. "No doubt she supposes I live a life of folly and dissolution."

Hertha von Löfven had a wicked tongue and knew practically all the old biddies in society. She avidly collected rumors to store them away like Pandora, then opened her metaphorical box to spread them far and wide. I probably featured prominently in her trove of gossip, for all those snobs were scandalized I'd dared to exempt myself from the rules of polite society.

"And what does your mother say to that?"

"Well, she would hardly have been pleased if Lisbeth had done the same, but all things considered, she is happy for you. In any case, she refuses to judge. She proclaims you a member of the feminine avant-garde, the gallant women who will someday shake out the stuffy old curtains of Swedish society."

"That sounds rather like a compliment."

Lennard smiled, and we stood there, regarding one another for a long while. How I'd missed him! He'd always brought a bit of light into even the darkest times.

"Shall we go back in?" he asked at last and pointed to the heavens. "There seems to be a storm brewing."

"The weather outside is not much different from the atmosphere inside the house."

"Oh, you exaggerate. They will all be happy with drink as they tell their stories about Thure and Hendrik." He offered me his arm. "This day will pass, and the sun will soon shine over Lion Hall again."

I hesitated, not wanting to provide more grist for the rumor mill. But then I took his arm and allowed him to escort me. I wanted to spend more time with Lennard, but when we went inside, my mother had returned and swept him away someplace.

Later, I was incapable of recalling the names of all who'd clutched my hand and expressed their sympathy. I learned in the course of the afternoon that the royal pair was bound for Copenhagen that same day and would overnight with the Danish royals. The news that they wouldn't be staying at Lion Hall was a great relief.

After the last visitor said good night, I dragged myself wearily upstairs. I wasn't used to playing hostess. That was rightly my mother's role, but after the royal couple's departure, she'd abruptly vanished.

Mother was waiting for me at the top of the stairs. She too seemed tired beyond words. "Agneta," she said in a low voice.

"Mother," I replied. "Are you all right?"

"I talked to Lennard Ekberg. He told me you two spoke."

"We did. It was lovely to see him again."

"I wish his father were in better health. It was terrible to hear everything his mother has to endure."

I gave her a perplexed look. When had we last spoken so freely? "Did he tell you Lisbeth is expecting?"

"He did," she said. "How unfortunate Lennard has still not found a wife." I couldn't escape the sensation that there was a hidden meaning within her remark. "You, however, should not let too much more time pass," she continued. "You are not getting younger. You are twenty-seven now, and—"

"Mother, can we talk about something else?" I replied. "Mr. Jensen spoke to me. He said that the opening of the wills is set for this coming Monday."

"That is our arrangement." She paused. "You are planning to return to Stockholm, I assume."

"That is not the subject for Monday's discussion, is it?" Yes, I longed to return to Stockholm, where, despite my meager circumstances, my life was less constrained. I yearned for Michael's kisses and his warm embrace. I had so much to tell him.

"No, it is not," my mother admitted, to my surprise. "This estate has to be properly administered. It is too valuable to be left without adequate oversight. Of course, that is all one to you. You have never given a thought to the future of Lion Hall."

The exhausted she-wolf had found the energy to renew the attack.

"That is not true, Mother. But I always knew Hendrik would inherit, not I. So I looked for something different. Something that was mine alone, so I could support myself as long as I lived."

Mother sniffed in derision. "As a starving artist! A woman painter! Without the allowance from your father, you would have been on the streets. You would have had to forget those studies of yours."

Weakened as I was, I couldn't stand up to that broadside. Why couldn't she simply leave me in peace on this of all days?

"I am going to bed. You can continue scolding me tomorrow morning."

I turned my back to her. My eyes instantly filled with tears—of fury, not grief. My mother knew Hendrik's destiny and mine had been different. She knew I should never have inherited the estate. My most likely prospect had been a dreary life on some other holding. Was that any excuse to claim I cared nothing for Lion Hall?

I fell heavily across my bed, almost insensible to the tight grip of the corset around my torso. Numb through and through, I wanted nothing but to sink deep into the oblivion of sleep. I yearned to wake up in Michael's arms in Stockholm. That was impossible, of course, but tomorrow was a new day. One when I'd either have to defend myself against my mother or endure her silence.

And on Monday we'd learn the last wishes of my brother and discover the destiny of Lion Hall.

One way or another, my life was about to change.

12

Monday was sunny and cool with only a couple of feathery clouds high in the sky. The birds were singing furiously, and the sun's rays had all but dried up the last puddles. A full week had passed since my father's death following the accident. Life had gone on. The sun rose each morning and set each evening, people died, and others were born.

My mother sat beside me in the coach. She'd said nothing at breakfast. That was all right with me, for her recent accusations had haunted my dreams. The worst of it was that she was right. Without my meager allowance, I'd have had to seek employment—or, penniless, find some even more miserable hole to crawl into. If the wills' contents gave her the authority, she'd restrict my privileges as much as possible.

I was jolted from my brooding by a sudden change in the rhythm of hoofbeats. Without realizing it, I'd been picking nervously at the fingertips of my gloves and had broken some of the seams. I did my best to hide the damage and glanced at her. She sat as stiff as a poker, her hands poised on the handle of her umbrella. She had insisted on bringing it, even though there was no threat of rain. I was thankful to see that Stella looked lost in thought, off in a different world. Perhaps she was reliving the past, those days when life had been simpler, predictable.

I gazed through the coach window as we rattled through the streets of Kristianstad. Affluent folks and servants alike bustled along the sidewalks, intent on their business. In Stockholm, I'd read of a shortage of servants throughout the country. The wealthiest families had hired maids and cooks to staff multiple residences, and other prominent families had difficulties locating qualified help. We didn't have such problems; young women from the village were eager to work for us. Employment at Lion Hall was much desired, for it allowed them to stay near home while offering a comfortable life not dependent upon the harvest.

I'd probably have felt the same, if I'd been in their shoes. I was even a bit envious of Lena. She was so young and unencumbered, and her eyes often had that dreamy expression. No doubt she was worried, wondering like the rest of the manor staff what was in store for them all. But her mother wasn't pushing her to rush into marriage. Stella hadn't yet gone back to that theme, but she surely would do so once we'd wrapped up the business with Mr. Jensen. Would that be the time for me to put my cards on the table and tell her I was going to marry a rising young attorney? For bourgeois families, a catch like Michael would be greeted with enthusiasm, but our set thought little of a suitor without a noble title.

The coach pulled up before the building. Jensen's law office, one of many here, was located in a building with a white facade featuring classically styled columns. It looked like a Greek temple. August opened the coach door and helped my mother out. I trailed her up the steps.

A current of cool air wafted through the entry hall. Our footsteps echoed against the marble tiles. My mother strode ahead purposefully, seeming to have forgotten my presence. I'd have liked to tarry to study the exterior and the paintings hung along the walls within. But we weren't here for the art. My mother took an instant to collect herself outside Jensen's door and then rapped on it. I was expecting her to warn me to behave, but she continued to ignore me.

Jensen himself opened the door almost immediately. He was again dressed in his dark suit, this time with a sapphire-blue tie.

"Ah, the ladies of Lion Hall! I am pleased to see you."

"The pleasure is entirely mine, Mr. Jensen," Mother said. "It is good you were able to find time for us on such short notice. When an estate like ours is in question, the circumstances must be made clear as quickly as possible so as to ensure the continued confidence of our business partners."

I was astonished by her declaration. How could anyone not trust the Lejongårds? Yes, people had certainly heard of Father's death, but his business partners would hardly be rushing to abandon the relationship. Everyone knew we were so closely linked to the palace that the crown prince himself had attended the funeral.

Jensen ushered us into his office, where two comfortable leather armchairs stood before his desk. Two envelopes were positioned on the desktop: Father's will and Hendrik's.

"Now that we are all here, we may as well begin." Jensen took his place behind the desk and made his formal declaration. "In my capacity as solicitor and royal notary, today, March 17, 1913, at eleven o'clock in the morning, I am breaking the seals and reading the last wishes of the deponents." He broke the wax seal of the first envelope and extracted a document.

I'd supposed Father's will would be longer, since perhaps our family had some distant relations he might have to take into consideration. The single sheet of paper made it clear he'd expressed his last wishes in very few words.

"The will is dated October 18, 1912, and it is the most recent declaration known to me. It reads, and I quote, 'I, Thure August Lejongård, direct in these my last wishes that the manor house and Lion Hall estate, including all livestock and inventory, as well as the villa near Åhus, will pass after my death to my son, Hendrik Olaf Lejongård. My daughter, Agneta Sophie Lejongård, receives a monthly allowance of thirty crowns, and if she should elect to return to reside at the estate, the allowance will be raised to one hundred crowns until she marries. In addition, she will receive as a dowry a one-time payment of fifteen thousand crowns. My wife, Stella Louise Lejongård, is entitled to reside on the estate as long as she lives and to receive an annual allowance of two thousand crowns.'"

Now came the second envelope with Hendrik's will. I still found it hard to believe my brother had thought to make one out.

I glanced at Mother. She seemed not entirely pleased by the terms Father had established. Was two thousand crowns a year not enough for her needs? It was a fortune, especially compared to the paltry sums Father had stipulated for me.

Jensen picked up the second envelope. "I now read the last will and testament of Hendrik Lejongård." He broke the seal. This time he took out two sheets. Had my brother written a will longer than Father's?

"This will is dated December 29, 1912, and it is the most recent declaration known to me. It reads as follows: 'I, Hendrik Olaf Lejongård, hereby direct that, in the event of my death, my fortune, the manor house, Lion Hall estate, with all livestock and inventory, and the summer house near Åhus are to pass to my sister, Agneta Sophie Lejongård.'"

December 29. He must have written it immediately after the argument at our Christmas ball. What had he been thinking? Had my father threatened to disinherit me? Had Hendrik wanted to protect me from my mother?

I closed my eyes. After the pledge he'd insisted I give, the will was really no surprise. Now it was official. My brother had briefly become the newest Count Lejongård, and his instructions had the force of law.

"In addition, he has included a personal note," Jensen added. He read it aloud.

Dear Agneta,

Do you still remember that day in the meadow when we talked about what we wanted to be when we grew up? You were seven or eight years old, and you were determined, come what may, to become mistress of the estate.

"Why do the boys always get everything?" you asked me, vexed, after Father explained, yet again, that you would not inherit.

We agreed that afternoon we would become joint masters of the estate.

Back then I already knew it could not be, unless you remained unmarried and lived at Lion Hall. I did not wish that fate for you, for you are far too beautiful to become an old maid!

I promised myself you would always have a share in the estate if you wanted it. I never told you, because I wanted you to find your own way, but it was true, nevertheless. I was very proud when you discovered painting and decided to seek fame as an artist. I hope you have achieved your goal by the time you read this.

I have no idea how old you are now. Perhaps we both survived to a ripe old age and led fulfilling lives before God called me home. Regardless, I hope with all my heart you will remember how attached to Lion Hall you once were. And that, as its new mistress, you will always take good care of it, so as to pass our thriving estate to the next generation.

Your brother, who loves you so much,
Hendrik

His words lingered in the room, sank deep into my heart, and exploded. I struggled for breath. Hendrik was calling to me from beyond the grave . . . How brief an interval there'd been between the drafting of his will and the accident!

"You are entirely free either to accept the inheritance or to turn it down."

Jensen's eyes bored into mine. I braved that challenge with an air of serene calm, even though I was fighting back tears. One person in this family had tried to understand me. At least one was proud of me and my actions. Why did Hendrik have to leave me so soon?

"I . . . I will inform you."

My mother intruded. "Do you really need time to think it over? Whatever for? You have inherited everything!"

Was that resentment I heard in her voice? She was well provided for and had no need to fear the future. But Father hadn't willed the estate to her. And neither had Hendrik.

"I presume, Countess, that you will accept the portion of the inheritance your husband has left you as a legacy?"

"I will." Mother looked at me. She didn't speak, but I got the message: *I, at least, am aware of what is required.*

I was just as aware.

"Then I hereby conclude the reading of the wills," Jensen pronounced. "I will expect your decision in the next fortnight, Miss Lejongård."

I nodded.

Jensen continued, saying, "I will have a transcription of the wills delivered to you. If you should decide to accept the legacy, additional matters will need to be discussed."

I nodded again and pressed my handbag to my chest. Now I was Countess Lejongård—if I wished to be. I felt no thrill at the thought; I had the feeling I'd just been locked inside the family mausoleum.

My mother stared out the coach window all the way back to Lion Hall. I could imagine what she was feeling. Everything had been laid at my feet—the title, the estate, the good will of the royal family, and our entire fortune. And I hadn't leaped to scoop up those gifts.

Mother would surely have wanted to see me sit down immediately with Jensen to review the Lion Hall inventory. But I couldn't, not yet. I needed time to think about Hendrik's invocation of that scene from our childhood, that distant moment when I insisted I wanted to be the mistress of Lion Hall.

The silence between my mother and me only emphasized our enormous undiscussed differences. I desperately wished I could explain how complicated I found this. Sacrificing deeply held ambitions was no easy thing. "Mother, I—"

Stella shook her head and held up a hand. "I am fatigued and wish to lie down. Tell me once you've decided to go back to Stockholm."

I felt as if I'd been slapped. Of course, I wanted to go back to the capital, but I was no capricious schoolgirl. I could have refused my father's legacy, but defying my beloved brother's dying wish seemed something else entirely.

I lagged behind as Mother stalked into the house. When I stepped inside, Marie was waiting for me. She wore a starched white apron, and a small cap covered her dark hair.

"Gracious miss, a police inspector is here. His name is Hermannsson. He wishes to speak to you."

"To me?" I echoed in surprise. My mother was already halfway up the stairs. She'd obviously told Marie I would attend to the visitor.

I recalled Langeholm's mention of an investigation. Perhaps the policeman had results to report.

"Where is he?" I asked as I finally shed my ghastly black gloves.

"In the salon."

Marie had apparently assumed Mother would receive him there. I had no intention of doing so.

"Escort the gentleman into my father's office and inform him I will be with him shortly. I need to freshen up first."

Marie curtsied and withdrew.

I watched her go and then went upstairs. I splashed cold water on my face, trying to flush away the headache that had been brewing on our return journey. I wasn't ready to give Jensen a response, but today I was going to rise to the responsibilities of my new role.

13

The police officer shifted from one leg to the other, turning his hat in his hands. He was in his midfifties, about the age of my father. The gray of his temples had begun to spread through the rest of his hair. He wore a somewhat shabby three-piece suit with a silver watch chain across the waistcoat. How many times had he checked the time while waiting?

I walked up to him. "Inspector Hermannsson?"

It was obvious from his expression he had no idea who I was. Our sleepy little community had no village policeman, for the master of the estate settled minor quarrels. If something serious occurred, the Kristianstad police could be summoned, but that almost never happened.

"I am Agneta Lejongård. Quite pleased to receive you."

Hermannsson took a moment to absorb this information. He extended his hand. "The pleasure is entirely mine. If one may say so in circumstances as unfortunate as these. Your father's death has shocked the entire region."

"Thank you very much, Inspector." I indicated the leather armchairs by the window where Father had always conducted his business. "Please take a seat. May I offer you something to drink?"

"Oh! No, that's not necessary. I simply wanted to inform you of the status of the investigation. Is your lady mother not presently at home?"

"My mother is currently indisposed. And, unfortunately, I have been informed of the incidents in only the most general terms. I was in Stockholm at the time."

The inspector nodded and took a little notebook from the inside pocket of his jacket. "I can describe what happened, if you wish."

I took the chair across from the inspector. "Please."

"Our investigation established that the fire broke out around eight o'clock in the morning. The local fire brigade was summoned to extinguish the blaze. Witnesses state that your father and brother were inside the building the whole time. Neither heeded the many calls to stay clear of danger. The fire became more intense as they drove the horses out of the structure. The roof collapsed. The stable boys were able to pull them both out of the burning wreckage, but your father's injuries were so severe that the physician called to the scene could do nothing for him."

His account corresponded with the stories from Langeholm and Lena, but it affected me powerfully nevertheless. Why hadn't they listened? Yes, the horses were expensive and beloved beasts, but that was nothing in comparison to life itself.

"Thank you, Inspector." I did my best to maintain control. "Are you in a position to close this case soon?"

"We must obtain additional statements, I regret to say. We've examined the debris and will probably be able to approve the clearing of the site in the next few days."

Statements? Hadn't the witnesses already told them everything?

"Upon close examination of the remains of the structure, we concluded this was a case of arson. The way the fire broke out indicates it was deliberately set in the straw stored in the barn. It spread slowly and almost died out, but then it reached the dry wood of the structure. We suspect a second fire was set under the roof, most likely with the intention of causing it to collapse."

I involuntarily pressed my hand to my abdomen.

"Are you certain?" I asked in a strangled voice.

"Fairly, yes. I'm afraid it will be necessary to carry out more detailed interrogations."

"Do you suspect someone from here on the estate?"

"We do not exclude anyone for the time being. Other than you and your lady mother, of course. We need to establish whether anyone might've had a reason to set fire to the barn."

"Please do what you must. And keep us informed of your progress."

"I will." The inspector rose and offered me his hand. "Again, many thanks." He took a business card from his wallet. "If you should hear anything, please contact me at this address or by telephone."

"I will send a messenger," I replied as I took the card. "We have no telephone here, unfortunately."

"As you wish, miss."

I escorted him to the door, then made my way back to the office, thinking it might be the best place to think.

I'd often crept in here as a child and hidden beneath the heavy oak desk. In Father's absence, I'd sometimes peeked at the contents of the drawers. The sight of the neat bronze handles, artfully crafted in floral shapes, made my fingers tingle. Emotion flooded through me. We'd had no chance to reconcile, but I missed Father, his decisive vigor, his warmth.

I hesitated, then opened the top drawer. Father had been a very orderly person, a trait he'd inherited from his mother. His pipe, exuding the strong odor of tobacco, was precisely positioned next to the silver pocket watch with the ornately engraved cover. He wore that timepiece only on special occasions, concerned he might lose it. Beneath those items were his most important papers, those he'd have rushed to retrieve if the manor had ever caught fire. Our patent of nobility, an extract of the register of heraldry, and the deed to Lion Hall were certainly all stowed away in a safety deposit box at the bank, but here he'd kept our collection of passports, the family birth certificates, and Lion Hall's bank statements. I spread them across the desk. My father's passport photo showed him in his midthirties, just as I remembered him from my childhood. His thick shock of black hair and vigorous chin reflected those of the ancestors depicted in the portraits downstairs. I'd inherited his blue eyes. And his ears—although, happily, mine were less prominent.

He looked formal and earnest in the photograph, but I had memories of him laughing and being carefree. He'd later become a distant, stern paternal figure, often annoyed by the mere sight of me. If I'd come back home and given in to his demands, perhaps I'd have rediscovered that loving father. But I would have always had the feeling that I'd betrayed myself.

A mist obscured his face, and a tear dropped onto the page. I snapped the passport shut. When I returned it to the drawer, I noticed a brown envelope that looked quite new. What else had Father kept with his personal papers? Curiosity overcame my grief. I opened the envelope carefully. Could it be a love letter to my mother? Or something else equally personal?

The paper I pulled from the envelope was no letter at all. It was a promissory note for five thousand crowns, dated just weeks before the fire. I was shocked.

My father had borrowed a fortune!

I stared at the document, my heart pounding. What did this mean? Was the estate in financial peril? Surely we had enough money; never before had a Lejongård been obliged to borrow—at least as far as I knew.

And yet there before me lay the contract, signed in my father's hand. Five thousand crowns! My ears thundered, and my hands trembled. Was Mr. Jensen not aware of this? Father discussed everything with him. I got to my feet.

Only one person might be able to throw light on this.

I knocked at the door of Mother's boudoir. Hearing no reply, I gingerly opened the door, only to find the bed untouched. She probably hadn't even contemplated lying down. I hurried downstairs to the salon, the other place she could usually be found.

Mother had ordered the salon decorated precisely to her tastes, which, curiously enough, had little to do with traditional Scandinavian decor. Perhaps it was merely a display of fashion to impress her friends, but I often wondered if under her cool exterior there might be a woman who longed for the brilliant sun and bright colors of southern and eastern lands—someone who loved exotic plants and would have happily ridden across Egypt on the back of a camel.

The salon was crowded with rattan chairs, heavy curtains, lacquered Asian boxes, paintings, and cushions upholstered in bright satin. Ranged about them were robust date palms, fragile orchids, and exotic bird-of-paradise flowers. My mother, the Ice Queen, seemed out of place in this room. Yet she preferred it to the rest of the vast house.

"What did the inspector have to say?"

"Not a great deal. He described the origin of the fire and said they will be carrying out some interrogations. They are investigating because this was a clear case of arson."

My mother shut her eyes. I could imagine why. A suspected crime would attract public interest the way pies cooling on windowsills attracted wasps. Before long, the provincial newspapers would be peddling all sorts of speculations.

"Did you demand his absolute discretion?"

"I am sure he is aware of the need. Besides, his investigation would be hindered if the arsonist were alerted by newspapers."

Mother looked horrified, as if I'd committed an unpardonable sin. She said nothing.

"If you like, I will take a trip to Kristianstad to remind him to muzzle his men."

Mother's expression changed hardly at all. "As mistress of Lion Hall, you must be careful in your choice of words," she said. "That is, to the extent you care. Considering that you live your life as a vagabond."

"Mother!"

"Was there anything else?"

"Yes. I . . ." I took the envelope from my skirt pocket. "I found this in Father's desk."

"What is it?"

I held it out. "A promissory note."

"For a loan?" she asked in astonishment and snatched it from my hand. She scanned the contents, recoiled slightly when she saw the amount, then read it to the end. Her face filled with indignation. "What is the meaning of this?"

"I was hoping you could tell me. The contract is dated three weeks before the fire. We—we aren't having financial difficulties, are we?"

My mother's face turned white. "You know your father never confided his business affairs to me."

"He did not mention some building project or a purchase he had in mind for the estate?"

That amount of money could have financed construction of a large structure. Why hadn't he told his wife? Did he have secret plans? Perhaps, though it seemed unthinkable, a love nest for a mistress?

"No. He had not spoken to me very much recently."

I sighed. This mystery made me acutely uneasy. I would have to sit down with our banker for a complete picture of our financial situation. Especially because we'd soon need an even greater sum to rebuild the horse barn.

"Where do you think this money is? If it has not yet been spent, we could simply reimburse the lender."

"I told you, I have no idea." Mother put one hand to her mouth, her eyes darting left and right.

"I could go to the bank and ask why he borrowed the money."

She waved her hand dismissively. "You would need to prove to them you own the estate."

"Mother, stop acting as if I turned it down," I said. "I need time to think, to decide the right thing to do."

"The right thing for you—or for the estate?"

"For both!" I took back the loan document. "We need to find out where this money is. And the financial condition of Lion Hall. It will be best for you to come to the bank with me."

Mother sat huddled in silence for a long while. At last she nodded. "Very well. We will take the coach back to Kristianstad to talk with Jensen and the bank. Perhaps your father told them something."

"Thank you, Mother." I got up, feeling a little dizzy. The promissory note was a leaden weight in my hand. Were more secrets waiting to be discovered? What if the estate was in financial crisis? Could someone really have set the barn on fire?

I mused for some time, then went to find Bruns. He was polishing the silver. "Would you be so kind as to tell August to get the coach ready? My mother and I must return to Kristianstad."

Bruns was surprised but instantly of service. "Very well, gracious miss."

"Thank you."

I hurried upstairs, unbuttoning my mourning clothes as I went. Everyone expected me to wear them for some time longer, but I needed garb less constricting for another trip.

I slipped into the traveling outfit I'd worn from Stockholm. It wouldn't please my mother, but I felt more at ease in it. And I needed confidence to confront whatever challenge was waiting for me.

14

The streets of Kristianstad were almost empty now. Shopkeepers had already begun to close up. My stomach was in turmoil. What was the meaning of this loan? I was shocked to learn Father had kept such a secret from Mother, and she apparently felt the same, considering her obvious state of agitation. What was going through her mind? Was she silently accusing her husband? What could have been going on between them over the past months and years? Had they become estranged? Was it my fault? I couldn't see how, but just then I was desperate for Mother to open up and offer me any possible explanations.

We arrived at the law offices, and Jensen appeared promptly.

"Good afternoon, ladies. How can I be of service?" He appeared pleased to see us back so soon.

"We are obliged to consult you once more," Mother said with a sideways glance at me. "Do you have a moment?"

"Of course," said Jensen. "For you, any time!"

We entered his office for the second time that day. The air was stuffy and dense with the smell of cigars. A couple of legal folders lay on his desk.

"Perhaps you wish to share your decision concerning the will?"

"Not yet," I replied. "We have come about another matter." Out of the corner of my eye, I noticed my mother looking grim.

I took out the promissory note and placed it on the desk. "I found this today. Do you know anything about it?"

Jensen frowned. He took the note from its envelope and examined it. When he at last looked up, confusion was plain on his face. "Your father did not mention this to me." He turned his gaze to my mother, whose stony expression betrayed nothing.

"Did my husband perhaps speak of some important business project?"

"No. Perhaps he formulated one but decided not to proceed. But this obligation should have figured in his will."

"Then it evidently is necessary to ask you if he was facing financial difficulties."

"Thure made no mention of anything of the kind. I do wish that he had taken me into his confidence."

"This contract was drawn up three weeks before the fire. He would have had time enough to inform you of it, would he not?"

Jensen pursed his lips but did not answer immediately. "My door has always stood open to Count Lejongård. I would have received him at any hour. Mind you, these five thousand crowns reduce the total estate by an almost insignificant amount, but—"

"But if financial problems do exist, my daughter could find herself burdened with them if she should accept the inheritance. Am I correct?"

I looked at my mother in astonishment. Was she actually taking my side? She was right: if I accepted a heavily indebted estate, I would find myself in trouble. But on the other hand, did I have a choice? Perhaps, I thought, Mother was using this as a pretext to press Jensen to confess if Father had sworn him to silence.

Jensen hesitated, then agreed. "If there are additional debts, that might be the case. I doubt there are, but since I was not kept informed of this one . . . Perhaps you should confer with the bank officials."

"My daughter needs the certificate of inheritance in order to do that."

"Countess, you have full authority until your daughter formally accepts. You have access to the bank account. In addition, your husband was on very good terms with the chairman of the bank. In a case such as this, the chairman will certainly recognize it is vital you both understand the financial picture before making a decision."

My mother nodded and turned her gaze to me. She was still upset, but the tight lines of tension had disappeared from around her mouth. "Very well, Mr. Jensen. We thank you for your time." She rose. "I trust we can count upon your discretion."

"Always. Nothing said here ever leaves this room."

Mother nodded and gave him her hand. I also took my leave. We left the law office, but we didn't immediately climb back into the coach. Mother stood outside and stared up at the gathering clouds, almost as if asking her husband why he'd put her in such a situation.

"Mother?" I called in a low voice.

She started.

"We should go, Mother. We need to get to Mr. Arenhus. I do not want to go back to Lion Hall without knowing where we stand."

Commerce Bank was one of Sweden's most powerful institutions, but at five in the afternoon, the Kristianstad branch was virtually deserted. The tellers in striped vests and cuff protectors looked done in. The bank was quite imposing and tastefully decorated. Portraits displayed on the wood-paneled walls, each identified by a brass plaque, lent an air of elegance further accentuated by modern gold-colored chandeliers. A dark-red carpet muffled our footsteps. It was far from certain we'd be able to get in to see Mr. Arenhus so late, but we didn't want to wait another day. I went straight up to one of the sleepy tellers and startled him by asking for the chairman. He gave me an astonished stare. They surely didn't see many women in here. I wondered what my mother thought of the man's attitude.

I'd never been initiated into the mysteries of accounting, and even in arithmetic, I'd regularly been the despair of my teachers. I could count, more or less, but for me, advanced mathematics was a book of seven seals. The silent, orderly atmosphere of the bank intrigued me, however, and I found it calming. Mother, by contrast, was nervously plucking at the sleeves of her dress.

Jonah Arenhus appeared almost immediately. He was a bald man in his fifties with a wiry beard and a pince-nez clamped to the bridge of his nose. He wore a custom-tailored brown suit, and the gold chain across his vest gave him an air of authority. I hadn't seen him at the funeral, even though he, like many other influential men, was a close associate of my father.

"Countess Lejongård!" he greeted my mother and turned to me. "Miss Agneta! Oh, my word, it has been so long since last I saw you."

That was true, for he hadn't attended our most recent midsummer ball. At least two years had gone by.

"I am very sorry the count and your Hendrik passed away. I could not be at the funeral, unfortunately, for we were attending to difficulties in the north of the country."

"That is understandable," my mother replied. "And thank you for your kind words. I will be sure to acknowledge them more at length in a letter to you and Betty."

My eyebrows rose. I'd never had the impression my mother was particularly close to the Arenhus family.

"Let me escort you to my office, where we can speak in private. I presume this concerns your husband's estate."

"Oh yes!" I blurted out. Mother shot me a look as piercing as an arrow. Perhaps this time I should stay in the background and see what developed.

Arenhus conducted us to his office upstairs and held the door for us. Dark wood paneling was everywhere, the same decor I'd found impressive downstairs. Up in this smaller space, it was a bit intimidating, although the heavy leather armchairs were spacious and accommodating.

"May I offer you something?" Arenhus inquired. "Tea, or perhaps coffee?"

"A glass of water will do." My mother shot me an admonitory look.

"Yes, water," I said, even though I wasn't thirsty. "Please."

The banker brought two glasses of water, each with a slice of lemon, and placed them on the low table before us. He also took an armchair. "What can I do for you?"

I handed him the envelope. "Inside this you will find a promissory note made out four weeks ago. Since neither my mother nor I knew of its existence, we are now wondering if the estate is in financial difficulties."

Arenhus extracted the note, carefully unfolded it, and studied it. "We did not draw up this note," he said, somewhat taken aback. "This is an arrangement with a private lender in Stockholm."

"Do you know this person?"

"Yes, I know of him. I am somewhat reluctant to say anything more."

"Because of something immoral?" Mother's voice was matter-of-fact.

"Well, hmm, not necessarily immoral, but Ohlsson is known to be a lender who does not inquire into the purposes for which funds are sought. He provides the cash, and those who do not meet the payment schedule suffer the most drastic consequences."

"Consequences?" Mother asked.

"You mean he uses violence against those who fail to pay?" I asked. I'd heard of such things in Stockholm.

"You might say that. An honorable man would find it best to avoid dealing with individuals like Ohlsson."

"Good Lord!" Mother's face lost all color. "Whatever could Thure have wanted from this man?"

"Perhaps he merely wished to keep the loan confidential? A secret, even from us? Your husband was my friend, as you know, and I am quite surprised he did not consult me. I would most likely have been able to assist him."

I pushed away visions of shadowy figures descending on my father. "Can you think of any reason for his secrecy?"

"Not really. A great deal of your father's wealth is invested, so not very much cash is readily available. A withdrawal of five thousand crowns would have been exceptional, and we would have asked about it. Perhaps he wished to avoid exactly that?"

Mother sat as still as a statue. Her forehead glistened with sweat.

"Are we in a position to settle this debt as soon as possible?" I asked. I somehow doubted we'd come across the cash stashed in Father's office.

"Of course, and that would help preserve your father's reputation. No one can keep Ohlsson from boasting about his clients, when—well, whenever the business relationships are less than stable. However, you will need to keep in mind that Lion Hall will require extensive investment soon. Surely the destroyed structures must be rebuilt and the lost horses replaced."

"As for the animals, the losses were minimal," I replied. "Of course, the barn must be rebuilt. And there are the costs of cleaning up after the fire."

"None of that should pose a problem. You still have horses, and you could sell some if needed. In order to do so, however, I would need the certificate of inheritance. I assume you plan to take charge of the estate, Miss Lejongård?"

I looked across at Mother. "I . . . I will be giving Mr. Jensen instructions shortly."

"Well, as long as we haven't established who is to inherit Lion Hall—"

"My daughter will," Mother answered. "And I hope she will make the right decisions."

"Very well, then! I will expect to see you again soon."

Afterward, we sat silent for a while in the motionless coach. I'd stopped Mother from rapping to tell August to start, for I knew the moment for a decision had come.

The skies dimmed, assuming deeper shades of red. Night would soon be upon us. I wrestled with my thoughts as the tower bells of Holy Trinity Church tolled six o'clock. We had to do something. Father had gotten into entirely unnecessary difficulties, and he'd left us a mystery we might never solve. Now it was a matter of protecting the estate before Ohlsson's thugs turned up to extort repayment.

I suddenly wondered if this Ohlsson might have something to do with the fire. On the other hand, the loan was only four weeks old. Even the most disreputable usurer wouldn't have sent his bully boys out that quickly. There was too much to do, and it was useless to expect some miracle to relieve me of the burden of a decision.

I could return to Stockholm and my life there, loving Michael, pursuing my art, and counting those water stains on the ceiling. But if I did, I would be tormented by a guilty conscience. I'd be hounded by the knowledge that I'd failed my brother. That I'd abandoned my family.

The alternative was to accept the estate, along with all the duties and obligations inherent to the title. I hadn't the slightest idea how to run things, and I'd have to go to war with Mother when I announced Michael was to be my husband. And on top of it all, I'd have to persuade Michael to leave Stockholm, at least once he'd finished his studies.

I weighed one choice against another and knew what I was going to do.

"Mother."

"Yes?" she replied, lost in thought.

I searched for the right words. "I am going to Stockholm tomorrow."

Stella said nothing.

I wanted an end to these icy silences, and I was determined not to put up with her reproaches. I took a deep breath and closed my eyes. "I will take care of whatever needs to be settled there. But first we must call on Mr. Jensen and inform him that, as far as the inheritance is concerned"—I sensed that Stella was holding her breath—"I will accept."

Mother's head swiveled toward me. She contemplated me for a long moment. An almost imperceptible smile flickered across her face.

I'd longed for that smile all my life, but now that it had appeared, I took no joy from it. The price I'd paid was far too high.

15

Heavy clouds hung low overhead when I emerged from Stockholm Central Station two days later. It seemed an eternity since I'd left the city. Grief over Hendrik and Father came at me in waves, but I'd begun to grapple with my situation. I would need a clear head to determine what was going to happen between Michael and me.

I decided to walk instead of taking a carriage. The day was fading as I reached my building. Electric streetlights had been installed around Stockholm's royal castle, but hired men walked their circuits in my neighborhood farther south, lighting one gas flame after another. How long would this ritual persist? Someday there'd be electric lighting everywhere, including at Lion Hall.

A shriek rang out from upstairs as I entered the apartment building. Apparently, the upstairs tenants were having another quarrel.

I opened the apartment door and knew Michael hadn't been there recently. He exuded such warmth that I always sensed his presence. I was alone in the apartment. He was probably at the university or in a tavern with his friends. I dropped my valise by the bed and turned to my easel. I went to the small table where I kept my painting tools. The turpentine had evaporated entirely from the dish, and the brush was stiff. I'd neglected to clean the palette, and now removing the clots of dried paint would be almost impossible.

My own paintings seemed unfamiliar, as if someone else had done them. This wasn't the first time I'd been surprised to find myself capable of producing art. I must have painted them in a trance.

The front door slammed, and I heard footsteps approach. Michael? Who else would be coming to the room of a woman painter? There was nothing here worth stealing.

"So. You're back."

I rushed to him, but his expression rebuffed me. He didn't seem at all pleased.

My smile disappeared. "Yes. I just came in by train."

Michael nodded. Where was his embrace? Where were his kisses? What had happened while I was away? I went to hug him, but he pulled back. "What's wrong?" I asked. "Didn't you get my letters?"

"Yes, I did," he said flatly. "And I am very sorry about what happened to your father and brother. But now your life will change. You are going back to your estate. Do you deny it?"

I hadn't expected this. My joy at our reunion disappeared instantly. "Michael, I—"

"Are you going to accept the inheritance and go back to the estate?"

I'd always appreciated his directness. His rational approach counterbalanced my imaginings; his realism complemented my fantasy. I'd always thought we were perfectly balanced. But this wasn't pragmatism. It was alienation.

"Yes, I must," I replied. "I have no other choice."

"I should have known," he muttered.

"Known what?" I reached out, but he brushed my hand away.

"I should have known you would never escape your family."

"Michael!" I grabbed his arm, but that just made his eyes flash in defiance. "You have always known who I am. Why do you suddenly think things have changed?"

"Before you left, you were a student who dreamed of becoming an artist. Now you come back here an heiress. What, in your opinion, is left of that dream? And how am I supposed to fit into it?"

The inheritance from my father was not the issue. I'd given Hendrik my pledge; I couldn't break my word to my brother.

"Michael, come with me. We can marry. This is not the end."

"In fact, it is."

That took my breath away.

Michael rubbed his face. "Listen to me: I will not leave Stockholm. That is too much to ask. Do you understand?"

"But why?" My heart pounded, choking me. "Would *you* deny your brother his dying request?"

"My brother would never ask me to renounce my whole life!"

"That is not what Hendrik asked. I can live on the estate and still paint!"

"How very lovely for you! And what about me? You never even introduced me to your parents. And now you expect me to give up everything here?"

"You don't have to," I pleaded. "Once you have your degree, you can work as an attorney in Kristianstad. We have contacts with law offices there."

Michael shook his head. "Thanks very much, but I intend to earn my own laurels instead of having them handed to me, the way you people do."

"That's not fair!" Wasn't there any way I could talk him out of this strange rancor? "Of course you can earn your own laurels!"

"And if I have no desire to live or work in your provincial metropolis of Kristianstad?" he replied, his eyes glinting dangerously. "If I plan to stay in Stockholm? How will that work, me here while you hold court at your estate?"

I'd never seen him like this. I trembled, fearing he'd walk out, and I wouldn't be able to stop him.

"You know what? You aristocrats think everything revolves around you." His voice was cutting and deadly earnest. "I cannot accept this! I want a wife at my side, not hundreds of miles away."

"A few hours by train," I said in a tiny voice. "We can see one another whenever we want."

"For the rest of our lives?" He shook his head. "No, not that. And you should think long and hard about what you want. Because if you go back to Lion Hall, you will be traveling alone." He turned and stalked toward the hall.

"Michael, wait!"

The door slammed behind him.

I stood there, paralyzed. I'd been so happy to come back to Michael, even though I'd known things would be complicated. I'd had no idea these few days would poison our relationship and infuriate him. Was it only because I'd accepted the family estate?

Before this, there'd been no thought of my returning to Lion Hall. We'd dreamed of a life together in Stockholm, where I'd be surrounded by gallery owners and maybe even exhibit my work at the palace. Michael would be a successful attorney renowned in the city and maybe a public prosecutor someday. Or even a minister of justice. Our dreams were unbounded. Until today. What was scaring him so much?

I sat down on the bed and stared into space. I couldn't believe my ears; had he really said those things?

My heart shriveled into a tiny ball. I began to weep, and my only thought was how cruel the world was.

I stayed awake for hours, hoping Michael would come back to say he hadn't meant it. I lay completely inert, my eyes raw from weeping. I started at every noise, but he never appeared. The neighborhood grew quiet. From time to time, a dog barked and someone yelled at it.

Again and again, my mind went over the strange confrontation. I came to the inevitable conclusion: he had fully intended to pick a fight.

Damn that fire! Whoever set it should roast in hell for taking my family, my dreams, and the man I loved away from me.

I needed something to contain all the pain, the grief, the questions with no answers. I got to my feet with difficulty and looked around for the brandy I'd been given by Thérèse, one of my fellow suffragettes. Her grandmother had distilled it, and Thérèse swore that it was strong enough to wake the dead. Or, conversely, you could turn yourself into the semblance of a corpse by drinking enough of it. I found it in the kitchen, next to the cleaning chemicals. I was determined to see if it really did have the power to wash away my disappointment and alleviate my anger.

I wiped the dust from the handwritten label and pulled out the cork. After sniffing to make sure it wasn't turpentine, I took a sip. It tasted foul and burned like hell. For a moment, I thought the fiery liquid was eating away the tissues of my throat. But by the third and then the fourth sip, Grandma's brandy started tasting better. I dragged myself back to the bedroom and threw myself onto the bed. I sat there for a while, nipping at the bottle. I hadn't had much experience with alcohol, but now all I wanted was to get good and drunk. To remove myself to somewhere far from the suffering of the last few days.

Her liquor quickly took effect. The world around me blurred, but my spirit was not consoled. I'd wanted not to care; instead I became incensed.

How had I gotten myself into this? Why couldn't I forget my ancestry? And Michael, why was he being such an idiot? I was the heiress to an estate, but so what! I wasn't going to turn into someone different! Did Michael think the money would change me somehow? I could take care of myself just fine. I'd previously scorned my privileges, but now I could command the vast resources of my family estate!

Or was that just it? Did my new power make him feel less of a man? Was he afraid he'd no longer be the stronger one? That was exactly the wrongheaded thinking we women of the sisterhood rejected! Maybe I'd have been better off if I'd never met him. Maybe I should never have come here . . .

My drunken gaze fell upon my paintings. The landscapes seemed just as desolate as my soul. I was a rotten painter! I'd been pursuing an illusion, a crazy dream I should have known I could never achieve. I was an heiress, not an artist. And I was obviously not worth enough for a man to put aside his own ego and deal with me honestly, face-to-face, for once.

With a scream of rage, I threw aside the almost-empty bottle. It struck one of the canvases and ripped a huge hole in it. That wasn't enough. If I was going to be stuck moldering away at Lion Hall for the rest of my life, it was better to eliminate every possible reminder of my halcyon days in Stockholm. I vowed I would never pick up a paintbrush again.

I shrieked in frustration and kicked over the easel. The painting fell to the floor but looked undamaged. I looked around feverishly for something I could use to rip it apart. The world tilted around me, and the alcohol boiled in my blood. Finally, I saw something glimmer. I grabbed a palette knife and plunged it into the canvas. I felt a momentary resistance, then heard a tearing sound. I looked down at a long, jagged tear. I reeled and tried to hold myself upright. My fury mounted with each stab.

I slashed and ripped until the world around me turned red. And then black.

16

I slowly became aware of an insistent rapping at the window. I wanted to tell whoever it was to go away. But maybe it was Michael . . . I sat up. Had he thought things over? Was he sorry he'd said such horrible things?

I pushed hair out of my face, unable to remember going to bed. The room smelled of turpentine and mold. The knocking continued. The silhouette at the window wasn't that of a man.

"Agneta, are you all right? It's me, Marit!"

I was a bit disappointed but relieved all the same. There was at least one person in Stockholm who still cared.

I shrugged aside the blanket, got unsteadily to my feet, and opened the window.

My friend was appalled. "You look absolutely awful!"

I felt awful. My temples were pounding, and there was a persistent dull ache at the back of my head. Not to mention the sharp pain on the top of my skull. My stomach heaved. I must have been green around the gills. My hair hung in sticky strands, and there was a sour smell to my nightgown. But what could you expect of someone abandoned by her lover?

"Thanks for the compliment. Would you like to come in?"

"I came to see if you were still alive. Now that's been established, I'm happy to come in. At least now I don't have to go to the police. They've been pretty standoffish since I scaled the wall at the prime minister's office."

I closed the window, went to the door, and waited for her in the hallway. Marit's wry comment had gotten me to smile.

"Darling, for heaven's sake, don't step outside your apartment looking like that!" she exclaimed. "What if the neighbors saw you?"

"The sainted lady across the hall doesn't care what I look like. She never gets out of bed before sunset. And the people upstairs don't know me at all."

Marit sniffed my breath. "Have you been drinking, my dear?"

"Yes, but that was earlier."

"You mean yesterday," Marit corrected me. "Michael told me you got back yesterday afternoon."

Was it really the afternoon of the following day? How had I managed to sleep so long?

"Enough!" Marit barked with the authority of an admiral. She grabbed me by my nightgown and hauled me back to my room. "You're going to wash up, brush your teeth, and put on decent clothes. Then we'll decide what to do."

The last thing I wanted was to consider what to do next. But Marit wouldn't take no for an answer. There was good reason she was mocked as the most rabid of suffragettes; she wouldn't have hesitated to tie herself half naked to a tree if it would advance the cause.

I threw on a robe and fetched water from the pump in the inner court and staggered back with the full bucket. I poured water into the washbasin and peeled off my clothes. My arms were weak and leaden, and splashing myself with cold water did little to change that. I found clean underwear and a new dress, then tottered into my workroom, where Marit stood, surveying the mess I'd created in my drunken passion.

"Oh my goodness. Weren't you in a rage!" she said. "If this is art, I'd have to call it expressionism."

"The paintings were worthless," I replied. "I will never touch a brush again."

Marit frowned. "Why not? You, who left it all to devote yourself to art?"

"Times change," I answered bitterly. "In fact, they already have."

Marit embraced me gently. "So what happened? I ran into Michael, but all he said was that you'd been very affected by the deaths of your father and brother."

"He didn't tell you he's going to leave me because I intend to accept the estate?"

He already left. Why did I say "is going to leave"?

Marit's eyebrows rose in surprise. "I thought you two were going to get married. It was always revolting the way you made puppy eyes at one another in public."

"Yes, it was. Because I was the rebel daughter who'd turned her back on the family wealth." I sniffled. "As if accepting my inheritance turned me into an entirely different person."

"Of course you'll be different," Marit told me. "You're a full-fledged member of the aristocracy now. A woman obliged to respect the social niceties."

I flinched. "That is what you think? Are you going to abandon me too?"

"That's not at all what I said," she responded. "Maybe you should start by telling me what happened."

She guided me to the bed she'd already made up, pressed a glass of water into my hand, and settled at my side.

My head still ached, as if trying to block out memories of the quarrel. And everything before that.

I told her of my arrival at the estate, the shock the sight of my father's body had caused me, and my grief at my brother's death. I told her about Lion Hall and how my brother had made me pledge to be his successor. How he'd written it into his will. I told her of my doubts, my desire for independence, and the violent emotions my time on the estate had aroused. Then I got to Michael.

Marit heard me out, occasionally patting my back. After I finished, she looked at me for a long time. Her expression was skeptical. "So nothing matters to him except his brilliant career?"

Marit always insisted that men rob us of our autonomy. She'd sworn never to let a man tie her down. When I first got involved with Michael, she'd told me to watch out.

I didn't want to be tied down, but I did want someone to be with. A man I could love, one who loved me back. It wasn't a question of sacrificing oneself, if only one could find the right man.

"Yes, that's what he said. I haven't really had time to think about it."

"No, you haven't, because you were busy destroying your artwork and your tools." Marit pushed a strand of hair out of my face. "You'll regret that, you know."

"I doubt it."

"You're being as stubborn as a spoiled child. That's not like you! Don't you think something can be done? Michael just overreacted. I'm sure you didn't jump for joy when you learned you were going to be mistress of the manor."

"Hardly," I answered. "It took me a long time, but no matter which way I turned it, I always came to the same conclusion: I have no other choice." I thought for a moment. "Besides, I still feel attached to the estate. I'd been denying that for a long time, especially because my mother is so unfeeling. But when the solicitor read Hendrik's letter to me, the truth came to me at last. I do love the place! It's full of memories of my brother. I can't just abandon it. That is unthinkable."

"In other words, you've definitely made your decision."

"I have. But Michael . . . I really thought he was the one . . ."

Marit placed her hand on my arm. "I know. And I also know it's horrible when love goes wrong. But perhaps it's all for the best. You know already I'm no friend of your pompous aristocrats. That lot are do-nothings as far as I'm concerned. But you, personally, are different. You've seen with your own eyes how ordinary folks live. Now you have the chance of a lifetime to change things."

"What do you mean?"

"We demonstrate in the streets, and what happens? We get arrested. Politicians laugh at us. At the university, they see us as a bizarre species. Men attack us at our rallies and hurl insults. They think that by reducing us to our body parts, they can rob us of our dignity."

Marit was on her soapbox again, but she was right. I'd experienced the same abuse. I knew the hurt such mockery caused.

Marit clutched my hands so hard she seemed to be holding me back from the brink of a precipice. "Now you have a chance to do something about it. On your estate, you can put into practice what we've been demanding. On the estate, in the village—"

I laughed bitterly. "That will do little to change the world."

"Who knows? You'll be in contact with other landowners. You can carry our message to their wives and daughters. By taking advantage of your situation, you've already achieved more than all of us who keep standing before the parliament and outside the palace, daring them to arrest us."

I was sure the wives and daughters of landowners wouldn't pay much attention to the concerns of the suffragettes. But why not give it a try? Perhaps my decision to leave the city might make some small bit of difference.

I freed my hands from Marit's grip and hugged her. "I'm so happy to have you in my life! Please promise you'll visit me at Lion Hall."

"I definitely will. Even though I can't stand the aristocracy."

"But you like me, don't you? And I have lots of lovely servants you can turn against me."

"As if I ever would!" she said. "And yes, I like you, more than anyone." She gazed at me for a moment, then planted a kiss on my cheek. "Do you think you'll be all right now?"

I looked over at the litter of splintered frames and torn canvas. The overturned brandy bottle was partly visible in the mess. The last drops of alcohol had spilled on the floor and dried up. It was no longer a threat.

"Yes, I think so. And I pledge never to drink hard liquor again."

"A little nip from time to time does no harm." Marit got up. "Do you know where to find Michael? That is, when you're ready to talk to him again?"

"He'll be at the university. Or with his friends. He won't return here."

Marit smiled. "I'm quite sure he'll regret his decision. He probably does already."

I nodded, and we hugged again. I held her close. "Thanks for all the support."

"That's what I'm here for."

Marit waved as she disappeared down the hall.

17

My heart was in my throat as I stood outside the main lecture hall of the law school. Michael should be coming out of class soon. I didn't know if it was any use trying to discuss things again, but I wanted to try. Our relationship shouldn't end in bitterness.

Marit would laugh when she heard I'd put on my best dark-blue dress for him. A tailor in Kristianstad had made it for me two years earlier, shortly before I'd left Lion Hall. It wasn't something a student would wear, but I'd kept it because it was beautiful. I doubted Michael would notice, but I very much hoped it would make me look attractive. And that he'd be willing to listen.

I'd waited half an hour as measured by the church bells when a bustle inside indicated Professor Rasmussen had finished his lecture. I stepped back and waited by the pillars.

Young men streamed out of the hall. Some carried their books strapped together, but many had no books at all. They'd probably used the lecture hour to catch up on their sleep. Eventually, Michael appeared, animatedly discussing something with a classmate. I felt a stab of pain. Our quarrel seemed very far away. I'd destroyed my paintings because of him, and here he was as if nothing was wrong. I gathered my resolve and walked in his direction.

"Michael!" I called as he parted from the other student.

He stopped short, his back to me. His friend stared as if I were a specter. Very few women turned up here. Michael must have recognized my voice, for he made no move to leave. Nor did he turn around.

"I'd like to talk with you, Michael," I said. "Please. It won't take long."

He turned to face me. His expression was unwelcoming. His friend saw this wasn't going to be a friendly chat, and he made himself scarce.

"How are things?" Michael asked in a frosty voice.

"It's about what we discussed yesterday."

He gave me a dark look. "What more is there to say? Have you decided to renounce the estate?"

"No. I . . . I thought that if I introduced you to my mother—"

"And then what?"

"Then we could think about planning our future." I felt a twinge deep inside. The Michael I used to know would have taken me in his arms. Our quarrels had never lasted long. This time he didn't budge.

"I already told you that if you go back to Lion Hall, we have no future together."

"Not even if we marry?" My wildly pounding heart was again in my throat.

Michael stared at me as if I were mad. "We never discussed such a thing!"

"You mean all your vows were true, provided I was penniless?" I felt my anger rising. "As long as I was a cute little painter girl with impossible dreams? As long as I subjugated myself to you?"

"I never said anything of the kind. But isn't it better for the man to be the breadwinner?"

I couldn't believe my ears. Only a few weeks earlier, he'd declared he admired me for demonstrating for women's rights. He must have been deceiving me.

"That is what you think, then? Have you forgotten who I am?"

"No, I haven't!" he spat at me. "You're a spoiled heiress, a girl who has everything. Let me say it again: Do you really think I am going to give up everything here to go stagnate in the provinces? As the consort to an heiress? What would I do all day long? Drown my woes in the wine cellar? Go hunting? You already know I don't come from the nobility. And if you've decided to go back there, I will never change my mind."

I stared at him in confusion. I should have known. A crushing weight settled over me. My knees started to buckle.

"Just look at you!" he went on, as if his rebuke hadn't already been enough to break my heart. "This is no place for you. Your clothing is old-fashioned, and so are you. You got your taste of modern life, but that obviously wasn't enough to keep you from crawling back to your reactionary ancestors. You'll find a man soon enough and spend your life with him. You have no need of me."

I almost fell over. I had so many words within me, but I couldn't utter a single one.

"It's over, Agneta," he said firmly.

"Michael . . . ," I sobbed.

"Goodbye!"

He left.

Half blinded by tears, I watched him go, my chest full of pain.

I spun around and ran along the path. I made it as far as the little garden next to the law school and curled up in tears on a secluded bench.

I don't remember making my way home. I must have walked in a trance, Michael's face before me, his words in my ears. My cheeks were stiff from weeping, and my eyes were swollen. Even so, my stumbling gait carried me directly back to my narrow street and humble apartment. I came to myself only after the door closed behind me. I felt the sudden chill of the room. The aftermath of my destructive frenzy lay all around.

I was ready to leave. Michael had released me. He was so much a part of everything I'd done here; I'd probably never again be able to look at a painting or pick up a brush. I'd thought my passion for painting would conquer all, for Michael had given me the courage to improve my art and become more than the amateur dabbler I'd been.

All that was over.

I took a deep, frustrated breath. Anger rose in me again, but this time it wasn't the wild, tearing rage of the day before. It was an anger I could master by force of will. Acting in a controlled, dispassionate manner, I would banish from my sight everything that might remind me of my time here. I had more paintings to destroy, or perhaps I would give them to Marit instead. She might be able to sell them and use the funds for the cause.

I began packing. I made two piles: one for everything to give Marit for the Salvation Army and the other for those few things I wanted to take with me.

I kept only one of my paintings, the one that had won me admission to the Royal Academy of Fine Arts. It was a landscape that showed Lion Hall, white and gleaming against banks of gathering clouds. There was a slightly menacing aspect to the summer light. The flowers stood out, garish and accusing. I'd titled it *Approaching Storm*.

That was appropriate, in two senses. First, I'd painted it as a storm approached—I was still proud of how well I'd captured that light. And second, there'd been a stormy, foreboding feeling within the manor house, for I'd recently told my father I wanted to study in Stockholm. The furious reactions of my parents had driven me to finish that deeply felt painting. It was strange how little it spoke to my current mood. I leaned it against the wall and carried on with my sorting.

I went to the wardrobe. I didn't want any of the clothes I'd worn here, but I knew the women sponsored by our circle would be overjoyed to have a new skirt, blouse, or dress. I put on a simple travel outfit I'd purchased from a Stockholm department store. Everything else I packed in my largest trunk. I borrowed a cart from the woman across the hall.

Soon afterward I set out for Marit's apartment.

There were inexpensive but acceptable apartments tucked away in corners of the neighborhood around the port, so long as one didn't mind seeing prostitutes nonchalantly strolling the street below. The houses were well past their prime. Plaster crumbled and paint peeled. From time to time, one might glimpse a sunflower in a flowerpot or see through the clotheslines a carefully tended gardenia on the ledge of a window.

It was almost evening. I was lucky, for Marit's window was lit, meaning she was at home. In addition to campaigning for women's rights, my friend worked in the Salvation Army kitchen and did piecework for a tailor shop. I knew she would have been happy to pursue higher education, but aside from the fact that women were very rarely admitted, she didn't have the financial means. Still, she made enough for her domestic needs, and I was always impressed by how clean and tidy she kept her tiny apartment compared with the chaos that often reigned in my own. I knocked, and she quickly came to the door.

"Hey, how lovely to see you!" she called. She embraced me but started when she caught sight of the cart in the street. "What is this?"

"All the clothing I possess. Except what I have on."

"And why are you trundling it through the streets?"

"To deliver it to you to distribute among the women. I have no more use for any of it."

She grabbed my arm. "You're not planning to do something stupid, are you?"

"Stupid?" I shook my head. "What an imagination you have! Michael has left me, yes, but no matter how deeply that grieves me, I would never take my own life. These things no longer interest me. They remind me how close I was to having a different life from the one planned by my parents."

Marit gave me a searching look. "Come inside. But first let's pull the cart into the hall. Otherwise it'll vanish quicker than you can cry 'Stop, thief!'"

She took the other side, and together we hauled the loaded cart up the front steps.

In a hall that stank of dirty diapers and stale food, she secured the cart with a rope and helped me get the trunk into her apartment. She didn't open it but instead took me to the large sofa she'd rescued from a house being demolished.

"So then, you spoke to him. No use?"

I shook my head and felt the anger begin to rise again. "I did. He wants to be the breadwinner, but he's calling *me* a reactionary. I will never see him again."

"Michael is an idiot."

I didn't try to change her mind. "I thought things would turn out differently. Or rather, I thought our love would be strong enough to keep us together through thick and thin."

Marit sighed. "You'll find the right man someday." She put her arm around my shoulders. "You're going back?"

I nodded and drew her close. "You're the most precious person in the world! Lion Hall will not change that. You'll always be welcome."

Marit leaned over and pressed her lips to my forehead. "I feel the same. Whenever your mother and the estate become too much to bear, write me or come stay on my sofa for a couple of nights."

"I look forward to that!"

I eventually said goodbye and left. I didn't feel lighthearted, for I dreaded what lay ahead. My grief was no longer focused on the loss of Father and Hendrik. Now I was mourning the months I'd had with Michael. His rejection had wounded me deeply, and it would take a long time for me to recover. But perhaps someday I could look forward to a less clouded future.

18

I'd had no idea how heavy the painting I'd brought to Stockholm would become. Perspiration oozed from my scalp and ran down my back underneath my dress. My feet ached, and I realized that walking home hadn't been a good idea. I could have sent Mother a telegram and asked for the coach to meet me, but I'd ridden the milk wagon to the village and hiked the rest of the way. I was glad to be in sight of Lion Hall at last.

I suffered each time the pain of the sudden rupture with Michael surged through me, but I did my best to think of the future. I had made my choice, and now it was up to me to make the best of it. I paused at the entrance to the estate—*abandon hope, all ye who enter here!* I was the mistress of this place now. I was determined to develop the estate and take it into a new era. I took a last deep breath of spring air, then stepped onto my property.

A pair of stable boys caught sight of me and scampered to announce the news. Miss Rosendahl met me at the front steps. "Gracious miss, how lovely to have you back again! But why didn't you advise us? August could have met you!"

I did my best to smile. "I wanted to walk a bit, thank you."

"Where is your baggage? Shall I have it fetched?"

I lifted the framed canvas I was carrying. "All I have is this and my handbag."

Miss Rosendahl looked at me in amazement. "I've already sent a maid running to inform the gracious lady of the house."

"Thank you very much, Miss Rosendahl. First I would like to go to my room to freshen up. Could you please have a bath drawn for me? I absolutely must wash off the stench of that train."

"But of course, gracious miss! I will set Lena to it immediately."

"Thank you." I gave her a nod and went upstairs. I shut the door behind me and examined myself in the mirror.

Marit would have found my appearance frightful. My hair had come loose from the bun, and my cheeks were pale. Deep, dark circles lay under my dull eyes, for I hadn't been able to sleep, despite my exhaustion. Not even the most artful makeup could conceal that.

Lena soon appeared. Her eyes shone as if she'd just gotten marvelous news. "You've returned, gracious miss!"

"Yes, I have."

"We're all so pleased! What may I do for you?"

"I would be glad to take a bath. And I wonder if the black blouse my mother lent me is available."

"It is," Lena answered. "Yesterday I hung it in the wardrobe myself."

"Very good. Then let us get started."

Lena hurried out of the room.

I pulled off my traveling dress, tossed it onto the bed, and examined it. Michael had seen me wear it only once. He'd found it enchanting, like every other garment he'd removed from my body. I still couldn't believe my inheritance had come between us. Obviously, I meant less to him than he'd meant to me, despite all his protestations. I brushed the rough fabric with my fingertips, tried to put aside my regrets, and decided to keep the dress, even though I wouldn't be wearing it anytime soon. It would sit, boxed up in the wardrobe. Someday, when I was old and gray, it would serve as a souvenir.

I bathed, changed clothes, and went downstairs in search of my mother. I felt somewhat better. The bath had revived my spirits and kept my unhappy thoughts at bay. I found Stella in the salon, seated on her favorite rattan lounge with a book on her lap.

"Mother?"

She snapped the leather-bound volume shut, took a deep breath, and inspected me. "Agneta."

I had no idea what my mother read in my face, but she looked even more fragile than before, though Mrs. Bloomquist had doubtless been doing her best to keep her well fed.

"You have returned. You could have called for the coach, you know."

"Someone offered me a ride, and then I decided to stretch my legs a bit. I needed time to think."

I knew Mother was suspicious about the suitability of my escort, but she didn't ask. "You have arrived just in time. I sent Susanna to fetch coffee. Would you like to have a cup?"

"I definitely would," I said gratefully.

"And have you tended to your arrangements?" she asked, as if addressing a person with one foot in the grave. She wasn't too far off the mark, for my life in Stockholm was now dead and gone.

I nodded. "Yes. I gave up my apartment and notified the university."

I did my best to speak lightly, but when writing out my resignation from the Royal Academy of Fine Arts, I'd broken down and sobbed aloud.

I'd had such high hopes two years earlier, overjoyed to be accepted where Anna Nordlander had led the way as one of the first woman students. To the school where Carl Larsson had refined his skills and become famous. How ecstatic I'd been when I got my letter of acceptance! Now I'd been forced to give all that up and put it behind me. I would miss the big white building on Fredsgatan.

Mother acknowledged my news with a nod, unable to conceal her satisfaction. "I am most pleased you decided in favor of your family and the estate. Now you will have many things to consider."

"Yes, Mother." I sank, exhausted, into an armchair. How I yearned to be comforted. But my mother wasn't the person to do it.

"Including the task of finding a man. An appropriate husband," she added sternly.

"For now, I prefer to begin by taking a look through Father's account books to get an idea of his business affairs. I suppose you still have no idea why Father took out that loan?"

"No, I do not. But fortunately, we were able to settle the debt."

After I'd notified Jensen that I intended to accept the inheritance, I authorized him to clear up any liens on the estate. The debt was paid off, and I hoped the loss would soon be recovered. But the mystery remained: Why had my father gotten involved with a shady usurer?

"It is not fitting for you, as a woman, to devote yourself to business," my mother said. "Your duty is to ensure the good standing of the family estate."

"To produce children, in other words?" My lips tightened in annoyance. "You apparently think I cannot do that while tending to the estate."

I'd had a faint hope she might say a mother always has to be there for her children. Hendrik and I had had nannies and governesses for as long as I could remember. On formal occasions, our mother played the maternal role, just as when we received visitors. We almost never saw her the rest of the time. I breathed deeply, gazing down, and then I looked directly into her eyes.

"I believe my primary duty is to see that Lion Hall is not adversely affected in any way," I said as calmly as I could manage. "And I hardly think there is anyone of noble blood in the region familiar with the circumstances of our estate. In addition, we are both in mourning. Do you really imagine that now, so soon after Hendrik's and Father's deaths,

I can bring myself to participate in festivities and balls, inviting gentlemen to come courting?"

"What about the son of Count Ekberg?" she asked. "You are quite well acquainted, or at least you used to be. He is unmarried. And I have the distinct feeling he would have no objection to taking you to wife."

"No objection?" I exclaimed. "Mother, do you really think marriage comes down to nothing more than the fact that neither partner objects? Do you not think they should love one another?"

I stared defiantly at her. Would she now claim that she herself had simply done her duty, and love had been no part of her own marriage?

"Mother," I said a bit more calmly, "you know, of course, how long he and I have been friends."

"And?"

"Did you consider that perhaps I might have already given him some sign if I had been the least bit interested? He is a friend, perhaps the best friend I have around here. But that is all he will ever be: a friend."

A loud crash in the corridor interrupted our discussion. I leaped to my feet, welcoming the interruption. "What was that?"

I heard a shriek as I raced to the door. I emerged to find Marie bending over Susanna, who was stretched out facedown on the floor, surrounded by shattered fragments of a porcelain coffee service.

"For God's sake, what happened?"

Marie shook her head. "I don't know, gracious miss. I heard a crash, and when I rushed to see, she was lying here."

I carefully turned Susanna onto her back and patted her cheeks. "Send Peter to fetch Dr. Bengtsen!"

Marie nodded and left.

My mother appeared at the salon door. "What on earth is wrong with her?"

"I have no idea. Is she subject to fainting spells?"

Susanna opened her eyes and looked confused. "What happened?" Her voice was slurred. She tried to get up.

I put my hand on her shoulder and gently pressed her back down. "You passed out. Are you in pain? Did you slip?"

"No, I . . . I don't know, suddenly everything went dark."

She cringed when she saw the smashed porcelain. "I'm so sorry, gracious miss! I didn't mean to—"

"Of course you didn't." I glanced up at Mother.

Stella Lejongård was fiddling with her pearl necklace. She seemed mildly intrigued but not particularly concerned.

Marie appeared. "Peter's on the way to fetch the doctor."

"Good, then help me. We must get her to her room."

"One of the maids can do that, surely?" my mother asked behind me.

I shook my head. "I am here, and I will help. There is no need to make a fuss." I addressed Susanna. "Do you think you can walk?"

She was shaking violently. "I don't know."

"Lean on us!" I took Susanna's left arm and motioned Marie to her other side. Together we got her to her feet, even though she was clearly still weak. We half carried her down the hall. It took forever to climb the stairs, but at last we reached the servants' quarters on the top floor. We put Susanna on her bed. She was bathed in sweat, and her skin was clammy. What could possibly be wrong with such a young girl?

I stroked her forehead in an effort to calm her. "Marie will take care of you until the doctor arrives. You should take off your dress; it is soaked with coffee."

Susanna gave me a pleading look. "Please, please—I didn't mean to break the coffee service."

Mother would survive. We had no lack of porcelain.

"Never mind that. You got dizzy; it was not your fault. Try to rest." I patted her shoulder and beckoned Marie out into the hall. "You will stay with her?"

Marie nodded.

"Has she mentioned not feeling well?"

"No, she was the same as always."

"And recently?"

"Nothing." Marie looked puzzled. "What could it be? Perhaps her heart? My grandfather just tipped over all of a sudden when he had his heart attack."

"I am not a physician, unfortunately," I replied. "But it seems to me quite unusual for a girl of her age to collapse like that." I sighed. "Go back in and let me know at once if her condition worsens. I am sure the doctor will be here soon."

Marie disappeared back into the room.

I stood in the hall for a time. My mind came up with all sorts of possibilities, but I refused to entertain any of them. Susanna's problem, whatever it was, would be for the doctor to determine.

I walked back downstairs and toward the salon. Lena had cleared away the broken porcelain. The scent of spilled coffee permeated the hall.

Mother had returned to her place on the lounge. "How is she?"

"Unchanged. Marie is staying with her."

"Perhaps she had nothing to eat. You know how these young things are nowadays."

"I doubt that is the cause. But we should wait to hear what the doctor says."

Half an hour later, there was a knock at the front door. Bruns responded, led Dr. Hanno Bengtsen into the dining room, and came to fetch me.

I went to greet him. "Thank you very much for coming so quickly, Doctor. Please follow me."

I took him upstairs to the servants' quarters. I knocked on the door of the room Susanna shared with Marie.

Marie opened it. "She's all better now!" It looked as if she'd been having an animated conversation with Susanna.

"That is for the doctor to decide." I turned to him. "Do you need anything?"

"A bowl with water, a hand towel, and some soap."

"Marie, would you please see to the doctor's requests?"

"Yes, gracious miss."

The physician nodded. "Thank you very much. I must ask you to remain outside."

"Of course, Doctor. I will wait here."

Bengtsen disappeared into the room. Marie soon returned with a washbasin and other items. She emerged a few moments later.

"It would be best for you to go downstairs and reassure the others," I said. "They surely will want to know what's happening."

"Very well, gracious miss."

I remained in the hall. This was a world generally off limits to the masters of the house. It was part of the estate, of course, and nothing barred us from coming here if we wanted. But only very rarely was a family member seen in the servants' quarters. When we were children, Hendrik and I often sneaked up to this floor until our governess tracked us down and scolded us. Later, we lost all interest in the cramped quarters.

Time seemed to stretch out forever, but it probably took only about half an hour. The doctor finally emerged from Susanna's room with a grave face. Was her condition really so dire?

"How is she?"

Dr. Bengtsen frowned. "There is really no need for concern. At least not in any medical sense."

"And otherwise?"

The doctor glanced around as if someone might overhear us. "Well, as a physician I am obliged to maintain patient confidentiality. You should ask your employee directly. She will explain, if she is willing to do so."

"I will do that," I replied. "Thank you, Doctor, for responding so quickly."

Bengtsen nodded and gave me his hand. "Goodbye. I gather we will be seeing you more often in times to come?"

"Indeed you will," I replied. "Although I do hope that it will not be for your professional services."

"I share that hope, Countess Lejongård." He smiled. "You will be a fine mistress to the folks here."

Countess Lejongård. The title sounded strange to my ears and somehow false. But he was right: I was the countess now.

The doctor went down the stairs, medical bag in hand. I watched him go. I heard muffled weeping behind Susanna's door. What was happening here? Especially if there was no reason to be concerned about her health? I knocked and listened.

The sobbing was stifled, and then I heard Susanna's choked voice. "Come in!"

She was seated on the edge of her bed, wearing her white nightgown, her legs pulled up and her arms clasped around her knees. She shuddered when she saw me and lowered her head.

I approached the bed. "How are you, Susanna?"

"Didn't the doctor tell you?"

I shook my head. "Physicians must respect the privacy of their patients. All I want to know is how you are feeling. You do not have to tell me anything unless you want to."

Susanna looked down for a moment, then raised her gaze to meet mine. "It probably can't be kept secret."

"Kept secret? What cannot be kept secret?"

Susanna pressed her lips together. Tears spilled from her eyes.

"Susanna?"

She struggled for words and then confessed. "I'm going to have a baby."

I stared at her. "You are expecting?"

That would normally be a reason for celebration, but Susanna wasn't married, and she was a servant in our house.

A cold shiver ran up my spine when I thought of the fate that might await her. I didn't share the view that women should be forced to marry as soon as they become pregnant, but I knew full well how little we'd been able to change the standards of our society. Without a husband, Susanna would be marked forever, and no one would court her. Women in her plight often had only two choices: suicide or prostitution.

"Is the doctor sure? Really sure? I mean, were you aware of this possibility?"

"I felt ill, but I managed to hide it," she sobbed. "And my day—I missed my day of the month."

I myself knew about the scare of a period that didn't come on time. I'd always done my best to keep exact count of the days, and just in case, Marit had given me an herbal remedy from an old woman on the outskirts of town. My monthly curse often arrived late, and even though I'd have welcomed the opportunity to bear Michael's child, I was relieved each time I found things could continue as before. All the more now that Michael had disappeared from my life.

I suppressed those thoughts before they affected me unduly. "How far along are you?"

"I don't know. Maybe one or two months. When the blood didn't come, I didn't worry too much. I thought it would come after a while, the way it sometimes does . . ."

I took a deep breath. "Do you know who the father is?"

She nodded.

"Someone from the estate?"

Susanna didn't answer my question.

"Susanna," I said, "even though I am your mistress and employer, your intimate relationship is entirely your own affair. But I hope you know that you will be in great difficulty if you do not marry the father of your child."

I'd never expected to hear myself say such a thing.

"He—he won't marry me," she said miserably. "It's all over."

"Even so, he is a father now! He should face up to his responsibility. Even if he already has a wife."

"He doesn't. But he won't. And I don't want to talk about it."

I took another deep breath. Society would never allow her simply to brave it out. And I didn't even want to imagine what was going to happen when my mother found out.

Susanna seemed to read my mind. "Please don't tell the gracious mistress!"

"Unfortunately, I will have to do just that," I told her. "Eventually. You can hide your condition for now, but she is bound to notice. For I have no intention of dismissing you."

She was amazed. "You don't?"

"No. Your work has been impeccable, and they tell me you are a dedicated employee. I have no idea how you managed to get with child, but I very much hope you loved the father, and he did not force you."

"No, he didn't." Her eyes filled with tears again. "I really thought I would be his wife someday. But now everything has changed."

What a heartless bastard! I thought. He'd exploited her love and then refused to marry her. I wondered if the father was someone on the estate. He could just as likely be from the village, a man with whom she'd spent her days off.

"Very well. I will see what can be done. But I warn you, the day will come when I have to inform my mother, if only because you will not be suited for heavy work. I do not want to see you collapse again."

Susanna nodded, looking anything but happy. I wished I could help. Some of the Stockholm suffragettes would have promptly recommended an "angel maker," but I pushed that thought away. If Susanna asked for help procuring an abortion, that would be different. But I would never propose such a thing, for fear of her thinking my support depended on it.

"And as for your child," I added, "we will try to find a solution."

"Thank you very much, gracious miss." Susanna reached for the covers.

I lingered on the staircase for a moment after leaving her room. A pregnancy couldn't be concealed for long, unfortunately, and Mother would be furious when she learned of it. Never before had we employed a serving girl in Susanna's condition. Young women who wished to marry always resigned. And those who became pregnant outside of marriage had always been discharged.

Perhaps I could put off my mother's anger while I searched for a solution for Susanna. But even if I succeeded in shielding her from Stella's wrath, the situation would remain delicate. At least we still had some time. Maybe I would think of something.

19

Early the next morning, I went into my father's office. In former times, not a single day had passed without some business appointment or other. Father's most important partners had been notified of the changes at Lion Hall, but perhaps they were awaiting developments.

The office had been thoroughly tidied and aired out since my discussion with the police inspector, but it still smelled of the cigars my father liked so much. Their odor lingered on the documents and files, the leather of the armchairs, and the wood of the bookshelves. Letters were stacked on the desk. Although they'd been carefully arranged, some had slipped to one side or the other. Perhaps that was where I ought to start. I settled into the tall chair behind the desk. It was uncomfortable. Father had treasured it because in his opinion there was no reason for work furniture to be comfortable. I went through the envelopes one by one. Some contained belated condolence wishes; others had the usual invoices and business correspondence. Father must have inquired recently about new stallions for the stud, for the pile contained several offers. I wondered if the breeders had already learned of the fire.

A knock at the door interrupted my thoughts.

"Come in!"

Bruns appeared in the doorway. "Excuse me, gracious miss. A certain Mr. Max von Bredestein is here. He says he had an appointment with your father. Perhaps you may wish to speak with him."

"An appointment? For what reason?"

"Well, in fact, your father mentioned to me that he was thinking of hiring the man as an estate manager."

"A manager?" Father had always had Hendrik to help him with the estate business. Why would he need a manager? Our last manager, old Gridholm, had died when Hendrik was fourteen. Shortly after that, Father began initiating my brother into the business.

"Very well. Ask him in."

I stood up and smoothed my dress. This was another project of which I'd known nothing. Had Mother known?

Soon there was another knock at the door.

"Come in!"

Mr. von Bredestein turned out to be a handsome man in his late twenties. His dark curly hair was a bit unruly and perhaps a little longer than currently fashionable. But my attention was caught by the bright blue eyes peering out from beneath striking arched brows. He'd have made an ideal painter's model. His athletic figure was garbed in black trousers, a white shirt, and a beige tweed jacket. He'd obviously arrived on horseback, for the riding boots that must have been highly polished that morning were now speckled with splashes of mud. His appearance was so remarkable that for a moment I forgot to greet him.

My visitor also seemed taken aback. Calling on "Countess Lejongård," had he expected to see my mother?

"Good day, Mr. von Bredestein," I said at last. "I am pleased to make your acquaintance."

"The pleasure is entirely mine," he replied with a faint German accent. "Though I was expecting to meet your father."

So the news hadn't reached him.

"Unfortunately, my father died two weeks ago."

Von Bredestein appeared genuinely shocked. "That—I am extremely sorry to hear it. I . . ." He gave me a confused look. "My most sincere condolences."

"Thank you."

"Then I have come at the wrong time, it appears?" He picked uneasily at a shirt cuff.

"Well, perhaps. Maybe we should sit down," I suggested. "And then please tell me what my father and you discussed. I have not been in charge of the estate for long; in fact, today is my first day."

"Oh!" His smile was so disarming that I found myself wishing we'd met in other circumstances. "Then each of us is in an awkward situation. Would you agree?"

I couldn't imagine this impressive man failing to rise to such an occasion. The fact that he was ill at ease made him that much more interesting. The men I'd encountered in Stockholm had been nothing like him. I gestured to the visitor's chair. I really should have invited him to the seating area by the window, but I felt much more secure behind the desk.

"I met your father in Stockholm just over a month ago," Von Bredestein said as he took his seat. "We fell into conversation during a horse auction."

"You wanted to buy horses?"

"Yes, for my father's estate."

I was intrigued. If his father owned an estate, why was he looking to manage someone else's?

"And my father offered to hire you?"

"Not yet, but that is what I hoped would happen today. I understand entirely if, after your father's death, you do not require my services. I am sure your husband will soon be taking charge."

"I have no husband. I intend to manage the estate myself."

"Ah! Then as the daughter of the house, you already have the necessary experience."

"That is correct. But it does not mean I might not require assistance."

I looked him over. His bearing had the slightest touch of arrogance, just enough to be agreeably provocative. "Tell me, if you will be so kind, why exactly you wish to leave your father's estate. He will certainly not be pleased to lose a capable family member."

A grim smile flickered across his face. His eyes glinted. "I do hope so. My father and I have never really gotten along. And there is the fact that I am his second son. My older brother will take over the holdings someday. I will be a mere employee, no matter what happens."

"Your relationship with your brother is not good?"

"It certainly is not! He will be more than happy to be rid of me." Von Bredestein paused for a moment. "Do you have other siblings? Your father did not tell me much about his family."

"I had a brother," I answered and felt a pang in my heart. "He died when my father did."

"Oh! I am so sorry."

I nodded. "He was the older child, and we got along very well. He would have inherited the estate. But now I am the next in line . . ."

"That hardly seems to please you."

"The price I had to pay was quite high." We gazed at one another in silence for a moment. I didn't know what he was seeing in my eyes. "In any case, I plan to take affairs into my own hands."

There was something odd about this man. I narrowed my eyes slightly.

"Are you German?" I asked. "Where do you come from?"

"From the area around Stralsund. In Pomerania."

"The area Wallenstein sought to conquer in the Thirty Years' War but could not," I responded. I recalled hearing in my childhood of the epic resistance of the people of Stralsund. And how our King Gustav II Adolf had intervened to help them triumph over Wallenstein's Catholic forces.

"True. Looking back at it now, we have good reason to be thankful to Sweden. But the Swedish troops were anything but gentle with the peasants. The brutal torture and other abuses drove many of them to rebel."

I contemplated him for a long moment. His familiarity with history pleased me. It was clear he had interests other than horses.

"Well, thank heavens those terrible times are long past. The people of Pomerania seem to have made their peace with Sweden."

Von Bredestein grinned. "My father married a Swede. That's why I can get by in your language."

He was fishing for a compliment; he knew how well he spoke my mother tongue. "Your Swedish is excellent."

"Thank you. You're very kind." His satisfied smile proved my intuition correct. "It was because I speak Swedish that my father sent me here to survey Swedish quarter horses. Our stud needs to be reinvigorated, and the animals here are superb."

I tilted my head. "Your father may have made a big mistake. It seems he now risks losing a good man. Was that a spontaneous decision, or had you been thinking for some time of getting the better of him?"

"I do not wish to get the better of my father, God knows, even if he deserves it. I want to stand on my own two feet, so I am not continually being compared to my brother. And since my mother is Swedish, I thought it would be a fine adventure to start anew in her homeland."

I leaned back and studied his face. He seemed not to have brought any credentials other than a distaste for his family. Yet my father had found him interesting enough to invite him to Lion Hall for a talk. And he wanted to stand on his own feet, a desire we had in common.

Should I give him a try? I found something about him attractive, though that in itself was no reason to take him on. Especially considering we'd just lost five thousand crowns to the repayment of a shady loan contract and were in no position to be extravagant.

"Do you have any experience managing an estate like this? How large is your father's stud farm?"

"We have about three hundred horses, all told. So it is not particularly large, but it is not small either. Of course, your estate is much grander, but I do not think the operations would be significantly different. I regret I cannot offer a letter of recommendation from my father; you will surely understand why I am not in a position to request one."

I nodded, leaned forward, and placed my hands on the desktop. "I will be candid with you. I was studying in Stockholm until a couple of weeks ago. My life was well ordered, and the path ahead was clear. But now I am here, and I will not conceal the fact that I could use some assistance. My mother was not involved in the business, and we have had no manager for a long time. Frankly speaking, I am a bit surprised to hear my father spoke to you about the position, considering my brother was being groomed to take over the estate."

I paused briefly to let those words work on him. There was curiosity in his face. He watched me closely, clearly keen to get the position.

"Things are as they are," I continued. "And I need someone to guide me in managing an estate. So let me ask you: When can you start?"

Von Bredestein's eyebrows shot up in astonishment. "You wish to hire me?"

"Yes, indeed I do. For a six-month trial. After all, you have provided no references."

"I promise you will not be disappointed."

"I hope not. We have a small cottage on the property you can use for now. Our former manager lived there many years ago. I will pay you eighty crowns per month, and your room and board are free. Where are you living currently?"

"Actually, I had hoped to be hired, so I am available immediately. Perhaps it would be better for me to stay at the inn. No doubt the cottage requires some work."

I nodded. "Excellent. Come here early tomorrow morning, and I will show you everything. The village inn is very good. Have the cost of the room charged to the estate."

"That is very generous of you," replied Von Bredestein, somewhat surprised. "Thank you."

"Not at all. If you fulfill my expectations, it will be money well spent."

"Said like a true businesswoman!"

I smiled. "I am nothing of the kind, God knows, but with your help, I may well become one."

"Until tomorrow, then, Countess Lejongård." My new estate manager bowed briefly and turned to the door.

"If you wish to advise your father of your new position, there is a telegraph office in the village. That is the quickest means."

"Ah, but who said I wanted to be quick?" Von Bredestein smiled and took his leave.

I looked after him and wondered what had possessed me. My father had an eye for talent, at least as far as the estate and the horses were concerned. He must have seen something in Von Bredestein, for otherwise he'd never have discussed taking him on. I hadn't been trained to run this place, and Von Bredestein would be a great help if he was really as good as my father thought.

I was gratified and in fact incredulous that Father had done me this posthumous service. But I couldn't help wondering why he hadn't planned to entrust estate management to Hendrik alone.

Someone knocked. Another appointment? I'd better check Father's agenda. But it wasn't Bruns, coming to announce a visitor.

My mother entered in response to my call. She held an envelope.

"Shouldn't delivering the mail be the maid's responsibility?" I teased her.

Mother refused to take the bait. She handed me the telegram. "Count Bergen has advised us he will visit today."

"The king's chamberlain?" Bergen hadn't visited us in quite a long time.

"He wishes to speak to the new Countess Lejongård."

"This seems a bit sudden."

The chamberlain usually communicated his plans weeks in advance, and the telegram gave no reason for his visit.

"Well, he is probably responding to our bereavement."

"But why such haste? I only just accepted the title."

"I assume this is simply protocol. You are the mistress of the manor, after all. No doubt he wishes to discuss palace affairs, so you should be on your best behavior. I will have Linda set out some of my garments. The clothing in your wardrobe is entirely too youthful. You need to do something about that."

Now she wanted me to commission a new wardrobe, as if I didn't have enough to do already!

"Perhaps Linda can find some things at the department store in Kristianstad," I suggested maliciously. I knew Mother was repelled by the notion of purchasing clothing off the rack. Appearing at an official function in a department store dress would provoke a middling scandal.

"You should summon my seamstress. That way, at least you would not be at risk of being mistaken for a common drab. If you wish, I can have her demonstrate the latest fashions to you."

I'd been delighted by her dressmaker's suggestions when I was a tender young thing. Everything she had to offer shimmered, shone, and glistened: taffeta, brocade, silk, crystal necklaces, and golden combs. I'd felt like a princess when surrounded by those beautiful fabrics and accessories. Now, however, those styles seemed distinctly behind the times.

But I had no desire for a clash with my mother right now. "Very well. Advise your dressmaker. I definitely need my own black dresses, since we are obliged to remain in mourning for some time yet. I cannot be constantly borrowing from your wardrobe."

"I will. And mind you, I expect no controversy this evening. No parading around like a mad suffragette!"

I was tempted to ask her to describe a "mad suffragette," but she didn't give me the chance.

"By the way, who was that young man who just left?" She studied me.

"Max von Bredestein," I told her. "Father met him in Stockholm and decided to take him on as a manager."

Mother's eyebrows arched. "Take him on? As a manager? Whatever for?"

"Perhaps to help with business affairs? This is the first I have heard of it."

"But Thure had his own son!"

I'd had exactly the same response. This development puzzled me almost as much as the unexplained loan had.

"Von Bredestein is from Pomerania, where his father has an estate. Father met him at the Stockholm auction and probably thought he could be useful."

"His father is an estate owner? Then why on earth would he be interested in working for us?"

"Mother, he is the second son and not on particularly good terms with his father. He told me he decided to strike out on his own. I understand exactly how he feels."

Mother glowered. "It is never acceptable to fail in one's obligations to a parent, whatever the circumstances."

I said nothing. I refused to be provoked.

"Do you intend to hire this man?" Mother probed.

"I have already done so. I know very little about running an estate, and I am sure he will be a great help."

Mother gave me a calculating look but finally nodded. She left the room.

20

As the hour of the chamberlain's arrival approached, I inspected myself in the mirror. The ruffled short sleeves, stiff bodice, and close-cut skirt were quite unfashionable. In Stockholm, I'd seen far more attractive cuts: Japanese cuts, loose wraps that resembled tunics, and elaborate cascades of fabric decorated with expensive lace and held snug at the waist with a wide sash. Corsets weren't needed for loose-cut teatime dresses. I'd attended the university wearing quite simple skirts and blouses. From time to time, Marit and I went window shopping, marveling at the latest fashions the tailor shops displayed. Fashion had long since ceased to be the exclusive province of the rich, a change Marit thoroughly approved of. Perhaps I should get the seamstress to dispose of that old fur muff from the back of the wardrobe, no matter what Mother thought.

But for now I had no choice. I had to wear this dress or cram myself into one of Mother's. I pulled on my elbow-length gloves and made my way downstairs.

Mother was already posted in the salon in her most elegant black dress. It was no more up-to-date than the one I wore. It would be a waste of breath trying to convince her that fashion was much less confining now.

She glanced at the clock. "He is late, and so are you!" She inspected me. "You urgently need new clothing. That is the attire of a seventeen-year-old."

"In many settings, that would be considered a compliment."

"Perhaps you could fasten your corset tighter. Your waist seems rather more ample than necessary."

"My waist is just fine. Instead, we can use this time to speculate why Count Bergen is late."

Mother grimaced. She found the failure to be punctual even more unacceptable than inappropriate clothing. "He intended to be here at eight o'clock. We are already fifteen minutes past that hour."

I was sure she wasn't going to reprove Count Bergen for tardiness. "Perhaps he stopped along the way. Or his coach broke down. You know the state of the roads around here."

Mother sniffed and glanced at the glass of soda water in her hand. The thin slice of lemon looked the worse for wear.

Just then, we heard a loud wheezing sound followed by a sharp report. We bounded to our feet. I knew that noise from Stockholm. I hurried to the window with the eagerness of a little child.

A motorcar came up the drive and rolled into the circular approach to the portico. It halted at the foot of the front steps. The car's dark-red chassis and brass lamp fixtures gleamed under the flickering gas lanterns of the forecourt. A young man in uniform and chauffeur's cap sat behind the wheel in a seat upholstered in red. Goggles dangled from his neck. The exposed valves of the engine glistened in the gaslight like the contents of a treasure chest. Count Bergen was at his ease in the rear upon a leather-upholstered bench that resembled a Chesterfield sofa.

This astonishing sight would have left Hendrik speechless. Even I couldn't help admiring such a vehicle. How heavenly it must be to race past the meadows with the wind in one's hair!

"Amazing!" I blurted.

"Look at that horse of the apocalypse!" Mother exclaimed. "In that dreadful conveyance, he is on display like a dandy on the prowl for a mate."

I hid a smile. She'd never have tolerated such disrespect for a member of the royal household from me. The automobile had put her in high dudgeon.

"It will forever be a mystery to me why the king would sit in such a vehicle." She shook her head. "Another caprice of his, like playing tennis. Did you hear he registered in a tennis tournament as 'Mr. G.'?"

I nodded, trying not to giggle. The Stockholm papers had been full of it.

"A thing like that pleases you? It is evidence of the decline of the Western world!"

"Mother, the West won't go under if our king plays tennis or even if his chamberlain travels by motorcar. We should ready ourselves to receive Count Bergen."

We returned to our seats. Mother muttered under her breath, then sipped her soda water. Bruns appeared moments later to announce the count.

Count Bergen had taken off his goggles and his duster. He was quite impressive in his gray traveling garb. His twirled mustache gave him a slightly decadent air somewhat risqué for a man in his sixties. My memories of him were nothing like this.

"Good evening, dear ladies!" He bowed, kissed my mother's hand, then bent over mine.

"Count Bergen," I responded. "I am delighted to welcome you to Lion Hall."

"Countess Lejongård, my most profound condolences for your loss. This certainly cannot have been easy for the two of you."

"Thank you."

Mother, unusually silent up to this point, spoke up. "Despite our bereavement, we remain attached to the glorious traditions of our ancestral line."

Bergen nodded. "We were relieved to hear you and your daughter were personally spared from the catastrophe."

I flinched. True, we'd suffered no bodily injuries, but the deaths had scarred us in less visible ways.

Mother stepped to the window and tugged the bell pull. I'd noted wonderful smells from the kitchen when I descended the stairs earlier, and I was eager to see what magic Mrs. Bloomquist had worked.

"The vehicle that conveyed you here is most impressive," I commented. I couldn't bear to reminisce about Father and Hendrik. I also wanted to keep that bizarre loan out of my thoughts. Bergen was here to pay his respects to the new countess. Not for sentimental reasons but purely practical ones.

"It is a Packard Eighteen Touring model," Bergen boasted. "In bad weather, it tends to bounce around, but when it comes to speed, not even the troll king could catch it. The king purchased three: one for the crown prince, one for himself, and one for the senior palace staff."

"What do you think, Mother?" I asked mischievously. "Should we get one like this? We could reach the city in the twinkling of an eye."

"Lion Hall is famous for its horses," Mother said tartly. "Not for automobiles."

He smiled. "You should take it for a trial ride. It is remarkably different from coach travel. One saves a great deal of time, and in my opinion, one is more comfortable."

"That is very kind of you, Count Bergen," Mother replied, "but we really do prefer travel by coach."

We? I bit back my objection.

Bruns appeared in the doorway. "The evening meal is ready, gracious mistress."

"Thank you, Bruns." Mother finished her soda water and rose.

When we entered the dining room, I saw the table was set differently. Mother had put me at the end, acknowledging me as head of the family. It was odd to be occupying Father's place. He'd seemed so Olympian in recent years.

Mother prompted me with a glance, for it was my duty to propose the toast. I found that disorienting as well. Marie appeared promptly and filled the wineglasses. Susanna was also in the room, still pale but apparently healthy.

"Let us drink to the royal family," I said into the expectant silence. "And to Thure and Hendrik Lejongård, my treasured father and my beloved brother."

"May the first flourish before God and the others find His peace," Bergen responded. He raised his glass and took a sip.

The servants brought the soup.

My head ached. If I were alone with Mother, we would have simply sat in silence. Tonight I was obliged to carry on a conversation. Mother expected me to entertain, whether we had a single guest or a hundred. I didn't know Bergen well enough to guess what might interest him. Father had always taken the lead in table talk while Hendrik and I had vied with one another in making grimaces and funny faces.

"Tell us, Count Bergen, what is the news at court?" I asked, once the soup bowls were filled and all serving maids had disappeared except Marie. She stood discreetly in a corner to attend to any requests.

"There is relatively little to report. The king is traveling quite a lot these days, and the queen needs more time than before in warmer climes. In part for that reason, the newest royal prince is growing up in excellent health. Bertil is a proper little ray of sunshine."

"I am quite pleased to hear it. Will Their Majesties be able to spend a few days with us this coming summer?"

He glanced at the maid. "Well, Countess Lejongård, that we can discuss in private after dinner."

"Is there any reason to be concerned?" Mother asked.

Bergen shook his head. "No. No reason to worry. I simply wish to discuss some minor details with your daughter. Matters I had discussed with your sainted late husband."

I didn't miss the fact that Mother's smile was rigid. Not because he'd mentioned Father but because she was to be excluded. Father had always disappeared with Bergen for private chats. That was all I remembered of the count's visits. He was relatively advanced in years, so he'd been of limited interest to me. Mother would retire to the salon with Bergen's wife, whom I could scarcely remember.

"How are things with your lady wife?" Mother asked in an effort to conceal her discontent.

"Not too well, unfortunately. Her memory has been playing tricks on her since last year. She is confused quite often, and when she goes out walking in the garden, she forgets how she came to be there. The physician believes she suffers from this new Alzheimer illness, and he prescribed a visit to Italy for rest and recovery. She is there now with my daughter."

"I am sorry to hear it. I hope the Italian air proves salutary."

His expression suggested he couldn't share that hope. A doctor's prescription of a stay abroad for rest and relaxation was never a good sign.

Bergen deftly changed the subject. "I hear you have had no fewer than twenty foals so far this year. A notable achievement!"

"Yes, Father acquired several additional mares. I have not yet seen all the animals, but the most recent foal, at least, seems superb." The thought of Evening Star brought the flicker of a smile to my face. If there was such a thing as the transmutation of souls, Hendrik's spirit had probably found a new home in that wonderfully beautiful little horse.

"Do you think you might be able to raise racehorses? You know, of course, that His Majesty dreams of establishing a racing circuit as respected as those in England."

That was news to me, though I'd heard of horse races in Stockholm. They were hardly of the class of those in England, but Hendrik had been very enthusiastic whenever they were mentioned.

"Our horses are very quick on the hunt, and I doubt you would find any better adapted to that purpose. How they might perform in competition on a track remains to be seen. In any case, I doubt it would be worthwhile to ship horses to England to compete at Ascot."

"Perhaps one day it will be. Imagine if the best racers in our own circuit were to succeed in England! Times are changing quickly, Countess Lejongård, and it is essential to keep up."

He was voicing the nation's opinion as defined by the royal family, but I didn't know if I could allow our horses to compete in such grueling events. I'd heard terrible stories about horses collapsing at the Stockholm race course.

Mother beckoned for the next course. "Well, if the king is in favor of it, a Swedish racing circuit is sure to be a tremendous success."

"How is he getting along with his tennis?" I asked, knowing she thought it wildly undignified for royalty to be leaping around a tennis court, even though the young set in Stockholm was enchanted by the sight.

"Oh, he is doing well. His new coach is quite satisfied."

"Will he be competing at Wimbledon?"

"Ah, who can tell? He has often attended as a guest, and he would certainly be pleased to match himself against players of international repute!"

"If he decides to do so, you must let us know. I have not visited England for a long time, and that would be the ideal occasion."

I'd last been to England in 1905 when Crown Prince Gustav Adolf married Princess Margaret at Windsor Castle. I was nineteen that year, and I'd found it all terribly exciting. I probably still had my sketch of the castle lying around somewhere.

The wedding celebrations had been breathtaking, and my mother had gotten it into her head to make our festival for the following midsummer just as splendid. She'd managed it at least in part, but the crown prince and his princess hadn't been able to attend because they were honeymooning in Ireland. Mother had been downcast about that for months.

"If His Royal Highness should actually participate in the Wimbledon tournament," Bergen replied, "an appropriate accompanying delegation would be called for, of course. I would personally propose your name."

"Thank you very much." I glanced at Mother, who looked as if she'd just found a fly in her soup. She would certainly have preferred a ball at the Court of St. James's to sitting for hours in the burning sun, eating strawberries with cream and taking the chance that a sudden shower might ruin her carefully done hair.

"We would be very happy to welcome His Majesty to our autumn foxhunt," Mother volunteered as we waited for the maids to serve the second course.

"Well, I assume he will not wish to forego such a thrilling event. But other things require our attention before then."

That comment brought the worry back into Mother's eyes. I found it strange that the chamberlain wasn't willing to elaborate. Hunting ran a close second to tennis among the king's passions. That surely couldn't have changed. Why was Bergen being so tight-lipped?

My mother took her leave after dinner. Count Bergen kissed her hand with a formal flourish, and I wished her good night as she retired to her chambers. I invited the count into the still-cluttered office, which seemed the only appropriate place to discuss the royal visit.

"Please excuse the disorder."

"It appears you have begun to review the business records, Countess."

"I have indeed. I wish to take the reins as quickly as possible. Every day of delay costs the estate." That wasn't me speaking; I was channeling my father. He'd drilled that admonition into Hendrik, who in turn had complained to me. I gestured toward the leather armchairs, fortunately no longer encumbered with documents. "Please have a seat."

The count sank gratefully into an armchair. "I must say that a great weight of responsibility has settled onto your shoulders now that you have accepted the title and the estate." He leaned back. "Your family has long been close to the royal house. But of course you know that."

I nodded. Father had instilled in me from my most tender years the Lejongård allegiance to the crown. I was puzzled by this preamble. "That will not change."

Bergen came calling whenever the royal family had a request to make, whether it be about a visit to break a long journey, the reception and housing of official guests, or a confidential meeting either private or political in nature. It seemed unlikely he'd come now only for a courtesy call.

I served some of the aquavit my father kept out of sight inside the globe. I set the count's glass within reach and sat in the armchair opposite him.

Fortunately, he wasn't a man given to wasting time with flowery speech. "You know of course that as chamberlain I am responsible for arranging the calendars of Their Highnesses Our Royal Majesties. I routinely discuss their activities with their individual secretaries. I was informed a few days ago that Princess Margaret anticipates spending a week here in August with the children."

"That will be a great honor," I replied, even though Bergen's grave countenance suggested there was a problem.

"Unfortunately, I would be required to express reservations about such a plan should it appear to me Her Majesty might be in danger."

"How might that be?"

"We are, of course, in ongoing contact with the chief of the national police. It has come to our attention that the authorities suspect the regrettable incident at Lion Hall may have resulted from arson."

Waves of hot and cold shot through me. This was something I hadn't considered, and there was nothing I could have done about it. The king and the crown prince had been advised of the police investigations because the Lejongårds were not just any family. Arson on our property affected the royal family, if only indirectly.

"That is correct. Inspector Hermannsson is looking at that possibility," I said. "But you can be assured we will do everything to keep Her Royal Highness safe. The debris of the burned building will be cleared away by that time and will pose no threat."

"My concern is that this may happen again," Bergen said bluntly. "If it indeed resulted from criminal activity, a second, similar incident might occur."

Suddenly my mouth was parched. "Ah! I would not expect anything of the kind."

"A hope we share, of course. But can you guarantee that?"

I shook my head, because I couldn't promise it.

"Another possibility would be for the palace to suggest Her Majesty stay at your seaside villa in Åhus."

"In that case, we would have to double the staff in Åhus," I mused. "Suppose, then, that my mother and I accompany them. Someone would still be required here to oversee the estate. Not that we have extensive personnel needs, but—"

"Her Royal Highness strongly prefers to stay at Lion Hall. Spring and autumn are the seasons for her visits to the seaside, as the moderate weather is more to her taste. If there is any danger to the princes and princesses, surely it would be no great inconvenience to you to make arrangements to ensure their safety."

"No, of course not," I replied, worried by his blasé assumption.

Hiring additional servants was a question of expense. I hadn't yet been properly initiated into the financial side of the estate, but rebuilding the horse barn would mean costs that we might well have to finance by selling horses.

"Good, then! She will be most pleased to hear it," Bergen pronounced, though he continued to scrutinize me. "That leads me to assume you will inform us as soon as the authorities complete their investigations?"

When they do, you'll certainly already have received the report piping hot from the chief of police, I wanted to respond, but I bit back that sarcastic response. One does not annoy the chamberlain if one wishes to stay in the good graces of the royal family. A few weeks earlier, I'd have laughed and dismissed that precept, but now I was going to have to be very, very careful.

"Of course, I will advise you immediately. And I will press the supervising police inspector for rapid results. They may identify the culprit quickly or find no foul play at all."

"We earnestly hope so, all of us." Bergen reassumed his usual genial smile. "Very well, then. I will not take up any more of your time."

"Won't you stay overnight? Our guest rooms are ready, and we will be very grateful if you grant us your company at breakfast tomorrow."

"I regret it very much, but I fear I must decline your hospitable invitation." He stood up and extended his hand. When I took it, he bowed and brushed his lips across my knuckles.

Bruns was waiting at the front door with the chamberlain's duster. The count slipped into it, and I accompanied him to the waiting vehicle.

"You really should reconsider acquiring a motorcar," he said. "Your mother perhaps may be a little bit distrustful of progress, but I assure you that once you take your seat in such a conveyance, you will never go back to actual horsepower." With that, he climbed into the back and gave his chauffeur the sign to crank the engine.

The motor came to life with a roar. Its racket filled the front court. I was sure the maids and stable boys were gathered at the windows for the spectacle. The driver moved a lever, and the vehicle began to advance. The tires kicked up gravel as it headed into the drive, then the white beams of the headlights and red gleams of the taillights disappeared into the night.

Bruns stood by the front door, ready for duty. The automobile had clearly impressed him, for his expression was as gleeful as that of a young child.

"Have you any other wish, gracious miss?"

I shook my head. "I am going to bed now. This has been a long, difficult day."

"I will inform Lena."

"No, do not bother her. After the maids finish their work, they may take the rest of the evening off."

I went upstairs. I needed time to myself. I had a terrible headache, and my neck was stiff. I undressed, washed in cold water, and pulled on my nightgown.

I'd just collapsed into bed when someone knocked. Had Lena come upstairs despite my instructions?

"Come in," I called in a drained voice. I sat up.

My mother appeared. She looked around the room she hadn't visited in years. "I hope the meeting with Count Bergen was mutually satisfactory?"

I nodded. "Yes, it was. The crown prince and princess will participate in the midsummer festivities, and Princess Margaret and the children will stay with us for a week in August."

She relaxed visibly at that news. "How wonderful!"

"Bergen's concern is that the question of arson be cleared up before August. He heard of the suspicions of the police. The palace wishes to make sure there is no threat to the princess and her children."

I extracted a couple of pins from my hair. How I disliked these elaborate hair creations! After a time, they felt like an ill-fitting wig. Why did women have to make such a fuss over their hair? I'd much have preferred to have mine cropped short, but I had so many other battles to fight. I had no stomach for confronting my mother over hairstyles.

"That is understandable," Mother replied with a sour expression. "And did he have anything useful to suggest?"

"He said that they might try to persuade the princess to use the villa in Åhus instead. I told him we would need more staff for that."

"We could find them, no doubt. You did not give him the impression, I hope, that we—"

"No, I did not. I made that remark in passing only."

"I hope he understood it that way! If people get the idea that our house cannot even organize a *séjour* for the crown princess, our reputation will be ruined. Our current king is not the one who granted us the estate."

"I am perfectly aware of that. But I do not see any reason for concern. Anyway, the princess still much prefers Lion Hall. In other words, we must make sure no more fires break out here."

"I will write Inspector Hermannsson and insist he move more quickly. I cannot imagine what is taking him so long."

"Only two weeks have passed. Proper police investigations must take time."

Mother looked as if she doubted that, but she didn't go so far as to accuse Hermannsson and his men of negligence. "Did Bergen have anything else on his mind?"

"No, that was all. The unexplained fire bothers them. That may be why he was noncommittal about the hunt." I paused. "The king will come. He enjoys our forests too much to stay away."

Mother nodded and turned away. "Good night, Agneta."

"Good night, Mother."

I looked after her, then sank back onto the bed. My heart was full of yearning. How much I'd have liked to be back in my Stockholm apartment with the water stains. And to nestle in Michael's arms. Both were impossibilities. I needed to make the best of the situation.

21

I stepped out the front door of the manor. "Well, well! You are certainly punctual."

Max von Bredestein looked up from the bottom of the steps. "And you are quite elegant this morning."

Was he mocking me? I was in a black dress with a broad sash. It rustled more than I liked, but Mother had told me at breakfast she would contact her dressmaker. Frau Larsson was zealous and quite prompt in attending to a client of my mother's status, but she couldn't perform miracles. Even if she took measurements before the day was out, it would take a week or more to produce a dress. Even with one of the modern electric sewing machines.

Von Bredestein carried a small valise.

"Is that all the baggage you have?"

"Yes, and I regret there will not be any more. Once I communicate to my father my intention to leave his employ, I expect he will have nothing more to do with me."

"Do you really imagine he will take it so ill?"

"Worse," he answered and hefted the valise. "And where might I find my new lodgings?"

His smile was touched by a shadow of concern. Despite his brave attitude, he appeared clearly dejected at the rupture with his family.

We walked past the stable boys' quarters. A couple of them, clearly curious, watched us go by. Langeholm turned up on our way. "Good morning, gracious miss. I was on my way to see you. We had two more foals during the night."

I shook hands with the stable master. "Good morning, Mr. Langeholm. This is Max von Bredestein, our new manager—Mr. von Bredestein, Sören Langeholm, the master of our stables."

"Delighted to meet you," Langeholm said with a broad smile. They shook hands.

I'd instructed the majordomo to inform our people I'd hired a new manager. The announcement was received with general approval.

"You will find life here on the estate very pleasant. If you need any help at all, please do not hesitate to contact me."

"Very kind of you. Thank you very much." My new manager beamed and fell into step behind me again.

The cottage was a small wooden structure surrounded by a fence. It was painted the traditional dark red. When Hendrik and I were small, we'd sneaked out there to plunder the apple tree in the yard while Gridholm was occupied elsewhere. He'd perpetually complained about crows, but I'd long been convinced he'd known exactly who'd been stealing the fruit.

I opened the garden gate. "If the isolation is not to your taste, tell me, and I will find other quarters for you."

"That will not be necessary." Von Bredestein smiled. "I like this very much. And I am quite glad to have time to myself. On my father's estate, I never did."

I unlocked the cottage.

The faint odor of Gridholm's cigars still permeated the wooden walls. I'd forgotten how snug and agreeable the place was. A tidy little fireplace with a stone chimney promised warmth in winter, and the windows were large enough to admit lots of summer sunshine. The dwelling consisted of two rooms: one with a small niche to serve as the kitchen and the other a bedroom with an ample bedstead and a metal bathtub behind a curtain. A toolshed stood in the garden. The estate staff were fed Mrs. Bloomquist's wonderful fare, but Gridholm had always supplemented it with his own supplies of tobacco, home-brewed brandy, and the fermented fish he liked so much. The tins of *surströmming* from his Norwegian cousin gave off such a putrid odor that he was allowed to open them only here, far from the manor.

"It is modest, but you are free to arrange things as you wish."

Von Bredestein surveyed the kitchen table, its two chairs, the secondhand wardrobe from the manor, and the hearth bench with a sheepskin throw.

"I believe I have everything I need," he said. "I do come from an estate, but I am quite self-sufficient. Properly rested and regularly fed, I will be quite content."

I looked him over. Indeed he looked nothing like the pampered offspring of a wealthy family. His features were strong and impressive. He was wiry, though not particularly muscular. His shoulders, arms, and gait signaled he'd grown up in the countryside and would be entirely capable of mastering and taming an unruly horse.

A horseman. Like Hendrik.

I shook my head to dispel the comparison.

"Should you need anything, do inform me or Mr. Langeholm. Meals are served in the manor kitchen at the common table with other employees. I will advise Mrs. Bloomquist to add another portion immediately. Meanwhile, I expect you in the office this afternoon. I will show you the accounts and discuss the details of the position."

I detected amusement in Von Bredestein's face. Was he not taking me seriously? Did he find it strange to be receiving instructions from a woman?

"Thank you, Countess Lejongård." He took my hand and pressed his lips to it. "I am very pleased to be working for you."

"The feeling is mutual."

We held one another's gaze for a moment, and then I turned away. I felt a sudden flutter and tickling deep inside. The sensation didn't go away as the cottage disappeared in the distance behind me.

22

The weather improved over the following weeks, and flowers bloomed everywhere. June brought splendid summer weather. Sweet perfumes filled the air, and the sun shone down from a sky of deep blue. Bees and butterflies competed in gathering pollen.

Max von Bredestein turned out to be a great help. He patiently explained the principles of bookkeeping, and he shared a great deal about the science of horse breeding. We even traveled with Langeholm to the Stockholm horse market. We didn't actually need more animals, but I was determined to learn about this aspect of the business. During my childhood, Mother had always kept me home when the men traveled.

Horse breeding was a masculine profession, and at the Stockholm horse market, I received many stares of absolute astonishment. It meant little that I was dressed quite simply and avoided appearing overly feminine. More than once the breeders assumed I was accompanying my husband—Langeholm or my manager, Max, as I soon began to think of him. Jaws dropped when I explained I was the interested party. Their reactions reminded me of the first time I'd walked into my class at the Royal Academy.

I began to enjoy my new role. I did weep late at night in my room for Hendrik and for Michael as well, but I kept a tight rein on my emotions during the day. Mother seemed to have softened a bit now that I'd given up my independence and accepted the yoke of family responsibilities.

I got myself new clothes, including a riding outfit so I could participate in the autumn hunt. Mother was scandalized and admonished me not to put myself on public display. But surely she couldn't expect me to ride sidesaddle during a foxhunt!

As time passed, I became more and more concerned about Susanna. Marit had agreed in early April to look for a prospective husband or at least a discreet physician, but I'd still had no word from her. Susanna wouldn't be able to hide her condition much longer. Though we didn't speak of it again, the pregnancy was clearly causing her difficulties. She had dark circles under her eyes and seemed to have lost weight, even though Mrs. Bloomquist provided her with plenty to eat. I had a bad feeling about the situation. Did the other maids suspect? Were they shunning her or talking behind her back?

Midsummer was approaching, and with it the date for the great ball. In our current circumstances, I wasn't sure if I should make arrangements and send out invitations. My father and brother had died scarcely three months before. Would it be socially acceptable to sponsor a ball so soon?

"Of course it's acceptable," my mother had declared at the breakfast table in early May. "Indeed, it is our obligation. Our peers and even the palace came to offer my late husband and son their respects. They expect us to reciprocate by sponsoring the ball."

It was completely beyond me why aristocrats and gentry who'd attended our family funeral would expect to dance on our tabletops only three months later.

"Very well, then, Mother. I will take the risk."

"What risk?" she erupted. "You cannot be serious! The midsummer celebration is sacred! We have never canceled it."

"But I fear people think it irreverent of us. We are in deep mourning."

Mother's jaw tightened. "We *must* give the ball. It can be a bit more sober and restrained, perhaps, but midsummer must be celebrated."

I sighed and set down my coffee cup. Was it worth it to take her on? Should I just give in? I liked the midsummer festivity, more than anything for the fresh herring and shot glasses of home-brewed aquavit.

"All right, Mother. We will celebrate midsummer."

"Excellent! We—"

"But we will make the festivities as simple and dignified as possible. No pomp! This will be an occasion to share a fine meal. Without dancing."

"Midsummer without dancing?" Her eyes went wide. "What sort of ball would that be? The villagers would never forgive us."

"Our guests may dance, of course. But we two should refrain."

That would pose no hardship for me. I had no reason to suppose that the eligible young men of the region would come running to court me.

Mother was miffed, but even so, she nodded. "Very well. We two will avoid the dance floor. But we should arrange for a full band."

"Why not just hire the village fiddler? He knows his craft, and the villagers will be delighted."

"Have you taken leave of your senses? What about His Majesty? Are you expecting him to cavort with peasant farmers?"

I couldn't hide a smile at that absurd image.

"Stop laughing at me!" my mother cried. "Why are you always so wrongheaded? You already scandalized my dressmaker. She almost quit because of your bizarre notions!"

"And what is wrong with having up-to-date fashions? It's important to keep abreast of the trends."

"Our social circles emphasize quality. There is no need to appear chic."

"Why not? I don't imagine your old bustles and crinolines will be coming back anytime soon. Modern women have liberated themselves from such restrictions."

"Oh, do tell! And will we next be shopping at department stores? I can just imagine motoring to Kristianstad to shop."

I couldn't hide my amusement at that, but my mother was entirely in earnest. "Oh, never mind, then," I told her. "Go ahead and hire the musicians. But I insist on having the fiddler as well. I am sure he will please the guests."

Mother heaved a sigh of exasperation. "For all I care!"

23

Everyone in the manor house was tense with expectation on the morning of the ball. They all wanted it to be a glorious success. The maids tittered constantly; even Miss Rosendahl and Mr. Bruns seemed less forbidding than usual. The midsummer sun was working its magic.

Lena appeared in my room. Her cheeks were bright red. She'd plaited her hair and put it up in a fashion I'd never seen before, probably with Susanna's inspiration and assistance.

"Good morning, Lena. Do you plan to search the meadows for seven types of flowers?"

Old folks in the village believed that if a girl picked seven different flowers on midsummer night and placed the bouquet beneath her pillow, she would dream of her future husband. Lena was only fourteen, of course, but perhaps she already had her hopes pinned on some young fellow.

"Yes, gracious miss. The rest of the village girls are just as excited."

"Do you hope to dream of someone in particular?" I asked, careful not to ask for a name, for divulging it would be bad luck.

Lena giggled. "Maybe. Anyhow, I don't expect he'll turn out to be my husband."

"Well, if the dream tells you so, it will come to pass."

"Are you sure?"

"If it does not, you can look to see what else the dream says. Maybe you will be surprised."

"But in addition to—" Lena looked down and blushed. "In addition, I work here at the manor, so I'm not allowed to get married."

"Who says so? Perhaps that was true in the old days, but times have changed. But before you ask for my blessing, you had best take care of my hair."

Lena laid out the brushes and combs. "Will you go pick flowers too?"

I studied myself in the mirror. If only I could go without the endless combing and pinning up of hair. But this was what was expected for the fête. You are required to sponsor a ball when you're in deep mourning, but a bad hairstyle will ruin your reputation. I really didn't care, but Mother would never let me hear the end of it if one of those old ladies claimed I was looking slovenly.

"I cannot say. We will see if I can find time to pick one or two." A comical vision of Max capering around the midsummer pole presented itself. "Perhaps this evening there will be one or another handsome man for my dreams."

I made my usual rounds after breakfast, though I didn't visit the stables that day. The garden, meticulously clipped and raked, was gorgeous. Even the pavilion looked rejuvenated. Why hadn't Mother ever arranged to hold the celebration in this section of the garden? Midsummer was a wild, primitive festival, an homage to nature. What other place on the estate was more splendidly natural than this one?

Max appeared just as I turned back toward the house. "Good morning. Are you celebrating already?"

"Tending to my hostess duties, rather. My own enjoyment is secondary."

"Well, I would never say that. My mother always told us a party falls flat when the mistress is in a bad mood."

"Did you celebrate midsummer in Pomerania?"

"No. My father did not care to do so, and the villagers would have found it strange. The Pomeranian population is not particularly enamored of the Swedes. After all, they colonized parts of our land."

"And people resent that to this day?"

I knew, of course, that during the Thirty Years' War, almost three hundred years earlier, Gustav Adolf had conquered towns in Pomerania. Those areas had remained Swedish after the Peace of Westphalia of 1648, blocking regional rulers' access to the Baltic Sea.

"Some do, even today. The 'Swedish era' wasn't a happy time. But fortunately, there is no longer anyone alive to tell tales of religious wars. People pass along stories their grandparents heard from their own grandparents."

"I must admit I have never visited Pomerania," I said. "What is it like?"

Max grinned. "To tell the truth, about the same as here, at least as far as geography is concerned. No significant hills; wide fields and deep woods. And to my chagrin, our villages are almost medieval compared to those here."

"Perhaps your mother should have remained in Sweden," I teased.

"Perhaps." He looked at me and seemed about to say something. But he didn't.

We strolled together for quite a while, and I wondered if I was keeping him from his work.

"Where do we stand with the master of the royal stables?" Max asked. "Has he answered your offer?"

"Yes, he did write, and he seems quite determined not to accept our bid. I cannot understand why not. After all, those are the best animals in the stables."

"Do we have competition?"

"There is always competition," I said. "But I am sure we can deal with that."

Max smiled. "When you speak that way, I recall your father."

"Well, I am his daughter, after all."

"We should be quoting even higher prices for our animals. The others might be selling for less, but our horses are unequalled anywhere."

"Are you quite sure of that? After so little time here?"

"If I learned anything from my father, it was how to recognize top-quality horseflesh. These are the best animals in Sweden. Your estate sells them to certain prized clients for much less than they are worth."

"My father always deferred to the royal house. As has every Lejongård."

"Granted, but times are changing. The currency continues to depreciate, and prices are rising everywhere. We should stop acting as if it's still 1880."

"Our prices are more than thirty years out of date?"

Max nodded. "Even in Pomerania, the large estates charge far more for their stock. Especially for purebreds. If you would like, we can discuss the matter when you have time. The issue of pricing is fundamental to this business."

"We will do so." I stopped and held up a hand to shade my eyes from the glare of the sun. I looked at Max. "In fact, we can do that right now."

"What about the ball?"

"It is still several hours off, and unlike my mother, I have no trouble deciding what to wear."

"It is a shame the deaths of your father and brother cast a shadow over the celebrations."

"Yes. I contemplated canceling the event this year. But the country people love the festivities, and we should not deny them their tradition because of our own bereavement. My mother made that abundantly clear."

"Your mother is a fascinating woman. I regret I have not yet had the opportunity for an extended conversation with her."

It was on the tip of my tongue to say he'd be better off if she kept ignoring him. But Mother could be quite charming and friendly—if she wished to be.

"You have not been with us very long. Things take time." I looked to the side and saw Lena running toward us. "Lena? What's the matter?"

"The gracious mistress wishes to consult with you about the menu," Lena gasped. "She says some things have been changed. They're different from what the guests usually expect."

"Oh? I did that deliberately. But of course I will attend her right away."

Lena turned and rushed away.

I gave Max an apologetic look. "Again, you see, duty calls."

"For me as well." He seemed reluctant to break off our chat. "I expect to be busy until this evening with the review of last year's accounts."

"Will I see you at the festivities?"

"You forget: I am not Swedish," he said with a mischievous smile. "Midsummer does not have the same meaning for me."

I saw he'd be happy to entice me into another playful conversation. But Lena turned back, impatient for me. Obviously, my mother had told her to make sure I came immediately.

"I am sure you would not want to miss a hearty meal with a splash or two of aquavit. Come join our crowd of local folk. You will enjoy it."

I turned and followed Lena back to the manor.

24

I'd concluded the discussions of horse prices and of menu courses well before the fest. To Mother's dismay, I was unyielding about my new plan for the midsummer evening meal. Everyone enjoyed traditional dishes of herring, new potatoes, and lingonberry cake, and I refused to set up separate tables for the villagers and our house guests.

After getting dressed, I gave myself the luxury of a few moments of quiet. The first guests would arrive before long. I watched through the window as the musicians set up their instruments in the pavilion. They moved purposefully, as if preparing to perform Beethoven instead of dance music. They began tuning their instruments. I listened for a short while but soon heard the clatter of an arriving carriage.

Time to go downstairs.

My mother was already stationed in the foyer. Her dress suited her splendidly. Linda had created an artful hairstyle, piled high and held in place with black lacquer combs.

She inspected me. "Your hair seems a bit casual. You should have asked Linda to do it."

I found it anything but casual, and Lena had done her best. Of course she didn't have the expert flair displayed in Mother's tresses, but she did quite a good job. In a couple of years, she'd surely prove as talented as Linda.

"I wanted it somewhat looser. You're lucky I didn't simply have it cut short."

"Cut short?" Mother shuddered at the thought. "Are you out of your mind? You're not a man!"

"True, Mother," I sighed. "Unfortunately."

She grimaced. "Someone might take you for an artist's model. All you lack are a hussy's shameless bare shoulders."

"Thank you for the compliment, Mother, but we have no time to quarrel. Look, here are the Gundersens."

We went to the door Bruns had just opened. The Gundersens were famed for their punctuality. Unfortunately, they'd witnessed the confrontation at Christmas, and at the sight of me, they looked as if they'd just bitten into a lemon.

"Welcome to Lion Hall!" I called, shaking hands first with Mrs. Gundersen and then with her husband. "I am pleased you found the time to celebrate with us."

The husband gave me a slightly offended look, as if my dress had indeed slipped down and bared my shoulders, but he did nod. "Thank you very much for the invitation. I see this noble family continues to respect its traditions."

Had he assumed I'd turn the place into a bordello? What sort of stories had been circulating in "our" social circles?

"That is exactly my intention," I replied with a friendly smile. "Come in. Marie will escort you to the refreshments table."

Mrs. Gundersen gave me a smile. Her husband continued to look distinctly put off.

Other guests arrived. I knew some from past events, while others had been invited because Mother's friends had identified them as active in philanthropic causes.

"One always needs new allies," Mother had commented when handing me the additions to the guest list.

Eventually, I saw someone whom I'd expected never to darken our door again.

Pelle Oglund and his wife mounted the stairs. I was relieved that their son, Daniel, wasn't with them. It was a wonder his parents had come at all.

I felt like fleeing. Old Oglund's eyes glinted with malice as they met mine. But he must have heard I'd taken charge of the estate. Had he come merely to gloat?

I thanked God I was in black so the man wouldn't notice I'd just broken into a sweat.

"Mr. Oglund! I am so pleased you and your lady wife accepted our invitation!"

"Well, well, look at this: the count's rebellious daughter!" Oglund's eyes narrowed to slits. "I remember you quite well. It is unfortunate there was no other way to assure the continuity of the estate after your father's death."

"Implying what?" I clenched my jaw. I'd just as soon have smashed this misogynist's head, but this was a formal occasion, and a queue of guests waited behind him.

"Mr. Oglund!" Mother interjected. I recognized the dangerous tone in her voice. "We did not invite you here to insult my daughter and the estate. Agneta is Countess Lejongård now. You will show her the appropriate respect or quit these premises."

I looked at my mother in astonishment. Her smile was grim, and her eyes flashed with menace.

Oglund stared at Stella as if struck by lightning.

I thought he would grab his wife's hand and disappear, which probably would have been best for everyone.

But then he relaxed. "I do apologize, Countess Lejongård. We are, of course, pleased to be able to share in your festivities. Accept our thanks for the invitation."

My face was hot and my eyes burned. I couldn't believe it. Mother had actually taken my side! I wouldn't have thought such a thing possible.

Susanna came to guide the Oglunds inside.

My heart pounded. I looked again at my mother but detected no warmth in her eyes. She'd mastered her own emotions with astonishing rapidity.

"Thank you, Mother," I whispered as the next guests came up the steps.

"No need. He attacked the mistress of the estate. It does not make up for what happened at Christmas. That dispute should never have occurred, but it cannot be helped now. One need not recall it on a day like this."

She stepped forward to greet the Södermalms, whose two excited daughters were blushing as furiously as if Cinderella's prince had just invited them to the ball. Lennard Ekberg appeared just a few moments later; I was surprised to see he was alone. The invitation had gone to his parents, his sister, and her whole family. Had they been delayed?

"Hello, my dear." We kissed one another's cheeks. "How are you? Is your mother coming?"

Lennard shook his head. "She decided to stay with Father. He is doing quite poorly."

"I am sorry to hear that. I had hoped to see them both."

"That would have pleased me as well." Lennard sighed. "But at least I am here. If you like, I can bore you with some of my stories."

"I will be happy to hear them," I assured him as I turned to welcome the next arrivals.

Sometime later, Professor Lindström and his elegant wife appeared. Irma was the daughter of one of his colleagues. She was fifteen years younger than her husband, a picture of beauty with dark hair and gray eyes. No one knew how it had come about that she, who could have had her choice of younger men, had fallen for Lindström instead. But it was clear they were deeply in love.

"Countess Lejongård," he greeted me and kissed my hand.

Mother was still chatting with the Södermalms, even though propriety demanded she turn her attention to the next arrivals.

An hour later, I couldn't have told you whom we'd received at the door. Couples with or without children filed past us, and gradually the garden filled with people and conversation. The band played undemanding string music in the background, and the sun shone down from on high. I looked at the grandfather clock. It was ten past eight, but the crown prince and princess had not yet arrived.

Mother was getting increasingly concerned. "I just hope nothing happened on their way here," she muttered. "Bergen would have certainly sent word if something had prevented them."

I tried to calm her. "Perhaps some family matter came up."

"Or the palace was so alarmed by the fire they decided not to attend."

The investigation had yielded no results as yet, unfortunately. Inspector Hermannsson was still following leads, and he'd promised to let us know if he got wind of anything new.

"The Bernadottes are not like that," I responded. "Someone would have informed us. They're likely to arrive at any moment."

No sooner had I spoken than a rattling and popping became audible in the distance. It got louder and louder, even threatening to drown out the music. In a matter of seconds, three gleaming motorcars sped up the drive. The guests still in the front courtyard gaped in amazement as the trio of bright-red vehicles pulled up to the front steps. One automobile bore the royal coat of arms, and the crown prince and princess were seated in the back. Their children weren't with them, even though their youngsters had always come with them before. This time the couple was attended by bodyguards in dark suits inappropriate for the warm weather. Count Bergen stepped down from the lead vehicle. He gave quick instructions to the bodyguards and then approached the royal couple.

"It's because of the fire," my mother muttered as she tried to work up a smile. "They're worried something might happen during the celebration."

"That's absurd. The ball doesn't take place anywhere near the stables. And I'm sure the old pavilion isn't going to catch fire."

Mother didn't respond, because the royal couple was approaching. Gustav Adolf wore an elegant black suit, and his tie was blue and yellow, the colors of the royal coat of arms. Princess Margaret wore long gloves, gold jewelry, and a blue satin dress trimmed with lace.

"Please excuse us!" The crown prince extended his hand. "Our motorcar broke down on the far side of Kristianstad. Unfortunately, there are few mechanics in this region familiar with this sort of vehicle."

"Think nothing of it, Your Majesty. The celebrations have only just begun." Mother was accomplished at concealing her resentment when she wanted to.

The crown prince kissed my hand. "Agneta, how enchanting you are this evening!"

"Thank you. You are entirely too kind, Your Majesty." I made a little curtsey and then offered my hand to the princess. "I am very pleased to welcome you to the midsummer ball."

"After all the difficulties you have been through, it is lovely to be here for a joyful occasion." She favored me with a friendly smile.

Even so, she projected an air of slight concern. Was she worried about her children? We accompanied Their Royal Majesties to the garden, where male guests bowed and ladies curtsied. Some were unmistakably envious, for they'd probably thought the Lejongård reputation had been tarnished by the fire and my acceptance of the estate. Old Oglund had a particularly sour expression, obviously put out at seeing we were still very much in the good graces of the royal family.

I'd already decided simply to ignore Oglund. Perhaps next year we would strike them from the invitation list.

Mother made sure Their Royal Majesties had taken their places, and then came the moment for me to deliver the welcoming speech, a duty I'd been dreading. At meetings of the Stockholm suffragettes, I'd had no trouble proclaiming our demands. I'd argued, debated, and often faced angry opponents. One time I was almost arrested, and only my eloquence spared me and others a trip to jail.

At this moment, however, I felt as awkward as a gymnast being tested on a routine he'd never been taught. I couldn't keep the guests waiting, though, so I ignored my stage fright and stepped onto the stage beside the musicians. They stopped playing, which brought all conversations to a halt. All eyes turned to me. My heart pounded as never before. I breathed deep, cleared my throat, and began.

"Your Royal Majesties, honored ladies, and gentlemen, I am very pleased to welcome you to Lion Hall, a place of rich tradition that Sweden's royal family has for many years both honored and visited. This manor has been the family seat for centuries; it is our home, a place of beauty, flourishing growth, and great joy. Although the absence of my father and brother grieves us deeply, my mother and I wish to celebrate with you this significant day on which the sun never sets. Let us raise our glasses and drink to those we miss and to the future of this place and all of Sweden. Long live the king! Long live Sweden!"

My hand shook as I raised my champagne glass, but I was reassured to see everyone respond to the toast. We toasted Father and Hendrik and then we toasted the royal couple. I stepped down from the stand, and the musicians struck up a lively tune. As I walked back to Mother, I saw her in conversation with Lennard.

"A fine speech!" he exclaimed.

I smiled. "Thank you for your generous encouragement."

He seemed unusually tired, which I hadn't noticed earlier. I detected a conspiratorial twinkle in Mother's eye. "Did you have a good chat?"

"A very good one," she said. "I will tell the maids to set out the meal."

She withdrew into the house. Bruns and several maids were moving along the ranks of guests with trays of drinks.

"You are flourishing in your new role," Lennard said. "Shall I fetch you a refreshment?"

"Why does everyone seem to flee from me?" I teased him. "It's not because I look like I am flourishing!"

"I promise to return as soon as I can liberate something from the butler's tray." He disappeared into the crowd of guests.

"Bruns would jump for joy if he heard you call him a butler!" I told Lennard when he came back with a glass of lemonade. "He has dreamed of that title ever since his time in England!"

"Just as well, then, that I did not say it where he could hear me." Lennard smiled. "Here."

"Thank you. That is so kind." I took a big gulp of lemonade. It was sweet and yet piquant, as only Mrs. Bloomquist knew how to make it.

"You know, I feel years older than I used to," Lennard said. "Running an estate is a heavy responsibility. I am sure you agree."

"At least you still have your father to give you advice!"

Lennard winced and seemed to shut down.

"What is it?" I asked. "Did I say something wrong?"

He shook his head. "No. It is just that . . . Father can no longer help me very much. Mother has to take care of him all day long."

"But you were able to get away?"

"I had to. My mother would not hear otherwise. After all, yours is the only significant midsummer celebration in the region."

"If only I had known—"

Corina Bomann

"No, you must not apologize. I confess it does me good to get away. My father is in such frightful pain. This lingering illness of his perpetually weighs upon me. It is terribly hard for all of us. You know, I wish so much the old superstition about the healing power of the midsummer morning dew were true! I yearn for Father to be with us for years longer. But my wish is unlikely to be granted."

"What do you mean?"

"The doctor told us recently that he has a year left at the most. And his failing health bears that out."

"That is terrible!" I wanted to embrace him but didn't dare. "Oh, Lennard!"

"Yes, the way things look, before long, I will be head of the family. As you are."

Was this what he'd been discussing with Mother? But she hadn't seemed to be reacting to a tale of woe.

Lennard looked about at the crowd. "Do you think we might take a moment for a private conversation? Before the celebration really gets going?"

"Of course!" I took his hand and pulled him away from the crowd onto the path toward the pastures. "No one will overhear us out here."

I was a bit disturbed by Lennard's request. Did he want to describe his father's difficulties in more detail? Did he need something from us?

"Agneta?" He spoke in a low voice and was looking at me with an expression I'd never seen before.

"Yes?"

"We have known each other almost our whole lives . . ."

Where was he going with this?

"We have indeed, Lennard. If you need help, you know you can count on me."

"I do know that," he responded. "But I was thinking about something else."

"And what is that?"

"Lately I have been thinking a lot about the future. We are in such similar situations, the two of us. My father is dying and yours has already passed away. We both are called to manage our estates. What . . . what would you say about taking the same path, together?"

I stared at him in disbelief. "Are you proposing?"

"No—I . . ." Suddenly he was the same timid boy I remembered from our childhood. "But—yes, I do think we would get along well. We could both manage such an arrangement. And we would not be so lonely."

He paused and waited for my response. I looked all around, completely at a loss. How had he come up with the notion that we should be spouses? Had his mother put him up to it? Had mine? We'd been friends for so long. But marry him? That was something else entirely.

"Think about it, Lennard. Surely it's wrong to get married just because you cannot think of anything else to do. Certainly, we both have heavy responsibilities. And we know each other well. But . . ."

"Is there someone else?" he asked. "If so, I can understand, but I—I just thought . . ."

"There was someone," I admitted. "In Stockholm. It was a secret, and it ended when Father and Hendrik died. I am really not in any condition right now to let another man into my life." I took his hand. "You are my best friend. But I believe marriage should be based on love."

"You do not think you might be able to love me someday?"

"I do love you! As a friend! But not as a man I could marry. Maybe someday I may realize you are the one for me. Who knows? But right now, my new life is unfamiliar and stressful, and I do not wish to tie myself down. You don't deserve that, and neither do I."

He looked down, disappointed. "As you wish."

I didn't know what to do. Perhaps I'd been too direct, maybe a bit harsh, but I'd told the truth. Michael had ended our relationship, and Lennard couldn't expect me to throw myself into the arms of the next man who came along.

Corina Bomann

But Lennard was a friend I didn't want to lose. I took his arm and was glad he didn't pull away. "Please understand. If I needed help, I would not hesitate to turn to you. And I am here for you—I will offer you any assistance. But marry? That would be an enormous mistake."

"Perhaps you are right." Lennard did his best to smile. "But that will not keep me from trying again. Someday."

I was absolutely certain he would never be my husband, but I didn't have the heart to tell him that.

"Meanwhile, would you give me the great pleasure of agreeing to dance with me?"

"Lennard, my mother and I agreed not to dance tonight. We are still in mourning. We did not cancel the celebration, but we should remain in the background. I do not mean to disappoint you again, but . . ."

"Agneta, that is quite all right." He leaned over and planted a kiss upon my forehead. "Life is long, after all." He did his best to keep his expression neutral. "We will have many other opportunities to dance. Do you agree?"

"Yes, we will."

We gazed at one another for a moment, then he turned and went back to the party. I shut my eyes and lifted my face to the midsummer sun. I mustn't allow the guests to see I was upset. I stood there in the meadow for a time, listening to the rustling of the tall grasses and the trees of the forest.

When I returned, the staff was bringing in heaping platters of food. Nips of aquavit had already elevated the spirits of some of the guests. I went to the table where Mother was waiting. Fortunately, our partners at the table—Lennard and the royal couple—were occupied elsewhere.

"Professor Lindström asked me to donate funds for some new medical equipment for the hospital," Mother said. "I said I would consult you. Since you are the countess."

"But you are on the hospital board! You can approve his request as long as our finances can handle it."

"Well, tell him that!" Mother took a long look at me. Her expression was indecipherable. "Did you enjoy your talk with Lennard?"

"I suppose—if you think it agreeable to learn his father is probably dying."

The incipient smile disappeared from Mother's face. "His father—"

"Has, if one is to believe the doctor, no more than a year left. Lennard will have to take responsibility for the estate."

Mother looked down and stared for a long moment at her plate and utensils. "Strange; he didn't tell me that."

"You two were talking. What about?" I asked, as if I didn't know already.

"He wanted to propose marriage to you. He asked my permission."

She seemed dismayed by the news of the decline of Lennard's father. Why hadn't he shared this with her?

"Well, I understand he wants to marry me because he thinks we could support one another. I told him that mutual support is not the same as marriage. The Ekbergs have always been our friends, and that will never change."

"You turned him down?"

"No, I talked him out of it. Contracting marriage in our current situations is a terrible idea as far as I am concerned."

Lennard walked up then, so Mother couldn't respond. He showed us a cheery face, but I knew he was concealing his feelings. After all, I knew him as well as I'd known my own brother.

"Ah, there you are again," he said and set down his empty aquavit glass. "Enjoying the night?"

"Yes! It's giving me quite an appetite. Will you please excuse me?" I strode off to the buffet table. I knew Mrs. Bloomquist's amazing cuisine would offer me solace from the rigors of the evening.

25

As the evening progressed, even the stiffest of our guests loosened up, enjoyed the music, and joined the dances around the midsummer pole. Mother and I kept our pledge and abstained. That may have surprised some of the guests, but we got looks of sympathy when we explained.

The crown prince and Princess Margaret chatted about their parents and the children, catching up on old times with their friends like regular people. Anyone could see our relations with the royal family were as close as ever. Mother was immensely relieved. After a while, the lighthearted chatter got to be a bit too much, so I rose and slipped away. As I strolled past the festive villagers, it occurred to me I hadn't seen Max all evening. I took the path to his cottage, carrying a lantern for my return.

I found Max leaning on the fence outside his house, looking up at the sky. No stars were visible; it was still too light for that. They would come out eventually, for unlike the northlands of Sweden, at this latitude the sun would sink below the horizon even at midsummer, if only for a short time.

"Good evening, Herr von Bredestein!" I called to him. "What are you doing here, all alone? Waiting for the first star to come out?"

"You caught me out, Countess!" he responded with that easy smile of his. "What brings you this way? I suppose the great ball is in full swing at the manor. Are you fleeing your Prince Charming?"

"If you refer to the crown prince, I have nothing to fear from him. I am not so sure about some of the others."

"I see you still have both your slippers, so no one is searching for you yet."

I almost giggled, for the punch had made me a bit giddy. "I just needed to get away. Besides, I missed you. I thought you promised to attend."

"To rescue you?" His eyes lit up. Suddenly I wasn't sure if it was the punch that I was feeling.

"To get to know people," I said. "No one here would mind your origins in the Pomeranian aristocracy."

"A landless aristocrat!" he replied. He gestured, inviting me to the cottage. "I believe I have something that might make the evening easier to bear."

I raised an eyebrow. "Something alcoholic?"

Max grinned. "You will like it. Come and take the place of honor."

The two kitchen chairs were outside on the porch. Apparently, Max was in the habit of contemplating the dark and impressive forest that stretched westward from the pasture. I took a seat while Max went inside.

He returned and held out a cup with a strong-smelling liquid. "Here you are!"

The sharp odor brought back unpleasant memories of Stockholm and the night I'd destroyed my paintings in a drunken rage. I'd abstained from strong drink since then, for I wanted to remain in full control.

"Home brew," he responded to my inquiring glance. "It was sent from home after I ran into a friend in Kristianstad not long ago."

"You did not mention that." I took a sip. The trickle of alcohol assaulted my throat like liquid fire.

"We rarely discuss private matters."

"That is true," I answered regretfully. "Why did you not at least put in an appearance at the ball?"

He took the chair beside me. "I told you already that such festivities mean nothing to me. I prefer my solitude." He took a sip from his cup and set it down next to him on the porch.

"You had no festivals on your estate?"

"Of course we did. That is why they do not interest me."

"Did they expect you to play the gallant?" I could imagine it: society ladies would mob a man like him. I'd thought the same thing of Lennard earlier in the evening.

"To a certain extent," Max said. "The hypocrisy was just too much for me. A smile on the face and a rock in the hand hidden behind the back, if you get my meaning."

"I can imagine." There was plenty of two-faced behavior at the ball, though fortunately we had more than enough genuinely pleasant guests to make up for it.

"I often wondered what it would be like simply to run away and start over. But I never had the chance—until I met your father."

"Fate invites us onto unexpected paths," I murmured and took another sip. A weight settled over me. It wasn't only the effect of the liquor; there was anger as well. And I felt terribly tired.

"And which path will you choose, Countess Lejongård?"

"Agneta," I said. "Call me Agneta."

"Is that wise? Your other employees might talk."

"Privately, then."

"Very well." He offered me his hand. "Max."

I'd already thought of him by that name for a couple of weeks, so it wasn't hard to agree to that.

"Well, Agneta? When we first met, you mentioned you had been studying. What would your path have been if things had turned out differently?"

I still felt that pain deep inside every time I thought of my days in Stockholm. I'd been away from the capital for three months now.

"I would certainly have come back for the midsummer celebration. That is family tradition. But I would probably be quarreling with my parents. My mother's attitude has not changed; she still thinks she has the right to tell me what to do. But I suppose, considering her situation, she is doing her best to be accommodating."

"What else?"

"I would have traveled back to Stockholm after the celebrations. To my seminar at the Royal Academy, and to—"

"A man?"

Had he read that in my face?

"Yes," I answered, feeling that I didn't need to keep any secrets from him. "Michael. I was with him for almost a year."

"What happened?"

"He could not bear the thought of living with a woman who had inherited an estate. He wanted nothing to do with life here, so we parted ways."

"He left you? Or did you leave him?"

"Does it matter?" I felt my temper start to rise. Why had Michael been so obstinate?

"Well, I think it does. You do not look particularly happy about the outcome."

"I am not. But that is how he wanted it. He was afraid our world would overwhelm him. He imagined himself as a prisoner eternally stuck in the provinces."

"You felt differently?"

"I grew up here. And I had no choice. I promised my dying brother I would take his place. To free myself from that obligation, I would have had to renounce Lion Hall forever."

"And you cannot."

"I loved my brother very much. And I love the estate as well. This is my home."

"Well, it sounds as if you could not have offered the fellow any alternative. You should forget him."

I studied Max's profile. He was scanning the sky for the first star.

"Saying it is one thing. Doing it is another."

He turned his gaze to me. "Well, do you not believe that life is too short to spend with the wrong person? They rob you of the energy you need for more important things. Your estate, for example."

"You are certainly right about that." I looked down and found the cup in my hand was almost empty. I didn't want to ask him for more for fear I'd wake up hungover the following morning. I placed the cup on the porch next to my chair. "I think I should be going."

Max was surprised. "So soon? Did I offend you?"

"Not at all. But I see there is no possibility of persuading you to accompany me back to the party. So I had better leave you here to study the stars."

I started to rise, but he gently grasped my arm. "Please do not be angry, Agneta."

"I am not."

"Then stay a little longer. Until the first star comes out. Or will they be wondering about you?"

I hesitated. If Mother discovered I wasn't circulating, she'd hit the ceiling. And Lindström would probably be scouring the estate for me to expound upon his list of proposed hospital improvements. But it was so peaceful here, and the night was so mild—I couldn't help but accede to Max's request.

"We can talk, or we can simply watch the sky," he said. "As you wish."

I settled back onto the chair. "Let us watch the sky."

We looked up for quite a long time. Streaks of red darkened overhead.

"Someone proposed to me today," I heard myself saying for no reason at all. I hadn't planned to share that with Max.

"It's a lovely night for that."

"Do you want to know if I accepted?"

"I am the estate manager, no more. I can work for you or for your husband."

My eyebrows lifted. Did I detect a touch of pique?

"Anyway, you may find it comforting to know there is no immediate prospect a master will take over the estate. I remain in charge."

His eyes widened slightly. "Then, to be truthful, I am quite pleased to be employed by the mistress of the estate."

"And being truthful in turn, I am quite pleased to be my own mistress. Even though I often miss being held." I shook my head, embarrassed. "Oh, what am I saying! You have your own troubles."

"I am always here if you wish to talk."

I felt his eyes upon me. Was he being truthful? His expression certainly seemed sincere. But Michael's eyes had also been filled with promises.

"Thank you."

He gazed up at the sky. "Look there. Do you see it?" He pointed. "There it is, the first star. It insists on showing itself, even though the sun is reluctant to set."

I did see a star. It was barely visible in the twilight, but its gleam would intensify as the sun sank below the horizon. And after midsummer day ended, it would cast a strong, steady light. Everything in its time; that was the essence of the universe: appearing, fading, coming back.

Back in the garden, the buffet table had been laid waste, as had the barriers between villagers and the well-born guests.

A hand seized my arm. "Where have you been all this time?"

I turned. Mother seemed genuinely upset.

"I took a little stroll to clear my head. I had the impression the guests were taking care of themselves."

She leaned in close and sniffed my breath. "You have been drinking!"

"Like everyone else," I snapped. Yes, it was probably irresponsible for a hostess to disappear even for a short time. But this was midsummer day, and the celebration would go on until the wee hours of the morning.

"Come with me. We have a problem."

A problem? Her words jolted me out of my mildly inebriated haze. What had happened? Was it one of the guests? My mother strode swiftly toward the house with me close behind.

We went to the smoking room, a place Mother rarely visited. She hated to berate people in her favorite rooms; that would defile those spaces and make her uncomfortable there afterward. But this was a place she disliked, the lair still pungent with the odor of Father's tobacco.

She shut the door behind us. "Susanna!"

That exclamation cut me like a whip. "What's wrong with her?"

Had she fainted again? Suffered a miscarriage?

"Did you know that girl is pregnant?"

Damn! I closed my eyes and took a deep breath. "How did you find out that—"

"I have a fine pair of eyes!" Her voice became shrill. "Dear God, I should have suspected it when she fainted!"

My hands were unsteady. I fought for breath.

"You should have told me!" Mother's voice was accusing. "You know I will not tolerate loose women in my house."

"But, Mother, the fact that she is pregnant does not mean she is wanton. We cannot know what promises were made to her."

"Promises? Well, those promises cannot have been worth much, since she felt she had to steal my jewelry!"

"What?" I felt as if the floor had just dropped out from under me. Susanna had stolen something? Even though I had promised to help her?

"Who claims such a thing?"

"No one is claiming anything. Linda caught her red-handed!"

Linda, my mother's fiercely loyal maid. This was the hour she always prepared my mother's bedchamber, even if Mother would be going to bed late. Susanna was familiar with the house routine, so she should have known she was likely to be caught. Or was Linda trying to frame the girl? Had she noticed the pregnancy? Susanna was in her fourth or fifth month by now . . .

"Not only is she a loose woman, she is a criminal!" my mother cried. "We must summon the police!"

I wanted to defend Susanna, but my mother was right. Stealing was a crime. Even if Linda had thwarted it.

"She must be removed immediately!"

"Not until after I have spoken with her," I said. "You cannot expect me to throw her out without hearing her version of events."

"Fine, then!" my mother spat. "She is in my room. Linda is watching her."

I rose and left the room. The guests outside were very merry, but my heart was pounding. Whatever could have prompted the girl to do such a stupid thing?

I found the disconsolate girl huddled on a low stool in Mother's room. Her swollen belly was obvious beneath her skirt.

Linda stood over her like a prison guard. My mother's personal maid was a thin, dark-haired woman with strong features. She'd been a housemaid when I was a child. Linda had become my mother's closest confidante, at least as far as the needs of the household were concerned, principally thanks to her single-minded loyalty. It was clear to me she'd been berating Susanna and had stopped only when I came in.

"Susanna!" I said, making her start in surprise. "What happened?"

Linda spoke up instead. "I was just getting the bed ready for the gracious mistress. When I came in, I saw her take something from the jewelry box on the dressing table. I challenged her, and she denied it. I made her empty her apron pockets, and the gracious lady's brooch came out. The gold one with the sapphire."

Mother's favorite brooch. How could she have imagined it wouldn't be missed?

"Is this true, Susanna?"

"Of course it is!" Linda interjected.

I raised a hand to hush her. "I want to hear it directly from Susanna."

"It's true," Susanna confessed, her voice breaking. "I—I was trying to steal the brooch."

Her candid avowal shocked me more than if she'd tried to deny it.

"Why did you try to steal it?" I asked, dismayed. "Were you afraid you were going to be discharged?"

Susanna pressed her lips together and lowered her head.

I glanced at Linda, who was glowering at the girl. "I wish to speak to Susanna in private."

Linda looked tempted to refuse, but she remembered her station. She curtsied. "As you wish, gracious miss."

She would certainly rush downstairs to report to my mother.

"Susanna?" I stepped in front of her. "Look at me. Please."

Reluctantly, she raised her eyes.

"Why did you do this? Because you were afraid of the future? Because of some pressing need?"

Susanna gnawed her upper lip. "I don't know . . ."

"'I don't know'?" I felt a rush of anger. Not because she'd tried to steal, but because she hadn't trusted me. "Did I not offer to help you? Have I not been protecting you from my mother?" I began to pace. "You could have come to me if you were afraid or in need!"

"You couldn't have done anything," she said darkly. "I'm still going to have a baby."

"Did the others find out?"

She bowed her head again.

"Susanna?"

"Yes." Her voice was almost inaudible.

"Linda?"

She nodded.

"When did she realize?"

"Today," Susanna replied. "I suddenly felt faint, and everything turned dark, and—when I sat down, she asked what was wrong and looked at my belly. So I told her."

I realized I'd been holding my breath. I released the air slowly. I should have foreseen this. It was my fault.

"Did she threaten to tell me or my mother?"

Another nod.

"And you thought I would throw you out, so you decided to take something to help make ends meet."

Susanna broke into a sob. "I'm so sorry! I wasn't thinking—"

"No, indeed you were not!" My voice rose in indignation. "You could have come and let me know Linda had found out! You should have asked me for help. I already told you I would never have discharged you for being pregnant. Now I have no choice!"

The door flew open. My mother appeared. Obviously, I couldn't ban her from her own room.

"And has this thief given you an answer?"

"Yes," I said. "But although I can understand her reasons, I have no choice but to discharge her from our service."

Mother clearly had been expecting me to defend the maid. Her posture lost some of its aggressive tension, but her next comment was snippy. "You understand her reasons?"

"She was expecting to be discharged because of the child." I looked at my mother's personal maid, who had just appeared in the doorway. Linda had probably threatened to tell the rest of the staff. "All too often, people let themselves get carried away and do stupid things. But that is no excuse for theft. She has to go."

I turned to Susanna, who had burst into tears. "You will leave the estate early tomorrow morning."

"Why not this instant?" my mother protested. "Are you offering her the opportunity to fill her pockets? What if she should steal from Their Majesties?"

"She will not. Will you, Susanna?"

The woebegone girl shook her head.

"Good. Otherwise I will be obliged to report this incident and anything else to the police. For the moment, I do not intend to lodge a complaint. Provided nothing else happens between now and tomorrow morning."

Susanna broke into a wail and doubled over in misery. Her vertebrae stood out like knobs against her pale skin. Had she been wasting away because of the pregnancy? Or had fear been consuming her?

There was nothing more I could do.

I turned to Linda. "Take Susanna to her quarters. She is to pack her things and stay there. And for God's sake, do not insult or accuse her any further. She has been punished enough already."

Linda nodded, but I could see by her expression she would keep hounding the girl, accusing her of betraying the family who'd provided her with a secure position, room, and board.

"Satisfied, Mother?" I asked after the two women were gone.

"You were entirely too soft," she grumbled.

"You have your brooch back, I think?"

"And Linda to thank for it."

"Good. We will give Linda a bonus for that. But we should not punish Susanna any further. Not only is she carrying an illegitimate child, now she has been dismissed and disgraced. I saw in Stockholm what can happen to such girls."

"That is none of your concern!"

"But it is. My friends and I struggled to make sure those girls and women weren't marked for life by a single mistake for which they were not the only ones to blame. And I would have helped Susanna. But now I cannot."

I turned on my heel and went to the door. Instead of opening it, I looked back at my mother.

"Linda told you, didn't she? That the girl is with child."

"There was no way of missing it. But no, she did not tell me."

"She would have done so this evening. But Susanna could no longer hide it anyway. She fainted."

I opened the door and left. My heart was still full of fury, but the alcohol in my bloodstream left me numb. I couldn't face any more festivities. I thought of Max in his cottage. He wouldn't learn of the incident until the next day. I wished I were out there with him, gazing up at the stars.

26

I awoke with a throbbing headache, and the sunshine through the curtains was unpleasantly harsh. I'd have preferred to stay in bed. But the royal couple, Count Bergen, and some of Mother's friends had stayed overnight, and we were due to have breakfast together.

I tottered out of bed with a groan. I splashed water on my face and glanced out at the meadow, where the manor staff were already cleaning up. Bruns had enlisted a couple of stable boys to carry away the tables.

Someone knocked.

"Come in!"

"Good morning, gracious miss." Lena seemed depressed. Hardly surprising; she'd lost a friend here.

"Good morning, Lena." Since I didn't want to ask whether Susanna had already left, I said, "How are you feeling after the midsummer festivities?"

"Very well," she replied. She looked as if she'd cried the night through.

"Susanna told you, didn't she?" It was useless pretending nothing had happened.

"Yes. She left early this morning."

"Did Linda or anyone else explain why?" I had no doubt Mother's personal maid had spread the news to everyone in the servants' quarters who would listen.

"It's said she stole something," Lena replied unhappily. "And she's going to have a child."

I felt the doleful impact of that news. Linda had been merciless. Worry gnawed at my insides. What if Susanna were to do something desperate? She wouldn't be the first girl who'd literally sought to drown her woes. She would be an outcast in the village, the "girl with the bastard child." None of the young men would marry her, lest he be seen to have taken leave of his senses.

"Listen to me, Lena." I took her hand. "I had no choice. Theft is no small matter, you know that. I was forced to act."

Lena nodded.

"But you must understand it was not because of the child. I would not hold such a thing against any of you, even though I urge you to wait until you marry before becoming pregnant. Our society is merciless with women whose children are not claimed by the father. You must always remember that when young men come courting. And do not be shy about telling me if any of them tries to force you to do something. You must always say no. Do you understand?"

Lena gaped at me in astonishment, but she nodded.

"And as for Susanna . . ." I paused for a moment, not sure if I should ask. "When you visit your parents in the village next Thursday, see if you can find out where she is. Please? I just want to know how she is doing, that is all."

"And what if she's having trouble?"

"Then I will find a way to help her. Somehow."

Lena nodded. A smile tugged at the corners of her mouth.

"Good. Thank you." I released her hand. "And now I want to know if you picked those seven blossoms."

"No," Lena replied. "Mrs. Bloomquist let me have a glass of aquavit. I fell asleep in the meadow."

I did my best to hide my smile. I could see it in my mind: how she'd lain in the grass until one of the other maids woke her in the gray of early morning. Last night's liquor was probably contributing to her listless mood today.

Losing Susanna was almost like losing part of myself. Without the animated chatter of the servants in the halls, silence reigned throughout the day. Miss Rosendahl tried once to raise the matter with me, but I wouldn't listen. I had no desire to elaborate upon the story, even as I brooded over the problems Susanna might be facing at home.

On Monday, Bruns appeared in my office. "A messenger just arrived with news I am instructed to deliver to you personally." He handed me an envelope.

It was from Inspector Hermannsson. Had the police finally made a determination? The month of August wasn't that far away, and I was extremely reluctant to inform His Majesty's chamberlain that the arsonist was still at large.

"Thank you, Bruns." Impatient, I ripped open the envelope.

The contents set my heart racing. I got up and went directly to my mother's room, where she was having her hair done.

"Would you give us a moment in private, Linda?"

Linda looked to my mother, but when her mistress didn't countermand the request, she curtsied and left.

My mother tugged at a strand of hair. "What is so terribly urgent?"

I held up the letter. "This is from the police." I summarized. "Evidently they have arrested a suspect."

Mother took it and quickly read it through.

"But their investigation is still ongoing."

"And thank heavens for that! Now it is just a matter of time until this man confesses."

"We can only hope they have the right man." I wondered who he might be. A villager? Hermannsson hadn't given the name, understandably, considering that they were still building their case. "He asks me to come to Kristianstad. They want me to see the suspect."

"What? He can hardly expect Countess Lejongård—"

"To talk to the suspect? I cannot say. It is likely Hermannsson wants me to tell him whatever I know about the individual. It may be advisable for you to come as well. You know the locals better than I."

"Your father knew the people here," she replied. "I would be of very little use. Perhaps you should take Langeholm. He is well acquainted with the villagers."

"All right. I will." I'd have much preferred to have Max, but he knew no one. "We will set out early tomorrow morning."

Mother nodded. "It will be splendid if they have caught him, surely?" Her voice was unusually gentle. "Then we could draw a line under all this at last."

"Yes. If only it would restore Father and Hendrik to us."

"Not even God will grant us that, but at least He can provide us justice."

"I hope so."

We looked at one another for a moment. I thought I saw the tiniest hint of a smile playing about her lips.

27

As the coach jolted toward Kristianstad, I remembered Count Bergen and the elegant palace motorcar that had conveyed him to us. The sum my father had borrowed would have sufficed to buy two of those. Maybe more.

I noticed Langeholm was unusually uncommunicative. I'd thought the news of a suspect would cheer him, but he was anything but enthusiastic. Langeholm was no gossip, but he was generally more open than this with me.

"May I ask what is on your mind?"

"I cannot help thinking of your father and brother," he said. "What happened was frightful."

"Well, if the police really have arrested the culprit, we can all feel relieved."

"I do hope so," he responded. "But perhaps this fellow will be proven innocent, and we'll be back where we started."

"Hermannsson wouldn't arrest someone without good reason. Especially since he wants to see me."

"Let us hope so, gracious miss." Langeholm looked out at the passing countryside and sank back into his gloom.

We reached police headquarters half an hour later. The white edifice gleamed in the sunshine, and the Swedish flag fluttered overhead. I caught sight of a face behind the barred windows, but I couldn't make out whether it was a police officer or a prisoner.

A typewriter was clattering as we entered. Fetid air smelled of damp wool, boot polish, and something indescribable. The officer on duty said the inspector was waiting in his office and escorted us there.

Hermannsson wore the same brown suit as at our first encounter, but his beard had grown out since then.

He shook my hand. "I'm glad you came so quickly, Countess Lejongård."

"Given the contents of your letter, I could hardly keep you waiting." I gestured to the man at my side. "This is Sören Langeholm, our stable master. I brought him because he knows the people in the region better than I."

Hermannsson shook his hand. "Very pleased! We can certainly benefit from his knowledge. Please follow me."

He accompanied us to the jail. It wasn't large, sufficient only to confine perhaps ten malefactors in a common cell as they awaited trial. The Kristianstad police appeared not to have a particularly heavy caseload. One man was sleeping off a night's drunkenness, and a uniformed officer was closely watching another young fellow. The only other prisoner was a shapeless, crumpled figure squatting on a bunk with his head down.

"You're fortunate today," Hermannsson told us. "This place is packed most of the time. I wouldn't wish any lady to be exposed to the usual conditions. Officer, cuff Hellersund and take him for interrogation."

The policeman unlocked the cell and went to the forlorn figure on the bunk.

"Come with me," the inspector told us. "We have a special room for this."

He guided us to a grim room a few steps away. A nagging sense of unease assailed me. The wall wasn't tiled, but otherwise it reminded me of the hospital morgue where we'd viewed Hendrik's body.

A small table and four chairs stood in the center of the room. The man they called Hellersund was shoved through the door and obliged to sit.

"I didn't do nothing," the man immediately protested, as if already before the judge. "Yes, I set fire to Larsen's haystack, but none of the rest was me!"

Hermannsson ignored his protest. "Perhaps you know this man, Countess Lejongård? His name is Ole Hellersund, born in Ystad, currently unemployed and homeless. He was arrested for setting fire to a haystack north of Kristianstad. We strongly suspect he may have caused the conflagration at your estate."

"I didn't do nothing!" the man howled. "I just wanted them voices to stop! They drive me crazy! They told me to do it."

I frowned. The man was out of his mind. Could my father and brother have fallen victim to a lunatic?

"Do you know him?" the inspector asked again.

I shook my head and looked to Langeholm.

He regarded the unknown man with distaste. "Might be he was loitering around our fields. We see people out there from time to time, but we pay precious little heed to them."

"Perhaps you should have. He is also accused of setting fire to three haystacks near Kristianstad. To be sure, none was near your estate, but it's conceivable he might have passed through your lands."

"If so, he would've had to sneak onto the estate."

The central buildings of Lion Hall were enclosed by walls and fences, but we never bothered to keep watch on them. Those who entered the estate did so through the main gate. I felt almost sick when I thought someone could have scaled a wall with the idea of committing a crime.

"Well, maybe he did just that," Hermannsson commented. "There is no other arsonist active in the region at the moment, so we believe he set the fire in your stables."

"The horses would've smelled him," Langeholm said. "His scent would have spooked them."

"Hellersund managed to sneak past two guard dogs to get to those haystacks. I'm sure he could have avoided detection by your horses."

"I swear I wasn't in no barn!" the man cried. He sprang up and stretched his hands out to me in appeal.

I jerked back in alarm. The officer standing behind the suspect grabbed him and forced him back into the chair. "Me voices didn't say nothing about a barn," Hellersund whimpered. "They told me about hay. Piles of hay!"

He was clearly insane, but was he responsible for the deaths of my father and brother? In my heart I didn't believe he was. The man across the table was pitiful and deserved punishment, but setting a haystack on fire was entirely different from deliberately burning down a large structure.

I turned to the stable master. "Mr. Langeholm, you were there the whole time during the fire."

Langeholm stiffened, surprised to be addressed. "Yes, I was. As were the stable lads."

"Did you see this man run out of the barn before the fire was discovered?"

Langeholm squinted, searching his memory, but at last he shook his head. "No. I saw no one at all."

I looked at the prisoner across the table. "How did you set fire to the haystacks? Did you stay to watch them burn?"

Hope began to glimmer in the man's eyes. "Aye, I did. And when I saw the fire, me voices stopped. It was lovely."

"What are they saying now?"

"They tell me to burn this place down!" He leaped to his feet again and yanked at the handcuffs. "Burn it to the ground!"

"Get him out of here!" Hermannsson told the guard. "Take him back to the cell."

The officer grabbed the suspect and dragged him to the door.

"It weren't me!" the tramp cried. "I didn't burn no barn! Me voices are saying it weren't me!"

The door slammed. His muffled cries quickly died away. I was shaken to the core. My mother had been right. Why on earth had Hermannsson asked me to see this madman?

"Well, what do you think?" I asked the inspector. "Do you really believe he was the culprit? Even though my stable master did not see him?"

Hermannsson gave me a look shaded with frustration. "That doesn't mean he couldn't have been there."

"Our people would have seen him," Langeholm objected. "We would have noticed any outsider nosing around."

"We will continue our investigation. Perhaps he used some other method. Maybe it didn't succeed immediately, so he left, and the fire broke out later."

We sat in silence for a moment in that bare interrogation room, then the inspector got up. "I am very grateful you took the time to assist me. Your statements were very valuable."

"Even though you will need to look elsewhere?"

"We want the truth, Countess Lejongård, no matter how long it may take to find it. We owe it to your family."

"And I thank you for it."

We shook hands. Langeholm and I left the station moments later.

I stood next to the coach, gazing blindly at the trees across the street. What was I to make of this meeting? Something told me we hadn't gotten to the bottom of things yet.

"Gracious miss?" Langeholm's voice jolted me from my reverie. "Are you not feeling well?"

"I am fine." I nodded. "We can go back."

I couldn't get the scene with the arsonist out of my mind. And the more I thought about it on our return journey, the less convinced I was he'd set the fire at Lion Hall. He'd freely admitted his other crimes, so why claim he hadn't set our stable on fire? Maybe he feared such a terrible crime would put him in prison forever? At least in prison his inner voices wouldn't be in control. And he already faced punishment for his other crimes. One way or another, he was going to wind up in prison—or an asylum.

We arrived, and I immediately rushed to my room. I was soaked in perspiration and in desperate need of peace and quiet. I removed my dress and threw on something lighter.

After a short rest, I went to the salon. My mother was laying out a game of solitaire and didn't bother to look up from her cards. "Well, then, how did it go with the police?"

"They've arrested a tramp who set fire to some haystacks in the area. He claims voices in his head made him do it."

"A madman! God help us all!"

"But he denies setting the fire here. It seems the voices did not tell him to."

"And does Hermannsson believe him?"

"That is hard to say. The police will hold him for the other fires, in any case, but Hermannsson seemed not entirely convinced they had the right man after all. Langeholm said they had never seen the man here."

"Who knows? Someone probably hid him," Mother replied. "The most vexing things have been happening. Maids getting pregnant out of wedlock, the mistress of the mansion not caring and letting them keep working . . ."

"Mother, there is absolutely no link between the fire and Susanna's pregnancy."

"She tried to commit a crime too."

"Because she was desperate!" I immediately regretted provoking my mother. I was somewhat more rested, but I still had a headache. "Linda threatened to expose her to everyone! She had nowhere to turn . . ."

"Whatever was she afraid of? You already knew, and the last I heard, you were the mistress of this estate. You have to make the hard decisions here."

"And I did. I would never have discharged her for becoming pregnant. But theft is another matter entirely."

Couldn't I steer this conversation back to the fire? I had the feeling the unpleasantness between Mother and me was about to explode.

"The servants would have noticed it sooner or later," Mother insisted, "and then the situation would have been no different. You cannot shield her from the censure of society. Or did you hope the father would change his mind and marry her, even though he's nowhere to be found?"

I told her the truth. "I hoped my friend in Stockholm would come up with some way to help. We often dealt with similar situations, and we were always able to help."

"I'm sure you did! But you are not in Stockholm, and your friend seems to have failed you. Perhaps she contracted some disease from those awful women your little band is so intent on helping."

"Mother, an extramarital pregnancy is not a contagious disease!" If I didn't leave immediately, I was going to smash something. I counted to ten. "Please excuse me. I have things to do."

I went to the door, fuming. My cursed mother had even managed to make me worry about Marit. Why hadn't she written since April?

"Send Linda to me!" Stella called.

I held back a cutting remark and yanked the door open. Linda was hovering in the hall.

"You may go in," I hissed as I stormed past.

I hadn't intended to spend the whole day outside the manor, but that afternoon I had Talla saddled, and I rode to the Kristianstad telegraph office.

The telegraphist was hidden behind a newspaper when I arrived, but he jumped in alarm when I came in and let it fall to the floor. "Good day, gracious lady. May I be of service?"

He was clearly pleased to have something to do at last.

"I should like to send a telegram," I told him as I took a couple of coins from my skirt pocket. "To Stockholm, to Miss Marit Andersson."

"Gladly, gracious lady. Please give me the address and the text of your message."

I recited Marit's address and handed him the message I'd written out in my office. It didn't mention Susanna by name or explain her circumstances. I inquired after Marit's health and about our "project." I said the situation had gotten worse.

Most of all I wanted to know that Marit was safe. Her assistance with Susanna was secondary.

The official accepted payment and went to work. As I listened to the metallic clatter of the telegraph key, my mind was far away, on the streets of Stockholm. Had something really happened to Marit? Had she fallen ill? Or had one of the demonstrations gotten so out of hand that she was languishing behind bars? The newspaper hadn't mentioned anything of the sort, but that meant nothing. Few reporters were interested in writing about such things.

"Aha! There, all done!" The telegraphist gave me a copy and a receipt.

Now there was nothing I could do but wait and hope for the best.

As I stepped out of the telegraph office, I looked up at the top branches of a tall spruce crowded with noisily twittering birds. Would being mistress of Lion Hall always entail such worry and problem solving? Was anxiety to be my constant companion from that day on?

When I got back to the estate, Max was waiting in the forecourt with a stack of folders. His broad smile chased away my worries, but only for a moment.

"Welcome back, gracious miss. I've finished reviewing the leases, and I really must point out that you are charging your tenants entirely too little. Landlords in Pomerania are nowhere near as indulgent."

"We already raised the prices for our horses," I grumbled. "I have no desire to provoke the tenants to march on us with torches and pitchforks." I regretted Max was seeing me in such a mood. He wasn't to blame for my encounter with the lunatic or for my mother's goading.

"Are you not feeling well? We can postpone discussing the leases until tomorrow, if you wish."

I shook my head. "No, let us do it now. Perhaps it will distract me from my worries."

"Does it have something to do with the suspect?"

"Did Langeholm tell you about that?"

"Me and the rest of the men. He said the fellow claimed to be hearing voices."

"Yes, he did. And I fear he is not the real culprit." I sighed. "I wish I could just close the book on all this. Nothing is resolved, and I've heard nothing from my Stockholm friend for weeks. That is quite unlike her."

"She will report in," Max said in a sympathetic tone. "And if I can help you, just tell me."

"You have already helped me a great deal." I felt a pang in my heart just looking at him. I needed a man like him at my side. Not only as an estate manager, but for everything else in my life.

"I am quite happy to assist with whatever you need."

"Thank you. I do appreciate that."

He gave me an encouraging nod.

"Very well, then. Come to the office with me. I will feel much better after we have coffee and a bit of pastry."

That evening, just after dismissing Lena for the night, I realized I'd neglected to put my identity documents back into the office drawer. I'd had them with me at the police station, thinking they might be required. I looked for my purse, but it was nowhere to be found. I hadn't taken it to the telegraph office, so I must have forgotten it in the coach. There was little money in it, but I didn't want my documents lying around. My grandmother had drilled into us the necessity of keeping passports and vital papers secure. She'd even made us stay up almost all night during a thunderstorm once, just in case lightning set the house on fire and we had to save both our papers and ourselves.

I'd had a fear of nighttime storms ever since. Hendrik had been no help, for he loved to spook me. He took every opportunity to play the ghost of some ancestor. When we got older, I preferred to stay awake and watch the lightning. I'd even tried to paint a nighttime thunderstorm, but I'd been so harrowed by those memories that I was unable to evoke them on canvas.

I went downstairs. I could hear the maids doing the washing-up in the kitchen. They would soon be dismissed to go to bed. I went out.

I approached the coach house and saw the door was open. That in itself wasn't unusual, for August was often occupied until late with adjustments and repairs. However, there was no light within. Had he simply forgotten to lock up? I stepped inside and was about to strike a match to light the lamp when I heard voices.

"I won't be able to come again for a while," a woman said. "Some things have happened."

"All right. But we made a deal, and you can't get out of it. You know that, don't you?"

The second voice was unmistakable. What was Langeholm up to? And the woman's voice resembled Susanna's. I hid by the coach and heard a belt being fastened. Skirts rustled, then I heard someone putting shoes on. I stooped and peered under the coach but saw only a dress and trouser legs.

The woman must have simply nodded, for they said no more and got up immediately. Did Langeholm have the key? If so, he might lock the coach house—with me inside!

But there was no way to slip out unnoticed. I caught sight of Susanna and Langeholm just before he shut the coach house door. Just as I'd feared, he locked it, and they left. I could have called out, but the enormity of what I'd just witnessed stopped me. My pulse thundered in my ears.

Was Langeholm Susanna's lover? The father of her child? I wished I hadn't heard his comment to her about a deal. What kind of deal? To meet in secret? In exchange for his pledge not to reveal he was the father of her child? Didn't Langeholm realize he was putting his own position at risk by allowing a person discharged for theft back onto the estate?

Incredulous, I stood by the coach, realizing I'd have to spend the night there in the dark. The coach house windows were nailed shut. My heart raced. Maybe I should cry for help? No one would be around at this time of night, except possibly Langeholm. I had no desire to come face-to-face with him here.

I was undecided for a while, then I climbed into the coach. The cushions inside were not overly comfortable, but they were better than the coach house floor. I could call for help early the next morning, if August hadn't already come in. I pulled the coach door shut and listened to my own heartbeat. It seemed unnaturally loud in that confined space.

What was going on? Why had Susanna come back? Had she begged Langeholm for help? Was she asking him to marry her?

None of this made sense. I intended to find out the truth—once someone freed me.

28

The coachman's voice shocked me from my sleep. "Good Lord, gracious miss! Why are ye sleeping here?"

I tried to rub the sleep from my eyes. At first I didn't know where I was, but the stiffness of my shoulders brought it all back—including the strange assignation I'd seen.

"Yer mother is sick with worry!" August exclaimed. I doubted that. Lena had probably discovered I wasn't in my room that morning. "She thought ye'd disappeared during the night. She sent me to take the coach out to look for ye."

"That is most unfortunate. But I am extremely glad to see you."

August gave me his hand and helped me step down.

"Thank you very much. It appears I had best reassure everyone before I ride off."

"Ride off?" August was baffled. "But where?"

"I have a matter to settle. Could you please tell the stable boys to saddle Talla immediately?"

"Gladly, gracious miss. But excuse me: What were ye doing in the coach?"

"I had forgotten my handbag," I said, holding it up. "I was getting it, but then the door shut, and someone locked up and left before I could call out."

August regarded me skeptically. He was probably wondering who else could have had the key. After all, this was his domain.

"Well, it's good it was nothing worse," the coachman concluded with an indulgent smile. "And as for the locked door, I'll have a couple of words with the lads."

"No, August. Say nothing. And please do not tell any of the staff where you found me."

"Why, then?"

"I—" I didn't want Langeholm to learn I'd discovered him! But what should I say? "There is something I would like to investigate."

August was puzzled, but he nodded. "Ye can count on me, gracious miss. Nary a word."

"Thank you, August."

I hurried to the manor. Luckily, the maids were busy elsewhere, and I didn't run across any of them. My heart pounded as I sneaked upstairs, trying all the while to get my thoughts in order. I had to reassure my mother, put in an appearance for the maids, and then ride to the village to locate Susanna without arousing any suspicions.

My mother called out as I walked down the corridor. "Agneta, wherever were you?"

"I fell asleep in the coach," I answered. I couldn't think of any better excuse.

She appeared at the end of the hall. "In the coach? What were you up to in the coach? August told me he did not take it out yesterday evening."

"He did not. And I will not be at breakfast. There is a matter I must attend to."

"Do you intend to inform your mother about this mysterious matter?"

"Yes," I responded. "But only once I have settled it." I disappeared into my room.

Soon thereafter, Lena appeared, quite upset. "Thank heaven you're back! We were all frightfully worried!"

"I just took a little stroll," I told her and tossed my purse onto the bed. "No reason to worry. Please take out my best riding outfit."

Lena's brow furrowed. I always told her in advance when I intended to sally out early the next day. But only a very good crystal ball could have predicted the scene I'd witnessed the evening before.

She bustled off and quickly returned with the outfit. "Shall I fetch you something to eat?"

I shook my head. "I will have something when I return. This is more important." I dressed and hurried downstairs to the forecourt, where Tim had Talla saddled and ready. I thanked him and rode off.

Talla and I galloped across the fields. I loved riding, and the morning was glorious, but I was distressed by what I'd seen. Sunk in thought, I scarcely noticed the beauty of the woods, where sunbeams dappled the mighty trunks and bathed everything in an early morning glow.

The Korvens tended a little farm on the outskirts of the village. I feared they'd be anything but pleased to receive me. They'd entrusted their daughter to us. Now she was pregnant, she'd been caught trying to steal, and God only knew what kind of trouble she was in.

Angry barking met me when I got to their farmstead. The dog raged so ferociously at the end of his chain I was afraid he was going to break loose. How long had the Korvens had such an evil-tempered dog?

Sven Korven came out of the house.

"Good morning, Mr. Korven!" I called over the mongrel's barking as I swung down from the saddle. "I am Agneta Lejongård, and—"

"I know who ye be!" the farmer roared. "And ye can go to the devil!"

That was more or less what I'd expected.

"Please, Mr. Korven. I need to speak with your daughter. It is important."

"Me daughter? If ye hadn't thrown her out, then sure ye'd be able to talk to her."

I looked around. Even if the dog hadn't been making such an uproar, our shouted exchange would certainly have brought the neighbors to the windows to see what was going on.

"Sven!" A woman's voice interrupted him. Mrs. Korven was a full head taller than her husband. She must have once been as good-looking as her daughter, but the years had taken their toll. "Go inside! I'll handle this."

I didn't know whether to hope he'd obey or refuse. She didn't appear any better disposed to me than he was.

Sven disappeared. Clearly Mrs. Korven was in charge.

She came out, itching for a fight. "So why do ye want to speak to the girl? Haven't ye made enough trouble for the lass?"

"I don't know what Susanna told you, but—"

"No need to tell us anything," the woman declared. "I saw it for meself. She went and got herself into a situation. Ye should have put a stop to it!"

"How could I have? I was in Stockholm!"

"Then yer father or yer mother should've! What would yer parents say to ye if ye came home pregnant with a bastard?"

I wouldn't have come back home at all, I thought, but I didn't want to provoke her even more.

"Well, we cannot change what has happened," I said. "I would like to help your daughter, but there is something I must tell her. Concerning the father of her child."

"Do ye know the name of the rogue?"

"No, but I suspect someone."

"And just who would that be? One of those good-for-nothing rascals ye lot have in yer stables? It can't be someone from the village. Or was it yer father who got his hands on her?"

That accusation took my breath away. Father had never paid any attention to the serving girls, as far as I knew. But on the other hand, there was that mysterious loan contract. Had he bought Susanna's silence?

The very thought made me sick, but I refused to let Mrs. Korven see that. "Leave my father out of this! We cannot make any speculations until I have spoken with Susanna."

Mrs. Korven shook a fist at me and turned to go inside. "If yer father had her, ye lot will pay for it!"

"Where is your daughter?"

"How would I know!" She disappeared into the house.

The dog had stopped pulling at its chain and was only growling.

Downcast, I mounted my horse and turned her toward the road.

"Gracious miss!" a voice called out. I hadn't noticed the elderly woman who'd obviously heard every word. "If you wish to speak to Susanna, she's in the little house by the lake. She couldn't bear her mother's scolding, and she fled out there. I saw her just yesterday."

I took a closer look. I must have been just a child the last time I saw that face. "You're Ida, the herb woman!"

She smiled. She'd lost a few teeth over the years, and the remaining ones were in frightfully bad shape. "Yes, indeed. And it's really terrible, what happened to the girl. All I can now do is watch over her until the baby comes."

Ida wasn't just the village herb woman. She also cared for pregnant women who sought her advice, and sometimes she was able to make pregnancies go away. No one in the village ever admitted she was an angel maker, but some muttered that she was a witch. In centuries past, someone would surely have tried to get her burned at the stake. Fortunately, those dark times were long gone, even though there was still much that needed to change.

It was a relief to hear she was taking care of Susanna. Ida wouldn't let anyone harm the girl.

"I would like to help her." I dismounted. "But first I need her to tell me something."

"Go visit her," Ida said with a calm smile. "She's not as stirred up as her parents. In fact, she's been waiting for you to come. Who can help her, if not you? No one in the village, that's certain. You know how folks are."

"Did she tell you she was caught trying to steal something from my mother?"

"She did. And she's frightfully sorry. Talk to her, and I'll see what I can do to help." The old woman put her wrinkled hand over mine. "You are a good woman, young Countess. Your father would have been different, but you are a gentle one. I don't mean to say I don't grieve for all that happened with the old count and his son. But they are in God's hands." With those words, she released me and limped away.

I stared after her, rooted where I stood, as if she'd cast a spell on me. It dissolved only after she'd turned the next corner and disappeared from sight.

I mounted my horse and rode toward the lake, my heart racing.

29

The hut by the lake was a tiny ramshackle structure devoid of comfort, but at least Susanna had a roof over her head, out of view of the villagers.

I tied Talla to a tree and walked through the tall grass. I heard the shrill whistle of a distant train. I knocked on the door.

At first there was no answer. *She must be out*, I told myself.

The door flew open.

I was shocked to see Susanna looking even more haggard than she had a couple of days earlier. Her skin was gray despite the abundant sunshine, and her face was swollen. Her eyes and hair had lost all their luster. The girl looked as if she'd had nothing to eat since leaving Lion Hall and hadn't slept the night before. How often was Langeholm forcing her to meet him?

"Countess Lejongård," she said with effort. She seemed afraid of me.

"Good morning, Susanna." I made no move to enter. It was up to her whether to invite me in. "I would very much like to talk to you."

"But I—"

"You were at the estate last night. Do not bother to deny it. I witnessed your meeting with Langeholm. Purely by chance."

Susanna swayed, and I thought for a moment she was going to faint. But she caught herself and stared at me as if I were an evil spirit come to haunt her.

"I didn't come to punish you, Susanna. But please talk to me! What is going on between you and the stable master?"

Her eyes gleamed with distrust. "Why?"

"Because I want to help you. I want to protect you and keep you from making another huge mistake."

Susanna snorted. "Just look at me! What mistake could possibly make things worse?" She held out her arms and displayed her now undeniably swollen belly.

"Perhaps something that would harm the estate? Something you will later regret?"

"I'm already a thief and a whore in the eyes of the people here," she replied bitterly. "Nothing could be worse than that."

"Susanna, you are *not* a whore!" I held out a hand, but she stood beyond my reach. "You must not think of yourself in such terms! Men simply want to persuade us women we are the only ones at fault when they make us pregnant. It's not true." I sighed in frustration and bowed my head. "Susanna, I really do want to help you. It looks as if your baby will be coming very soon. You need a good midwife, at the very least! And as for your attempted theft, I understand it. A woman in a situation like yours—"

"You don't understand anything!" She flung the accusation at me. "You were never in a situation like this."

"No, but in Stockholm I knew several women in similar predicaments. They joined the women's rights movement because they wanted change. And we were able to assist them."

Susanna sniffed in derision. "So you want me to join those women's rights people?"

"Not at all. I want you to let me help you. I am not your mistress or employer any longer, so of course you can do whatever you wish. But I still have my Stockholm acquaintances. They can stand beside you."

"I suppose that's only if I give you the name of the father?" Susanna shook her head and pursed her lips. Tears glistened in her eyes.

Was Langeholm indeed the father? Was that why she was afraid?

"We would do everything possible to have the man brought to court," I told her, silently promising myself I would personally lecture Langeholm on the chapters in Leviticus about sin and atonement. "Our attorneys can make sure he provides child support. No one can force him to marry you, but he must accept the consequences of his acts."

She gave me an odd look. Suddenly all the tension went out of her body. She seemed to collapse into herself.

"I'm afraid that's not possible. He will never be in a position to face a judge."

My face betrayed my surprise. "And why not? Langeholm—"

"Langeholm?" she repeated in astonishment. "What about him?"

"I thought he—"

She shook her head. "It was your brother," she said at last. "Hendrik Lejongård fathered my child."

Time stopped. Her words blasted through my mind like shots from a revolver, and it took a very long time for me to catch my breath.

"Hendrik and you?"

Susanna's eyes filled with contempt. "Yes, that's hard for you to believe, isn't it? That your hoity-toity brother got involved with a maid?"

"That is not it," I quickly replied. "Hendrik—I mean, he told me nothing of this."

"He wanted to keep it a secret, until . . ."

"Until what?"

"Until we married. He wanted to defy his father."

Again I was speechless. Hendrik had promised to marry Susanna! I knew him well; he wouldn't have stopped until he had his own way.

A harrowing thought struck me. Had Father known of this? Had he sought to silence Susanna by offering her the borrowed money? If so, why hadn't she taken it and disappeared?

"Susanna, I have a question. A very delicate question." My heart rose into my throat.

"Yes?"

I didn't know where to begin. "Please forgive me, but I must ask. Did my father know about your relationship? Did he offer you money to forget my brother?"

Her eyes opened wide in alarm. "No! Hendrik hadn't told him. He said we should wait until the spring. And I didn't get a cent. No one knew. I swear it to you!"

I nodded. "Thank you."

Susanna stared blankly into the distance.

We stood there a long time without speaking. I tried to imagine my mother's reaction to hearing that her exemplary son had gotten a servant pregnant. And had even wanted to marry her! But could it be true?

I was assailed by doubts for a moment. Then I recalled that Hendrik's first love had been the blacksmith's daughter. He'd been attracted by the simple girl's freshness and innocence. And Susanna was a real beauty! I now understood why she had wept in Hendrik's room after his death. It wasn't because of some dreamy infatuation with her master; it was grief for her beloved.

"Why didn't you say anything to me?"

"I couldn't. You probably wouldn't have believed me." A tear trickled down her cheek. "When I heard he was badly hurt, it tore me apart. Every day I prayed and hoped he would make it. I already feared he wouldn't marry me. Your mother is too strict. But he promised to take care of me, no matter what. And getting pregnant—we got carried away. He told me he'd be careful, but it happened anyhow."

Marit would have torn her hair at that. Her constant complaint was that men promised women they'd be careful, then forgot themselves in the heat of the moment.

"I went to old Ida quick as I could for herbs, but they didn't work. As you can see."

I looked at Susanna. She was such a bright and sweet girl. My brother might well have taken the revolutionary step of actually marrying her. As master of the estate, he could have done whatever he wished. I wondered if they could have been happy.

"Susanna, please listen to me."

She looked up, and my heart almost broke when I saw the suffering in her eyes.

"My brother would certainly have provided for your child. Since he can't, I will do so, as best I can."

"You want to take my baby?"

I shook my head and raised my hands. "No, not that! You misunderstand me! I'm only saying I'll assist you. Will you allow me to come in and tell you what I propose? If it doesn't please you, you can refuse, and I'll leave you in peace. But give me the chance to make up for Hendrik's failing!"

Susanna nodded. "All right, come inside."

The interior of the hut was a bit untidy, but what could one expect of such a neglected structure? It was no place for Susanna to bring up a child.

Oh, Hendrik. What were you thinking?

I put that thought aside and settled on a low stool.

"I have nothing to offer you," she apologized. "I even ran out of wild nettles for tea."

"There's no need. So tell me, how far along are you?"

"I'm probably in my sixth month. I don't know exactly. Hendrik and I . . . we . . . several times—"

I raised one hand. "There's no need for details. Let us assume that in fact you're in your sixth month. You need a physician or a midwife who'll ask no questions when it comes to delivery."

"I . . . I have no way to pay," Susanna stammered.

"Never mind that. I'll take care of it. I've contacted my friend Marit Andersson for assistance. She knows many people. And some members of the movement for women's rights are midwives. A number of physicians sympathize with our aims."

"That means I have to give birth in secret. Then what?"

"Well, I don't know what Marit will suggest, for she hasn't responded yet. You may need to enter into a marriage of convenience—on paper only, so that you won't be known as an unmarried mother. Think about it; would you be willing? And it would probably be advisable to move to Stockholm to escape the rumors here. I'm not suggesting this to get rid of you but because you can find work there. There's great demand for qualified servants, and you already have experience. You can start anew."

She shook her head. "I don't want a husband!"

I understood. But society's code was strict. A woman with an illegitimate child would never find proper employment. And employment was Susanna's only hope of salvation.

"It wouldn't be a real marriage. There are certain men in Stockholm who, let us say, have no interest in marrying a woman. They're willing to help women in difficulties, for they know all too well the kind of reprisals society can take. Such a man wouldn't oblige you to satisfy him as a true wife. And if you should ever fall in love, he would quickly agree to a divorce."

"But isn't that a sin? Marriage is supposed to last until death!"

I gave a short, disdainful laugh. "Times have changed, especially in the big city. Women there have begun to insist on marriage contracts that guarantee their husbands cannot appropriate all their property in the event of divorce. It will be a long time before that becomes the norm out here in the countryside, but there is a great deal of progress. Women like my friend Marit are making sure of that."

Susanna nodded, concerned. It was clear she needed time to ponder what she'd just heard.

"Now would you please tell me what you were up to with the stable master? Were you trying to convince him to marry you?"

"Me, marry Langeholm?" Susanna shook her head in horror. "I wouldn't do that for all the gold in China!"

"Then why were you meeting him?"

"Because we had a deal."

"Which was?"

I couldn't imagine arranging a secret rendezvous with a man I disliked as much as Susanna appeared to despise Langeholm.

"I was supposed to—" She blushed and refused to say more.

"You were supposed to . . . go to bed with him?" I frowned. Could this be true? Langeholm was a man, after all. Might he be so unprincipled as to demand sexual favors from a disgraced young woman?

"Yes," Susanna replied, her tears again beginning to flow. "I know how that sounds, but I had no choice. And when I became too pregnant to satisfy him, he wanted me to steal."

"Why would you do that?" I asked, horrified.

"To keep him from telling people who fathered my child."

"He knew?"

"Yes. He cornered me one evening and claimed he'd seen Hendrik and me." She bowed her head in shame. "He threatened to tell the gracious mistress. And everyone in the village."

This was nothing short of monstrous! The stable master had blackmailed Susanna? Turned her into his personal whore and forced her to steal?

My gorge rose at the thought of it. "You will not meet the stable master again. Do I make myself clear?"

"But if he—"

"He will not breathe a word to anyone in the village. I will make certain of that."

"But your mother—"

I placed a hand on her shoulder. "Nothing! She will do nothing. Other than rant and rave, but that will not affect you."

Susanna grabbed my hands. "But Langeholm will do everything he can to hurt me. And Hendrik—"

"Nothing will happen to you, I promise!" I took her hands in mine and pressed them. "You will be safe here. And I will make sure you have plenty of good, nourishing food."

If I enlisted Ida and gave her some money, she would surely see to Susanna's needs as long as the girl stayed here. And I knew I could count on the herb woman's discretion.

30

I left Talla with Tim, the stable boy, and swiftly strode to the mansion.

I was still stunned by Susanna's confession. Hendrik should have foreseen the consequences of his actions! At least he wasn't a heedless, contemptible swine, like so many other men.

The coaches waiting in the courtyard were evidence that Mother's friends were visiting. All the better! That meant she wouldn't bother me before I could put my thoughts in order.

"Good day, Miss Lejongård!" called a voice.

Langeholm. My hand clenched around the riding belt, and I shuddered. I wanted to slash the leather strap and steel buckle across his hypocritical grin, but I controlled myself.

I answered as calmly as I could. "Mr. Langeholm, good day." I vanished into the house.

I was furious. He'd seemed so trustworthy, but he'd acted so unscrupulously! Forcing a maid to service him sexually and steal from her mistress!

I'd been entirely too naive about the men on the estate. So I went to the kitchen for counsel from the woman who knew them better than anyone.

I found Miss Rosendahl sitting with Mrs. Bloomquist, Marie, Svea, and Lena at the long kitchen table. The inviting scent of coffee and pastries hung in the air.

The women rose as soon as I entered.

"Oh, gracious miss, may I offer you a delicacy?" Mrs. Bloomquist asked. "I just brewed coffee. And the first pastries for this afternoon have just come out of the oven. If you'd like a taste . . ."

I couldn't resist the alluring smell of her baking. "Thank you very much, Mrs. Bloomquist. I would gladly accept a small cup of coffee and a couple of your dainty sweets."

Our cook's baked goods were magical. She and cooks on nearby estates competed in elaborating ingenious new recipes. Our long-standing custom at Lion Hall was to enjoy afternoon coffee with an assortment of seven different baked delights. Mrs. Bloomquist jealously guarded her recipes and banned the servants of other households from her pantry of precious ingredients.

"I can take them up for you!" Lena said dutifully and rose to fetch them.

"Thank you, Lena, but that is not necessary. You have all earned your break. I will carry the tray myself."

Lena turned to appeal for Miss Rosendahl's support, only to be met by a stern stare of reproof. But I saw nothing in Lena's behavior that merited reproach. In Stockholm, I'd learned to brew my own coffee.

"I just came by for you, Miss Rosendahl. To ask if I could have a word."

"By all means. What is it?"

I shook my head. "Enjoy your coffee, and I will do the same. You will find me in the office. Please come see me when it is convenient." I heaped a small silver tray with baked goods and carried it upstairs.

For a while, the aroma of the coffee covered the office's familiar smells of cedar and leather. I leaned back in an upholstered leather armchair, tore off a morsel of pastry, and let the buttery deliciousness melt in my mouth.

The sweetness of the pastry and the powerful effects of the coffee did much to improve my mood. I looked through the window, contemplated the clouds, and tried to put my thoughts into some semblance of order.

There was a knock at the door. It was, of course, Miss Rosendahl, unable to wait and visibly concerned by my summons. "Is this a convenient moment?"

"Of course." I gestured toward the armchair. "Please have a seat, Miss Rosendahl."

The housekeeper stepped forward a bit hesitantly and sat down. "I do hope there has been no incident with the staff."

"No, that is not it," I answered, since one couldn't properly label it an "incident." It was worse; it was an outrage. "How well do you know Mr. Langeholm?"

"Our stable master?"

"Yes. What do you know of him? I am aware he has been employed by the family for some time, but I have not been in residence for two years. Has Mr. Langeholm, shall we say, come to your attention in any way?"

The housekeeper gave me a puzzled look. "No, not that I can recall. He has always conducted himself correctly."

"Really?" I raised my eyebrows. Someone capable of blackmailing a servant girl couldn't have gone bad overnight.

"That is—I don't know if your mother mentioned the matter concerning Juna."

"Juna?"

"She was taken on as a maid in January. And not long after her arrival, she became involved with the stable master. The affair was discovered, and your mother discharged the girl."

Why hadn't Hendrik mentioned this in any of his letters? Had he thought it insignificant? Or had the fate of that maid given him pause, considering his own affair with Susanna?

"You called it an affair," I said. "As far as I have been informed, the stable master is not married."

Miss Rosendahl's expression darkened. "Perhaps. But neither your mother nor the master, your sainted father, tolerated relationships belowstairs. They were of the opinion it did no good for employees to be distracted by personal relationships."

I examined Miss Rosendahl. During my childhood, I'd always admired her beauty. If any woman around here might have ever attracted my father's amorous attentions, it was Miss Rosendahl. But she'd always been above reproach. Had she subordinated her longings and natural desires to her duty as an employee?

I took a deep breath. "Well, it appears that as the new mistress of the estate, I must make some changes."

The housekeeper's expression was one of disbelief. "What do you mean?"

"I have no objection to an employee having a sincere, loving relationship with another person. It must not get in the way of the work, of course, and I will not encourage illicit affairs. But when two single persons with feelings for one another are considering matrimony, no one has the right to come between them."

Marit would have cheered. Some of our sister suffragettes were employed as servants and strictly enjoined from seeking husbands during the term of their employment. A woman could choose to give notice, of course, but frequently a relationship was broken off before the knot was tied. And all too often the woman ended up on the street.

"But that would be in complete contradiction to what your father always stipulated!" the housekeeper protested. "What would our guests think if all the maids around here were great with child? Not to mention it's the woman's obligation to keep house for her husband."

"Miss Rosendahl, I am in charge here now." I spoke as calmly as possible. One of the principal grievances of our movement was the contention that women couldn't tend to their own families and household duties if employed elsewhere. I'd long found that assertion absurd. "We are now thirteen years into the new century. Are you not of the opinion that, with all the progress made to date, there should also be changes in the obligations forced upon women?"

"But there are reasons for those rules."

"Indeed. One reason is to keep women in their place. Another is to convince women they merit nothing better." I looked at her closely. "You have been employed by our family for quite a long time."

"For almost thirty years."

"That is a very long time. And as far as I know, my parents have always been satisfied with you. Tell me, does your work give you pleasure?"

"I—I am not certain one's work must provide pleasure. We each have our place and duties we must fulfill."

"Well, that is true, but one should be wholeheartedly devoted to one's place, am I right?"

"Of course."

"Are you wholeheartedly devoted?"

Miss Rosendahl seemed quite upset. "That goes without saying, gracious miss. If you assume otherwise . . ."

I raised a hand to reassure her. "I do not assume otherwise, for I have never noted you to be anything but knowledgeable and efficient. I am addressing a different matter. Have you ever wished to have a husband and a family?"

"No, I—I have always sought only to provide the best service I could." Her face flushed, a hint she wasn't telling the whole truth.

"And that you do, but I ask you sincerely: Did you ever have that thought, at any time in your life? Every woman longs to be loved. Or am I mistaken?"

"Well, that is a private matter," she responded hesitantly.

I nodded. I really had no place inquiring into her intimate thoughts and feelings. But I couldn't imagine Miss Rosendahl had never in her life longed for affection.

"Personal indeed, and we all deserve to have parts of our life be such. Henceforth, I will be applying new rules here. Including the stipulation that a person in our service may enter into marriage without losing her position."

Miss Rosendahl nodded, assuming that our conversation had ended. She started to get up.

I stopped her. "Getting back to Mr. Langeholm: Since the young lady's departure, have you noticed anything unusual about him? Did he mention he was displeased, or was he upset with my father?"

The housekeeper sank back into the armchair. "Well, of course he said he was unhappy Juna left, but he never complained about your father. He got over it after a time. The girl went back to the village and broke off the relationship."

"Where does this Juna live? What is her family name?"

I should probably look into this passionate intrigue. Perhaps Langeholm had wanted Susanna to steal the brooch so he could give it to his inamorata.

"Holm," Miss Rosendahl said. "Juna Holm. But I don't know where she lives."

"Thank you very much, Miss Rosendahl. That will be all for now."

The housekeeper nodded, got up, and left the office.

Filled with misgivings, I gazed moodily out the window. There was a distinctly fishy smell to all of this.

31

I went to the salon after my mother's visitors left. I knew Mother would still be there, at ease in the restored peace and quiet.

I was right. She was sitting on the rattan sofa with a glass of cranberry lemonade before her, deep in thought as she gazed out the window.

"Mother? May I disturb you for a moment?"

She slowly turned her head to regard me. "You have returned! I thought you were riding around the estate."

"I was. There is something we need to discuss."

"How long have you been back?"

"Not very long," I said. Otherwise I knew she'd scold me for not coming to greet her friends. "Have you had a pleasant day?"

Stella's eyes glinted as if she'd just caught me in a lie. Perhaps Linda had advised her immediately of my return. "It was quite entertaining. What did you wish to discuss?"

My mother had never been one to share the gossip she heard from friends. She might have contributed to it though, maybe even revealing my refusal of the marriage-minded son of Count Ekberg.

I settled onto a chair still redolent of the previous occupant's perfume.

"I called on Susanna."

Mother was immediately on guard. "What did you want from that horrid, immoral woman?"

"Yesterday I witnessed something that left me quite unsettled."

"Did she try to steal something else?" Her pitch rose.

"No. But she was here on the estate."

My mother's finely plucked eyebrows lifted into two scornful arcs. "What was that little tart doing? Why did you not inform me immediately?"

"I had no time. Her encounter was brief and took place in . . . quite unusual circumstances."

"Her encounter? With whom?"

"With Langeholm."

"The stable master?"

"Yes. And it appears the man has quite deceived us."

"In what way?"

I told my mother exactly what I'd seen in the coach house, as well as what Susanna had confessed—but I omitted the allegation that Hendrik was the father of her child. I kept that in reserve.

My mother became increasingly infuriated as my account progressed. If we'd had bloodhounds like those of our ancestor, Axel, she would have unleashed them on the poor girl.

"She claims, then, that he incited her to steal and to . . . engage in immoral behavior?"

"Yes."

"That is absurd! Langeholm is one of our best people! He has always been a good and faithful servant of this family!"

"I would not be so certain of that, considering how Juna lost her job. Surely you have not forgotten Langeholm had a relationship with that maid."

Mother grimaced in disgust. "A comical liaison! The girl was probably trying to get her claws in a good husband."

I tilted my head, sickened by what I heard. "Her claws? It is not entirely unusual for two people to fall in love. Did that ever occur to you? And love can lead to reckless behavior!"

"Stop it!" She waved me away. "There are rules of conduct in a house like ours. Relationships between employees must not infringe upon moral standards."

"The only person who infringed upon moral standards was Langeholm, when he spied on Susanna and blackmailed her. And God only knows how many times he has behaved so deplorably."

That dodgy five-thousand-crown loan came to mind. Had it been hush money to keep Langeholm from revealing Hendrik's affair with a serving girl?

"Susanna should not have allowed him to exploit her!" my mother declared, making me flush with anger.

"In your world, it's always the woman's fault," I said hotly. "No matter what men do, they are innocent little lambs. They make a woman pregnant, so the woman must have led them astray. A man blackmails a woman, and you consider it the woman's fault!"

"Most of the time, it is."

"How can you possibly say that?"

Mother clenched her jaw. "In Susanna's case, it is perfectly clear. She got herself mixed up with some philanderer."

I dropped my bomb. "You cannot call Hendrik a philanderer."

My mother's face turned ashen. I must admit it was a delicious moment for me, even though I knew the rest of our conversation was going to be extremely difficult.

"What did you just say?"

"That surely Hendrik was no philanderer. And yes, you heard me right. Susanna's child is his."

"Is that what she claims?"

"Yes, and the mother of a child knows where it came from."

Mother hit the roof. "It's a lie! She is looking to tarnish our reputation and get something out of us!"

Exactly the reaction I'd expected.

"If that were so, why didn't she say so when her pregnancy became obvious? Or later, when we discharged her? She didn't say a word because she didn't want to compromise Hendrik."

"Oh, and then she tells you when you turn up?" My mother could hardly contain her rage. "She is plotting something, and she is exploiting the stable master in order to gain access to the mansion!"

"And that is why he has been abusing her for his sexual needs? That is the reason he threatened to reveal the father of her child? That was why he lurked around, watching to see with whom Hendrik was having a liaison?"

We glared furiously at one another. The air between us shimmered as if someone had lit a fuse.

I took several deep breaths and eventually resumed in a somewhat quieter tone. "You know, Mother, after Hendrik died, Susanna was sitting in his room, sobbing. She told me she'd come to air it out and only then was struck by the reality of his death."

"That child and Hendrik, a couple? The notion makes me laugh!"

"Mother, please," I appealed to her. Why was I always forced to raise my voice to make her listen? "If I hadn't gone to her hut today, Susanna would never have revealed her secret. She could have told her parents who the father was, and Mrs. Korven would have marched straight to our front door. But Susanna said nothing. Instead of blaming her, we would do far better to ask ourselves what Langeholm was scheming and why he involved Susanna."

"If that were true, why would he blackmail her when he could have blackmailed us?" she snarled. "If he had wanted to punish us because of that little slut Juna, he would have threatened to disgrace us!"

"Can you be so sure he did not? Or that he is not prepared to do so now?"

Suddenly something occurred to me—no, it struck me like a bolt of lightning. There was something I had to do immediately.

My mother was in a terrible temper. "This is arrant nonsense! And you refuse to listen to reason. You always have!"

"You know very well that is not true. But I must determine what happened. I can do nothing else."

"Determine whatever you please. Accusing Langeholm of blackmail! But I want no more talk. I am tired and want to lie down. You will excuse me."

She stalked away, opened the door, and shut it behind her with more force than was necessary.

I was quaking. Had I won this battle? I couldn't be sure.

Mother was nowhere to be seen when I left the salon some moments later. No doubt she was stretched out in bed, her eyes covered with her sleep mask as she tried to assimilate the news. That would keep her busy whether she believed me or not.

I went back to the office. It still seemed strange each time I entered, almost as if Father would come in at any moment and ask what I was doing there. With trembling hands, I opened the desk drawer and took out a sheet of the stationery with our family coat of arms. My eye fell upon the loan contract that still lay next to the writing utensils, and my pulse again began to race.

This was the original. We had no copy, so I would be taking a risk if I sent it to Kristianstad. But Hermannsson needed to see it; he needed to know what had gone on here. And a letter sealed with the wax impression of our family crest should arrive safely.

My note provided the briefest possible summary of what had happened with Juna and Susanna. I asked Inspector Hermannsson to take that information into consideration in his investigation. I slipped my letter into a small envelope and put it and the loan contract into a larger one. Across the front I inscribed the address given on the policeman's visiting card. I went downstairs two steps at a time, left the house, and crossed the courtyard.

Fortunately, Langeholm was busy elsewhere, so I didn't have to face him. Our errand boy was cleaning the hooves of one of the horses.

"Peter, take this letter to Inspector Hermannsson in Kristianstad. It is very important."

"Yes, gracious miss."

"You had best get on the road right away, and if he gives you a letter in reply, please inform me the instant you return."

The boy nodded, slipped the letter into his interior jacket pocket, and went to fetch a saddle.

I looked after him. My hands were icy with worry and anger, and my heart was racing. If my suspicion was correct, we would soon be able to welcome the crown princess without any fear of future mishap.

32

I couldn't sleep that night. Over and over I heard Susanna's description of what had happened. And, in my mother's voice: *Was Hendrik the father, or is she trying to swindle us?*

I couldn't simply dismiss my mother's points. We had no evidence Hendrik had fathered the child. But I didn't believe Susanna had offered the stable master her body simply to get back into the manor.

Mother sent a message the next morning advising me she wouldn't be at breakfast. I wasn't surprised, considering our previous day's discussion. I brooded over coffee and thought of Inspector Hermannsson. What would he make of the information I'd shared?

The swish of the opening door interrupted my thoughts. I looked up to see Bruns enter with a silver tray. News? So early in the morning?

"A telegram has been delivered," Bruns said, bowing slightly as he held out the tray.

Concerned, I ripped open the envelope. Was it from Hermannsson?

ARRIVE TOMORROW 5 PM KRISTIANSTAD
TO EXPLAIN ALL +STOP+ HOPE YOU ARE
PLEASED +STOP+ MARIT +STOP+

And I was indeed so wonderfully pleased! It seemed Marit was safe and sound, and now she was on the way to visit me.

"Thank you, Bruns," I said as I left the dining room, telegram in hand. In the kitchen, I found the maids were busy with preparations for dinner.

"Where is Miss Rosendahl?" I asked, for she was nowhere to be seen.

"Your mother wished to speak with her," Mrs. Bloomquist answered. "She will be in the mistress's room."

"Thank you!" I hurried upstairs.

Miss Rosendahl appeared in the corridor, having left the room to which my mother regularly retired when she was "indisposed."

"Miss Rosendahl, we will have a visitor tomorrow evening. Would you please have our best guest room prepared?"

"With pleasure, gracious miss. May I inquire as to the visitor's name?"

"My friend Marit Andersson from Stockholm. August should be at the Kristianstad train station at five p.m. to receive her. She will not have much luggage. But she should be given as welcoming a reception as possible."

"We will do everything we can to assure her satisfaction." The housekeeper bowed slightly and went downstairs.

I pressed the telegram to my breast. Marit would have all sorts of news for me. And though it was ridiculous, I did so hope at least one of her tidbits would mention Michael.

From time to time, my heart still ached, but my responsibilities here had left me little time to brood on lost love. And then there was Max; I enjoyed his company a great deal. I would have to introduce the two of them. And I'd tell her about Lennard's awkward proposal. I was thrilled to know she was coming.

The next evening, I was pacing back and forth, peering constantly out the window in hopes of catching sight of the returning coach.

The hands of the clock crept to 6:30 p.m. Of course, the trip from Kristianstad always took a while. Afternoon rains had left the road muddy, and August was always careful to avoid risks. The train might have been late as well. Maybe a tree had fallen across the tracks.

"Are you sure your friend was on the train?" my mother asked. She was seated at a little desk in the foyer, looking like a clerk inventorying sacks of flour.

"She was on the train. Why else would she have written that she was coming today?"

"Well, it may be that she changed her mind. Agitators like her assume the rules do not apply to them."

I rolled my eyes. If only I hadn't told Mother about Marit's dedication to the rights movement! "I grant you that maybe *we* don't accept some of the rules, especially the ones men impose upon us." I emphasized the "we" just in case my mother had forgotten I too was one of "those" women. "But time, as far as I know, wasn't invented by men, so Marit will not flout it. Anyhow, she can't be punctual if her train was delayed."

I heard horse hooves clattering on pavement. August was steering the coach around the circular drive.

"There, see. She is here!"

"Perhaps Bruns should be the one to receive her?" Mother called out behind me.

"Marit is my friend," I replied. "Nobody will think less of me if I'm the first to greet her."

She was climbing the front steps as I emerged from the house. She carried a small carpetbag.

I was pleased to see she was wearing garments I'd given her. The close-fit white blouse and burgundy-colored skirt had never looked as good on me as they now did on her.

"Hello, darling!" I grabbed her in an embrace so enthusiastic that she lost the dark-red hat perched above her neatly knotted bun. "It's so lovely to be together again!"

Marit returned the hug warmly, then pulled back to inspect me. "It looks as if Countess Lejongård hasn't changed a jot."

"Are you so sure? I was thinking I must have some white hairs by now."

Marit peered at me. "No, not that I can see. You must disguise them very well."

"Like so many other things," I replied. "Come, I will introduce my mother to you!"

"I do hope I'm appropriately attired," Marit said with a twinkle as she stooped to recover her hat and then took my arm.

I'd expected Mother to retire to her quarters, but there she stood in the hall, observing us.

"Mother, this is Marit Andersson. Marit, may I introduce my mother, Stella Lejongård?"

Marit stepped forward, made a little curtsey, and extended her hand. "I am very pleased to meet you. Agneta has told me so much about you."

Mother glanced at me. "Well, then, I can imagine what she said. But I doubt that is the reason for your visit."

Marit was a bit taken aback. My descriptions of my mother hadn't prepared her for even half of the real thing.

"Let me show you to your room," I said. "And you must tell me everything I have missed since I left."

Marit and Mother nodded to one another, then I pulled my friend away from Cerberus, the mythic guard dog, before my mother could bare her fangs.

Miss Rosendahl had done a beautiful job setting up the guest room. Lit candles stood on a mantelpiece scattered with rose petals that filled the air with their perfume. The windows were just washed. The bed was made with sheets of cotton batiste and a patterned damask bedspread. A soft morning robe was laid out on the bed, and slippers decorated with intricate needlepoint were placed on the carpet. On the writing table by the window, a bouquet of sunflowers glowed in the muted light of early evening.

Lion Hall offered generous hospitality to every guest, regardless of rank.

"This is unbelievable!" Marit exclaimed when she saw the room. "You grew up here?"

"Not in this very room," I said. "This is one of the guest rooms."

"Do the others look like this?" Marit stepped into the center of the room and looked around.

"Yes, more or less, but we take special pains for our guests. The candles and slippers come out only for our most esteemed visitors."

Marit looked amused. "And I'm esteemed, is that it?"

"Who else, if not you!"

We hugged one another again, and she again looked me over. "You seem to have settled in quite well. Despite all the difficulties."

"I am doing my best. Every day it seems I have to defend myself against new and unwelcome surprises. I am getting used to it. And to battling with my mother."

"I see you weren't exaggerating when you described her."

Someone knocked.

"Come in!"

Marie appeared in the door with fresh hand towels. "Excuse me, please; I just wanted to ask if our guest is in need of anything."

"Thank you, Marie. I am sure Miss Andersson can rely on your help."

I saw Marit's look of dismay. "You'll have to get used to the constant presence of our staff. Marie will assist you in everything, and she will find you a dress appropriate for this evening's dinner."

"Appropriate?"

"We want to avoid setting Mother off when you turn up in the dining room costumed as a suffragette." I gave her a wave of farewell.

Marit appeared half an hour later in the dining room looking like a completely different person. The dress suited her marvelously, and Marie had put her hair in braids decorated with tiny flowers. She would have caught every eye if she'd appeared at the midsummer festival dressed like that. Marit wasn't entirely at ease in the outfit, but not even my mother would find anything to complain about.

Mother addressed her after the maids had served the first course. "You are from Stockholm, then." I tensed at once. Now what? "Were you studying at the university with my daughter?"

"No, unfortunately, I didn't have the money for that. I work at the Salvation Army and do some mending. Your daughter and I met through our mutual interest in women's rights."

Mother gave me an ever-so-subtle glance, then resumed her interrogation. "And do you have a husband?"

Marit choked on the soup and actually had to cough. She wiped her lips and apologized. "No, I have no husband. I'm making my own way through life."

"But would it not be easier if you were married?"

"Mother, I think Marit is the best judge of that. It is up to each woman to decide whether she wishes to marry."

"Well, possibly, in these modern times. Perhaps I have no understanding of the wider world."

I caught the hostile glint in Marit's eye. This was precisely the sort of discussion that drove her to flights of eloquence.

"The world is caught up in change," she said, clearly taking pains to remain polite. "One cannot say women are incapable of leading their own lives. Society erects one obstacle after another before them. Many women have known nothing other than family life because that is how they were brought up; others find themselves obliged by their circumstances to seek a husband. And then there are women like me, who want to venture through life on their own."

"And how long do you expect that will last for you?"

Shivers ran down my spine. The last thing I wanted was adversarial debate across the dinner table, but Stella Lejongård seemed to be doing her best to provoke exactly that. Would she have done so if my friend had come from "polite society"?

"For a very long time, I hope. Salvation Army pay is not good, and my seamstress work will never make me rich. But my income is my own, and I am independent. There is no need for me to put up with an unfaithful husband who beats me, as many women of my class must do."

"You therefore are of the opinion that men are, without exception, coarse and vulgar?"

"Mother!" I said in a warning voice. "Perhaps we should change the subject."

But my mother wouldn't hear of it.

"No, but I believe that almost all men have been raised badly from the very beginning," Marit riposted. "They are told from a tender age that women are worthless, that at best we should be relegated to having children and keeping house."

"Nature ordered it so!" my mother countered. "And so it has been for thousands of years!"

"Perhaps it is the will of nature. And indeed many women do have children and take care of them. Women do the housekeeping. And yet, they should be free to decide if that is what they truly want. Every woman has the right to have children and stay at home, if she finds that fulfilling. But a woman who seeks something else in life should be empowered to achieve her goal."

Mother examined Marit for a moment in thoughtful silence. She probably suspected she'd identified the inspiration for my Christmas harangue. "And what is it you want from your life? To spend it caring for the ill and the poor? Remaining forever ill and poor yourself?"

"I want rather to make my own decisions. I take joy in helping others and caring for the needy. Your social circles greatly appreciate charity and benevolence, don't they?"

"But we practice them from a different point of view. We share a portion of our wealth."

Marit snorted and for a moment appeared about to throw down her spoon and storm out of the room. "Do you really suppose I was forced to accept employment at the Salvation Army? I was not. I do it because I am convinced my contribution makes a difference. That is why women like your daughter and I take to the streets to demand our rights. And while we're discussing dreams: I dream of traveling to America someday. It won't be right away, and after what happened to the *Titanic* last year, I certainly don't intend to travel in steerage. But I will make it happen. On my own and without the blessing of a man."

A painful silence ensued. My mother's face relaxed into a smile. What did it mean? Whenever I made such declarations, she scowled, but Marit appeared to amuse her. Perhaps because she assumed my friend was doomed to failure.

"I don't believe we will be able to accommodate one another on that subject," Mother said at last. "But I do admire those who aim to conquer life on their own terms. Only time will tell whether they emerge victorious or defeated, but they can always pride themselves on having made the effort."

I stared at Mother. She admired those who followed their own star? Then why hadn't she ever shown it? Why had I been forced to endure so many frightful debates over my desire for independence?

Marit seemed equally astonished. She'd been preparing for a lengthy, bitter debate, but that now seemed unlikely.

My mother rang the little bell next to her place. Marie and Svea quickly appeared with the second course. Now that Susanna was gone, the kitchen maids had to assist in the serving. We needed to replace her—yet another task on my list.

After dinner I went out into the garden with Marit. The evening was mild, and the skies were clear. We strolled to the small pavilion still decorated with midsummer colors. Crickets chirped in the background.

The rest of dinner had gone off surprisingly well. My mother had made polite conversation, and we'd followed her lead. Afterward Mother had withdrawn to her suite.

Marit looked around. "It's breathtakingly beautiful here. You never told me about your garden."

"I didn't recall how beautiful it is. I noticed it again only when I stood here with Lennard after the funerals."

"Lennard?"

"A friend from my youth. I hadn't seen him in years. After the funeral, I couldn't bear to stay in the house, and I found him here when I came out. We recalled all the good times we had here as children. And just imagine: he proposed to me!"

"What? Why didn't you mention that in your letters?"

"Sorry—I suspect Lennard asked on a whim. His father is very ill."

"That can't have been the only reason."

"He thought we would both have an easier time if we walked the same road. Not exactly romantic! I value him as a friend, but love should be the basis of marriage."

Lost in my thoughts, I reached up to touch one of the streamers hanging from the pavilion roof. Should I ask her about Michael?

"You should have come earlier," I said as we mounted the steps and went under the shelter of the hexagonal roof. "Our midsummer fest was interesting."

"The way you described it, it doesn't seem to have been a very merry celebration."

"It was merry—until the girl I mentioned in my letter tried to steal Mother's brooch."

We seated ourselves on the bench in the pavilion.

"I'm very sorry I wasn't able to help sooner," she said. "It was difficult to find a doctor willing to deliver her baby and say nothing."

"What about Dr. Strondheim?"

"He passed away unexpectedly a couple of weeks ago."

I stopped. "What? But he was only sixty!" The man's kindly face rose before my eyes, clear and vivid. Even though he was quite old-fashioned, he'd always stood ready to provide his services to women in trouble and never breathe a word.

"His heart," Marit said. "We were all deeply shocked. From one moment to the next, we had no one to help us. It was difficult to find someone, even among the younger physicians, who wasn't a slave to convention. And in this case, we also needed to find a man willing to enter into a marriage of convenience."

"And did you?"

"Yes, a bookkeeper named Sigurd Wallin, arrested a few weeks ago because he'd been accused of sodomy. They claim he made an indecent proposal to a man at the railway station. Elsa found him for us. He's ready to marry Susanna as a way of protecting his elderly parents from scandal."

"Marriage according to our conditions?"

"He'll require nothing from her, other than to keep the house clean and smile sweetly whenever his parents visit. I assume the girl is pretty?"

"What does that matter?"

"A pretty girl has a better chance of being accepted by the in-laws—especially when she's already survived other circumstances."

"And who can we get to take care of the delivery?"

"This will please you: a woman. She received her medical degree just a couple of weeks ago, and you can imagine how all Stockholm is abuzz. But that simply makes her more determined to help us. Let's hope she's been blessed with a strong heart."

"Yes, let us hope so. Thanks for investing so much effort in this. I was worried something had happened to you."

"Well, strictly speaking, something did." Marit met my eyes. "I was very ill. The doctor suspected it was some sort of influenza that has been making the rounds."

I stared at her in alarm. "And you did not write? I would have—"

Marit shook her head. "You couldn't have done anything. And besides, I was far too weak to lift a pen. All I wanted was just to stay alive, and somehow I managed. Many have been ill recently, and you were fortunate not to be there."

"Even so, you must write to me if anything like that happens!"

"And give you even more worries? You have more than enough to deal with. And as you can see, your friend has emerged from the valley of the shadow. Elsa and the others took care of me, and I promise I won't let the grim reaper get that close to me ever again."

I couldn't bear the thought that Marit could have died. I wouldn't have survived losing her so soon after my brother's death. I hugged her.

"Have you heard anything about Michael?" I suddenly heard myself asking. Even saying his name aloud felt like tearing my heart in two. "And thank you, by the way, for not mentioning him to my mother."

"After that discussion about women and marriage? I had no desire to throw myself into hell's fiery furnace!" She was quiet for a moment, then she reached for my hand in a way that made me fear what she was about to say. "They announced his engagement a few days ago. I saw it in the paper."

An engagement. He'd found someone else already, a woman he considered worthy of becoming his wife. I shut my eyes.

"Do you want to know her name?" Marit's voice was cautious.

"No."

Marit nodded and looked toward the house. "I know you loved him. But from my point of view, you made the right decision, everything considered. You're independent and you're powerful. You had to give up Stockholm, but now you can live your life exactly as you choose."

"Well, if it were up to my mother, I would be standing before the altar tomorrow morning."

"You need a man for that. A strong man, one who won't fence you in. You need someone who will stand by you. Michael wasn't right for that. He would have never lasted out here. Or something else would have broken up the relationship. Who knows?"

"Yes," I said and pulled her a bit closer. "Who knows?"

I would've contradicted anyone else but not Marit. She was right. Michael would have been miserable here. And considering how quickly he'd found comfort elsewhere, he probably would have been unfaithful.

Furthermore, I couldn't shed my own skin. I knew that now. No one on earth could magically transform Countess Lejongård into the dutiful wife of an attorney. The countess was condemned to make her way alone.

"Putting aside your childhood friend, is there no one who interests you?"

I shook my head. "Nobody is looking for a woman like me."

"And how about your own needs? I certainly prefer to live without a husband, but I'm not you! Is there no one you could halfway tolerate? No man who touches your heart?"

I was about to deny it, but suddenly I saw a face. Brilliant blue eyes, a confident smile, distinctive features . . . Max! We got along famously, and I'd often thought he really understood me. But to be honest, I still felt too bruised to open myself to someone new. Max was an aristocrat, but he was also my employee.

"There is one person who might be able to touch my heart. But I have no idea of his sentiments. I am not ready to enter into something unpromising. My heart still aches—a little more now, to learn I was so quickly replaced."

"But when you see an opportunity, you'll take it, won't you?" Marit was very serious. "Don't allow your responsibilities to keep you from your happiness."

"I will not. But I need time. And when there is someone in my life, you will be the first to know."

Marit smiled and tightened her grip on my hand.

We sat that way for a long time, but at last we went back to the manor house. We had no idea what lay ahead, but the next day was bound to be stressful.

33

My friend was afraid of horses and didn't know how to ride, so we took the old landau carriage the next morning. I was at the reins. Traveling this way, we couldn't cut across fields or meadows and had to walk the last stretch to Susanna's hut.

Marit huffed and puffed as we made our way through the high grass. "I absolutely cannot understand how you can live out here in this wilderness."

"If you'd been willing to mount a horse, we'd be there already," I replied, feeling yet again what a pleasure it was to lark about in nature.

"No country girl I, nor ever will be," she said. "But I'm eager to meet the young woman."

"And I'll be forever thankful for that. I hope everything will work out. After all, I'm the baby's aunt."

Marit stopped and stared at me.

"Susanna is carrying Hendrik's child."

Marit almost gagged. "The usual affair between master and maid?"

"Marit!" I knew all too well her attitude toward employers who lured their servants into bed with false promises.

"You're saying this was different? You know I love you, but now I have to admit my opinion of the rest of your family has changed very little."

"Except now I have the position of authority Hendrik would've had."

"I know that, and believe me, I'm glad. Otherwise this poor woman would wind up in the gutter."

"You cannot know that, and I cannot judge their relationship. But I do know one thing: Hendrik would never have been so callous as to abandon Susanna and their child. She thinks he was going to marry her. He just didn't have the opportunity."

Marit's lips tightened. I saw she was holding back her opinion out of consideration for me. "Are we almost there?"

"Yes. Look there, ahead. It's not far." I pointed to the little hut mostly hidden by high grass from our vantage point.

"What a hovel!"

"I would have gladly taken her in, but after the attempted theft, I couldn't allow her back into the house."

"Does your mother know it's your brother's child?"

"Yes," I replied. "I told her, but she hasn't said a word about it since."

"Why didn't the girl say something earlier?"

I outlined what I'd learned about Langeholm. "She wanted to protect Hendrik's reputation—to the point of sacrificing herself! I can scarcely imagine going so far myself. She must have loved him immensely."

When we reached the hut, we found the door wide open. Susanna was nowhere to be seen. Was she out scrounging for something to eat? Had Ida moved her elsewhere?

All my senses were on alert. "Let's look around." I turned toward the lake. "Maybe we can find her."

We struggled through the tall grass and came across a narrow path. We followed it to the lakeshore.

"I learned to swim in this lake," I told Marit. "My brother and I often came here when we were small. We built a raft from old logs and rowed it out there once. It sank beneath us. Fortunately, we already knew how to swim, but we had quite a fright."

"I wish I'd had a lake nearby when I was a child. I've spent my entire life in Stockholm."

"The Baltic was your own private lake."

"Yes, but it was no place to learn to swim."

"Come spend the summer here, and I'll teach you. Right here!"

I stopped short at the sight of a figure on the jetty. Her blonde hair moved with the wind, and she held her arms spread wide, as if ready to take flight. I recognized her immediately.

"Wait here!" I told Marit.

I cautiously approached the jetty. Was Susanna about to throw herself into the water?

"Hello? Susanna!"

She dropped her arms and spun around in alarm.

"Gracious miss," she said, bewildered. "I—what are you doing here?"

"You asked me that a couple of days ago. And my answer is the same: I came for your sake." I gestured toward Marit. "This is Marit Andersson, the friend I mentioned. She has come to help you. Perhaps we could continue this conversation in your habitation?"

Susanna glanced at Marit and then followed me back to the shore.

My friend extended her hand. "I'm Marit. May I call you Susanna?"

Susanna nodded.

"Lovely!" Marit said in that winning manner of hers. "We've found a way to help you. I can take you to Stockholm right away, if you like."

"To Stockholm?" Astonished, Susanna looked back and forth from me to Marit.

"Yes, Stockholm!" I said. "You can accept or not; it is entirely up to you."

Susanna nodded apprehensively but led us to her shelter.

We sat around the rickety table. Marit explained the plan and showed her a photograph of Sigurd Wallin. I must admit I found him handsome. If his character was as good as his looks, he would certainly keep his word.

Susanna's expression was skeptical as she heard us out. Marit explained she would lodge Susanna with a suffragette friend for several weeks. She'd introduce her to the physician and to her future husband.

"Dr. Strömstad will provide care and attend the birth. Sigurd will acknowledge the child and thereby give you a respectable place in society."

"And this Sigurd—what if he doesn't treat me the way he should?" She looked to me for assurance. Unfortunately, I had no reply to that.

"He will," Marit interjected. "We will make sure of that. You have nothing to fear."

"And what about my family? My parents? Will I see them again?"

I thought of the furious Mrs. Korven. Susanna's eyes glistened with tears.

"You will be able to visit at any time," Marit reassured her. "If they desire it and you do as well. Or you can choose not to give them your new address. You need be in no hurry to decide."

"In any case, no one will accuse you or gossip about you," I spoke up. "They will leave you in peace, and you will be the respectable wife of a bookkeeper."

Susanna didn't seem particularly pleased at the prospect.

"Think it over. It is no easy thing to take such a drastic step, but you can imagine the alternative."

Susanna said nothing. I silently prayed she wouldn't turn down the offer.

She sat for a long time, staring down at the table. Then she looked up at me. "What do you think?" she asked. "This is your brother's baby. Is your family not going to claim the child?"

I looked at Marit. I hadn't expected that question. "That depends on you. Will you want to tell your child the name of the real father? Or will you let your husband be seen as the father? It is up to you."

Susanna nodded.

Marit responded, "I take it, then, that you agree to the marriage?"

"I do," Susanna replied. "I don't really have any other choice, do I?"

"None that will keep you and the child safe from harm." Marit placed her hand on Susanna's arm. "You will like life in the city. No one knows you there, and you can start over. You can have a good life, a better one than if you stayed here alone with your baby at the mercy of the villagers."

We didn't say a word on the way back to the carriage. Marit had assured Susanna we would pick her up early in the morning on our way to Kristianstad. She would prepare in the meantime and visit her parents if she wanted to.

"She'll do fine," Marit said, taking my arm as we walked. "This was the right thing to do."

"Yes," I responded. "And I'm glad. Even if—"

"If what?"

"This is Hendrik's child as well. My nephew or niece. I will never get to see the child or know what happens."

"Oh, as far as that goes, I'll be happy to keep you informed. I doubt Susanna will object, after all you've done."

I snorted. "All I did was throw her out!"

"And you made sure, through me, that she'll have a good life. Not every employer would have done that."

I nodded but was far from satisfied. I would have preferred to handle the matter differently, even though I knew society wouldn't tolerate brazen honesty.

"How long will it be before a woman is permitted to bring up her child alone?" I mused.

"Or allowed to seek an honorable partner to help her raise the child, which I know many would prefer. Unfortunately, the Church recognizes only those children born to married couples, and society will follow its dictates for a long time yet."

"But it seems to me the Church is committing a terrible sin when it makes people exclude women and children. Don't you disagree? You know as well as I that most of those poor women must eventually turn to prostitution. And many of their children never escape that underworld."

"I know, and that's part of the reason for our struggle. But it's a goal that may take a hundred years to reach. Or more."

We returned to the carriage, and I turned the horses toward home. Clouds raced across the sky and threatened to hide the sun. A strange light fell across the fields. Was it about to rain? We needed to get back to the manor.

We said nothing on the return trip, each sunk in private thoughts.

As we rolled up the drive, we caught sight of Max on his way back from the fields. He wore tall boots, and a folder was tucked under his arm. The farm overseer accompanied him. I was surprised to see them in lively conversation. Torge Breken, the farm manager, was rarely that forthcoming with anyone.

"Now there's an attractive man," Marit commented, tilting her head.

"Max von Bredestein, our new estate manager. My father found him not long before his death."

Now she was watching me with an inquisitive expression. "So tell me, what's he like?"

"Quite amiable, though he prefers to be alone most of the time. He is estranged from his father. And he likes to study the stars."

"Have you been stargazing with him?"

"Only once, when I was trying to persuade him to join our midsummer festivities. There weren't many stars out that evening. I didn't succeed in convincing him either. Nothing would persuade him."

"You should try again." She gave me a meaningful look. "Stars are rumored to have a very strong influence."

"Just listen to the woman who swore never to marry!" I teased her.

"Really, I might not be so adamant as you think. A person just back from death's door starts to see things differently."

My eyebrows rose. "Do you have someone in mind?"

"No."

I had a sense she wasn't being entirely truthful.

"And I'll always fight for women's rights, whether I find a husband or not. He'd have to accept that—applaud it—in order for me to care for him."

Max saw us and strode over. "Good morning, Countess Lejongård!" he exclaimed. "Who is the lovely lady at your side?"

I'd never seen Marit blush before this.

"This is my friend Marit Andersson. Marit, Max von Bredestein, my manager."

Max kissed her hand. "Very pleased to meet you."

I was surprised to feel a momentary twinge of jealousy. *Don't be ridiculous,* I told myself.

"Are you enjoying your time here at Lion Hall?"

"Yes, very much," she said. "But I wouldn't want to live here. I'm a child of the city."

"Which city?"

"Stockholm."

"Stockholm is beautiful," he said. "Although it has its dark side. You must be careful."

"I always am."

"Then I am reassured." Max turned to me again. "Mr. Breken and I have just inspected the fields. The wheat crop is doing very well."

"I am glad to hear it. Were you aware Mr. Breken always has a little nip with his companions after an expedition to the fields?"

Max laughed. "So he said. When I reminded him it is unseemly to drink during working hours, he explained the tradition."

"It is indeed a tradition and therefore tolerated. My great-great-grandfather introduced the practice, in the belief it kept bad weather away from the crops."

"And did it?"

"Sometimes, perhaps."

Max laughed again, and our eyes met. I felt a rush of warmth. My distress at the news of Michael's engagement had passed, and in fact I now felt relieved of a heavy burden. For the first time in a long while, I was experiencing physical longing for a man.

I was thankful no one could read my thoughts. Personal involvement with an employee was dangerous.

"Enjoy yourself," I added. "And hold on tight. Breken's home brew is said to be strong indeed."

"I believe I will survive. If not—if my legs fail me—you will find me at Torge's lodging." He turned to Marit. "Take care of yourself, Miss Andersson."

He kissed her hand again and left. She stood there for a moment, as if she'd just seen an apparition. She watched him until he was out of sight. It seemed that even my committed suffragette got weak in the knees when she came face-to-face with such a handsome man.

"You're infatuated," Marit declared as soon as he was gone.

"Me? You're raving!"

"You are! Your conversation is so free and easy—you sound like a couple who've known one another forever."

"I hired him three months ago. You can hardly call that an eternity."

"But it's more than enough time to lose your heart. That takes only a moment." Marit took my hand. "Forget Michael. Despite what you thought, he was never the one for you. I'm convinced you'll find true love."

I looked in the direction where Max had vanished. I saw him clearly in my mind.

Was I really falling in love? Everything had been so clear with Michael; now it was all confused.

Perhaps in these matters my friend's eyes were better than mine.

34

A light morning mist hovered over the fields. The sun would soon drive it away and herald a glorious day. Marit was still asleep, and even the servants weren't up yet.

I washed, quickly donned my dress, and left the manor. It had been some time since I last visited the family vault, and before we took Susanna to Stockholm, I wanted to tell Hendrik his child was in good hands.

As I walked, I tried to imagine how he might have responded to that news. And what he'd have done about it. I refused to see him as a sordid seducer. Perhaps he really had intended to wed Susanna. That would have caused a scandal, and Father certainly would have threatened to disinherit him. But things would have calmed down eventually. And even if polite society was bound to turn up its collective nose at her, Susanna might have become Countess Lejongård. Their triumph of love now would never be realized.

The grass along the path to the cemetery was wet with dewdrops that sparkled like diamonds. I passed the graves of two elderly villagers who'd died a few weeks earlier. We'd heard the tolling of the bells. I'd called on the families to express my condolences, as was expected of the head of the estate. The flowers on their graves were withered now.

Our mausoleum dominated the cemetery. The gate to the crypt squealed in quiet protest as I unlocked it and pushed it open. I went to the niche inside where my brother had been laid. Stone tiles bearing his name and that of my father had been cemented in place after the funeral. The rose engraved above Hendrik's name was based on a sketch I'd made. I placed my palm against the tile and tried to sense the presence of my brother. I couldn't, of course.

"I . . ." My strangled voice echoed in the chamber. "I wish you had told me."

I didn't mention her name, as if somehow it was still necessary to keep the secret from Father.

"I believe I would have understood." I paused and then added, "You must have worried about her. Maybe she meant nothing to you? I cannot believe that. Your heart was pure. Your child will grow up in Stockholm and will probably never know your name or the truth about our family history."

Tears filled my eyes, and it was some time before I could speak. My heart fluttered. For a moment, I felt again all the anguish of Hendrik's death.

I took a deep breath and straightened up. Even if Susanna's baby would never be recognized as a real Lejongård, something of my brother lived on in that child. Perhaps I might be able to keep track of my nephew or niece as the years went by.

"Farewell, Hendrik," I said at last and ran my finger along the contours of the engraved rose. I turned and left the mausoleum.

Birdsong rang out from the trees around the cemetery and wrapped me in its celebration. I paused for a moment, enchanted, my eyes closed as I gave myself to the music. It was like stepping into a fairy tale in which the feathered kingdom was either welcoming me or sounding the alarm about an intruder. But when I opened my eyes, I was still in the village cemetery, the mausoleum at my back. I left that sanctified ground and meandered across the fields.

The cemetery was far behind and I was approaching the meadows of our estate when a figure appeared. As he came nearer, I recognized him. What was Max doing here? Was he on his way to the village? Perhaps to post a letter?

He stopped and took me in. "Good morning, Agneta."

He hadn't forgotten our pact to use first names when no one else was present.

"Good morning, Max," I replied. As I met his eyes, I again felt that warmth rising in my breast. If only I could have peered into his innermost self to know what he was thinking!

"What are you seeking so early in the morning?" he asked at last. "I do not recall seeing you about at this hour."

"I needed to visit my brother," I told him.

Max nodded.

"And you?" I asked. "Do you always wander through the meadows in early morning?"

"Actually, I do," he said. "It gives me the strength to face the day."

"Really?" I gave him an amused smile. "Are you about to offer me your arm again?" That frequent gesture of his had made many a gray day more tolerable.

"Not unless you wish," he replied and approached. "I enjoy taking long walks. I get to know the area. And it's agreeable to be awake while so many others are still sleeping."

"The farmers and villagers surely must be stirring by now."

"But out here, we see only foxes and rabbits." He looked at me for a moment. "Here's an idea: How about taking strolls together from time to time? You could tell me a story or two. Something about trolls and elves, for example."

"I thought you were looking for quiet before you had to put up with my questions and instructions!"

He reached out and took my hand in his. Its warmth spread through me. My heart pounded, and my body became weightless. I felt like I might dissolve into pure sunlight.

"You're no burden to me, Agneta, either as Countess Lejongård or as yourself. I could spend hours, even days, with you, whether in the woods or in some shady grotto. And it would make me very happy to have you accompany me in the morning. That would be an ideal start to the day."

We stood looking at one another. I racked my brain for a reply worthy of his candor, and I felt myself swaying toward him. How easy it would be to kiss him. Or to accept his kiss.

But he pulled back slightly. "Perhaps you might find my company unwelcome."

I looked at him, confused, then shook my head. "Oh! Not by any means! And I—I would be very happy to walk with you."

He released his breath in a little puff of relief and smiled. "Really?"

"Yes. Really. If you like, we can start right now."

"Gladly. But you were on the way to the manor. Do you have time for a stroll?"

"A short one," I answered and pulled him after me into the meadow. "I imagine this path is new to you. With some luck, we will see trolls."

"In all seriousness?"

"My brother and I were almost certain of it when we were children. Perhaps our hearts are still innocent enough to catch a glimpse of them."

We followed the narrow path for a while, me leading and him behind, until we reached a gathering of tall spruce trees. I sensed his eyes upon me and felt the heat of his body. I had to keep myself in strict control not to burst into giggles like some silly schoolgirl. It was lovely to find a man interested in me. I was aware I was falling for Max. I didn't know if it was love, but perhaps I'd soon get the opportunity to find out.

I returned to the manor an hour later. Max had taken his leave a few minutes before to return to his cottage. I felt lightheaded and elated, almost as if the dark days had never happened. But as soon as I got back into the house, the weight of responsibility fell upon my shoulders again.

Susanna. Langeholm. My mother. Lion Hall. Would I ever again feel unburdened?

Marit and I got into the landau after breakfast.

"Shouldn't I drive ye?" August asked.

I didn't want the staff to know we were picking Susanna up. I could swear August to silence, but it would be better if he knew nothing at all. Sooner or later, our errand boy would hear that Susanna had disappeared, and I wanted no one to know how. I was particularly worried about Langeholm, but the villagers were a concern as well. It was vital that no one be in a position to harm her as she started a new life.

"No, August. That is not necessary. I would like to practice driving the team. My father was a very accomplished driver."

"Aye, that is certainly true," the coachman said. "But do take care. Yer gracious lady mother will tear me to pieces if anything should happen to ye."

"I am a responsible adult, August!" I protested.

Once Marit had her carpetbag safely stowed aboard, I cracked the whip over the horses' heads.

We took a little byway to the lake so as to escape the eyes of the villagers. Susanna was waiting for us at the roadside. She wore a coarse knitted jacket, despite the heat. She'd woven her hair into a neat braid. The circles under her eyes were still dark, but the prospect of traveling to Stockholm had invigorated her. We helped her into the carriage, and I took her bag.

"Do you have anything else?" I asked.

She shook her head in reply. "This is everything I own. I'm sure my parents would not give me anything else."

"Have you spoken with them?"

She shook her head again. "No. I will write them a letter after I get there."

I glanced at Marit, who nodded to signal she'd take care of everything.

I climbed back onto the driver's seat.

The trip was uneventful, for the ground was dry and the warm sun shone upon us.

I pulled up at the Kristianstad train station and set the brake. Passersby gave us curious looks. After all, a carriage with three women, one of them in the driver's seat, was an unusual sight.

We helped Susanna down, and I embraced Marit. "Next time you are ill, you must tell me," I admonished her. "I will send you the best doctors in the land. And you can come here to recuperate anytime you like."

"Thanks. That's lovely of you," she replied. "But I have my work cut out for me now." She glanced at Susanna, who stood next to us, eyes wide.

I reached out to embrace Susanna, but she pulled back. "But gracious miss, I—"

"You are no longer my employee," I replied. "You are a free woman, and soon you will be a bookkeeper's wife." I smiled to encourage her. She nodded and allowed me to hug her. "Take care of yourself and the child. I wish both of you the greatest happiness!"

Marit picked up her own bag and Susanna's. The two stopped just outside the entrance to the station and looked back. I waved and climbed up into the landau.

My mother came to see me not long after my return to Lion Hall. I was surprised to see she was upset.

She plucked at the ruffled sleeves of her dress. "Was the train on time?"

"Yes, everything went smoothly."

Stella nodded. "Quite a shame your friend had to leave. She rather pleased me. In truth, she is not a woman with whom you should often associate, but she is both strong and strong-willed, a person who chooses her own path and relies on no one. If she manages to find the right husband, she may rise quite high in society. She has the character for it."

"She might rise in society without a man's help at all," I riposted, but Mother's positive evaluation pleased me. The little dispute with Marit over dinner had turned out well after all. "And Marit took Susanna with her. That was the main reason for her visit."

Mother's expression stiffened.

"Mother, please try to understand!" I said. "This is about the child, Hendrik's child. I know we have only Susanna's word that he is the father, and perhaps you still consider her a thief. But you should have seen her when we spoke of Hendrik. She loved him deeply."

My mother had nothing to say to that, but I saw her take that information on board.

"She will marry a bookkeeper and have her child in the care of a capable physician. The man will declare the child to be his own, so you need not be concerned they will make any claim upon us."

"And what about our own claim?" she asked. "If Hendrik was in fact the father, then the child is a Lejongård."

"The child may have Lejongård blood, but a bookkeeper will be the father," I replied. "There is no other way to proceed if we are determined to avoid scandal."

Deep lines appeared on her brow. "And what if this child is the only offspring of our family?"

"We will find a way to deal with that eventuality. If necessary, I will decide what is required."

We regarded one another for a moment. Mother nodded at last. "You are right. This is for the best. I will not disturb you any further."

She retired. I somehow had the feeling she had more on her mind.

35

Three weeks passed. Late summer came to the countryside, and the crown princess's visit was imminent. Knowing Count Bergen was impatient for progress, I'd let him know the police had identified a suspect. I would much have preferred to inform him the culprit had been arrested, but I hadn't heard further from Inspector Hermannsson. Whether Langeholm had any connection with the arson or not, at least he could no longer coerce Susanna. He wouldn't dare ask the Korvens for her address. I was monitoring the man very closely. He did nothing to arouse suspicion, although late one evening, I saw him leaving the stables in a foul temper. Was he going out to look for Susanna? Or was he just on his way to the tavern?

A few days later, I was absorbed in drafting a letter to our feed supplier. We'd traditionally fed our horses from our own farm's production, but Max had suggested a special variety of oats for the pregnant mares.

Hurried footsteps interrupted my concentration. Someone knocked at the door.

"Come in!"

"Gracious miss, come quickly!" Lena called in alarm. Her face was flushed. "These police gentlemen want to arrest Mr. Langeholm!"

Her words shot through me like tongues of fire. Had Hermannsson found evidence against him?

"I'm coming!" I dropped my pen on the desk and rushed past Lena.

When I emerged from the manor, I found two uniformed policemen struggling with the stable master, who was doing his best to break free. The stable boys were huddled together outside the horse barn.

"Gracious miss!" Langeholm cried out as soon as he saw me. "This is a terrible mistake. Tell them I've done nothing."

I pursed my lips. The men dragged him down the drive toward a bulky prison wagon.

"I'm innocent!" Langeholm roared, but the policemen paid him no attention. Nor did I. I could hardly believe that just a few weeks earlier I'd placed myself in the coach next to this man and ridden off to see a suspect.

"Countess Lejongård," I heard Hermannsson say next to me. I turned and saw his grave expression.

"Inspector Hermannsson. It appears the contents of my letter were relevant to your inquiry."

"They certainly were, and I thank you sincerely. Perhaps we could take a walk around the premises? I am afraid this affair is more complicated than you may know."

I stared at him. What did he mean? I wrapped my arms about my waist to hide the fact that I was shaking with emotion.

We walked in the direction of the English garden. Mother seemed to have forgotten to supervise the gardener, for wild clover had spread across the lawn separating it from the mansion.

"Thanks to your letter, we took a closer look at Sören Langeholm. And we found that he had gambling debts at an establishment in Stockholm. We also paid a call upon his former paramour, Juna Holm, who is living in a house on the outskirts of Kristianstad."

"And what did you find?"

"The young woman claimed Langeholm had purchased the house for her—for the price of a thousand crowns!"

"A thousand crowns? That is significantly more than he earns from us in a year," I said, drawing on my newly acquired knowledge of employee salaries.

"We assumed as much. And we found other incongruities. The gambling house had until recently listed him as owing them four thousand crowns."

"Four thousand!" I couldn't help exclaiming. That was a fortune!

"He was so far indebted that the owner of the gaming house threatened him with violence if he failed to pay. Mr. Langeholm settled his debt in February, some three weeks before your barn burned down."

"The loan to my father was made in February."

"Exactly as we thought. We contacted the lender, who had no idea why your father took out the loan. But the amount of five thousand crowns corresponds quite well to the concerns of our investigation."

"But why did Langeholm press Susanna to steal an expensive brooch? He could have just as easily blackmailed my mother."

"Well, perhaps he found it easier simply to threaten the maid. Your mother was far more likely to turn to us."

"Then why didn't my father? He was on good terms with you, I believe?"

"Yes. But it seems Langeholm may have had some other hold over him."

"Something else?" I gazed over Hermannsson's shoulder at the manor. It seemed that whatever had gone on within its walls during my absence was far worse than the alleged immoralities I'd encountered in Stockholm.

"We asked the young woman, Juna, and put some pressure on her. She was reluctant to get involved but finally admitted that once, in anger, Langeholm told her he'd like to burn down the place and that haughty Count Lejongård with it."

My jaw dropped in horror. The inspector paused and looked away before continuing.

"The proof of blackmail and the threat expressed to Miss Holm led us to conclude that we should arrest Mr. Langeholm."

I sank slowly onto a moss-covered marble bench. One of the carved angels seemed to be weeping green tears. "So he was the one who set the fire?"

"Remember, please, that we need incontrovertible proof. Still, imagine the scenario: Langeholm's salary wasn't sufficient for his needs. Most likely because he'd fallen in love with Juna and was planning a future with her. Maybe he wanted to impress the girl. He thought he could get rich by gambling, but instead he incurred debts and found himself in great difficulty. The owner of the gaming house demanded payment."

I frowned. "And then Juna was discharged when the relationship between her and Langeholm became known."

Hermannsson nodded. "He was beside himself with rage, and he threatened his employer in the presence of Miss Holm. We can assume that, meanwhile, the gambling thugs had discovered where he was living. Langeholm saw his employer's son with Miss Korven and had an idea. He blackmailed your father for the amount of the gambling debts, plus more he could use to provide for his lover. Your father paid up."

My mother lay stretched out on her bed, her hands primly folded across her stomach, her eyes covered with her mauve-colored sleep mask to block the light. At first glance she looked like a corpse, but I saw her breast rise and fall.

"Mother, I must speak with you," I said. From my earliest childhood, I'd known that Mother snored as loudly as Father. When she didn't, that meant she was using the mask to shut out things she didn't want to see.

"I am taking my midday nap," she replied. "Can it wait?"

"Inspector Hermannsson has just arrested Langeholm."

Stella pulled off the mask and sat up. "On what grounds?" she cried, clearly astonished.

"I wrote to inform Hermannsson of the matter concerning Susanna. And I told him about Father's unusual loan. They investigated, and he—"

"You told the inspector about your father's debt? How dare you!"

"I had my suspicions, Mother!" I said. "As soon as I found the loan contract, I wanted to know if Father had some secret purpose for the funds. If he had taken that much from estate funds, Hendrik would have noticed."

Mother flinched at the mention of her son's name. She still blamed Susanna, of course, but I hoped she'd begun to see her son wasn't as innocent as she'd thought.

"Even so," she hissed, "you cannot simply run off to tattle to the police about it. What if Kristianstad society should hear of this?"

"They will not."

"Oh but they will!" she insisted. "If not immediately, then certainly when the newspapers report this case."

"And what should I have done? Stood by in silence and let an arsonist go free?"

"What does the fire have to do with Langeholm?"

I sighed. "Let me finish telling you, Mother. May I?"

Stella pressed her lips into a thin, bloodless line, but she let me go on.

"Hermannsson spoke with Juna, the maid you threw out because of her affair with Langeholm. It turns out he bought a house worth a thousand crowns for her, just like that! And there's more: Langeholm had four thousand crowns in gambling debts. The police conclude Langeholm discovered Susanna and Hendrik, and he used that knowledge to blackmail Father."

"Your father would never have yielded to such a demand."

"No? I believe he did in order to protect his son. But then Langeholm threatened Father again. I am sure Father refused, for he had paid more than enough. No one knows for sure yet, but it is probable that Langeholm set fire to the barn to punish Father. Juna heard him threatening to do just that."

"These shameless girls are perfectly capable of lying!" Mother shot back.

"Why would she lie? Langeholm gave her a beautiful house, a residence far beyond the means of any serving girl."

"But if she was so indebted to him, why did she say anything at all?"

"Because she was afraid of the police!" I realized I'd shifted into an aggressive stance. I took a deep breath and lowered my shoulders. "Hermannsson's people are searching Langeholm's quarters. And they will go through the house where Juna lives. We can assume that they have correctly identified the arsonist, who turns out to be our own stable master."

I watched Mother, expecting a reaction, any reaction. But there was none. I knew she'd always thought highly of Langeholm. But the evidence could not be denied.

Her voice, when it came, was lifeless. "That means your father brought this misfortune upon us."

"That is one way of looking at it."

Or, if you wanted, you could say Hendrik brought it upon us. His liaison with Susanna had given Langeholm the perfect opportunity for blackmail.

"You may be interested to hear," I said, "that the only reason Susanna tried to steal your brooch was because Langeholm forced her. But fortunately we are no longer menaced, so the crown princess has no need to feel threatened. I will inform Count Bergen."

Mother nodded, reclined, and covered her eyes with the sleep mask. I'd expected a much stronger reaction, but it seemed she needed time to absorb all this. I felt overwhelming relief knowing we'd finally gotten to the end of it.

36

That evening, I set out for Max's cottage. He'd witnessed the arrest, as had everyone else, but we hadn't had the opportunity to discuss it. Now there was indeed something to discuss, and I was in a mood to celebrate. I'd taken the bottle of aquavit out of Father's globe.

I gazed up at the stars as I walked along the meadow. Marit's comment echoed in my mind, and the memory of the near kiss made me blush. Might there be some possibility of a relationship between us?

Max was sitting on the porch. The flickering flame of a solitary candle reflected in his little wire-rimmed glasses. He reminded me of a student cramming for an exam.

"Good evening, Max," I called, startling him.

"Agneta!"

"Are you reading something spellbinding?"

He held up the book. August Strindberg. The sight of that name made me shudder, for it reminded me of the Christmas confrontation with Oglund. That argument seemed from another century, as did my life in Stockholm.

"You are aware, I assume, that Strindberg abhors women." I stepped up onto the porch. "I hope you do not plan to endorse his views."

"To tell the truth, I find him difficult to read. But I have nothing else here."

"You can borrow books from the manor house. I fear Father's library is not terribly current, but nonetheless it contains a number of interesting books. Strange as it may seem, my father had a weakness for detective stories."

"Well, then! I will be happy to take a look. But what brings you here?" He pointed to the bottle in my hand. "Did you come to drown the turmoil of this afternoon?"

"I wanted to celebrate with you the fact that our ordeal is at an end. You have certainly heard that the police believe they've caught the arsonist."

Max nodded. "I have, and to be honest, it took me entirely by surprise. There was never any clue Mr. Langeholm wanted to harm your family."

"No direct proof, but there certainly is evidence. Do you remember Susanna?"

"The maid who had to leave?"

"Yes. He obliged her to steal. Luckily, nothing came of it."

I was tempted to tell him more about Susanna but decided against it. Marit had written that they'd arrived safely, and Susanna was slowly becoming accustomed to the city.

"Have a seat," Max said and indicated the chair next to his. "I will fetch cups for our libations." He rose and vanished into the cottage.

Over the past three weeks, we'd met from time to time for early morning walks. Every time I thought Max was about to loosen up and use the terms close friends fall into, he pulled back, as if warned off by my noble title.

He soon came back with two ceramic cups and placed one before me.

"I should ask Mrs. Bloomquist to provide you with some glasses," I commented.

"No need," he said. "These cups are perfectly adequate. And besides, they have a sentimental value for me."

"Sentimental?" I echoed in surprise. "Unless my memory is mistaken, these were sent here from the manor a long time ago because there weren't enough of them for a full dinner service."

"But you drank from one of them," he said with a teasing smile. "So I can always imagine that your lips touched the rim."

My cheeks flushed, and I suppressed a giggle. "But only if you happen to pick up the one from which I drank." I held one up. "They all look alike!"

"Indeed, and that is why I intend to offer you one each time you visit. Eventually, you will have used every one."

I uncorked the bottle with a grin. "This is from the globe in the office," I told him as I poured.

Max was intrigued. "A bar inside a globe?"

"Have you never seen such a thing? Every self-respecting mansion has a globe with a liquor cabinet concealed inside. Or at least that used to be the custom."

"My father had nothing like that. He hid his schnapps in his room, where only he and his valet could touch it."

I regarded him. He said that in such a free and easy fashion! My father had been the same; never in his life had he allowed anyone other than Bruns and my mother into his bedroom. He couldn't have kept them out, even if he'd wanted to.

Max knew what it was like to grow up in a manor house. Unlike Michael, he knew what it was to be a member of a titled family and how difficult it was to liberate oneself.

"Shouldn't we speak more familiarly with one another?" I asked as I raised my glass.

"Would that be wise?" he replied. "The servants would talk."

"Not if we do it when we're sitting together alone."

"Only when we're sitting?"

"No, I just mean . . ." I paused and blushed, catching his entendre. I waved it away, embarrassed. "In my opinion, there is no reason to speak formally. We are of the same social class, after all."

"But your family is closely allied with the Swedish royal family. Mine is of the rural aristocracy."

"As are we." His reluctance made me nervous. Had I gone too far? Perhaps our easy conversations on our morning walks had meant nothing at all. "But if you prefer otherwise, we can leave things as they were." I looked down. Disappointment gnawed at me. I'd thought he had some feeling for me. Had I been wrong?

"I do prefer otherwise," he said. He reached for my hand.

I looked up, and in his eyes I saw a fire I'd last seen in Michael's. In the early days, when we'd first gotten to know one another.

"I want to avoid subjecting you to the annoyances of petty gossip," he added. "You have more than enough on your plate."

"I know. But I would not find it at all uncomfortable if the two of us . . . were to behave in a friendlier fashion. Quite the opposite."

Max took his time thinking that over, and then he nodded. "Very well. There is no need to be formal in private. We will see later what comes of it."

"Yes," I said. "Let us see what develops."

We clinked our cups, then he leaned over and kissed me.

I started. But then I put down the cup and wrapped my arms around his neck. Our kiss was hesitant, like one between persons who need more practice. I felt him struggling against a boiling passion. I shivered in sweet anticipation and felt with each heartbeat how much I longed to hold him close in a naked embrace.

He suddenly pulled away and fixed his fierce eyes on my face. "We should take this slowly," he said, his voice husky with desire. "I know you are a modern woman, but I prefer old-fashioned ways. I wish to court you, to explore our mutual desires."

"Very well," I gasped, breathless from his kiss. My blood boiled, and for the first time in an eternity, I felt aroused. All the longing, grief, and anger I'd been suppressing now flooded through me. It felt as if the ancient, cramped container of my soul had opened to make space for something new.

"Good." The conflicted expression on his face was replaced by one of relief. He held up his cup and toasted me. "To you, my beautiful countess of the horses!"

"To you, noble cavalier."

The cups clinked in harmony, and the aquavit trickled smoothly down our throats.

At last Max put his arm around me and let me settle back against his shoulder. We gazed up at the stars multiplying overhead. The night grew darker. A meteor blazed across the sky.

"When I stop to think that every star up there is a world unto itself," he said after a time, "it makes me wonder how many people like us are looking up at the heavens."

"Are you sure each one is a world?" I teased him. "What if it is just a huge curtain hung with jewels?"

He shook his head, not catching my joke. "No, God knows it is not. Each of those stars is a sun, and each sun has planets. And, who knows, maybe people like us live up there."

"The village priest would argue that this is the only world where God created life."

"The Church may have forced Galileo to recant his theory that the earth is round and orbits about the sun, but the astronomer's battle has long been won. And I would never yield in my belief that there is life somewhere else in the universe. And love as well."

I heaved an enormous sigh. He sounded so wise, so gentle . . . I would gladly have stayed there listening to him for hours. And though I'd sworn never to pick up a paintbrush again, I suddenly wished I could paint unknown worlds no one had ever seen. Perhaps someday I would.

Instead of confessing this, I groaned. "Now I need a new stable master. Langeholm is gone, and I do not think any of the stable boys has learned enough to replace him."

Max looked down at me. "Well, I think Lasse's a valiant lad. He's smarter and quicker than the others. Maybe he is young, but he has an excellent knowledge of horses."

"Perhaps, but I need someone with experience. Someone like you."

"But I am your estate manager. Or had you forgotten?"

"No, of course not. But I wonder if you could train Lasse. Only for a while, until he can manage by himself."

Max grimaced. Adding the responsibilities of the stable master would mean a double burden for him. There was no doubt about that. But I couldn't think of anyone else qualified.

"That is a great deal of work," Max said.

"I know, but I think I'm ready to take over more of the management responsibilities." I gave him a pleading look. "And I'll pay you Langeholm's salary on top of your own."

"All right, then," he finally conceded. "As a temporary measure. Until Lasse can take over the position."

Ecstatic, I hugged his neck and kissed him. "Thank you! You are my savior!"

Max appeared amused but flattered as well. "Does that mean I have to give up the cottage?" he asked. "You know how much I like this place."

"You can stay here." I nestled into his arms again. "It is amazingly beautiful here, and I doubt we would be able to meet in Langeholm's quarters. Besides, I wouldn't want to. My memories of him are much too unpleasant."

Max kissed me again, and then wrapped his arms around me. They felt as if they'd never been destined for anything else.

We sat there a long time as the broad expanse of the Milky Way emerged in the heavens.

"I must go," I said and rose from my seat. The warmth from his body disappeared far too quickly, and I'd much rather have stayed. But I had no desire to throw Lena into another early morning panic.

"You can sleep here, if you like," he said.

I shook my head. "No, it's best to leave now. I seem to recall we decided to take our time. If I stay here, I might get ideas."

Max laughed, then kissed my forehead. "I will be quite happy to hear about your ideas someday."

He gently caressed my arm as I pulled myself free. That was almost enough to make me stay. But I didn't want to destroy the moment.

"Until tomorrow," I said softly and left the porch. I walked away, and when I looked back, he was standing there, watching me go.

I waved and plunged into the dark. I felt like I was walking on a cloud. My whole body was tingling, and on the way to the manor, I tried to recall and relive all the caresses and kisses of the evening.

I closed my eyes and savored them again—gentle, warm, and full of longing. I would dream of them after I slipped beneath the covers.

37

A couple of weeks later, just before the crown princess and her entourage set out for our estate, Inspector Hermannsson wrote to inform us Langeholm had confessed both to setting the fire and to blackmailing my father.

"*He stresses he did not intend to harm the count and his son*," I read aloud to my mother that evening. "*He wanted only to threaten the estate because his demand had not been met. The authorities will probably charge him not only for the deaths but for much more, since he was willing to stop at nothing to achieve his wicked ends. We will inform you as soon as the date for a trial is set. It is possible you may be called to testify.*"

I lowered the letter and looked at my mother. She sat as rigid as a marble statue, glowering with hate.

"Such a despicable man!" she burst out. "He should be put to death. I am appalled I took him in."

"Unfortunately, people can be quite misleading." I put away the letter.

I felt deep relief. Hope was dawning in my soul. We were safe, and so was Hendrik and Susanna's child. There was no reversing the catastrophe we'd suffered, but at least now we had the chance to put it behind us. "The threat has been averted, and Count Bergen need not worry about Princess Margaret."

My mother frowned, then lifted her eyes to meet my gaze. "Agneta, you made the right decisions. Both with Langeholm and with the child. I apologize. The past months—years—have made me deeply pessimistic about everything and everyone."

I stared at my mother. This was a tone I'd never heard from her before. It was so astonishing, I was determined to commit it to memory.

I took a moment to recover, then said, "I would never do anything to hurt our family. When I decided to declare myself independent of the Lejongårds, I knew Hendrik would be here to continue our line. When that was no longer the case, I returned."

"If you would only marry—"

I raised a hand to stop her. "Please do not destroy this precious moment. This is the first time the two of us have found ourselves in complete agreement. I hope you do see that? We can wait until later to debate whether and whom I should marry. And many other things as well, I am sure. But please give me time. I will make the right decisions. The Lejongårds will not vanish from this earth."

Mother choked back whatever she'd been intending to say. "Good. We can leave it at that for now. At last your father and brother can rest in peace. And we will carry on. Lejongård women have never played leading roles, but perhaps it is time for that to change." She lifted her wineglass and silently toasted me.

I reciprocated, glowing with pleasure.

PART II

1914

38

The mild, golden late summer of 1913 had given way to a foggy, dark autumn. The crows and ravens had flocked in the fields. The woods had turned red and yellow, while pines and spruces stood like gloomy sentinels awaiting the snows.

Langeholm was brought to trial quickly, doubtless because of the prominence of our family. We weren't spared the unpleasant task of testifying against him, but we spoke in closed session. The news that he'd been sentenced to life in prison was cause for great satisfaction among the estate staff. We celebrated as well, though more soberly. Officially, we were marking the inauguration of the new horse barn, but all of us knew the real reason.

I'd informed Marit immediately, of course, so Susanna might have the news. Marit had written in late November to tell me Susanna had given birth to a healthy little girl. They christened her Matilda. Marit promised she would arrange for me to see the child.

She reported that Susanna's marriage with the bookkeeper was a satisfactory arrangement. The man was a hard worker, often absent in his free time. Susanna was alone most of the day in their tiny house in

Södermalm, in central Stockholm. Marit wrote that Susanna's role as housewife suited her, and she'd made no complaint.

With all these things assured, Mother and I were able to have a quiet Christmas celebration despite the upsets of the year. We also sponsored a splendid New Year's Eve party.

There was no heated argument with any guest that year. Max didn't want to attend the event, so I visited him in his cottage. We had a drink together and kept each other warm, but otherwise he held back, just as he'd said he would during the summer. Other than that, our regular morning walks continued, and Max became an increasingly dear companion, courting me slowly and gently.

The spring was cold and wet, but May brought us warmer weather. Our year of mourning finished, Mother and I were free to dress in brighter colors. Many of our garments were old-fashioned, but the seamstress from Kristianstad made sure we'd be elegant and appropriately updated for that year's midsummer festival.

New horses were born; grown horses were sold. Some of our business partners had initial misgivings about dealing with a woman, but with the help of Max's impressive knowledge of horses, I quickly overcame their reluctance. One after another, they acknowledged that Thure Lejongård's daughter had inherited his head for business and that Lion Hall was in good hands.

Early on the first of June, I was called urgently to the barn. Young Tim, the stable boy, told me in great distress that something was wrong with Evening Star, the horse that promised to become the best purebred we'd ever raised.

Max was already there. Evening Star's belly heaved. His nostrils were tinged with blue.

"I fear he will not survive." Max's eyes showed his deep concern. "He has been listless for several days, and his condition is getting much worse."

I looked at our horse and saw no other obvious signs of weakness except a certain fatigue in his eyes. "He is a full year old now," I said. "And there have been no problems before this."

"It has nothing to do with age. Even very young horses can fall ill. This may be something passing, but the chances are that Evening Star has developed a heart condition. We need to call a veterinarian."

"Did you see heart ailments at your own estate, Mr. von Bredestein?" I asked, caressing Evening Star's mane. We still hadn't brought ourselves to use first names with others present.

"Not often. Our horses tended to have problems with their hooves. But on neighboring farms, I saw instances where horses suddenly developed signs of fatigue that eventually degenerated into full-fledged heart conditions. We had better get an expert diagnosis. We do not want to see him collapse beneath a rider someday."

That news pained me. I now knew by heart the records my father and grandfather had created for all the horses raised here. Lion Hall stables had seen no significant incidents of ill health for a very long time. There'd once been an epidemic of hoof-and-mouth disease and a later episode when a number of horses had come down with a strange colic. No horse here had ever been afflicted by heart disease. But anything was possible.

"We should send someone for old Linus. He oversaw Evening Star's birth, and he knows horses better than anyone in the region."

"Even better than I do?" Max asked with that teasing little smile I'd come to know so well.

"Linus is very wise, and my father and grandfather trusted him implicitly. It's not that I discount veterinary science, but the old man's intuition has never failed. He can detect something as serious as a deteriorating heart."

"And can he provide a thorough diagnosis?"

"Why do you doubt him?"

"I confess I'm skeptical when it comes to these so-called seers. Our ailing villagers used to avoid the local doctor and consult a healer woman instead. Until one time the old woman made a misdiagnosis that nearly cost a patient her life. We were lucky the doctor was able to save her."

"You knew the patient?"

"She was my mother. The healer claimed her potions didn't work because Mother didn't believe in them. My own belief is that the old woman's herbs were good only for aches and pains. Anything more serious should have been attended to by a physician."

I nodded, wondering what kind of ailment had afflicted his mother. He'd told me very little about his family.

"I share your faith in medicine, but I do think we should call Linus. I value his judgment. There will still be time to seek other experts."

"As you wish." Max didn't sound particularly enthusiastic, but maybe the old man would change his mind.

The usual correspondence was waiting for me back at the office: bills, requests for stud services, and statements from Commerce Bank. But at the bottom of the pile, I found a weighty letter that seemed out of place. The small cream-colored envelope was of handmade paper. Intrigued, I turned it over. The return address was in an odd, spidery hand, with no mention of the sender. I felt a moment of dread; perhaps it was from Langeholm. Prisoners were permitted to send letters, and what was to stop him cursing us from afar? I slit open the envelope anyway, and before I could extract the letter, a small photograph fell out.

The image was of a baby girl dressed in a frilly dress decorated with old lace. She was propped up on a pillow. The photographer had captured a broad smile that struck me like a bolt of lightning. My eyes filled with tears, for that was Hendrik's own smile.

I stared at the photograph and gently caressed it with my thumb. Matilda. My niece. That thought flowed through me like honey through milk. Hendrik's daughter. She was a marvel.

I wasn't able to put down the photo for several minutes. When I took out the letter, the awkward handwriting told me that Susanna herself had written it.

Dear gracious miss,

I hope you are well. I am sending you a picture of Matilda, who is in wonderful health and has started to crawl. She is my heart's joy, and I can hardly believe what great happiness you made possible for me.

Sigurd is a very pleasant husband. When he is with Matilda, you could almost believe he was her father. He takes very good care of her and me. I often wish he was able to show his affection in other ways, but I know I cannot expect that.

A few weeks ago, I invited my parents to visit. They wrote they would not come. That made me very unhappy. I know I disappointed them, but the worst is they do not want to see their grandchild.

I know I am asking a lot, but would you show the picture to my mother? I so want her to see Matilda.

How is little Lena? I am sure she is now more comfortable at the house. I remember how nervous she was when she first started. And Marie? And Mrs. Bloomquist? I was even thinking about Miss Rosendahl the other day. Many times I want to write to them, but maybe that would cause too much excitement.

I wish you every good you can imagine and hope fortune has returned to Lion Hall.

With great respect,
Susanna

I put down the letter. I was very pleased that Susanna was doing well, and I hoped her good fortune would last a long time. The news of her parents made me sad. Couldn't they forgive their daughter? Couldn't they be happy she wasn't an outcast? That she'd bettered herself in life, and good had come from a situation that had seemed impossible?

My thoughts turned to my own mother. Our relationship had improved, even if we still had occasional differences. She rarely mentioned my time in Stockholm, except when I talked about some social development she wasn't inclined to applaud.

And what about Susanna and Hendrik? Stella wasn't angry with her son, and she still blamed the girl. The very mention of Susanna's name was enough to set her off. I looked down at the photograph. Would Matilda's physical appearance be of interest to my mother? I decided not to pursue that for the time being. I would wait for the right time, a moment when she'd take the news calmly.

Linus responded to our call that afternoon. He rode up on his stout, slow pony, as always. I saw Max's silent displeasure. But perhaps there were things that only a man almost a century old could perceive.

"Good day, Linus," I said and extended my hand to the horse wizard. He seemed to have gotten even more frail since his last visit.

"Good day, young countess. I am pleased to see ye again. It has been quite a while since we met. Ye haven't had any foals born in all these months?"

"Yes, we have," I admitted and looked at Max, who'd stopped the stable boys from sprinkling bits of broken mirror along the windowsills when mares were giving birth. I'd told him it was traditional, but he'd said it increased the risk of fire. It had emerged during the trial that Langeholm had used a fragment of mirror to concentrate sunlight and kindle the fire. After that, I'd left it to Max to oversee the births. Not a single one had been difficult, and the young horses were soon frolicking in the pasture.

"We hesitated to disturb you," I told Linus. "After all, you are not so young anymore."

"Bah!" the old fellow replied. "It's because of that new fella there. He thinks he knows better than us old folks do."

"Not at all," Max protested. "But I grew up with horses, as did my father, my grandfather, and my great-grandfather. I have horse lore in my blood."

"Lad's still green behind the ears," Linus muttered to me. "But let's see about yer horse."

I beckoned to Linus. Max trailed behind.

We found Evening Star kneeling in his stall. He sat back on his hindquarters and simply couldn't find the energy to rise. I encouraged him, but he only quivered and shook.

"Could it be his heart?" Max asked from behind us, but the old man paid him no attention. He went to Evening Star, bent down, and spoke in the ancient palaver he always used when tending to horses. He opened the horse's mouth, peered at his gums, and sniffed his breath. He checked the nostrils, eyes, and ears. Finally, he straightened up and dug something out of his pocket.

"Take this and sprinkle it along the windowsill to keep night goblins away. I'll put together some other herbs to strengthen him."

"Is it his heart?" I asked.

"No, no, he's just a little weak. Seems he ate something he shouldn't have."

"Ate something?" I gave Max a baffled look.

"Might have been a poisonous plant. Sometimes they get mixed in with the hay. Me herbs'll draw out the poison and make him stronger."

Max's expression was skeptical. "I would suggest we also call in a real veterinarian."

Linus narrowed his eyes. "Yer not trusting me?"

I spoke up quickly. "Of course we trust you, Linus; there is no problem. Fetch your herbs."

I accepted the amulet bag. Tiny symbols were inscribed along the edges, runes from long ago. It was probably nonsense, but who knew?

"I'll come back this evening," Linus said at last. "I'd ask ye to be so kind as to make sure the herbs are given to the animal before midnight."

"I will. Mr. von Bredestein will see to it."

Linus came close to scoffing at that as he stepped out of the stall.

Max rolled his eyes, resigned. "Shall I go with you?"

"No, youngster. I can find me way without help." Without another word, Linus mounted his pony and rode away.

"Are you sure you want to listen to him?" Max asked. "I understand why he distrusts me, the new employee and a foreigner, to boot. But that mumbo jumbo with the night goblins—"

"I know, and I agree, at least as far as spells and goblins are concerned. But Linus's herbs have always helped our horses. And he has been good at birthing foals."

"Of course," murmured Max, "with his magic spells! The truth is, mares can give birth without any assistance. We are called to intervene only when there are complications. Which I did, twice, in recent months."

"And you managed splendidly. But please, let us give his herbs a try. If they do not help, we can still call in the veterinarian."

Max nodded. "Very well, then. We will. But I want you to remember I suspect a heart condition."

"It may be both," I responded, a bit annoyed at my own lack of knowledge about equine diseases. "Surely there must be plant toxins that affect the heart."

"There may well be. But I doubt Evening Star ate anything of the sort. And I know something about plant toxicology. I will take a close look at the herbs the old man wants to give the horse. If I find anything inadvisable, I will let you know."

"Thanks. I would expect no less." I looked into his eyes and was tempted to kiss him, but at that moment two stable boys walked past. I pulled away and cleared my throat.

Max read my meaning and stepped back. "Will you return this evening?"

"Yes," I told him.

"Fine. I hope Linus is quick with his herbs. I cannot bear to see an animal in such torment."

"Nor can I. We will do the right thing," I said and brushed my fingertips across the back of Max's hand. The warmth of his skin stilled my worries for a moment, but they returned as soon as I left the stall. I was desperate not to lose my Evening Star.

39

"You seem distracted," my mother said at breakfast the next morning as the summer sun poured through the windows. "Has something happened?"

"I am worried about Evening Star," I answered. "There's something wrong with him."

Linus had brought his herbal remedy as promised, but it had no visible effect. Evening Star had continued to weaken, and I'd agreed that Max should summon a Stockholm vet.

"And what, exactly, is the problem?"

"Max—that is, Mr. von Bredestein—suspects that our horse may be developing a heart condition. Linus was here yesterday. He thinks Evening Star ate something poisonous."

"There's a curse on that horse," my mother muttered. "It was born the day Hendrik died."

"I know that, but I do not believe in curses. There must be a rational cause. Perhaps it was a toxin too strong for Linus's remedy."

"What if another of the maids has compromised herself?" Langeholm's manipulation of Susanna had made my mother more paranoid than ever.

"There is no sign of that. Believe me, if I catch anyone using poison, I will tear his—or her—head off." I bit savagely into my square of crisp bread with cream and jam, my usual breakfast.

"If you truly suspect poisoning, call your police inspector. He will establish the facts."

"I think Inspector Hermannsson has more important things to do than to look for a phantom horse poisoner."

A sudden thought struck me. If something poisonous had gotten into the feed, why hadn't any of the other horses manifested similar symptoms? Did some stable boy have a particular dislike for this horse? Or maybe Max was right and something was affecting Evening Star's heart. Evening Star's mother was in perfect health, so if this was a genetic condition, it came from the stallion. That meant I'd need to inform the owner and warn him not to put it out to stud anymore . . .

Mother interrupted my thoughts. "We are not just anybody," she reminded me. "Hermannsson will come if we summon him."

I shook my head. "No, we should wait for the time being. We will know more soon."

A bicycle bell clanged outside. I got up and went to the window.

"That will be the newspaper boy," Mother said. By now she'd become resigned to my habit of abruptly departing from the table before the meal was done. Father used to do the same thing, leaving Stella indignant and fuming.

I saw a young man in brown knickerbockers hastening up the steps. "Actually, this may be the young man from the telegraph office."

We waited in silence for confirmation. The door to the dining room opened. Bruns entered, carrying a silver tray, and went to my mother. "A telegram for you, gracious lady."

A telegram for Mother? Had something happened to one of her friends? I knew telegrams brought bad news all too often.

As had this one, for my mother gasped and put a hand to her mouth.

"What is it?"

Motionless, her hand still covering her mouth, Mother wasn't capable of answering at first. But finally she murmured, "Gustav has died."

"What?" I cried, and for a long moment, I feared our king had passed away. But then I remembered: Lennard's father was also named Gustav.

I went around the table to see. "Poor Lennard," I said in a low voice, as my mother and I read and reread the brief message that conveyed so much. Now the friend of my youth was obliged to shoulder his family responsibilities, just as I had been.

I'd last spoken to him during the Christmas season. He'd sent word he felt obliged to skip our festivities and stay at Ekberg Manor because of his father's condition, so I'd traveled to him instead.

The situation there had affected me greatly. Distinguished, imposing Gustav Ekberg had become a mere shadow of himself, hardly aware of his surroundings. When he saw me, he cried, "Stella! Why are you here?"

I'd never thought there was any particular resemblance between me and my mother, but Lennard's father saw one. His wife, Anna, told him I was Agneta, Stella's daughter, but he insisted otherwise. I saw how much that pained Lennard and found myself hoping his father would soon be relieved of the sad burden of existence.

"Poor Anna," my mother sighed. "She must be devastated."

"Yes, she must. But Lennard is there. He will support her."

Mother looked at me. "That may be. But Lennard has no sense of purpose. And I fear that he won't be able to manage the estate as well as his father."

"I did not have the impression Lennard was directionless," I replied. I knew where she was going with this, and I wouldn't hesitate to lecture her exactly as I had Lennard at midsummer. I could not and would not betray my heart. Not ever.

Stella's gaze bored into me. "He would be a better master of his estate with the right woman at his side."

I returned to my seat. "I am sure Lennard will look for a bride as soon as it is appropriate to do so. He has hardly left Ekberg Manor for the last three years."

My mother waved this off. "We both know who would be the best wife for him."

"No, Mother. You think you know. But you are mistaken. I will not marry my oldest friend. Besides, what would become of Lion Hall?"

"You would support each other," she contended. "I have always dreamed that you two would marry someday."

Really? When Hendrik and Lennard and I came back from the woods covered with twigs and leaves, our knees green with moss stains, had she actually pictured such a thing?

"Lennard can always count on my help. And I will stand by him, no matter whom he marries. Provided he does not choose me, for I refuse to marry him."

"Then, pray tell, who *will* you accept?" Mother was definitely annoyed.

"We will see when the time comes."

"You are already twenty-eight years old!"

"Astonishing, is it not?" I said.

I thought back to my twenty-fifth birthday. My parents had invited a hundred guests to celebrate. Lennard wasn't there because his father was doing poorly, and I hardly knew the rest of the guests. I took advantage of the occasion to announce that the judge had approved my petition for legal independence that very day. My parents were aghast, and so were the guests. If anything, they'd expected an engagement announcement instead.

Last year's birthday had been far more pleasant. I'd held no party, but when Max heard it was my birthday, he'd bought me a star atlas. "To convince you I know what I'm talking about," he'd said. He even threatened to quiz me on the names of the stars, most of which came from Greek or Arabic. He never did, but I kept the book tucked away beneath my pillow. It was my hidden treasure, a way of pretending Max was with me in bed.

"Before we start planning my wedding or declaring me a spinster," I continued, "we should probably discuss what to do about Gustav. We will attend the funeral, that goes without saying, but perhaps we should go to the Ekbergs ahead of time. Assuming that is not indecorous."

Mother raised an eyebrow. "You, of all people, pay heed to social convention?"

"Yes, I do," I declared. "At least in matters as unhappy as the demise of an old friend. Do you think they would consider a visit from us an unwelcome burden? They did not come here when Father and Hendrik died, but that was certainly because Gustav was in such poor health."

"I will think about it," my mother replied. "You should start planning what to wear."

"How many days will we be staying?" Lena asked as soon as I told her we would visit the Ekberg estate, a full day's journey from us. She was excited by the prospect of going along as my personal maid. I would need Lena's help because Mother would insist I be properly attired, out of respect for Countess Ekberg.

"Five," I said, doing my best to hide my misgivings. That seemed an eternity to me, too long to be separated from Max. And I was still deeply worried about Evening Star. "Keep in mind that this is no pleasure trip. The count was very ill for a long time. We go to pay our respects and attend the funeral. Your behavior there must be just as correct as here in the manor."

"It will be," Lena promised. Even so, her eyes sparkled in anticipation.

I understood her delight, but I could not share it. First of all, because I was genuinely sad old Count Ekberg had died. In addition, I dreaded Lennard would propose again. Together Lena and I went through the mourning clothes stored away in the wardrobe and picked out the finest ones. I shuddered when I touched the dress I'd worn for the funeral of Father and Hendrik.

"Definitely not this." I handed it to Lena. "I want never to wear it again."

My maid curtsied obediently and whisked it out of sight.

Once we'd finished packing, I dismissed Lena and took a moment to gaze out the window. Max walked across the courtyard with a couple of stable boys, deep in discussion.

I put aside my worries, got up, and went to the office. I had business to deal with before traveling—mail to answer, instructions to Miss Rosendahl for the time we'd be away, and much more. I wouldn't be able to check on Evening Star until late in the day.

The moon had risen by the time I finally set out for the cottage. I'd seen Max only very briefly that morning, and I wanted to discuss the horse's treatment during my absence.

No light burned in the windows. Was Max already asleep? I stepped up on the porch and knocked. The sound echoed inside, but nothing stirred.

I turned and went to the barn. Warm smells of horse and straw met me, and I saw a flickering light. I advanced to Evening Star's stall and found our horse sleeping on his side with Max curled up next to him. I cleared my throat. Max started and sat bolt upright.

"Agneta!" he exclaimed. "What are you doing here?"

I crouched next to him in the straw. "It is almost eleven o'clock."

He rubbed his face. "Dear Lord. I must have dozed off."

I plucked a piece of straw from his hair. "You did indeed. I went to your cottage and found it empty."

"I am sorry about that, but I wanted to be with Evening Star for a while. He is getting worse. His nose is hot with fever."

"We must get the veterinarian here as quickly as possible!" I was angry with myself for not heeding Max's warning sooner. But why had Linus failed to diagnose the horse's ailment? Was Max right about a heart condition?

Max stroked Evening Star's side. "I will send a telegram first thing tomorrow."

"Tomorrow I leave for the Ekberg estate. The old count just passed away."

"The father of your childhood friend?"

"Yes. He had been ill for a very long time. Last year his doctor gave him a year to live. The man was right."

"That must have hit your friend hard," Max said pensively.

The relationship between Max and me was still relatively undefined. We hadn't fully made physical love, for he refused to allow me to take the risk Susanna had. I'd told him I knew the signs of my own body and could tell when I was fertile, but that didn't reassure him. "We must wait for the day we are certain we belong together," he'd insisted. I'd sensed him struggling to maintain that vow of self-discipline. And whenever Lennard's name came up, Max grew insecure, seeming to regard my friend as a rival for my affections.

"Yes, I'm certain he is devastated," I answered. I was determined to hide nothing from Max; we had to be completely open with one another. I'd also told him all about Michael. "If Lennard proposes again, I will refuse him. There is no one but you."

I reached for his hand and felt it close around my own. I sensed his tension and arousal, but I knew he would keep his vow. I leaned over and kissed him, then settled back against his shoulder.

"You need rest," Max said after we'd been lying together for a while. "You had better go back to the manor. I will let you know if anything changes."

How much I wished I could take him to my bed! But I knew he was right. I sat up. "Very well. Good night!"

"Good night, Agneta. Will we see one another tomorrow before you set out?"

"Yes, we will."

We exchanged another kiss, a passionate one this time, and then he allowed me to slip out of his arms.

40

My heart was heavy as I climbed into the coach. Max had assured me that he and Lasse, our stable master in training, would take care of everything, but I was afraid the time I'd wasted going to Linus would result in Evening Star's death. I knew the notion was absurd, but it seemed almost that I was about to lose my brother a second time.

I listened with half an ear as Mother complained that one of her best black dresses had a tear Linda hadn't had time to finish mending. Unmoved, I looked toward the horse barn, hoping to catch a glimpse of Max. He was nowhere in sight.

August shook the reins and set the team in motion. I gazed longingly back at the manor.

I would miss Max. That morning we'd met to walk, but we'd spoken hardly at all, instead holding each other close and kissing. Now I wished I'd made love to him right there in the meadow. It seemed the full act of love would be postponed until marriage, when we fully belonged to one other. That vexed me.

"You are so quiet," my mother commented after a while. "Are you worrying about that sick horse?"

"Yes," I fibbed. "I insisted Mr. von Bredestein send a telegram to the veterinarian."

My mother looked out into the distance. "If it dies, there will be others. The same with human beings. One dies, another takes his place."

"Still, I would be sorry to lose Evening Star."

"Agneta, the creature is merely a horse. Your brother's soul is in heaven, and you had better not think otherwise. That would be heresy."

I turned away. Lena hunched up as if the reprimand had been meant for her; Linda pretended to have heard nothing, but that didn't mean she wasn't paying close attention. For that reason, I chose not to argue with Mother and gazed out the window instead. We were still on our own property, but the manor was far behind us. And so was Max.

I would have to force myself not to wallow in frustrated desire for him, at least not as long as anyone else was present.

We arrived at the Ekberg estate in the late evening. The sun was just above the horizon, and its rays reflected off the windowpanes of the rococo edifice. The manor had been extensively damaged by a fire in the eighteenth century, and much of it had been rebuilt. A seashell motif typical of the time appeared throughout the facade: above the windows and doors, in the tresses of the female figures in bas-relief that looked down upon visitors, and in the carvings of flowers that twined up the stately columns. Ivy adorned the walls. The mansion was delicate and graceful, in contrast to our more substantial manor with its imposing lions. But if Ekberg Manor had been much larger, one could have called it a proper castle.

Moments after August reined in the horses, Thomas Lundt, the majordomo, hurried out to receive us. He was shorter than Bruns and about the same age. His thick hair was already gleaming white.

Close behind him came two young male servants I'd never seen before. Lena blushed furiously when the blond, freckled one smiled at her. The coach door opened, and I suppressed a groan as I climbed down. My rear was numb, and my legs were stiff.

"Welcome to the Ekberg estate." Lundt bowed. "The family is expecting you."

Lennard and his mother appeared at the front door.

Countess Anna Ekberg had been a beautiful woman. The portrait of her in the Ekbergs' salon always took my breath away. Now Anna's appearance was still striking, but her husband's long illness and its sad outcome had visibly affected her. Mother had always been notably more energetic. The two had entirely different temperaments.

"Anna, my dear," Mother exclaimed as she embraced the countess. "I am so terribly, terribly sorry."

"Thank you," Anna said, her voice heavy with grief. "It is so good of you to come. With you here, I can forget, at least for a few moments."

She took me into her arms in a motherly hug.

Then it was Lennard's turn. The hours of grief had left their mark upon him as well, but after gallantly kissing Mother's hand, he favored me with a smile and an embrace. "I am so very pleased to see you again!"

"The same for me." I stoically accepted his hug, feeling cornered. I was afraid he'd raise the subject of marriage again, as he'd warned me he would. Nothing had changed—except that now I'd given my heart to another. If I told Lennard, would he accept my refusal? Would it make me feel better? I pushed the thoughts from my mind.

"We were hoping you would arrive in time for dinner," Countess Ekberg declared. "I told Lundt to have the large table set. Our Martha is pleased to have the opportunity to prepare a real meal at last."

"If she needs any help with the preparation, our maids will be happy to assist," Mother volunteered magnanimously.

I hid a smile. What would Linda think of that? Lena was happy to lend a hand anywhere, but Linda had a privileged position among the servants. If Mother's offer annoyed her, she showed no sign of it.

The lady of the manor and Lennard accompanied us to the guest rooms.

Mother strolled down the corridor, arm in arm with Anna. "Where is your daughter?"

I walked at Lennard's side, both of us clearly feeling awkward.

"Lisbeth arrives tomorrow," Anna answered. "Her husband's duties made it impossible to come sooner."

"And how is your grandson?"

"The little fellow is thriving splendidly. It is so sad that Gustav will not be here to see him." Anna's voice became muffled as she pressed a handkerchief to her mouth. Lennard placed a hand on his mother's shoulder, a gesture so tender it moved me as well.

"Please don't mind me," Anna said. "These thoughts come upon me unexpectedly. I am sure they will do so for some time. When Gustav was alive, I always clung to the hope that some miracle would restore him. But death reminds us that hope is bounded and life must reach its end."

Looking at the countess, my own grief came rushing back. She was correct, as heartrending as that was for us all.

Linda excused herself and took Lena downstairs to the Ekbergs' kitchen.

Mother and I changed from our traveling clothes and went to the dining room. The two large mirrors there were draped in black, a mourning custom we no longer observed at Lion Hall. The lengths of fabric seemed like two ghosts looming over us as we ate.

The cook had in fact trotted out her best recipes and furnished us with marvelous pâtés, a succulent roast, and a colorful vegetable dish accompanied by baby carrots dripping in butter.

"My husband merely pecked at his meals toward the end. He could digest almost nothing," Anna said unhappily. "I wish some sort of food could have better fortified him."

"That simply was not possible," Lennard commented gently. "You heard his physicians. You must not torment yourself, Mother. Father is now in a better place and no longer in pain."

Anna nodded, again in tears. Lennard gave us an apologetic look, but I signaled there was no need for that. Mother and I had been struck by many moments of sudden grief in the days and weeks following our loved ones' deaths.

"You are entirely correct, Lennard," Mother commented. "Your father is no longer obliged to suffer. That must be a consolation to you. He died with the knowledge that the future of his line was assured."

"Yes," sobbed Anna. "If only—I wish Lennard was already married."

"Mother," Lennard intervened, "that is not a topic to be discussing at this time."

He glanced at me, his face red with embarrassment. I almost grinned. It was obvious our mothers were in cahoots.

"I am sure," Stella declared, "that your son will make the right decision."

There was no mistaking her meaning, for she gazed first at him and then at me.

"Do excuse me," Anna Ekberg said. "I am still so upset. My world has turned upside down from one moment to the next. The future seems so uncertain. One wishes everything was definite, already settled."

"Remember, Mother, you have a grandchild," Lennard said. "Elisabeth would be hurt if you did not take account of her as well."

"True, but you are the heir to the estate," my mother interjected. "A mother always hopes a title can be continued by direct succession."

"Suppose Lennard does not marry," I responded. "In that case, Lisbeth's child will be the heir and take over the estate."

"But our family name would die out," Anna protested. "Unless her husband should be willing to adopt it."

Would a man really consider taking his wife's family name? I wondered. I thought of Michael, how he'd left me because I'd accepted my inheritance. Feeling a little queasy, I glanced at Lennard and hoped he was aware how uncomfortable this discussion was making me. I wanted to put a swift end to it, but any firm words would be considered inappropriate in the face of our friends' immense grief.

Anna turned to me. "You and your family face a similar dilemma. If you were to marry, then your name would change, and the Lejongårds would disappear. Unless . . ."

"When the time comes," Mother added, "we will do what is required to assure the continuity of our name. If the husband were to come from a respected noble family, he would certainly understand."

"Of course," Lennard said, knowing he'd been directly addressed.

I felt my temper rising, despite my best efforts. I wanted to honor Anna's grief, but having to listen to her and Mother discuss a future for Lennard and me was distinctly unpleasant.

"In such a case, I imagine that they could both retain their names and titles," Lennard continued with a straight face. "Or choose a combined name to continue the family lines."

"That would be possible," Stella replied, "but the parties would have to come to an agreement on the arrangement."

The situation was deteriorating rapidly. At any moment, Mother would initiate a frontal attack.

Fortunately, Lennard finally took control. "How far along are you with preparations for the midsummer celebration?"

"Given the circumstances, we unfortunately will not be able to participate this year," Anna commented, although Lennard's question had been addressed to me.

Relieved to discuss something other than aristocratic marriages, I said, "We have almost finished. Will you really not be with us, Countess Ekberg? It will not be an elaborate celebration but rather a friendly gathering. True, we are no longer in formal mourning, but we are determined to keep things modest."

Those negotiations had taken a long time. Mother had favored returning to the traditional pomp, but I thought it better to keep the celebrations as simple as those of the previous year. The only exception would be that this year she and I would participate in the dancing.

"People will say we're having financial problems," she'd objected unhappily.

"No," I'd replied, "they will see I wish to be thrifty. Our house is doing well, the new horse barn is larger than the old one, and no one will detect any sign of penury. If we hold a simpler midsummer celebration, they will understand we are not spendthrifts and that the new countess knows how to manage the family business. Society can offer no greater praise than that."

"Provided they really do interpret it that way," Mother had muttered, for she still wanted to sponsor an extravagant ball. But times had changed and would continue to do so.

"They will understand. And if there is malicious gossip, we will simply turn a deaf ear." I'd long been used to high society's judgment.

As I looked into Anna Ekberg's eyes, I knew simplicity had been the right choice.

"In that case, we will consider it," she said.

"Perhaps a change of scenery will do you good," my mother said. She had not sought any such refuge from our recent grief, although she could have opted to stay at our beach property near Åhus.

"We would be very pleased to host you for as long as you'd like," I assured Anna. "Simply let us know."

Anna smiled at me. "That is very generous, Agneta. I will discuss it with my son."

Lennard smiled as well.

We spent the rest of the evening calling up memories. From time to time, Anna's eyes glistened with tears, but because we were sharing happy memories, the day's end was anything but sad.

We then went upstairs to our rooms. I could see that Lennard would have gladly invited me on an evening stroll, but I told him I was fatigued from the long trip and ready for bed.

"Perhaps we might meet in the morning for a short ride?" he asked, his eyes hopeful.

"I will be glad to." After all, I couldn't simply shut myself up in my room all the time. And I didn't want to join Mother and Anna grieving for Gustav in the salon.

Lena came to my room a few moments later.

"How was your evening?" I asked her. Just then I heard something fall to the floor. I twisted around and saw a book on the rug. It must have come from Lena's pocket.

"I—I didn't steal it!" she said quickly, picked up the slim volume, and held it out with trembling hands. "The cook lent it to me. So I'd have something to read, she said, in case I got bored."

I inspected the book. It was a collection of detective stories.

"You read this sort of thing?" I asked, amused. "I always thought girls preferred romances."

She blushed furiously. "I like them. My father had some. I read them so many times, they came apart in my hands." Lena smiled at that recollection, and I felt my own heavy mood lift a bit.

"Well, then, perhaps I should try reading detective stories sometime."

"But you are never bored, gracious miss."

"No, but I could say the same of you," I told her. "We should not read only to fill the hours, but also to develop our minds. I am happy to see you reading. It is the key to a better life."

Oh how I missed Marit! Those were her very words. I suspected she'd been quoting someone, but that admonition was true, nevertheless.

"I could lend you books, if you like," I said. "So you would not have to spend your savings."

"Oh, gracious miss, I don't know if—"

"They are not jewels, are they? I would be pleased to share them. Provided, of course, you return them in the same condition."

"But what will the other girls say?" Lena's voice betrayed apprehension, but her eyes shone with anticipation.

"It does not concern the others. And should someone ask, you can refer them to me." I took her hand. "I am happy to do it, and God knows this land needs learned women."

Lena nodded happily. "Thank you very much, gracious miss. You are very kind."

"Take your time, think it over, and decide which book will be your first. Tell me, and I will give it to you."

I could tell from Lena's wide eyes that she'd find it hard to sleep that night. She wouldn't be disturbed by the stillness of Ekberg Manor as I was; she would be thinking of all the books at home in our library.

After she left, I got up and went to the wardrobe. Lena had brushed off my travel dress and hung it carefully. I slipped Susanna's letter and the photo of Hendrik's daughter out of the pocket and took them back to bed. What a charming little girl! It pained me that Mother had no idea how beautiful Hendrik's child was. I even recognized some of Mother's features. The bookkeeper's declaration of paternity meant that Matilda was not Mother's granddaughter in the eyes of the law. But before God and nature, she certainly was.

I doubted Stella would still be up, but even so, I left my room and softly knocked on her door.

"Come in!"

I stepped inside. Flames were flickering around a couple of logs in the fireplace. Mother sat in an armchair, and from where I stood, the firelight seemed to cast a halo around her head.

"May I have a word?"

"Of course. What is it?" She turned to regard me. "Do have a seat."

I took my place in the chair next to hers and held up the envelope.

"This letter arrived a short while ago." I offered her the photograph. "I thought you would like to see your granddaughter. Doesn't she look just like Hendrik at that age?"

Stella's face went rigid. She made no move to accept the photograph, or even to look at it. When she finally spoke, her voice was cold. "Did that girl send it to you?"

"Yes, and she thanked me for everything I did for her. Wasn't that nice?"

Mother stared at the fire. "It was appropriate of her to say so, at least."

"Mother," I said gently as I leaned forward a bit and held out the photograph, "this is your granddaughter! You heard what Anna said: that she was aggrieved Gustav would not see his grandson grow up."

"That child is not my granddaughter," Mother replied. "She is the daughter of a bookkeeper. There is no reason for me to care whether the child grows up or not."

Disappointment sank deep into me, heavy as a stone. I took a deep breath and lowered my hand; there was no use trying to force her.

"You know very well that he's the father of record only. Hendrik is the father of this beautiful creature."

"Perhaps, but she will never be part of our lineage. She will never know. And it would be far better if she had never been conceived. I still cannot understand Hendrik. I will never understand."

Those were such bitter words. I felt angry, but at the same time I pitied my mother. She'd placed such great hopes upon Hendrik, and in the end he'd disappointed her as much as I had. Perhaps even more, considering that at last I had given in to my family responsibilities.

What would have happened if the fire hadn't occurred? Everything would have been different at Lion Hall, one way or another.

I pitied the little girl as well, even though she would never learn of this discussion. It was horrible to be unwanted by one's own grandmother and even worse when someone wished you'd never been born.

In the past, this would have provoked righteous indignation in me, but I'd come to understand that no angry reproach would ever get my mother to change her mind. It was probably better for the child to go through life never knowing anything of Lion Hall. I slipped the photo and letter back into my pocket and sat wordlessly across from my mother. She continued staring at the fire.

"It is time for me to go to bed," I said at last and got to my feet. "You should too."

Mother nodded but didn't reply. She seemed to be watching something in the embers that I couldn't see. Perhaps a brilliant future for Lion Hall? An alternate world in which there'd been no fire and no illegitimate granddaughter?

I went to the door.

"You are right," I heard Mother say behind me. "She really does resemble Hendrik."

I looked back, but she was still staring into the fire.

"Good night, Mother."

"Good night," she said.

41

The morning crept dark and leaden over the manor house. I awoke from a dreamless sleep, feeling as if I hadn't closed my eyes at all. The bedcovers were clammy, and I missed the familiar rustle of curtains being drawn. The grief that lay heavy on this house seemed to have muted even the twittering of sparrows and the bustling of servants.

I was used to rising early to walk the fields and forest trails with Max. Three more days without him! The funeral was scheduled for the next day, and we'd stay the day after that so Mother could support the newly widowed dowager countess. I threw aside the covers and got up.

The house was chilly despite the summer weather. Lennard was probably used to it, but I was freezing. I wondered if this chill emanated from the history of the place.

Several of Lennard's ancestors had died violently. One was shot in the back during the Scanian rebellion of 1658, for people believed he'd betrayed them to the Swedes. The Ekbergs were originally from Denmark, though they accepted Sweden's King Charles and swore their allegiance to him. Lennard's murdered ancestor probably haunted the mansion, along with other Ekbergs who'd died in unusual circumstances.

Lena wasn't up yet, so I splashed my face with cold water from a pitcher and slipped into one of my plainer black dresses. Though made of light muslin, it weighed on me like armor—my armor against mourning, the armor I'd commissioned months before. Thank God I'd have to bear it only as long as we were at the Ekbergs'.

I left my room. The manse was dark and foreboding, but I knew every corner of it by heart. Lennard, Hendrik, and I had often sneaked into the attic in search of ghosts. I went downstairs to the entrance hall and stood beneath the enormous crystal chandelier. The first hints of thin morning light from the tall windows fell across the parquet.

"Are you up for a ride?"

I spun around to see Lennard in the shadows, rising from a chair by the stairs.

"Whatever are you doing here?"

He looked exhausted, and his eyes were puffy. Even so, a little smile played about his lips. "I couldn't sleep. So I decided to sit in the hall and watch the sunrise."

"I had the same idea," I said. "But outside."

"Well, that is just as good a notion. Do you mind if I accompany you?"

I'd have preferred to go out alone to muse about what Max might be doing, how he was probably pacing our familiar paths, and whether he'd been longing as intensely for me as I had for him. But I couldn't simply order Lennard back to bed. This was his home; he could do—or not do—whatever he wished.

"Not at all," I answered. I pointed to his bare feet. "But perhaps you might need your shoes."

"Oh!" he responded. "Indeed that had escaped me!"

"And while you're at it, perhaps put on something other than your morning robe. There is no use giving your staff a fright. Especially in the company of a lady!"

Lennard hurried upstairs and soon returned in dark trousers and a white shirt with the sleeves rolled up. He'd put on his riding boots.

"Much better!" I said with a smile.

The morning air was cool, but it was sure to warm up quickly. We walked in silence for a time. I was feeling uncertain of myself. On one hand, I was afraid he might start talking about marriage again; on the other, I felt reassured by his presence. Why was I caught in such contradictions? Was I afraid I might be attracted to him?

But my feelings for him were not new! Lennard was my friend, the only remaining link to my childhood since the death of my brother. If Max hadn't come into my life, might I have fallen in love with Lennard? Would I have rejected a second proposal just as vehemently?

Lennard interrupted my thoughts. "It is really quite beautiful here. I'd completely forgotten how much I love being outside to watch the sunrise."

"These recent weeks must have been very difficult for you," I said. "And a sunrise was probably the last thing on your mind."

"That is certainly true," he replied. "These last weeks put everything else out of my mind. They were . . . horrible."

"I believe it."

"I have to admit I wish Father had not lingered so. You were probably devastated when you received the unexpected news, but grief has hovered over this house for years. And things just got worse as time passed. I found Father's last hours almost unbearable. He wanted us by his side at the end, but I desperately wanted to get away. Witnessing such a long and painful passing is an ordeal I would wish on no one."

"Why was your sister absent?" I asked.

Lennard shrugged. "Oh, you know. Her husband, her child."

I heard the bitter undertone and could easily discern his resentment. Lennard's mother was pressing him to find a wife, and she probably saw me as the perfect candidate. Meanwhile, Lennard hadn't had the opportunity to meet any others. He'd had no time for courting or wooing, for he'd been too busy caring for his parents. I found that sad; it even angered me a little. Elisabeth, who already had a husband and child, should have been much more present in those dark days. She could have given Lennard time and opportunity to discern his own path, to find someone to cling to through those terrible times. The poor man had been reduced to making a heavy-handed proposal to a childhood friend he hadn't seen in years.

I was right not to accept. I'd kept him from making a huge mistake.

"Well, though it is sad, and I grieve for your father," I told him, "I should point out that all sorts of possibilities are now open to you."

"I have to take over management of the estate," Lennard replied, sounding despondent.

"But you knew you would. It was inevitable, you prepared for it, and you have been in charge since your father fell ill. Surely you are not going to tell me you would rather be a steamship captain!" I caught his fleeting smile out of the corner of my eye.

"No, of course not," he said. "Forgive me. I am beginning to sound like a cranky old man."

"More like a conscientious son who fears the future. But listen to me: you will have it easier than I have. Many people are quite miffed that I took over estate business. Some will accept my authority only once I eventually marry. You have no such constraints. I know your mother keeps pushing you to marry, and my mother does the same to me. But we both should stand fast until we find the right person."

Lennard looked at me. "And what if I have already found the right one?"

The wash of warm emotion took me completely by surprise—and alarmed me. I looked straight ahead and refused to be charmed. "No, you have not. You cannot have, for you have been completely cut off from society." I looked up, saw a pleading expression on his face, but insisted. "I advise you to travel a bit once the mourning period is over. Accept invitations. Survey the unmarried daughters of your parents' friends. Spend time in Stockholm. You will meet so many women, your head will spin. And you will understand that your childhood friend is not the one for you. I am certain that somewhere there exists a beautiful young woman who will be delighted to become your wife. And when that happens, I will be honored to serve as witness to the ceremony." I rose on tiptoes and planted a firm kiss on his cheek.

Lennard nodded yet appeared anything but reassured.

As we completed our round of the garden and returned to the manor, Lennard was downcast. I had the impression I'd hurt his feelings—but shouldn't friends be honest with one another?

"Shall we take a ride later?" he asked.

"Of course," I replied. "Provided you agree to start looking for a bride."

Lennard laughed but shook his head. "I will see you later."

"At breakfast!" I replied as I headed back to my room.

After breakfast, I slipped on a dress loose enough for riding sidesaddle. I'd much have preferred my riding outfit, but I hadn't brought it. It had prompted a great deal of astonishment the previous autumn when I'd first worn it but had also elicited many compliments.

I went downstairs as soon as I was dressed. Lennard was already there. He was in the midst of a tremendous yawn.

"Sorry," he said. "I slept very little."

"Hardly surprising, considering how early you were up this morning."

He yawned again. "How can you possibly be so bright-eyed?"

"I am used to it. I rise at four for a walk before things get going at the manor." I glanced at him uncertainly. "You don't need to entertain me, if it is a burden."

He shook his head. "Believe me, my invitation was for purely self-ish reasons. I need to get away from this house. I must clear my head."

"If that is your aim, I am happy to accompany you."

In truth, I was just as glad to escape.

When one is grieving, it's easy not to notice the atmosphere of gloom hanging over a house. But for those affected only indirectly, pain lurks in every nook and cranny. The pervasive grief depressed me terribly.

The Ekberg estate was renowned for its fertile land. The family's income had always come from its crops of wheat, rye, barley, and oats. There was probably not a soul in all of Sweden who hadn't eaten bread made with flour from here. While the Lejongårds were the aristocrats of horse breeding, the Ekbergs were unquestionably the lords of grain.

As for wealth, the Ekbergs' fortune was greater than ours. Grain was always in demand, while horses were becoming less and less important as mechanized transport became more common. What's more, the times of vast military cavalry were ancient history now. Not that I regretted that historical evolution. Still, I saw clearly that our descendants would eventually need to find other means to support themselves.

Lennard accompanied me to the horse barn. A brown horse and a dappled gray stood saddled and ready.

"Which is calmer?" I asked, feeling a sudden pang as I thought of Evening Star. How unfortunate that telephone lines hadn't yet reached the southern regions and I couldn't call home for news. If there was any recent innovation I wanted for Lion Hall, it was the telephone.

"Take the gray. He is an ideal horse."

"What is his name?"

"Rajah. My father named him for an acquaintance from India."

Old Count Ekberg's voyage to India had been a frequent topic whenever our families visited one another.

"And the brown?"

"Goblin, and he lives up to his name. Sometimes he gets over-wrought for no reason at all and nips a stable boy, but he's superb for riding. If ever I hunt again, I will be riding him."

"You're not planning to miss our autumn hunt again this year, are you?"

"Probably. Such pursuits will have to wait until next year. Life must go on." A brief, pained smile passed over his face. By the time he next participated in our foxhunt, he'd have been Count Ekberg for more than a year. I expected he would then be changed, as I had been, by the responsibilities of running an estate.

We swung into our saddles and rode out of the courtyard.

The fields lay before us like carpets of gold tinged with shades ranging from bright yellow to yellow-green, sparkling like brilliantly lit gems.

It had never occurred to me to paint this landscape, but now as I rode through the fields, they presented themselves as a glorious composition. I reminded myself that those days had passed, but I found my fingers still itched to pick up a brush.

"Tell me, how long before you harvest the rapeseed?" The Ekbergs' land was north of Lion Hall, so their harvests were generally later in the season.

"Oh, a month yet. Perhaps a bit more. It depends on how much sun we get."

I kept glancing at him as we chatted. He'd seemed stressed and uncertain when he proposed to me the previous summer, but now he sounded as authoritative as his father. Before the year was out, he would make a better landowner than I.

We rode along a trail through the woods toward a small lake.

"Remember this place?" Lennard pointed toward a little house almost hidden by the reeds.

I frowned for a moment, and then it came to me. The little fishing hut! It hadn't been overgrown with weeds back then. Whenever Hendrik and I visited, all three of us would come here and make up stories about wicked pirates and sea monsters. The lake looked vast as an ocean to us then, and our fantasies soared past its banks.

"It appears it's no longer possible to sit on the shore." I cautiously urged my horse forward. The undergrowth was thick, and the marshy ground was treacherous.

"No, unfortunately not. But I often come here anyway. After Hendrik died, for a time I came out here almost every day to relive our silly adventures."

"I often visited our haunts around Lion Hall," I confessed. "I almost expected to come across Hendrik's ghost, but I always found myself alone."

"You are not alone," Lennard responded. "I am here. Even though I do not live nearby."

"Lennard . . . ," I protested.

"Fear not! I do not intend to propose." He leaned over to take my hand and gave me a searching look. "At least not yet."

I'd have preferred to look away, but I couldn't. Lennard was my friend, and I cared about him deeply.

"I simply want you to know," he said, "that you can count on me in any difficulties. No matter what is required. I will be there for you."

"That is very kind. But right now, you are the one in need of comforting."

Lennard barked a sharp laugh. "I very much doubt anyone other than you is concerned about that. My mother is too deep in her own grief. I am so glad that Stella is here to provide consolation."

"And I am here for you," I pointed out. "Just as Hendrik, you, and I promised one another."

"Oh dear, you still remember that? Swearing before the sea god statue?"

"Of course!"

Our families had spent summers together at our vacation home at Åhus, on the coast. Well, not everyone, since the fathers stayed behind to manage business. But both countesses were there with their children and servants. Somewhere in the woods close to the beach, we'd found an ancient post with a face carved into it. Hendrik claimed it was a fearsome, ancient Viking god and the perfect place to pledge eternal loyalty. And so we did. The three of us clasped hands and swore everlasting alliance.

"Do you think it is still out there?" Lennard mused.

"The statue?" I shrugged. "Perhaps. The wood seemed as hard as stone." I glanced at him. "We should take a trip to look for it—and a bride for you. Åhus has some very beautiful girls."

Lennard's eyes lit up. "I would be delighted to take such a trip. Though I am afraid I will not be able to get away from the estate anytime this year."

"Then we should plan it for next year," I suggested. "Promise me, please, that in the meantime you will make an effort to meet eligible women who live nearby. Take a close look at each one, and do not compare them to me. None is like me, and I resemble none of them. Once you have a likely candidate, someone who pleases you, point her out to me. I will decide if she is worthy of you."

Lennard leaned over and kissed my forehead. "As you command! I will do so."

I wasn't sure if he would keep his word. But at that moment I felt quite relieved.

42

There was a great deal of lamenting at Gustav Ekberg's funeral, but many affectionate things were said as well. I was enchanted by anecdotes about the old count at his best. Even Anna broke into smiles from time to time. One thing I'd learned from our own year of mourning was that joy does return eventually. Memories help diminish the pain, a healing for which I was deeply grateful.

Two days later, I ran into Mother in the hall early in the morning. She was already dressed for our departure. Her conversations with Anna had clearly affected her, and her makeup couldn't quite conceal the dark circles under her eyes.

"I cannot understand why you must be so obstinate," she said as we went to the stairs. "I see the way Lennard looks at you. You turned him down, but he would still marry you in an instant."

"Mother, please. This is a discussion we can have at home."

"A quarrel, you mean," she said sharply, but then she sighed. "I know Anna wishes with all her heart the two of you would wed. She always has."

"That may be, Mother. But I beg you not to raise that topic this morning. I have no desire to disappoint Anna yet again. It is a marvel she treats me with such affection after I rejected her son last year."

"Lennard probably did not take it as a rejection. You told him you were not ready. He must endure the customary period of mourning, but afterward I imagine he will renew his proposal."

I took a deep breath in order to maintain my calm. "I discussed it with him again and charged him to look elsewhere. He has had so little contact with society in recent years, he cannot possibly compare me with others."

My mother was indignant. "You told him to find another woman?"

"Yes, one he loves. Our lineage and estate do not depend upon my making a brilliant match. It is simply not necessary."

"Nor should the Lejongårds marry beneath them. The Ekbergs are our equals in rank, unlike virtually everyone else in the region."

"Well, suppose I go hunting in the frozen north?" I suggested mischievously. "I might find a man up where the summer sun never sets and the winter sun never rises!"

My mother appeared genuinely shocked. "You? In the north? But who would manage Lion Hall?"

"Mother, I was joking."

She shook her head. "I doubt you will find a man content to let you live on your own estate while he sits alone on his."

"These are modern times, Mother. Perhaps soon it won't matter where married partners live or even if they have the same last name. Besides, I find it absurd for a woman to lose her home when she marries and for her husband to get everything she owns."

"That is tradition. Life has always been that way."

"Exactly! And I will never accept it. If I ever do marry, a binding contract will spell out my conditions." Though I spoke from deep conviction, I couldn't help thinking of Max. Would he be willing to marry under those circumstances?

"A contract!" my mother echoed, but the Ekbergs' maid appeared on the stairs, so she fell silent and followed me to the dining room.

Anna seemed tired and ill, scarcely able to eat. Now that the funeral was over, both the tension and all her energy had drained away. Lennard didn't look much better. I was glad when breakfast ended and we could leave.

At the front door, Anna took my hand and pulled me aside. She ushered me into a secluded niche the architect had created for private conversations.

"Agneta, I want you to know you will always be welcome in this house. Stella told me you remain determined not to entertain any suitors because the deaths of your father and brother have so affected you."

"Estate business is demanding as well," I replied, suddenly feeling an uncomfortable warmth. "Managing the breeding and sale of horses is very challenging. It is a man's world."

"Ah, but once your heart has gotten over its grief, you should reconsider. I know my son proposed already, but you were in no position to accept at that time. Just give him a sign whenever you feel the time might be right. My husband and I have always loved you like a daughter, you know that. You have always been the right one for Lennard. I am sure he feels the same."

What I wanted to do more than anything at that moment was to tear free and run screaming out of the house. But I couldn't. I stood there, petrified. How should I react? Confess I had no desire to wed my best friend? Say I'd urged him to find another woman, someone more suitable for him? Assure her that Lennard, with his friendly spirit and handsome appearance, could have his pick of any girl in Sweden?

"I—I will think about it and let him know. When my heart is no longer so burdened. If the day comes when I can permit myself to contemplate marriage."

Anna gave me an encouraging nod. She wasn't entirely satisfied, but she knew the mistress of Lion Hall was determined to have
her own way. "Have a safe journey, Agneta, and take care of your
mother."

"I will," I replied. "Many thanks." *No one needs to worry about Stella
Lejongård,* I thought. Mother was made of far sterner stuff than Anna.
But Lennard's mother seemed visibly heartened by my half promise as
she bid us farewell.

I looked back at Ekberg Manor with mixed emotions as the coach
got underway. That impressive edifice had always fascinated me, but
now I was leaving it with a distinctly uneasy feeling. I wouldn't be
coming back anytime soon, unless there was no way of avoiding it.
Not because of the mournful shadow cast by the death of the count but
rather because of the hopes of the countess.

If only I could tell someone about the pressure I was under! I
glanced at my mother, but that wouldn't do; she was part of the problem. Right now, she was probably mentally outlining a lecture about
marriage contracts. Thank heavens she couldn't hold forth in the presence of the maids.

As soon as we got back, I rushed to Evening Star's stall. Voices came
through the open door, including one I didn't recognize. I stepped in
and saw a tall man, probably in his fifties, wearing dark trousers with
suspenders. His shirtsleeves were rolled up, and he was washing his
hands. His sparse hair was grayish-blond, and his wire-framed spectacles
had slipped down his nose.

"Ah, here is the mistress of the estate!" Max said, standing next
to the stranger. "Dr. Falk, let me present Countess Agneta Lejongård.
Countess, this is Dr. Arvid Falk, Stockholm's best veterinarian."

"Very pleased to meet you," I greeted the veterinarian and offered
him my hand after he'd finished toweling off his own. I looked at Max
expectantly. He seemed worried.

"The pleasure is entirely my own, Countess," the distinguished visitor said with a little bow. He beckoned to me. "Let us take a look at the patient together."

I went in and saw Evening Star lying on his side. He was wheezing, and his eyes rolled in panic. Every breath cost enormous effort. Was he dying? Fear shot through me. *If I hadn't started with Linus, the veterinarian could have been called much sooner.*

Evening Star was in torment. I felt a rush of anxiety and pity for the poor beast. It broke my heart and brought back visions of my dying brother. "What's wrong with him?"

"An infection caused an inflammation affecting the heart muscle. He is suffering. His heart is greatly enlarged."

So it was a heart condition after all, just as Max had suspected. That confirmation brought me little comfort.

"Can anything be done?"

"I have already begun treatment. Your stable master tells me this is a very expensive horse. Many an owner would simply put the beast out of his misery. The damage may be permanent. The animal might be permanently enfeebled."

I shuddered. "We very rarely carry out mercy killings on this estate. Only when suffering becomes so intense we see no other choice. And I assure you, this horse is extremely valuable to me."

The veterinarian nodded. "I am no proponent of putting down a horse in this condition. There is still a realistic possibility of healing the animal."

"Really?" My heart bounded.

"Indeed. It is essential to keep the animal from any and all exertion. I administered a mild sedative for that reason. I barely brushed his side with my fingertips, and he became frantic. The sedative will help."

"Evening Star senses he is dying?"

Falk nodded. "Who would not panic at a wildly irregular heartbeat? The horse must rest. I also ordered a compound from a respected pharmacist, a friend, to be administered over the course of two weeks. You must understand that the horse may remain very weak even after that. But I hope he can live a normal lifespan if my advice is followed."

"Could he have a relapse?"

"You are wondering if you will be able to ride him?" the animal doctor asked. "Hmm, that depends on whether he recovers completely. If all turns out for the best, you will have nothing to fear from routine pleasure riding."

"And how about hunting?"

"I would not ride the animal hard this year. But if he recovers, then autumn of the following year will probably present no problem."

I nodded. "Good! Thank you very much, Dr. Falk."

"If you allow, I will remain on the premises until the compounded medicine is delivered. Your stable master has been so kind as to offer me lodging."

I looked at Max, who was standing in the shadows. He seemed just as relieved by Falk's comments as I was.

"That will not be necessary, Doctor. You are visiting the estate, and we will of course put you up in one of our guest rooms."

I wasn't going to agree to arrangements that would keep me from meeting Max in private.

"That is very kind of you. Thank you very much."

"Permit me to accompany you to the manor, where I can present you to my mother. Unless your services are still required here?"

Falk shook his head. "I doubt they will be, at least for the time being. Mr. von Bredestein and Mr. Broderson are fully capable of caring for the animal."

The men exchanged nods, and the veterinarian came with me to the manor.

"Dr. Falk, this is Stella Lejongård, my mother," I told him. "Mother, this is Dr. Arvid Falk, one of Stockholm's leading veterinarians. He is caring for Evening Star."

Mother took a moment to inspect the veterinarian and then offered him her hand. "Very pleased to make your acquaintance."

The doctor gallantly kissed her hand. "As I am very pleased to be your guest. The manager's cottage is not at all uncomfortable, but I am delighted to be invited into the agreeable circumstances here, if you will be so kind as to permit it."

My mother was charmed by his artful reply. She beamed as I hadn't seen her do for a very long time. "It is a pleasure to receive such a culti-vated guest. And if you are not currently engaged in our equine affairs, I would be pleased to welcome you into the salon."

"Indeed you honor me!"

As the two regarded one another, it occurred to me that perhaps their mutual attraction was like that between Max and me. I didn't believe in love at first sight anymore, but there was a definite affinity between Mother and this man she had only just met.

"Come, Dr. Falk. First I will show you to your room. Our major-domo, Mr. Bruns, will provide you with whatever you may need."

The veterinarian followed me somewhat reluctantly. Out of the corner of my eye, I saw my mother standing in the hall, watching him go. I had a mad notion: What if she were to fall in love again? Might that get her to stop devising elaborate schemes to marry me off?

43

During that evening's dinner, I enjoyed watching Mother struggle not to flirt openly with our distinguished visitor. Afterward I went to the horse barn. I was very much hoping Max would be back in his cottage, but he was just as likely to be watching over Evening Star as he had on the night before we left for the Ekberg estate.

Lasse was asleep in the straw at Evening Star's side. Our horse lay unmoving, but I heard him breathing regularly. I left for the cottage, with Anna's urgings echoing in my ears. Was it time at last to tell my mother the truth? To confess I was in love with Max?

I saw light in the cottage windows and stopped worrying about the Ekbergs. My heart surged with joyful anticipation of Max's kisses. I knocked and listened. Was he expecting me?

He opened the door after a moment. "Excuse me. I was tidying up," he said. "Thanks for taking charge of our visiting practitioner. I did not feel authorized to offer lodging at the manor, and I was reluctant to offend your mother by asking."

"Well, considering how much she enjoys the good doctor's company, your offense would quickly have been forgiven!"

Max tilted his head, intrigued.

I described their conversation over dinner, and laughed. "I am tempted to call it a case of love at first sight."

Max came closer. "Really?" He enfolded me in his arms. "Does such a thing exist?"

"Someone once persuaded me it might."

"And was that me? Your love at first sight?" His kiss was fiery on my lips and, as always, it sent an exquisite shudder through my whole body.

"I will admit there was a certain attraction. But love? Probably only at second sight."

He feigned disappointment.

I kissed him. "But I understand that kind of love lasts longer. They say it is more dependable than a sudden, short-lived blaze."

"I am relieved to hear that."

We kissed again. I opened my eyes, looked past his shoulder, and noticed he'd changed the linens on the bed in the next room. How alluring that bed was! I happily would have curled up there and held him tight.

I leaned back to look at him. "Thank you for summoning the veterinarian."

Max smiled, relieved. "I was haunted by the thought of your reaction if the horse you loved should die while you were gone. I called in the best man I could find. I really regret he couldn't come sooner." He brushed a lock of hair from my face.

I felt a fluttering in my breast. "Are you aware Evening Star was born the very day my brother died?"

Max shook his head.

Mother had known, and so had Langeholm, but evidently no one else had connected the two events. The stable boys probably hadn't thought to mention it.

"I was there. Linus brought him into the world. Evening Star was gorgeous from the moment he arrived."

"Linus can assist in the future, if you wish."

I put a hand across his lips. "Never mind about that. I only wanted you to understand why I feel so attached to this horse. I know it is foolish, but I like to imagine that Hendrik's soul entered the body of that little foal. That would have been just like him, you see. He told me several times long ago that, if reincarnation existed, he would want to come back as a horse."

"The priest would not have been pleased to hear that."

"Hendrik never told him; he told me instead. We were real romantics back then." I peered into Max's eyes. "How about you? In what form would you like to be reincarnated?"

He shrugged. "The thought never occurred to me. I live in the here and now."

"Did you never wonder what it would be like to have a second chance?"

"No doubt I would make exactly the same mistakes." He drew me close and kissed me again. "But I would still get the important things right."

This kiss was different—hungry, more demanding. Desire welled up in me. I pressed against him, and my hands moved across his back. This was the point at which he usually disengaged. But not tonight; he threw caution to the wind. He abandoned my lips and planted burning kisses on my neck as he lifted me to him and ran his fingers down my spine.

I couldn't have fended him off even if I'd wanted to. A frenzy of passion seized me. My fingers fumbled at the buttons of his shirt, and I inhaled his masculine scent. I was afraid he would break free at any moment and leave unsatisfied my fever of desire. But no; he swept me up in his arms, carried me to his room, laid me across his bed, and ripped open my dress.

I wrapped my legs around him, hungry and impatient, but he withstood my wordless plea. Only when we were both completely naked did he begin caressing my breasts, my belly, the soft skin of my secret parts . . .

I burned with desire and expectation. His kisses and caresses brought me to a fever pitch. When he thrust into me at last, I lifted my hips to receive him. My first orgasm was quick and earthshaking, faster than I'd expected. I gasped and begged for more.

One moment he was on top of me, the next I was over him. I loved riding him, and he loved pushing himself slowly, deliberately, into me, driving me to ecstasy. A simultaneous orgasm overwhelmed us. We clung to one another as if about to fall over a precipice. I'd never experienced anything like this with Michael. Our love had been passionate, but my surrender to Max yielded an immense, intense pleasure I wanted never to end.

Late that night we lay against one another, exhausted and deeply content. Outside, night insects swarmed in the moonlight.

My lids were heavy, but my mind was wide awake. My body throbbed. I felt truly alive for the first time in ages.

Max caressed the hollow of my throat. "Now I know what my incarnation should be."

"I thought you did not believe in such things," I teased.

"You just changed my mind," he said. "I would be happy to be reborn as a butterfly." He leaned over and kissed my left breast. "I could alight right here."

"Would that be enough for you?"

"I believe it would. Better than roasting in the hell the priest keeps railing about. Perhaps you disagree?"

"But maybe we two could grow old and die at the same moment. What then?"

"You would be reborn as the same gloriously beautiful woman. I would find you, no matter how far I had to fly. I will always find you."

He bent over me again. I threw my arms around him and pulled him into another sweet delirium of love. Eventually, we lapsed peacefully into slumber.

Night enclosed us like a soft blanket. I would have happily remained in that land of dreams, but habit woke me. I had no need to check the time.

I gently nudged him. "We must get up. It is four o'clock already. I must be back in my room before the maids are up."

Max sat up, took me in his arms, and kissed me again. "I would rather have you here with me."

"I know. Perhaps someday you will not have to let me go. But today I have no choice."

Max murmured unhappily, but then he released me and rolled onto his back. I surveyed him with a smile. The first glimmer of the rising sun fell across his chest where my head had lain.

Mother would be furious when I told her I was in love with my estate manager. But why should I care? I'd found the love of my life, a man I could be happy with for as long as I lived!

Max watched me dress, then got up and wrapped himself in his morning robe. It was an old thing, mended in many places, as if it had been stitched together from random pieces of leftover fabric. A robe of many colors, it would have been perfect for a circus magician.

"Why do you keep that funny old thing?" I asked. "We can pick out a new one for you."

"I wouldn't give it up for anything in the world." Max wrapped it comically tight around him. "It belonged to my great-grandfather."

"Your great-grandfather?"

"Yes, and what a man he was! Drank like a fish, cursed like a drover, flirted like mad. His children and grandchildren adored him. He lived to be almost a hundred, so I was blessed to have known him personally. He would take me on his knee, usually wearing this robe, and he would bark, 'Aha, youngster, how're ya doing?' and when I told him I was good, he would jiggle his knee like a horsey and make me laugh my head off. The day he died was the saddest of my life."

"Yours seems to be a long-lived family."

"Oh yes, at least as far as the men are concerned. My grandfather is still alive, but he's a bit soft in the head. He doesn't recognize my parents a lot of the time, but he's interested in the strangest things. It's too bad I have no son to present to him." He gave me a suggestive glance.

I wasn't ready to have children yet. The estate took up too much of my time. And if I had children, I wouldn't want to turn them over to nannies and governesses; I'd take care of them myself.

"We will see," I said and blew him a kiss.

Max pretended to catch it and tuck it into the pocket of his robe. "My great-grandfather would certainly have appreciated that."

"That is why I sent it your way! I will see you soon, my love!"

Smiling, I left the cottage. The sun was peeking over the horizon. I felt like I was racing above the clouds. Halfway to the manor, I threw my arms up, whirled around, and shouted so loud, the woods echoed. I skipped along, elated as a child.

Once the mansion was in view, I consciously contained myself. If any of the stable boys noticed my exaltation, he'd want to know why. And, just as bad, my authority over them might be undermined.

I crept into the house, quiet as a mouse. I heard rapid footsteps up on the top floor and knew the maids were already up. Lena wouldn't appear in my room for another two hours, but she mustn't see me on the stairs. That would have posed no problem normally, for I could have been returning from an innocent stroll. But on that special day I worried she might detect signs of lovemaking. My blissful expression would rouse her suspicions, and she might even smell Max on me. I wanted to avoid that at any cost.

I nipped into my room, undressed, and lay my clothing over the armchair. Then I slipped under the covers. My skin tingled. Deep inside, I felt happier than I had for a very long time.

44

Throughout the morning I did my best to contain the smile that kept breaking out on my face. I usually failed. Joy dwelt there, unmistakable, and tucked itself away in my heart, waiting for the next opportunity to blossom.

My mother never noticed, for she had eyes only for Dr. Falk. He turned out to be a superb storyteller with endlessly entertaining anecdotes about his practice. Mother listened to him, entranced, and I encouraged him to tell us more. At some point she disappeared into the salon with him. They remained there until Dr. Falk joined Max and me in the horse barn, where the compound had been delivered.

We'd been waiting for him for a while, exchanging covert glances and knowing smiles.

Dr. Falk administered the medicine to Evening Star. Max and I watched, hoping to see immediate effects.

"It may take a day or two to see changes," Falk advised us. "This medicine acts gradually."

But the miracle occurred faster than expected. Within hours, Evening Star was back on his feet. At first he rose to a squatting position, then he got all the way up. He swayed slightly, unwilling to walk, but we were encouraged by the signs of recovery.

"Give him this compound morning and evening. Do not let him leave the stall," Dr. Falk told us. "Two weeks from now, you can lead him outside on a bridle. Slowly. I would wait another two weeks before attempting to saddle and mount him."

I felt like hugging the veterinarian. Evening Star was going to live! My heart bounded with joy, this time purely because our horse had escaped the clutches of death.

Dr. Falk packed his bags the next day, for his presence was no longer required. He bid us farewell and assured me he'd be back in a couple of weeks to check up on the patient. August drove him to the Kristianstad railway station in our coach. Estate life resumed its routine, though Mother seemed to miss the conversations with her new acquaintance.

At dinner that evening, I was terribly impatient to finish so I could go see Max. My mother had insisted both of us keep company with Dr. Falk until late each evening. I went to my room immediately afterward.

But not tonight. I ate without tasting the food, for my passionate thoughts were elsewhere. I pretended to have an appetite so as not to arouse Mother's suspicions.

"You had agreeable conversations with the doctor," I commented.

"Extremely agreeable," she answered. "He is a man of superior intelligence. Perhaps one might expect a veterinarian to be somewhat unusual; after all, he treats and dissects all sorts of animals. But he is not at all odd."

"It sounds as if you may have taken a fancy to him," I said hopefully.

Mother snorted. "I find him amusing, that is all. My heart still belongs to your father. There will never be another man for me."

"Why not?" I asked. "You could find a companion. Our mourning has ended, and the doctor seems a very nice man."

"He is nice—and married. He told me a great deal about his wife and two daughters. One of them is currently expecting her first child, and the other will marry soon."

My eyebrows rose. "He revealed all that?"

"Yes. And I told him about my husband, Hendrik, and you."

"Oh dear! I hope you left out the spiciest details." I flushed hot and cold as I imagined what tales she might have spun about my studies and our disputes.

"You can be reassured. I know what is appropriate. One shares some things and one keeps other things to oneself. I would be very happy to receive Dr. Falk again. We could engage him for an annual inspection of the horses."

"That is an excellent idea." Somehow I wasn't entirely convinced she liked the veterinarian only because of his sparkling personality. But not even a master torturer would be able to pry that confession from her. "By the way, if you happen to develop an interest in a man, you won't have to worry whether it suits me. It would be lovely to see you happy again."

Mother stiffened in disapproval. She frowned and said nothing. At least she didn't urge me yet again to go hunting for a man for myself.

45

Midsummer came and went. Lennard and his mother didn't attend the festivities. It was another lovely celebration with herring, aquavit, and a maypole. Max stayed away again, and I stole off to him like a thief in the night. This time our stargazing had to wait until after we'd made passionate love.

"What would you say to living in the manor?" I asked a week later, the last Sunday evening in June, as I lay in his arms.

"As your lover?"

"As my husband."

I rolled over and propped myself up on his chest. My hair fell across his belly. It was wonderful to be able to wear it loose instead of having to subjugate it with hairpins.

"Must we discuss such a thing," he asked, "when we can simply enjoy what we have?"

"That may be fine for you, but I am under constant pressure, day after day, to find a husband. The visit to the Ekbergs was an ordeal, but that was no surprise. This midsummer party was even worse. I felt like a mare at auction. I have no idea what my mother told her lady friends, but their sons swarmed around me like flies. I was seriously tempted to tell them off exactly the way I did Lennard."

I'd held nothing back when I told Max about Lennard's declaration of a renewed interest in marriage. Or of my refusal and insistence he look elsewhere.

"Maybe you should have," Max said, twisting a ringlet of my hair around one finger.

"I will not hesitate to do so if necessary." I ran my fingertips across his chest. "Tell me, do you think marrying me would bring a curse on you?"

"Of course not. Though I do wonder how your mother would react."

"Oh, she would be quite enchanted."

Max laughed. "Surely you jest!"

"She would have to get used to it. She could not argue that you come from a lower class. You are a Pomeranian baron."

"Penniless and landless," he added. "She would see me as an adventurer out after your title. And money."

"Please note, however, I was the one to make the proposal." I rested my head on his chest and heard the quiet, powerful beating of his heart. "Correct?"

He caressed my hair. "Yes, indeed you are the one proposing. But I do not know how to respond."

I pushed myself up, feeling a pang of disappointment. I thought of Michael's refusal to join me in my new life. "Do you not wish to be with me?"

A little wrinkle of displeasure appeared between Max's eyebrows. It marred his appearance. "More than anything in the world! But there are complications. My family—"

"Would they object to your marrying a Swede?" That seemed hardly likely, considering his mother was Swedish.

"No, they would find the idea quite attractive. But—"

"But?" I echoed.

"But then you would belong to them."

I gave him a baffled look.

"My father would require you, as his daughter-in-law, to live on our estate. And I would be subject to their constant surveillance."

"Then we should get married in secret!" I exclaimed. "If you want never to see your family again, that is entirely up to you. You could even take my family name."

"Agneta," he said in a low, unhappy voice, "I prefer not to make a decision now. Let us continue as we are. We can let things take their course. Who knows if you will want me six months from now."

I sat up. My disappointment was as profound as my ecstasy had been only minutes before. I pushed my hair back from my face. Looking around, I sought something to fix my gaze upon, for at that moment I couldn't bear to look at him. I started to get up. "I should go."

Max grabbed me and held me fast. "Please do not be angry. We can talk about this again later. In a month or two. Or in half a year."

"Oh? Six months from now, your father will not insist I move to his estate? In half a year, your feelings will have changed?"

My indignation mounted, and I realized I was about to throw a tantrum. I burst into tears, tormented by my yearning.

"Agneta, please understand," he said. "I cannot make you a promise I may not be able to keep."

My eyebrows rose. "There is some obstacle to marriage? Do you have someone else?"

"No."

"Perhaps you just want to move on? Had enough of Lion Hall, have you?"

"That is not it."

Something in him had changed.

"What, then?"

"I cannot tell you. This is not the moment."

I pushed him away. "As you wish. Excuse me for pressuring you. That was not my intention."

I saw him relax, but I was ready to explode. I'd thought the time was right. But it looked like I'd again become involved with a man who didn't want to commit, who didn't want to spend his life with me. How could I go to bed with him again as if nothing had happened? I needed time to think, time to deal with my anger. I needed to decide what *I* wanted.

Fighting to maintain my composure, I got dressed. I was expecting Max to break the silence, but he didn't.

"Are we going to take a walk in the morning?" he asked at last as I went to the door.

"No. I need to deal with my work."

My curt refusal prompted him to get up. He gathered me in his arms and kissed me.

I was in no mood to respond.

"Please understand," he breathed in my ear. "We will discuss it. Later. When we both know for sure."

"Understood," I replied and pulled away. I managed to shut the door behind me before my tears welled up again.

I ran, wanting to put as much room as possible between me and the cottage. I raced across the meadows and through the night until I was certain that no one could see or hear me. Then I slowed to a walk and sobbed bitterly.

I returned to the mansion in the gray hours of early morning. I was tired and defeated, disoriented and moody. Bitter disappointment burned within me, and I shuddered to think of my morning duties. I could see only two possible reasons for Max's refusal to marry me: either he didn't really love me and thought our involvement was bound to end soon, or he was intimidated by my social standing, fearful he wouldn't be accepted as head of the family.

Upstairs in my room, I peeled off my dress and lay down. My head ached, and my eyes were leaden. My body gave out almost immediately; exhaustion overpowered me.

I woke with a start to someone shaking my shoulder. I'd been dreaming I was running through the forest. Now bright sunshine blinded me. I looked around in confusion, then finally recognized my own room.

"Excuse me, gracious miss," Lena said. "I wanted to wake you earlier, but your mother said it was better for us to let you rest."

I bolted upright. "What time is it?" The sun was high, and I could feel the heat of the day.

"Eleven o'clock."

"Good Lord!" I threw aside the duvet and sprang out of bed.

"Is there water still?" I cried as I rushed to the bathroom. No matter how late it was, I had to wash away every trace of last night's activities.

"I set it up already," Lena said. She appeared seconds later with the hand towel.

Water washed me clean, and my fatigue disappeared, but my heart felt no lighter. Max's refusal had affected me deeply. I'd made a fool of myself.

The dining room was empty. I went to the kitchen. "Good morning," I said. "Might you still have anything left from breakfast?"

"Good morning, gracious miss," Mrs. Bloomquist answered. She put down her ladle. "Your lady mother told me you would be visiting."

My eyebrows rose. My mother had asked the cook to prepare something especially for me? That was unheard-of, a completely new development.

"After a late night, you need a proper meal," she added. She set a place for me and put out the breadbasket and jams.

"Excuse me?"

Mrs. Bloomquist turned, suddenly embarrassed. "I only mean—you woke up so late. The gracious lady told the girls not to disturb you. After all, you work such long hours."

My skin prickled as if attacked by angry ants. "Yes," I said. "It was very late last night."

"Your sainted father would sometimes sit up very late, working at his desk. From time to time, I would prepare him a breakfast like this."

She was doing her best to make nothing of it, but I still felt uneasy. What if the servants knew I was having an affair with Max? What if they were talking about me?

And even worse: What if Mother knew?

I took a seat at the kitchen table, horrified by my own recklessness. "Thank you, Mrs. Bloomquist. This is very kind of you. What would my father have for breakfast after his late nights?"

"An egg, sunny-side up; bread with blueberry or plum sauce; and good, strong coffee."

I yawned with all my might. "Oh, that sounds splendid!"

I heard the maids giggling outside, but I tried to ignore them. I would make sure I didn't oversleep again, no matter how late I stayed with Max.

After breakfast, I took the stairs to the attic. I didn't encounter Mother on my way, which was a relief. I didn't care to explain why I'd stayed in bed so late.

The steps of the narrow staircase creaked beneath my weight. They'd done the same when Hendrik and I sneaked up here, usually when people we didn't know visited, and we didn't want to be stuck with their children. In the attic we were safe from games we didn't want to play and chatter we didn't want to hear.

As I opened the door and put my head through, it was almost as if I could see the two of us there, playing among the boxes and trunks. We'd made up stories, usually about faraway lands and often about ghosts.

We'd pretended we *were* ghosts. While people talked and laughed downstairs, we were gloriously invisible.

Bright sunshine fell through the window slits and threw pools of light across the floorboards, but they couldn't drive away the ghosts of memory. I stepped around a heavy trunk packed with my grandfather's holiday outfits and terribly ancient clothes that had belonged to my great-grandmother Roben. Hendrik and I often pulled those garments out and frolicked through the attic. The clothing was far too large for us, of course, and Mother would certainly have given us a proper scolding if she'd found out, but she never did. I wondered if anyone else had been up here since then. Surely only the maids, when they carried up other things to put away.

I'd have loved to spend the whole day up here, but I was no longer a child. And not yet a ghost. I worked my way over to a small chest tucked behind a steamer trunk.

I lifted the lid and rummaged through it until I located my maternal grandmother's alarm clock. She'd always been a stickler for punctuality, a virtue she considered second only to Christian discipline. The large, slightly rounded table clock had always struck me as slightly menacing, but now it was exactly what I needed. I blew away a coating of dust, wound it up, and set the time. It came to life, ticking quietly. My heart warmed as I remembered my kindly grandmother. She'd always made sure her grandchildren received proper schooling and instruction. And now I imagined she was watching over me to make sure that I didn't neglect my responsibilities.

46

I labored over the accounts through the afternoon. Mother was receiving friends again, but I had no desire to look in on them. Fatigue made it difficult to concentrate, and the discussion with Max kept haunting me. I regretted my proposal and wished things could have gone differently.

But I couldn't just pretend that nothing had happened. It was clear now that Max didn't want to marry me. At least not yet. Maybe never. We could sleep together and take our walks, but if Max had his way, that would be all. No matter how much I tried to convince myself that as a modern woman I had no need of a permanent relationship, my disappointment would not go away.

A knock on the door brought me out of my confused brooding. I was suddenly apprehensive Max might have come to see me. But it was Marie.

I rubbed my eyes and suppressed another yawn. "What is it?"

"The gracious lady wishes to speak with you in the salon. She says it's important."

Important? What was the reason for this summons? Had one of her lady friends brought along a son who absolutely had to be presented?

Marie's expression was grave. I gathered she'd get a stern reprimand if she failed to produce me right away.

"Very well. In just a moment," I said.

I stood and stretched, though that didn't much help. I was exhausted, and I wasn't about to change my clothing merely to appear briefly in the salon. Mother would just have to say whatever was on her mind. I'd have a coffee and then come back to my work.

"Ah, there you are!" my mother exclaimed as I pushed open the glass door to the salon. "Join us. We saved you a place."

She beckoned me to sit next to her on the rattan sofa. Opposite her sat Mrs. Söderlund, Mrs. Axelson, and Mrs. Niebro. They weren't Mother's closest friends, but they were all sufficiently well acquainted for her to invite them as a group once a month.

I greeted each of them. Their faces were as solemn as if the king had just died.

I joined my mother, glad there was no promising young man present. "I hope you are enjoying your visit, ladies."

"Oh yes, indeed," the first one said.

"You seem quite fatigued," remarked the second.

Stella threw me a critical glance. "My daughter has been working a great deal, staying up quite late."

Was she on to me? That was the last thing I needed.

Fortunately, none of those present suggested I find myself a man who could take some of the burden from my shoulders.

"There is horrific news," Mrs. Söderlund said.

"What has happened?" I asked. "I must admit that I have not looked at today's newspaper."

"Well, you should call for it," Mrs. Söderlund said. "Yesterday in Sarajevo, the Austrian crown prince was murdered. Along with his wife. All Europe is in shock."

My eyes went wide in surprise. In our modern age, attacks on members of royal families were quite rare. But when they did occur, it was as if one's own family had been targeted.

"That is frightful!" I exclaimed. "Do they know who did it?"

"According to what we have heard, it was a Serb belonging to a group opposed to the Austrian monarchy. I am very afraid this will soon have terrible consequences."

"Let's call it by its name," Mother intervened. "War! There will be war. Austria will not let such a horrible deed pass unpunished."

"The kaiser has demanded the Serbian authorities carry out a ruthless investigation," Mrs. Söderlund said. "And if the results are not satisfactory, Austria will take its own measures."

"The assassination of a crown prince is more than enough reason for reprisals," Mrs. Niebro proclaimed. "In the old days, such criminals would be drawn and quartered."

I tried to make sense of the remarks flying around the room. Of course, assassination should be punished, but was war really looming?

And how would war affect us? Sweden hadn't been at war for more than a century. We'd proclaimed ourselves neutral long ago. Would the king change that policy because members of another country's ruling family were assassinated?

Plunged in these thoughts, I only half heard the women's comments. They vied with one another in suggesting ways to avenge the murder, each worse than the one before. My mother did not participate, and at last she rapped on the table to call the debate to order.

"We no longer live in the Middle Ages," she said. "Murders can no longer be avenged according to the ancient laws."

Mrs. Söderlund turned to me. "What is your view?"

"Unleashing a war is no solution, in my opinion. I hope the kaiser feels the same. War brings suffering to thousands. I would hazard a guess that not a single Serbian peasant wished to have the crown prince shot. Those innocent folks will bear the brunt if war should break out."

The elderly Mrs. Axelson was clearly thrilled by the prospect of conflict. "But my dear, don't you agree that a prince's life is worth more than that of a peasant?"

"Every human life is worth the same, from the moment of birth," I asserted. "Every person bears the same responsibility. A peasant tries to protect his family, a king his people. If a peasant's child is attacked by a bear, the father will do his best to kill the bear or drive it away, but he will not seek to exterminate all bears. The same is true of a king or a kaiser. If an individual commits a despicable crime, that does not justify attacking a whole race or nation. The murderer should be arrested, tried, and put in prison. The world has no need of another war."

After I'd unburdened myself, I became aware my heart was pounding. The women gaped at me. I'd elicited a similar reaction once during a Stockholm demonstration. Both women and men had been scandalized by my full-throated declaration that it was unjust to grant men every possible privilege yet deny women basic rights.

I stole a glance at my mother. Despite her grim mien, a sly smile played about her lips. Had she been waiting for me to shock these female proponents of war? Expecting me to read them chapter and verse from Leviticus? Well, I'd just done exactly that.

My head ached as I left the salon.

All this talk about war! Father had told me our ancestors had always fought at the king's side. I'd never known anything of armed conflict, but his accounts were more than enough. He'd told me about our early ancestors from the seventeenth and eighteenth centuries, when Sweden was perpetually invading other countries and waging war. Those were stories of blood and suffering, for frequently more was destroyed than was gained. Kings had died in wars, and thousands of families lost fathers or sons. Soldiers raped thousands of women. Countless children starved.

I calmed down somewhat once I was outside on the stairs. The sun shone, and the birds twittered. A horse's whinny reached my ear from far away. A hot breeze swept across the gravel of the circular drive. Here in Sweden, nothing had changed.

Still, I had an intuition that our lives would change in the coming months. Would the king maintain neutrality, or would he dispatch our forces? Would our national life change from one day to the next?

That evening, I walked to the cottage. The news of the assassination made my brooding seem trivial, and I couldn't go on sulking and feeling rejected.

I knocked on the cottage door but got no response. "Hello?" I called into the darkness, but there was no one there.

Maybe Max was drinking at the village tavern? I stood on the cottage porch for a long time, tempted to ride to the village to look for him. But I dismissed that notion. He'd probably heard the news from the stable boys or the coachman of one of Mother's friends. If Max was in the tavern, it was because he wanted news. Kaiser Franz Joseph of Austria didn't rule Pomerania, but Max's homeland was part of Prussia, ruled by Germany's Kaiser Wilhelm II, and therefore bound to Austria-Hungary by a formal alliance. If war came, Max would be obligated to fight on Austria's side. I refused to contemplate the possible conflagration.

Just as I turned to go, a figure strode vigorously out of the forest. Max! He accelerated when he caught sight of me. "Hello, Agneta!"

"Hello," I responded after a moment.

An awkward silence followed.

"Have you heard? Crown Prince Franz Ferdinand of Austria was shot in Sarajevo."

Max nodded. "One of the coachmen told us. And now, of course, everyone is speculating this will mean war."

"Sweden has not been at war for a very long time. I know our king, and I doubt he will get involved."

"That may well be, but things look different for Germany. If Kaiser Franz Joseph decides to attack the Serbs, Wilhelm will join him."

"Then let us hope such things do not come to pass."

Again we fell silent.

Max was the first to speak. "About last night. I greatly regret that—"

"Shh!" I put my finger across his lips. "There is no cause for regret. I should not have pressed you. I still have no idea what made me do it. All this talk from my mother about marriage . . . Everyone seems to be impatient for me to choose a husband. I suspect I simply wanted to be done with all of it. It was wrong, I see that now, and I beg you to forgive me."

Max didn't respond directly, but those worry lines appeared in his face again.

Suddenly he stepped forward and pulled me into his arms. "There is nothing to forgive. You responded to your heart. When the time is right, I will be the one to propose. Grant me that time, I beg you."

I agreed, but something deep inside me had been laid waste. I loved him. I looked at him and wanted to lose myself in his eyes. But his rejection was a dark shadow between us that I could do nothing to dispel. We kissed and made love as we had before, but when it was over, I gazed mindlessly through the window and wondered what was in store.

47

That warm June was followed by an even warmer July. The wheat ripened as the horses sheltered under the willow trees, stolidly waiting for the evening breeze.

I often went to the pasture to watch Talla and the others. Evening Star had almost completely recovered, but I was reluctant to tire him. I had him put out to the pasture, free and unsaddled. I might never ride him again, but I did hope we would be able to breed him.

Life continued its routine despite the threat that hung over us like an ominous cloud. I read every word of the newspaper reports. Our local paper said very little, so I arranged for delivery of a Stockholm publication filled with current events.

I was alarmed that the Serbian regime showed no inclination to prosecute the guilty parties. There was speculation that the Serbian authorities even approved of the murder as an excuse to drive the Austrians out of Bosnia and reclaim the land for Serbia. The newspapers called this the "July crisis" and predicted war if negotiations failed. The dire expectations of Mother's friends seemed to be coming true.

Late on July 28, I looked out the office window to see our errand boy, Peter, racing across the front courtyard. What could be important enough to send him scrambling straight up the front steps instead of through the servants' entrance? The knock at the door came moments later.

"Come in." I looked up to see our highly excited young messenger clutching his cap.

Peter bowed hastily. "Gracious miss! The Austrians declared war on Serbia!"

"Who told you this?" I asked. We'd heard rumors of war for days, but the newspaper hadn't confirmed them.

"Olson, the telegraph office messenger. Somebody got a telegram. The telegrapher was terribly upset and called his family together right away. Olson jumped on his bicycle and got to the village just before I did. Everyone is shocked."

So was I. I remembered vividly the days at the Östermalm Secondary School for Girls when we'd had to memorize the links between royal families and the resulting national alliances.

It was quite likely that an Austrian declaration of war against Serbia would oblige the Germans to lend their support. The Serbs, on the other hand, were allied with the Russian czar, who in turn had ties to France. That could potentially put five major European countries at war with one another. And more might well join, as Belgium was allied with both France and Great Britain. It was like a row of dominos. Once the first tile fell, the others would follow.

How long would Sweden be able to stay clear of that deadly sequence? Relations between our royal family and the German kaiser were good, but there was no formal alliance. Would the Danes be dragged into supporting their German neighbors? And what about Norway, independent of the Swedish crown since 1905? Or the Finns, threatened by Russia?

"Gracious miss, are you all right?" Peter sounded worried.

Only then did I realize I'd been sitting there for a long while, rigid and unresponsive.

"Yes, thank you, Peter. And thank you for the news."

The boy bowed and left the office.

I stared for a time at the place where he'd been standing, then rose and left the office. I went downstairs, crossed the garden, and plunged into the woods that surrounded the mansion grounds.

I sat on a rock in a mossy area and stared up into the sheltering leaves.

War had begun.

Yet nothing seemed to have changed. The leaves rustled in the wind; the birds sang their summer songs and taught their fledglings to fly. The sun was shining, and clouds drifted across the sky. The grass bent gently before the breeze. Beetles and ants scurried in search of food.

Human beings were the only creatures who understood what it meant to declare war. Human beings alone were aware of the disastrous consequences.

Our manor was steeped in silence that evening. The maids whispered to one another, and Mr. Bruns and Miss Rosendahl exchanged wordless glances that spoke volumes. It was obvious they wanted to know more, but I had nothing to tell them. Mother was the same, silent and sunk in her own thoughts.

I went to Max after the maids were in bed and all lights were out.

His cottage was lit. I took a moment to watch him through the window before announcing myself. He was sitting at his desk, absorbed in some document. Was it a letter? If so, when had it come?

Max appeared very focused on the document's contents, and he'd clearly not taken the time to change from his work clothes. His suspenders cut into his shoulders, and his shirt was wrinkled. A smile passed over my face as I started up the front steps. One wooden stair creaked loudly. That had become our sign.

He opened the door before I could knock. His uncombed hair hung over his forehead, and his smile seemed forced.

"Hello, Agneta. Come in."

I searched his face. "I hope I'm not intruding."

He took me in his arms and kissed me. "You never intrude. And anyway, I know you'll come to me every evening."

He held me close, and I could tell his heart was racing. Was it because of me or because of what he'd been reading?

I glanced at the desk. "Did you get a letter?" It was back in the envelope, which he hadn't bothered to put away.

Max released me, turned, took the envelope, and shoved it into his trouser pocket. His expression was indecipherable when his eyes met mine. "Yes, but it's nothing of importance."

"It seems to be on your mind."

"War has broken out. You can imagine how that is affecting people."

"Yes, I can," I said. "But there's nothing for you to fear. It will not affect you here at Lion Hall, and if it does, I will make sure you do not have to fight."

I moved to embrace him, but he stepped back.

"What if I decide to volunteer?"

I stared at him in disbelief. "You would choose to go to the war?"

"Why not?" he replied gruffly. "Many men my age are volunteering already. It is our duty to support Austria."

"Our duty?" I shook my head. "You are half Swedish, or have you forgotten?"

"Of course not. But what if the Swedish king orders a mobilization?"

"We have been neutral forever! I hardly think Sweden would join a war that has nothing to do with us."

There was an agitation in him I'd never seen before. "It is not always a question of being directly attacked, is it?"

I was appalled. I'd never have imagined Max could be so caught up in this fervor.

He read my reaction, for his shoulders sank and suddenly he looked exhausted. "Forgive me, please. This is no reason for us to quarrel."

He embraced me, but I didn't return the gesture. I stood as rigid as a wooden pole. I'd come here looking for calm and quiet, and I could no longer face this.

"I am very tired," I said at last. "It would be better for me to go back."

Max nodded. I almost hoped he'd ask me to spend the night with him. But he made no move to hold me back. I went to the door.

"Agneta," he said.

I looked back. My throat tightened, but I did my best to hide my feelings.

"Please give me some time."

The same request he'd made four weeks earlier, when I'd suggested we get married.

"Very well," I said. I didn't even have the heart to ask him the reason for his request.

I said good night and went outside.

The night was alive with sound, and thousands of stars burned overhead. This was the spectacle we had enjoyed so often over the previous year. But there I was, outside, and he was in his cottage. I turned back one last time, only to see him sit down at his desk again, unfold the letter, and devote himself to studying it.

I didn't want to admit it, but somehow I had the feeling the end was near. Maybe it was just the letter; maybe he simply didn't want me to be disturbed by its contents. But as I was doing my best to rationalize Max's behavior and excuse it, a little voice in my mind warned me he was slipping away. Was there anything I could do to prevent it?

I didn't know. Maybe something would occur to me once I was back in the quiet of my room, where the only sound was the ticking of my grandmother's alarm clock.

48

Germany declared war a week later. The dominos were falling. Which would be the next to go?

Our king refused to be drawn into the conflict. He said Sweden had not been involved in a war since 1814, and he wasn't going to end a century of peace by declaring support for Germany. Gustav was accused of weakness, but I was grateful and relieved.

Even so, I sensed a change, especially in Max. He was moody and sullen most of the time. When I spoke to him, he would look up as if seeing me for the first time. I asked what was on his mind, but he never replied.

Max read about the war for hours on end, and I knew he was debating whether to enlist. It was incredible to me that a man who'd left his family estate to escape their demands now wanted to submit himself to the discipline of the military. A man with a good, comfortable life now desired to endure the pain and misery of the battlefield. It seemed I'd never understood him.

This change meant that we only seldom met for our morning walk. At first I sought him out and persuaded him, but the walls he put up grew ever higher. One day he didn't appear at our meeting place, and not long afterward, I stopped going as well. He again said he needed time to himself and suggested it would be enough to see one another in the evenings. His words hurt me deeply, for the meaning behind them was clear. He no longer desired my company. We still made love, but the thrill was gone.

That upset me greatly, and often, after visiting him, I would cry myself to sleep. I didn't know how to get him to love me as before. So I plunged into my work and read everything about the war I could lay my hands on.

In late August, I received an inquiry from Germany that made me profoundly uneasy. A certain Count von Kranitz communicated his interest in our Swedish warmblood horses. He flattered me in his letter: *I was informed that your horses are the best, the most robust, and the sturdiest in Europe.*

A disquieting euphoria seemed to have swept Germany. Many men hailed the war as glorious and saw no purpose in life more sacred than throwing themselves into armed conflict to prove their valor. Max's interest in that propaganda disturbed me, but I trusted he wouldn't abandon his duty to the estate.

Despite my misgivings, I agreed to receive the count and his entourage. We made assiduous preparations for the visit. My visitor arrived in an open landau drawn by four handsome dapple grays. I was taken aback by the sight of four men in uniform alighting from the carriage. The count hadn't mentioned any military involvement. Had war fever gone so far in Germany that everyone was in uniform?

I went to receive them, glad I'd chosen to wear a severely formal dark-gray dress. It was vital to avoid giving such visitors any sign I might be naive in business affairs. White muslin would have sent the wrong message.

"We wish you a warm welcome to Lion Hall," I said in acceptable German. I'd regularly practiced it over the last year, thanks to Max. "I am Agneta Lejongård, countess of this estate."

The count clicked his heels together, bowed, and kissed my hand. It was all I could do to hide my distaste. We'd rarely had any business with the military, but even Swedish military officers put me off. Their bristling, aggressive attitude intimidated me. My friends in Stockholm had regularly decried such absurdly exaggerated displays of masculinity.

"Countess Lejongård! Here I have my stable master, Weber; my deputy, Köster; and my friend Baron von Stein."

The men saluted in turn. Even the stable master was in uniform.

"I am very pleased you agreed to receive us," he continued. "Truly, your horses have a superb reputation."

"You are very kind," I answered. "Perhaps I could offer the gentlemen some refreshment?"

"Please do!" Von Kranitz said. He fell into step behind me, and the others followed.

I escorted them to the smoking room, the usual venue for business meetings. The tobacco smell exuded by the walls lent me greater credibility and had helped conclude even the most difficult negotiations. The tactic worked with Swedish clients, so why not with Germans?

The men looked around in admiration. They seemed especially attracted by the still life of a hunt that showed slaughtered pheasants dangling from nooses. In the foreground lay a deer shot through the heart, surrounded by the typical tableau of foliage and evergreen branches. I didn't know if Father had cared for the painting, but for me it had provoked grisly childhood nightmares. I would have banished it to the attic, but I'd seen its effect on certain male visitors. Death and blood excited them. The painting spurred them to engage and negotiate seriously.

I invited my visitors to settle into the leather armchairs and rang for Bruns. He appeared immediately with a tray laden with a coffee service and a platter of Mrs. Bloomquist's pastry creations.

"Our Swedish tradition is to offer seven varieties of baked goods with coffee," I explained. "The coffee hour, our *fika*, is sacred. Help yourselves, gentlemen. My cook will never forgive me if the tray is not empty upon its return."

Bruns poured the coffee, and they raised their cups. I took a sip. The strong aroma and robust taste warmed my mouth and pleased my palate.

"It is quite unusual to find a woman administering an estate entirely alone," Von Kranitz commented after savoring his first taste of coffee. I'd told Mrs. Bloomquist to brew it strong. Business discussions were often tiresome, and I wanted to avoid any hint of fatigue. "But in Sweden, the women have always been robust, true?"

"If you refer to our Norse history, you are entirely correct," I replied. "There are many examples. Our early sagas tell us that women retrieved the bodies of warriors from the battlefields and carried them to Valhalla."

"Yes, we know your Valkyries. Your mythology is most admirable."

"Thank you." I would have preferred to go straight to business, but courtesy required spending some time on small talk. "Our family line is proud of its history of some two hundred and fifty years of serving our kings and running our estate."

"I am proud to report," Von Kranitz replied, "that my forefathers rode with the knights of Karl the Great. I know one of your greatest monarchs bore the same name."

"I understand you to refer to Carolus Rex. Indeed, Charles XII was one of our fiercest kings. Unfortunately, his fate was to be slain by a rifle bullet. A number of his contemporaries did not regret his passing. His campaigns cost the land more than they yielded."

Von Kranitz was assessing me, and his reference to our country's warlike past was anything but innocent. I was increasingly sure he wasn't seeking horses for civilian purposes.

"What do you think?" he asked at last. "Will Gustav V support the kaiser?" The mood in the room became noticeably tense.

"You must ask the king himself," I said. "Our family is closely aligned with the House of Bernadotte, but we do not engage in politics. My ancestors chose to concentrate on horse breeding instead."

Von Kranitz pursed his lips. He reflected for a moment. "I am most eager to see your horses. Might you take us on a tour of your stalls and pastures?"

"With the greatest pleasure," I said. "Once we have finished our pastries."

Half an hour later, I escorted them out to our pasture and from there to the horse barn. Von Kranitz had nothing but praise for our animals.

"Horses like these!" he declared with a sweeping gesture, as if taking possession of the barn and pasture. "This is what the kaiser needs!"

In that instant, I knew we would not come to terms.

Max awaited us at the horse barn. I'd told him of the visit of his compatriots, and he seemed genuinely pleased by their uniforms. "Max von Bredestein!" he introduced himself.

"Pleased to make your acquaintance!" Von Kranitz said. "You are German? What is your opinion of the most recent events?"

"I believe the kaiser has made the correct decision," Max answered. "Austria must not allow this cowardly assassination to go unpunished."

Von Kranitz took his measure. "You seem quite capable. And, no doubt, of a good family as well. A gentleman like you, with a good knowledge of horses, would be of great use to the army."

Max glanced my way. It was extremely difficult to conceal my displeasure at hearing the count openly attempt to lure away my manager. But I would wait for a more appropriate moment to send the man and his followers politely on their way.

"Thank you," said Max. "However, I am contracted to oversee the breeding of these animals. I am needed on the estate."

His reply didn't sound particularly enthusiastic. He was trying to hide it, but I'd seen his admiration for our male visitors and detected the longing in his eyes.

"The animals would be used for military purposes?" I asked. "Where would they be assigned? To the battlefield?" I didn't immediately realize I'd raised my voice.

"We will of course give the animals training so that they will not be frightened in battle, but I assume most of them will quickly learn to tolerate the sound of gunfire."

I took a deep breath. "And how much are you prepared to pay—and for how many animals?" Since he'd concealed his intentions, I was hoping to accuse him of trying to swindle me. I'd also have been happy to accuse Germany of seeking to bribe Sweden to support its war.

"The kaiser offers fifty thousand marks for the entire herd."

"Fifty thousand?" I echoed. That was a huge sum.

"For five hundred horses," Von Kranitz added, quite pleased with himself. "That is a retail price of one hundred marks per animal." He clearly assumed I was incapable of simple arithmetic.

I left him hanging and looked at Max. "What do you think, Herr von Bredestein?"

"A very good offer, in my opinion!" Max responded enthusiastically.

I turned to Von Kranitz and met the dark eyes of his angular face. "Thank you very much for the generous offer. I am afraid, however, that Swedish horses have been sheltered so long from the sound of gunfire that they will never again become accustomed to it. Please convey to the kaiser my thanks for his interest; however, I will not sell my horses. They are not suited for war."

"But, Countess, I do not understand! I said—" Von Kranitz glanced at the other men. They'd obviously been expecting to conclude the sale quickly. "We can raise the offer somewhat, if you wish. We will pay you sixty thousand!"

I shook my head. I was not going to send my horses to die on the battlefield. "I greatly regret it, Herr von Kranitz, but that is my last word. I am grateful for your visit and your interest, and I wish you all the best."

Von Kranitz looked at me as if I'd lost my mind. His jaw worked, and he seemed to be waiting for me to change my mind. But I did not.

Enraged, he turned abruptly and stamped back to the carriage. I trailed after them, but the men did not even do me the courtesy of saying goodbye.

I went to the office as soon as the Germans were gone. Max stormed in, beside himself. "Why did you turn them down?"

"You heard me; I don't want my horses sent into battle. They are too valuable. And the entire herd? Sacrifice our entire breeding line?"

"But he offered you an enormous sum!"

"The danger to which the horses would be exposed is equally enormous," I told him. "In addition, we Swedes will not betray our neutrality so easily."

"But this doesn't infringe upon Swedish neutrality!"

"Oh no? These horses would carry German soldiers into battle! That absolutely constitutes support for their war."

My heart was pounding. My feelings for Max had been cooling for some time, and the fact that he was willing to send our horses to be mowed down on the battlefield filled me with inexpressible fury.

"These horses are important to the war!" he protested. "And we need the money! It's a fortune you cannot refuse! I will ride after them and bring Von Kranitz back!"

"As far as I can recall, I am still the mistress of this estate," I informed him in an icy tone. "And I refuse to send my animals into this war!"

Max's eyes narrowed. He involuntarily knotted his hands into fists and looked ready to attack me. I'd never seen him like this, and suddenly I felt truly afraid. Why was he so obsessed with this war? Why did he want to turn our horses into cannon fodder? These beautiful beasts we had so carefully brought into the world, raised, and cherished?

"Would you be saying this if your king had ordered general mobilization?" he asked. "If the English attacked?"

"The king has done no such thing," I snapped. "And he is smart enough not to do so in the foreseeable future. Do you really believe the country can afford to sacrifice thousands of men? Those days are long gone. Every child here learns in school how much suffering our wars caused. By now we should be beyond rejoicing at the prospect of war!"

Max glowered at me. I thought he was going to say something more, but he turned on his heel and angrily left the office.

I stared after him for a moment and then sagged back against the desk. I'd always seen Max as a gentle man, one who spoke in moving terms of the skies, butterflies, and other worlds in the stars.

The man who had just left my office was a stranger to me. Sweden hadn't embraced the European war, but, incredibly, the war had reached out and altered Max's heart beyond recognition.

49

I didn't visit Max in the weeks that followed, either mornings or evenings. I didn't want to see him. I was furious about the horses and his views on the war, and I spoke no more to him than absolutely necessary. I couldn't believe he could be so adamantly in favor of ordering men to their deaths on the backs of our horses.

One morning in September, just before the big annual foxhunt, Tim rushed up to me as I was walking to the horse barns.

"Gracious miss! Herr von Bredestein didn't come to work this morning! We looked everywhere, and when we didn't find him, we ran to the cottage, but everything there is locked. We didn't want to break down the door, so I thought maybe I could ask you . . ."

My heartbeat accelerated. What had happened? Had he taken our differences as a reason to disappear? Had he put his plans into action and gone back home to volunteer? The thought made me sick.

"You did exactly the right thing," I said. "I have a duplicate key for the cottage. We will both go have a look." I rose as calmly as I could, struggling to keep panic at bay.

Suicide wasn't unknown in our region. I remembered all too well the farmer in the village who hanged himself in his barn after the doctor told him he had cancer.

Had Max received a similar report? I couldn't help thinking of the letter that had concerned him so much. But why hadn't he taken me into his confidence? I put my hand to my mouth, but quickly lowered it again. I didn't want to give the stable boys any reason to think that Max meant more to me than was appropriate.

I was careful to act as I would in the case of any other employee. It was difficult, but I took the key in hand and walked to the cottage, accompanied by some of our workers. On the way there, I had to listen to the wildest speculations. When a stable boy voiced his suspicion that the police were looking for Max, I could take no more.

"Do not spread rumors! Please!" I rebuked him. "We must find out what happened. Only then will we have something to discuss."

The men gaped at me. I'd almost never raised my voice before, but I couldn't permit them to drag Max's name through the mud.

I went up the porch steps at last. I knocked and called out. When there was no answer, I unlocked the cottage.

Chilly silence. All of the furniture was in place, but every personal item was gone.

I went into the bedroom. It was as if he'd never existed. The bed was neatly made. His great-grandfather's robe wasn't in the wardrobe. The valise he'd brought with him was gone.

I stood rooted to the spot for some time. My heart hammered against my ribs, and the blood surging through my body gave me a terrible headache.

I couldn't believe my eyes. Max had simply left. I looked everywhere but found no letter of farewell. Hadn't he owed me at least that much? Couldn't he at least have left me a note?

I felt pangs of guilt. Had I driven him away? Or had Count von Kranitz's remarks won him over?

Some time passed before I realized the men were waiting for my reaction.

"It appears that Mr. von Bredestein has left," I announced, confirming the obvious. I turned around. "Lasse, do you feel ready to take over as stable master, without assistance?"

"Yes, of course, gracious miss." Lasse sounded nervous, but I knew Max had trained him well, and, after all, Lasse had already been working at Lion Hall for twelve years.

"Good. Let us go back to work. And should anyone happen to discover the whereabouts of the gentleman, inform me immediately."

"Yes, gracious miss," the men chorused. They dispersed, each back to his own responsibilities.

I remained in the cottage for a while. *Max, what have you done?* I lifted my eyes to the beams overhead and silently appealed to him. *Why didn't you talk to me? What drove you to betray us?*

I went back to the manor to think about what had happened.

"What was all that commotion?" Mother asked as soon as I entered the house.

"Our manager has disappeared." I said no more and walked past her.

"Disappeared?" she called after me.

"Yes, he has vanished," I said without looking around. "Lasse is ready to take over as stable master. I will assume all management responsibilities." Without another word, I quickly strode upstairs.

I closed the office door behind me, and the dam broke. I curled up, trying to stifle the sounds of my pain. Tears streamed, hot and heavy. I trembled all over. I dragged myself to the desk and fell heavily into the chair behind it. There, I sobbed and wept, pressed my hands to my forehead, and let tears drench me. My ears roared. My heart raced and contracted in pain at the same time.

Why had he left? What had happened? Gradually my grief and bewilderment gave way to worry and apprehension.

I looked up when I heard a knock. No one must see me in this condition! Not Bruns, not Miss Rosendahl, and certainly not my mother. I breathed deeply to regain control and frantically wiped my cheeks. If it was Bruns or the housekeeper, the person would go away if I didn't answer. But it was more likely that Mother was outside, intent on demanding an explanation.

The knock came again and then the door opened. Stella entered, clearly concerned.

My eyes were burning, and I knew my distress was obvious.

"Are you ill?" Mother asked as she closed the door behind her.

"Yes—no!" I took a deep breath and expelled it, wishing Marit were there to help me. I hadn't written to her during the recent strange events. Now I wished I had. I needed someone to open up to. Mother was certainly not that person. "I cannot understand how he could simply disappear."

Mother came around the desk to take a closer look at me. It wasn't any use pretending I hadn't been bawling like a baby.

She took a handkerchief from her sleeve and held it out. "Here. Take this."

"Thank you." I wiped my eyes, blew my nose, and wadded up the square of fabric.

"Well, you already know my views concerning men who abandon their homes," she began in a gentle voice. "That was an obvious sign the man could not be counted on. I will not assert that he achieved nothing for the good of Lion Hall, but you should have taken as a warning the fact that he walked away from his father's estate. I can only assume that is his flawed character. And you have no claim upon him. Why would he have had any more reason to respect you than his own family?"

I felt the urge to scream that I'd been far closer to Max than his father had. I wanted to tell her I'd been vitally important to him.

But that surge of resentment ceded to the revelation that she was right.

Max hadn't respected his own family, and I'd been nothing but his employer. I'd assumed that the ties between us would keep him with me, despite our differences. But clearly I'd been mistaken. If only he'd left me a note, I might have seen things differently, but given the circumstances, I had to face the fact that he'd abandoned me, just as he'd walked out on his own family.

"The next time you appoint an estate manager, you will do better to trust someone you know."

"But Father interviewed him. Father chose him."

"Bruns said Father chose him."

"How else would he have been aware the manager's position was open?" I didn't want to believe Max had conned his way on to our estate. That would mean I'd also have to question his feelings for me. I refused to believe he was that manipulative.

"Your father allowed himself to be blackmailed by a stable master." She spoke in a tone harsher than I'd ever heard her use when mentioning Father. "He took out a loan without telling me of the circumstances that prompted him to do so."

"He wanted to protect Hendrik. You would surely have done the same."

"I would have insisted Hendrik put an end to the affair."

"Langeholm would have smeared our family name."

Mother shook her head. "He would have failed. But Thure was headstrong. It is unfortunately the case that men do what they think is right, even when it is not. And it is also a fact that a woman too often seeks in vain to put her husband on the right path. For a time, he pretends to understand, but in truth he considers her weak and stupid, and so he embraces his fate."

Those words almost convinced me Mother knew about my affair with Max, that she'd realized something was going on. But I'd been careful, and she'd never shown any sign of suspecting.

I clutched the handkerchief even tighter. "Thank you, Mother."

Stella nodded. "You are my daughter and the mistress of this estate. You will deal with this loss and soldier on. The Lejongårds always remain steadfast, no matter what happens."

After all those years of seeking her encouragement, I'd finally received it. She wasn't effusive and she wasn't warmhearted, but at least she was on my side.

Stella left the room with her head held high. I looked down at my hands after the door closed. How was it that both of the loves I'd had in life had simply slipped between my fingers? Was I unfit for real love? Was this my destiny—to make the wrong choice again and again?

50

After an almost sleepless night, I took a morning ride to the village. I didn't really know where to turn, but I hoped someone could tell me where Max might have gone.

I headed first to the tavern. Friedjof had run the public house as long as I could remember. The man had served lemonade to us when we were children, but I hadn't been inside in years. I opened the door and entered a mysterious den where the walls reeked of cigarettes.

"Well, look here! What brings the mistress of Lion Hall to visit me?" That friendly mutter came from a nook behind the bar. Friedjof emerged. He'd aged. His hair was still thick, but now it was snow-white, as was his beard. He'd always been stocky, but the weight of time had added a stoop.

"Good morning, Friedjof. It has been a long time."

"Right ye are. Far too long. But nobody expects a young miss to come looking for a stein of beer and coarse talk from the farmers."

"My father visited often though, didn't he?"

The tapster nodded. "Aye, though not too oft in the months before he died. He was a regular before that, here every week. What happened to him was a misery to us all."

I tried to imagine my father rubbing elbows with the peasants and field hands who came here for a drop after a hard day's work. I couldn't. Father stopped bringing me here when I turned twelve. Agneta would be a grown woman soon, he'd declared, and a tavern was no place for her.

Friedjof inspected me with his watery blue eyes. "But I'm sure ye haven't come to talk about yer father. Am I right?"

"You are," I answered him. "My estate manager disappeared yesterday. I wanted to ask if you had seen him."

My host's eyes narrowed. He seemed to be searching through a collection of his clients' faces, like scanning over titles of books on a shelf.

"Ah, that's right. The German fella!" he said at last. "He come here a time or two. Talked to the folks, friendly-like. Surprised his Swedish was so good."

"His mother is Swedish."

"Is that it? He never said. But the man never said much about himself, now I think of it. More interested in the region and the people. Talked about the estate a lot, how he was glad to know ye, admired how ye took on yer father's business and were running it all by yerself."

I held still, expressionless, resisting the urge to close my eyes or otherwise betray emotion. The man across the counter had known so many people, he could read a face like a book. Any hint that the mistress of the estate had feelings for an employee would become the talk of the village.

"Did he say he had to go somewhere? Has he been in the last few days?"

"Nay," the proprietor replied. "Last time he come was a week ago. Wasn't a regular anyhow, so I didn't think much about it."

"So you don't know where he may have gone?"

Friedjof shook his head. "Sorry. Haven't heard anything about the man."

I had another question I was burning to ask: Had he ever seen Max in the company of another woman? But I held back. I didn't dare expose myself any more than I already had.

"Thank you very much, Friedjof."

I ducked out of the tavern, and looked up and down the street outside. The sandy surface of the road was crisscrossed with tracks. Were Max's footprints among them? Had he passed through the village, or had he traversed the forest? Perhaps he wasn't far away. Not a single horse from our stables was missing . . . but he could easily have bought a horse from one of the local farmers. He could be in Stockholm by now or aboard a ship bound for his homeland.

I mounted Talla again and urged her forward. My skin prickled, and a burning sensation was growing deep within me.

I would have to get over this. I'd already lived through the end of a love affair. But could I forget a man I'd truly believed to be the great love of my life? A man whose sudden transformation was so inexplicable?

I walked to the cottage every night that week. Driven by the hope that Max might somehow turn up, I persuaded myself it was worth checking one more time. But when I found the windows dark; when I knocked on the door and got no reply; when I opened the door, went in, and found nothing but bare furnishings, I had to face reality. I looked in vain for a farewell letter each time, rummaging in the pantry, the wardrobe, and the desk. It was as if everything we'd shared in this place was nothing but a dream. The only vestige was the scent of him in the bedclothes.

I lay on the bed, wrapped the blanket around me, inhaled it, absorbed it. That didn't help. It merely intensified my suffering and disappointment.

I lived two separate realities in the days that followed. One was as the manager of the estate, investing all my energy in its affairs, and the other was as the abandoned lover, grieving and staring through the window for some sign of her beloved's return.

I'd filed a missing person report with the police, but they doubted anything would come of it. "If he took his things, that's a sure sign he was leaving for good. As long as he hasn't committed a crime, we can't go looking for him."

I riffled through each day's mail with trembling fingers. I was hoping to find a letter without a return address written in Max's hand or awkwardly tapped out on a typewriter so as to give no indication of its origin.

No news came, and my life grew more and more dismal. My work required ever closer attention, but I neglected anything that seemed to be taking care of itself. I was a sleepwalker waiting to be awakened.

I finally decided to write to Max's father. I'd once seen his address on an envelope lying unopened on Max's desk. The letter wasn't recent; he'd brought it with him from Stockholm. His father had been under the impression that Max was still living with a friend, as was his custom when visiting Sweden. Max told me he intended never to open that letter because he knew what it would contain. His father would condemn him for staying away and in the very next line entreat him to return. Max wasn't intimidated by his father's pique and had no desire to go back. I clearly remembered the name of the district where the Von Bredestein estate was located. Max and his father didn't get along, but even so, maybe Max had gone home.

I wrote his father a polite but impersonal note to tell him Max had been working for me and disappeared without a trace. I asked for news, so we wouldn't have to worry, and I ended with a respectful complimentary closing.

My hands shook as I sealed the envelope. I was hoping against hope, as I constantly did in those days, that he would come back. But on finishing the letter to Max's father, I was plagued by additional doubts. What if he'd already received news of Max's death? Max could have plunged into some battle and gotten killed. Any such report would be conclusive but would provide no explanation. My heart would break, but even that seemed better than living with perpetual uncertainty. I got up, left the room, and went to the kitchen. Peter was there, chatting with Marie.

I handed him the envelope and told him to ride directly to the post office. I sent a silent prayer after him for some sign Max was still alive.

51

The following two weeks were no better. The approaching autumn colored the woods in brilliant reds and yellows. I deeply loved that spectacle, and I'd often painted those scenes, but now it seemed a gray mist was masking the reds, yellows, and oranges, robbing them of their brilliance.

My spiritual pain was matched by a listlessness I couldn't explain. I had no appetite and tired quickly. I grew weaker from day to day, and eventually all I wanted to do was stay in bed. But I forced myself to get up. When concentrating on work, I was able to set aside most of my burdens.

One morning toward the end of September, I suddenly awoke feeling miserably ill. I was drenched in a cold sweat. Panic sent my heart racing. The ticking of Grandmother's alarm clock thundered in my head. What was going on?

An instant later, bitter gall rose into my throat, and I frantically rolled out of bed. I barely managed to reach the empty bucket from the previous night's bath. I threw up very little, mostly a nasty dark liquid, but I wasn't able to straighten up for quite a while. Gasping in pain, I squatted by the bucket as spots flickered before my eyes. My mind went blank, and terror possessed me.

Had I contracted a disease? Was it my broken heart? I struggled to my feet and tried to go back to bed, but my head began spinning again. I grabbed the edge of the tub to steady myself and held tight until the dizziness passed. My knees were weak. I was covered from head to toe in a cold sweat. I felt a stab of fear that turned into panic when I realized Lena would soon come and see what was in the bucket.

It was hard, but I summoned enough strength to stand up. I dumped the contents of the bucket into the toilet. Nausea washed over me again as I sloshed water from the pitcher after it.

Back in my room, I seated myself before the mirror.

At that moment the gray veil of heartbreak was torn away. I saw what the past weeks had done to me. There were dark circles under my eyes, as if I hadn't slept since Max's disappearance. My hair was in wild disarray, and my lips were dry. My skin had taken on an ashen cast.

I had no idea how Lena had managed to fix me up so no one had noticed my ravaged condition. It came to me that I'd seen another face like the one in the mirror. That time in the maids' quarters with Susanna! Could I be pregnant?

That thought paralyzed me. How often in Stockholm had women told us they'd vomited their guts out before realizing they were pregnant? But how could it be? I'd always carefully calculated the days of risk and given myself to Max only when it was safe to do so. According to my days of the month . . . But recently, I'd paid no attention to my cycle. The sad weeks had passed in a blur, and I hadn't kept count. And now . . .

There was a knock. I shuddered. Lena!

"Come in!" I called and forced myself to sound casual. *Lena mustn't suspect,* I thought, even though I knew she would never intentionally betray me. But one false step, a single slip, could set tongues wagging to devastating effect. I couldn't do anything before making certain of my condition. Only Dr. Bengtsen could tell me what I needed to know.

The doctor's office was in the far south of the village, almost on the outskirts. The first physician had set up shop in the red-painted wooden house in 1795, and his many successors had staffed it continually since then. The building was badly in need of extensive maintenance, but Dr. Bengtsen was too busy with his patients.

My feeling of terror intensified as I looked at the house. I'd have preferred being seriously ill to being pregnant with the child of a man who'd left without a word. If Mother learned of it, the hell I'd thought was behind me would be nothing compared to the torture to come.

I'd evidently chosen a good time, for the waiting room was empty. A shimmering silence hovered in the house, with not a sound to be heard. Was the doctor away on a house call? The wall clock showed it was ten minutes after two, so lunchtime had passed. Perhaps the office was closed?

I was walking back toward the door to check the office hours when a stair creaked behind me. I spun around and saw the doctor descending. He stopped when he saw me.

"Countess Lejongård," he exclaimed in surprise. "What brings you here?"

"Good day, Doctor. I would like to speak with you. Provided you have the time."

The physician frowned and then nodded. "Come into my consultation room, gracious miss."

Bengtsen went to one of the doors. As he opened it, I caught a glimpse of an examination table and a tall, glass-fronted cabinet filled with many brown glass bottles.

"Now, Countess, what can I do for you?" the doctor asked as he pulled on his laboratory coat.

I followed him into the room hesitantly, for I'd never been in a doctor's office before. Even when I was little, Dr. Bengtsen had always come to us.

That would have been more comforting, for his consultation room sent a little shock of fear through me. An elaborate sketch hanging on the wall depicted a skinless cadaver, its muscles and arteries labeled. Another drawing was a cross-section of the human head. The plants on the window ledge were dusty and wilted, and the inscriptions on the brown bottles were illegible scrawls. The star attraction of this chamber of horrors was the skeleton that hung from a stand by the window and leered at patients with its lipless mouth.

I shuddered but forced myself to focus—and not flee. "You are obliged to maintain patient confidentiality, are you not?"

"Of course. Whatever it may be, I will never share it with anyone."

"Not even with my mother?"

"If that is your wish."

I vividly remembered how he'd carefully explained confidentiality when I'd asked about Susanna.

"Very well, then." I perched on the edge of the small chair before his desk. "I have been tired for some time, and now I feel quite exhausted. And this morning, out of nowhere, I vomited."

The doctor nodded and made a note. "Have you ever experienced this before?"

"Yes, a couple of times in the past, but I quickly got over it."

"And did this always occur in the morning, or was it also at other times of the day?"

I thought back. When was I least interested in eating?

"Mornings," I heard myself declare. "Yes, in the morning. I would have much preferred to skip breakfast, but my mother never permitted that."

The doctor nodded. My cheeks burned.

"Now I must put a delicate question to you," said Bengtsen. "In recent weeks, have you had contact with a man?"

Contact? I'd had contact with many men. But I knew very well what he was asking. "You mean, did I sleep with someone?"

Plainly discomfited, the physician made a face. "Um, I do."

"Yes," I answered. It was no use lying. One wasn't simply visited with a child the way the Virgin Mary had been. "And if you also wish to know whether my menstruation occurred afterward, the answer is no. Not in the last month. Or, to be specific, I lost track of the dates, for there was a great deal of estate business to manage, and then there was the war as well . . ."

Bengtsen furrowed his brow. "Understood. In order to be certain, I must ask you to provide me with a urine sample. I will get a container, and you can go behind that screen."

Urine sample? I gave him a surprised look. Had he done this with Susanna?

Dr. Bengtsen stepped out and soon returned with a glass jar. He left the room. I went behind the screen and squatted. The awkwardness and absurdity of this kept me from producing anything initially, but eventually I managed a small quantity. When I rose after finishing, my vision clouded over. Tiny stars burst before my eyes. Before I was able to call out for help, everything reverted to normal. The spell of vertigo was over in a flash.

I called Bengtsen and handed the container to him. He asked me to wait and disappeared into his laboratory. I wondered what on earth he was doing with my urine. Was he evaluating its density? Checking to see if it was flammable?

Quite a while passed before he returned. His expression was serious. "Well, Countess, I have confirmed that you are expecting a child."

For a moment, I even forgot to breathe. My heart skipped a beat, and my hands began trembling.

I'd suspected it, but even so, the confirmation hit me hard. My stomach cramped up. I knew what his diagnosis meant even though my mind was in a whirl.

Bengtsen returned to his seat behind the desk. "I do not know whether congratulations are in order, and so I will not comment. But I will counsel you to arrange for regular medical care during the upcoming months so the pregnancy can proceed normally. And you should not ride on horseback in the meantime, for that might cause a miscarriage."

So the pregnancy can proceed normally. Those words spilled across me like water splashed across a leaf.

I'd been impregnated by a man who stole away in the night. I was expecting his child!

"Thank you, Doctor." I got up, feeling entirely numb. Somehow I had the presence of mind to assure Bengtsen I would be inviting him to call on me. I gave him my hand, took my leave, and stumbled out of the office.

Outside I saw several women walking in my direction. They were probably wondering what on earth the countess was doing here. I tried to keep my composure and greeted them as I went to my horse. I swung up into the saddle.

Hadn't the doctor just said I should refrain from riding? But what if I wanted to tempt fate? I rode out of the village, across the field and into the forest.

Let it be so, then. I'll go find old Ida. Though even she couldn't guarantee the child would disappear.

But did I really want it to? It was Max's child, and I still loved him. I couldn't turn this budding life over to an angel maker.

Nor could I go to my mother and announce the joyful news. Despite my blue blood, I'd be subject to the same withering contempt Susanna had faced. People would smear my name. And this would also devastate the business dealings of Lion Hall, the activity that supported everyone here.

What could I do to avoid ruining my reputation?

I was so wrapped up in these thoughts, I paid no attention to the route we took back to the house. Fortunately, Talla found her own way.

Marit! I had to write to her for advice. She'd helped so many others, and perhaps she could help me as well. Surely it was an irony of fate that Marit's best friend had made the same mistake all those other women had. Hadn't I known better? *Oh, damned heart of mine! Why did you persuade me to believe in a future with Max?*

Back in the courtyard, I swung down from the saddle and ran up the front steps. In the hall I almost collided with Miss Rosendahl, who was on her way to Mother's salon.

"Excuse me!" I called as I hurried to my room.

I closed the door behind me and paced back and forth. Anxiety and agitation racked me, and my heart was pounding madly. The worst of it was having no one to turn to, no one to whom I could pour out my heart. My mother wouldn't have understood, and I couldn't say anything to the maids. Not even Lena. Or Lennard . . . to him, least of all! And Marit was in Stockholm, so terribly far away . . .

I'd never felt as isolated and lonely as I did in that moment. The walls of my room seemed to be closing in, but I desperately didn't want to leave it. I was afraid everyone would see right through me. I feared their censure and condemnation.

It took me a long time to rouse myself to go to the office. My knees were so weak, I felt I was on the heaving deck of a ship. I installed myself at the desk and with trembling hands began to compose a letter to my friend. I could have sent a telegram, but in such a constrained format, I couldn't possibly describe what I was feeling.

Could I even manage to put it into a letter? All of it? Wouldn't it be better to travel to Stockholm? Maybe I could tell her everything and seek refuge in her arms. I put the pen down next to the inkwell and reviewed what I'd written so far.

No, written words wouldn't suffice. I might have some talent as an artist, but it would have taken a poet to convey the state of my profoundly shaken soul. I could manage that only in the presence of my friend. When I could look into her eyes, feel her closeness, and know she was opening her whole heart to receive me.

I crumpled up the sheet of stationery and threw it into the trash basket. I sat in thought for a long moment. Then I got up, went to the window, and rang the bell.

Bruns appeared promptly. "Your desire, gracious miss?"

"I wish to travel to Stockholm tomorrow. Please make all the arrangements and tell Lena to come assist with the packing."

The majordomo was astonished and somewhat indelicate as a result. "Is there a specific reason for your trip?"

"No. Or, rather, yes, there is." I had to tell him something. "It is a business matter."

"As you wish. I will see to everything."

I stared out the window after he'd gone. There would be talk, and I wouldn't escape a grilling by my mother, but I vowed she'd not get anything out of me yet. I had to consult Marit first.

52

An overcast Stockholm received me. It felt like an eternity since I was there last. Nothing seemed to have changed, but everything was different. I had changed. I wasn't a girl anymore; I was a woman. I was pregnant. I was no better than the women who gave themselves to some man in hopes of a better future and were cruelly disappointed instead. Did my social class make any difference? At the end of the day, I was still just a woman . . .

I'd sent Marit a telegram from the Kristianstad train station. I hoped she wasn't too busy. In a letter a couple of weeks earlier, she'd told me she'd met a young physician. He was only a little older than she was and had recently been taken into the practice of a colleague planning to retire. The young man expected to take over the practice. I'd been astounded that Marit, who'd refused to allow any man at all into her life, sounded so enamored of this one. But I was happy for her and wrote to say so despite the revelation that I'd been abandoned by my own love. Marit and I had exchanged no letters since. Hardly surprising; the young doctor was probably the focus of her existence, just as Max had filled mine.

I firmly grasped the handle of my valise and walked the length of the train platform. I'd deluded myself into thinking she would meet me at the station. I crossed the echoing interior with a curious sense of homecoming. I wondered in my heart what my life would have been like now if only Father and Hendrik had been alive, if that terrible fire the previous year had never occurred.

"Agneta!" someone called. I looked around and spotted a hand waving above the heads of the travelers. It took Marit some time to make her way to me, but at last she emerged from the crowd.

She'd cut her hair and was wearing it much shorter, a style that seemed almost defiant. The dark-gray summer dress with a white petticoat suited her splendidly. She no longer looked like a Salvation Army employee who did mending after hours. Her young doctor must have been taking good care of her.

A year earlier I'd never expected to see her living the contented life of a bourgeois city dweller. But I wished her good fortune with all my heart.

"Marit!" I called and ran toward her.

We fell into one another's arms with happy familiarity, as if it hadn't been a year since we'd last met.

"I missed you so much!" I hugged her close. It was a wonderful feeling. Why had I waited so long and come only when I got into trouble?

She pulled back to look at me. "It's wonderful to see you again!"

"You mustn't say I am looking good," I chided, anticipating her. "I am not. Nor do I feel well."

Marit frowned. "What happened?"

"We should find some quieter place to discuss it." I slipped my arm through hers. "I am so sorry it took a problem to get me to visit."

"That's what friends are for! Come this way. I know a café where we won't be disturbed. And then I'll show you my new apartment. You can stay with me if you want."

"A new apartment?"

"Yes, in Old Town. Peer insisted I give up the last one."

"Your doctor friend?"

"Yes, exactly. I told him I didn't want to depend on him, but when it came to the apartment, he insisted."

"You, in fashionable Old Town!" I smiled. "Would you ever have dreamed you would live there?"

"Absolutely not," Marit replied. "And as for men, I'd never have dreamed I'd find one who met my standards. But I did. That doesn't mean I've changed my ways. We still organize our demonstrations, and I still work at the Salvation Army. That's where we met. Peer is a dedicated socialist. He fully supports my efforts to secure rights for women."

"You certainly have been fortunate!" A warm flush of joy for my friend filled my heart, even as I was on the verge of bursting into tears of self-pity.

"Come, we'll take a carriage," she said. She hauled me to one of the vehicles waiting alongside the station.

On the way to Old Town, I noticed more automobiles on the streets. Obviously, many wealthy city folk were following the king's example and buying motor carriages.

"Isn't everything that's happening south of the Baltic just frightful?" Marit said as we rode through the narrow streets. "We were terribly shocked to hear about the war."

"We were shocked as well," I told her. "I only hope the king stays the course and refuses to get involved."

"Peer says he has to stay out of it. Many in the government are insisting we support Germany. But if the king sends Swedes to war, he will lose his people's support."

"Your Peer sounds like a smart man."

"Yes, and more than anything, he's someone who refuses to follow the herd."

"Has he introduced you to his parents?"

"Not yet. We're planning that in the next two months."

"Is he from the bourgeoisie?"

Marit shook her head. "No, he's working-class. His father is a carpenter who resents the fact that his son decided to study medicine. He'd wanted Peer to take over the workshop."

"Does he have brothers and sisters?"

"One sister, but her husband is a government official."

"What a shame for Peer's father."

Marit dismissed my remark with a wave. "He has a talented assistant he can turn the business over to someday. Peer says the fellow's a better carpenter than his father."

"But he is not a member of the family."

"True, but that's hardly relevant, don't you think?"

I shook my head and tried to imagine my own father finding himself obliged to turn over management of the estate to some outsider. I couldn't. But then Lion Hall wasn't the same as a woodworking shop.

"No, I suppose you are right," I answered. "And who knows? Perhaps he will have a grandson interested in cabinetmaking."

"Well, first they'll have to consent for Peer to marry me. His sister has two girls, and the father thinks women aren't capable of mastering the craft."

"Someday we will prove him wrong," I responded with a confident smile.

We paid the carriage driver in front of a little café Marit assured me was within walking distance of their apartment. We settled in a nook, and Marit ordered coffees. After the waiter set the steaming beverages before us, I began the story of the past year.

I told her how I'd gotten close to Max, we'd become intimate, we'd dreamed of a life together, and how he'd changed when he heard war had been declared. I described the German officers' visit, Max's disappearance, and my consultation with Dr. Bengtsen.

"And what it comes down to is that I am pregnant," I concluded. "I never thought something like this would happen to me."

Marit frowned. She became very serious. "That fellow is really the last straw," she said. "I'd have expected anything from him but not that."

"I feel exactly the same way," I replied. "I trusted him. I looked forward to spending the rest of my life with him! He was so rebellious, so free . . . I really thought he was a kindred soul."

My eyes were full of tears. Was I destined to spend the rest of my life without someone to love?

Marit put her hand on my arm. "It's human nature to make mistakes," she said gently. "Especially when it comes to men. You know I never wanted to marry. But then Peer came into my life. I'm sure you'll find a man who will stand by you and never abandon you the way Michael and that Max person have."

"But perhaps I will be forced to take a sham husband," I whispered, "just like Susanna." My tears overflowed.

"We'll come up with something," said Marit. She leaned over and kissed my brow.

Later, sitting on the red sofa she had moved to their new apartment, Marit reviewed my options.

"You could go to an angel maker," she said. "But that's extremely dangerous, and it could cost you your life."

"No," I said. The thought of it filled me with terror, for during my time in Stockholm, we'd known women who'd died at the hands of abortionists. And herbal treatments were ineffective all too often. Anyway, the thought of having my child killed . . . No, my heart would never allow me to do that!

"Adoption is another possibility. You would give birth in secret and then hand it over to another woman. No one would know."

"I cannot."

"You want to keep the child?" Marit asked quietly. "Despite the difficulties?"

I nodded. "Yes. I do want to keep the baby." My voice rose. "And I find it unacceptable that people consider a woman wanton and unfit when she has a child but no husband."

Anger boiled up within me. Why was there all this pressure? Why did everyone make it so difficult for women to choose for themselves?

Marit sighed. "You're right. In a just world, it wouldn't be any problem, especially not for a woman like you. You have the money to hire a nanny. You can provide the child with a wealthy home. And the child will carry on your family line. But society is merciless. Scandal would certainly prejudice the estate, especially since you depend upon the sale of your horses."

"If I were a man, none of this would be a problem. I would just hide my lover in some outbuilding. Or in a secret garden."

"But you are a woman. You're expected to marry appropriately and fulfill your duty. The very fact that you're running an estate on your own, without a husband, is already unheard-of."

"Then perhaps it is time to provoke a scandal. Who is going to prohibit me from having my child to continue my family line? The truth is that Hendrik's child should be doing exactly that."

"Susanna's child is safe, sound, and loved. If you like, you can visit tomorrow morning and meet your little niece." Marit stroked my hand. "And of course, no one is going to stop you from giving birth. A pretend husband isn't an absolute necessity. You come from a different class, and you have the means to take care of your child."

"Yes, but my reputation would be ruined."

"Certain people won't attend your receptions or invite you to theirs. Does that sound so bad?"

"True—I guess I wouldn't mind that at all!" I tried to laugh.

Marit looked at me with concern. "But it would create difficulties for the estate, wouldn't it? A black mark on your family. I know you must take such things into consideration." She pulled me into her arms and held me. "I'm afraid the only way to get out of this situation unscathed is actually to get married." She paused. "It'll be a challenge to find someone of your own rank. Ordinary women have it easier, as far as that's concerned."

"I imagine Lennard will not want to have anything to do with me once he learns of this."

"Lennard?"

"The friend who proposed to me," I replied. "He doesn't deserve such humiliation."

Marit suddenly straightened up. "Even so, you should consider it! If he *is* truly your friend, he'll probably be willing to enter into an arrangement. You could offer to let him keep a mistress. Or to let him divorce you eventually. Once enough time has passed."

"I could never propose that to Lennard," I objected. "And, anyway, I'm afraid that what he really wants is me."

"So? What's holding you back?"

"I cannot fall in love with him."

"Plenty of marriages have precious little to do with love," Marit insisted. "I've never been married, but I've known quite a few couples. Lifelong partners quite satisfied with one another but never in love. They respected one another and made their marriage work. Why couldn't you do the same with Lennard?"

I stared at her in disbelief. She also had changed over the year I'd been away from Stockholm. She'd matured. She sounded significantly more grounded. Much more than I was. To her eyes, I must look like an immature child.

"I cannot tell," I sighed. "I simply wish—not to forfeit my freedom."

"Would he be one to deprive you of your freedom?"

"No, but—"

"Then try it at least. If he declines, we'll have to come up with something else. And talk to your mother!"

I recoiled at her mention of Stella. That ordeal was still ahead of me. And I certainly was far more afraid of Mother's reaction than I was of having a few snobs refuse to call at Christmas or dance at midsummer.

"My mother would be absolutely horrified," I said. "She would pack her trunks the very same day. To tell the truth, that would probably be fine with me."

"I don't think she would. In fact, I'm sure she would be more than pleased by the suggestion you might marry the childhood friend she's been trying to foist upon you. You should float that idea immediately."

I shook my head. "What if I just run away? Exactly the way Max did?"

"Of all the options, that is by far the worst," Marit explained patiently. "You wouldn't get very far. And what would become of Lion Hall? You accepted the inheritance, and now you're responsible for far more than yourself alone. You owe it to all those people who live or work on the estate. They count on you; they need you. If Lion Hall goes bankrupt, not only will the Lejongårds cease to exist, the people there will lose their livelihoods. That would inflict more misery than you can possibly imagine." She thought for a moment. "And how about all the change you want to make? If it weren't for you, Susanna and her child would be living on the street! Thanks to your intervention, the police caught the arsonist responsible for the deaths of your father and brother. And who knows how much more you'll be able to accomplish? Maybe one day your estate can offer shelter and refuge to mistreated women. Lion Hall could be an example that could change minds in this society."

Marit's lecture plunged me into despair. She was right. Once again I'd been selfish, thinking only of myself. I leaned against her, wanting only to howl.

"Come, now," Marit said at last. "Let's drink a glass of lemonade. And then we'll talk about this some more."

I nodded, but I knew that the only options were adoption or marriage. I'd dismissed the former out of hand. Perhaps my child would never know its father, but I was determined its mother would be part of its life.

I remembered Susanna. Her child would never know the true father either. Perhaps I should visit her to understand this better.

53

Birds twittered everywhere the next morning. Marit had told me the bookkeeper always left for work at eight o'clock, so I'd be able to talk to Susanna undisturbed after that. I didn't want to get her in trouble.

The house was located on Brännkyrka Street. This stretch descended steeply, and the houses stood aligned like the steps of a staircase. Susanna's house, tiny but two-storied, had been painted matte yellow. The windows were adorned with climbing vines, an old-fashioned touch. Susanna had installed curtains that gave it an air of simple, homely comfort. The front garden was carefully tended and very colorful. The abundant gladiolas, roses, and sunflowers dazzled passersby.

Susanna could never have aspired to such a house if she'd stayed on the estate. Her involvement with Hendrik was the strange means to this outcome. Was she truly happy here? Or was she asking herself whether things should have turned out differently? I stood before the gate for a time but finally summoned my courage and pushed it open. A dog inside the house immediately started barking. I stepped back in alarm.

"Down, Petterson! Go sit!"

Susanna! I smiled in pleasure. She sounded confident and commanding. Moments later she came to the front door.

She'd regained weight over the past year, and it suited her; she was beautiful. She didn't recognize me at first, but then her eyes widened in surprise. "Gracious miss!"

"Call me Agneta." I extended my hand. "Hello, Susanna, how are you doing?"

She stood petrified for a moment, then released her breath in one long exhalation. "Wonderfully well! I—I wasn't expecting you."

"I wanted to surprise you and see your little one. I hope this is not an inconvenient time."

"No, of course not!" She hesitantly took my hand. "Please come in."

I heard the baby babbling as soon as I stepped inside. Then came the sound of something hitting the floor.

Susanna turned with an apologetic smile. "Full of energy. She's always going on in her own secret language and throwing her building blocks. She hit the dog with one just now, but luckily I was there to separate them."

Susanna hurried across the room to the highchair at the kitchen table. Matilda clapped her hands, then looked up at me. Her eyes opened wide. The sight of that little face, so similar to Hendrik's, pierced my heart. It felt like a miracle that something of my brother still lived on in her tiny form.

And now this marvelous little creature was probably going to have a cousin, a boy or another little girl. The question was whether the next baby would be a Lejongård.

"Come in here, Agneta, please," Susanna said and ushered me to a small seating arrangement in the living room. The armchairs were old. Sigurd had probably brought them from his family home. But the ensemble exuded a sense of happy comfort, reinforced by the fact that the leather was polished to a high luster.

After a moment Susanna returned with a coffeepot. She put out settings for two on the table between the armchairs, and she took the seat across from me. I was again impressed by her healthy appearance.

But appearances can be deceiving. "Is your life here going well?"

The brilliant smile Susanna instantly gave me was a clear indication that she not only looked healthy and vigorous but felt that way too. "Very well!" she answered. "Matilda is growing wonderfully, and I have everything I need. And I'm finally getting enough sleep again because she doesn't wake up so often at night anymore." She radiated warmth. "I can't thank you enough!"

For just a moment I had a vision of the enthusiastic maid returning to Lion Hall.

But that was demeaning, both to her and to me. She was a free woman now, a member of the Stockholm citizenry. She no longer had to serve anyone but herself and her family.

"I did not come seeking your thanks," I told her gently. "You have already thanked me time and again, most generously. And now that I see you, your child, and the way you live, I feel blessed. You made the right choice that day."

"And so did you."

I shook my head. "No, I did nothing at all. You were solely responsible. You could have turned down the offer."

"No," she said, "I couldn't have. There was no other way out. I didn't want them to take Matilda away from me. Or for the two of us to endure an awful fate. As soon as you and Marit contacted me, I knew you'd found the solution I needed so badly. Otherwise I'd probably be dead now. And Matilda with me." She looked across the room into the kitchen, where the tiny girl was happily sorting her blocks.

I nodded. "As I said, you made the right decision."

I fell silent, puzzling how I might discuss my own quandary without giving too much away. Susanna certainly would take no pleasure in my plight or in knowing I was in the same trouble. But I worried that if she mentioned something to her husband, the story might eventually get out.

"I have a very personal question," I began. "You need not answer if doing so makes you feel uncomfortable. Or if you think it is inappropriate . . ."

"Ask your question, Agneta," she said, and I felt as if she could see into my heart.

"Tell me what it is like to be married to a man like Sigurd. A man you did not know and whom you did not love." My heart rose into my throat, beating furiously. I didn't know if I'd have been capable of answering such an intrusive question.

Susanna thought for a few moments. "Sigurd is a very orderly man. He's friendly, and he provides for us very well. But . . ." She stopped, and a shadow passed over her face. "But his own inclinations don't let us really get close. That upsets me now and then, for he has won my heart with the way he treats us. I must reconcile myself to the fact that I will never have a place in his."

"You cannot assume that," I offered. "It is possible he may have a similar affection for you."

Susanna nodded. "Yes. Perhaps. But if so, he understands it in a way that's completely different from mine. We'll never be a real couple. I'll probably never know love again. Spiritual or physical . . ."

Those words betrayed a terrible loneliness. We'd sheltered her from the contempt of society but condemned her to a life bereft of intimacy. Her husband would never fulfill the duties of the matrimonial bed. But that would not be grounds for separation or divorce, for he was providing a home and had given her child a father. A mutually advantageous agreement.

Could it possibly turn out that way with Lennard? He was no stranger, of course, and if I invited it, he would probably engage physically with me. But could I ever love him? Or would any relationship be merely a business arrangement?

A gurgle of laughter from Matilda brought me out of my musing. Something hit the floor, and she crowed in delight.

"Just a moment. I'll bring her here." Susanna got up. Watching her go, my questions still tormented me. She returned almost immediately with Matilda on one arm. The little one wrung her hands when she saw me, and again gave me that wide-eyed look. She seemed about to burst out in tears. Susanna placed her on my lap. "Look!" Susanna told her daughter. "This is Miss Lejongård! She came to visit!"

The little girl gave me a curious look, not knowing what to make of me. Then she stretched her little hands up toward my face.

She felt so warm and soft. Anyone would have to love her. Sigurd probably felt the same way when he held her. And Hendrik would have as well, if he'd only had the chance.

The thought of my brother brought tears to my eyes. More than a year and a half had passed, and I'd wept for him every day. Time reduced the pain but couldn't heal the wounds entirely.

Susanna placed a hand on my arm. "I promise you, when the time comes, I'll tell her about her father."

I looked up and wiped the wetness from my cheeks with the back of one hand. "Is that wise?" I asked. "It may confuse her."

"She has a right to know. She needs to know who her father was. The only man who truly loved me. He would have loved her too."

Suddenly I wondered what would have happened if Hendrik had survived the fire. Or if the barn hadn't been set ablaze at all. Susanna spoke sincerely of their love, and I had no desire to contradict her. Perhaps she dreamed late at night of Hendrik. Maybe she even imagined herself as the mistress of Lion Hall. But she'd come to terms with her fate. Hearing that Matilda would one day know the identity of her father, even though there was no advantage to it, made me happy.

I spent some time gossiping about the estate and the other maids, and eventually took my leave. At the front door I looked back again at Susanna with Matilda in the crook of her arm. When would I see them again? Surely not soon. But I promised myself I'd never lose track of them.

54

"Tell me right away how it turns out," Marit said on our way to the train station.

The southbound train was due to leave, and we didn't have much time. We'd poured out our hearts to one another until late the previous night. I still doubted whether I'd be able to see the plan through, but Marit's advice and encouragement had braced me to face the coming days.

"I will let you know. And I'll do my best to write more often."

"That would be lovely. And if there's a disaster and everything falls apart, just come back to me."

"The same for you. Bring Peer with you the next time. He's a doctor, so surely he can arrange for time away in the country."

"We'll see if he's ready for the famous Lion Hall." Marit laughed and hugged me. "Everything will turn out. I know it."

The locomotive rolled into the station, wrapped in a cloud of steam.

We embraced. I climbed aboard and took my seat. Marit stood outside on the platform, and I waved. I knew then that, one way or another, I would be a different woman the next time I saw her, and the prospect filled me with dread.

The train got underway and left Marit behind, obscured by steam. I leaned back, realizing how tired I was. I'd had morning sickness again and still had a sour aftertaste in my mouth. How long would I have to put up with this? How much had the child inside me already developed?

I picked at the sleeve of my blouse. The passengers sitting across from me might wonder why I was so nervous, but I didn't care.

I watched the passing scenery. A swarm of crows took flight from a harvested field and seemed to chase the train. Morning lengthened, then afternoon turned to evening. As we approached Kristianstad, the sun diminished to a small red smear on the horizon, and I made my decision.

August and the coach awaited me at the station. "Fine to have ye back, gracious miss," he said as he took my valise. "Yer mother will be very pleased to see ye."

"We are not going to Lion Hall. Take me to the Ekberg estate."

August was astounded. "To the Ekbergs? Now? But—"

"No questions, August, please. Simply do as I say. This is very important."

"But yer mother is expecting ye! If I don't come back, she'll worry. And soon it'll be dark. It means driving all the night."

"That is of no consequence to me," I replied. "And as for my mother, we will stop at the telegraph office and ask them to deliver a message. It is vitally important I speak to Count Ekberg."

August nodded, harrumphed, and gave in. "As you wish, gracious miss."

"Have no fear. My mother will not hold you responsible. I will explain everything to her."

With that, I climbed into the coach, stifling my anxiety. I was taking a risky course, but I saw it as the only possible escape from my plight.

Morning mists shrouded the Ekberg estate as the coach rolled into their forecourt. I'd decided against sending Lennard and Anna a telegram. I didn't want them speculating about the reason for my visit.

"Thank you, August, and please, go get some rest." I knew there were quarters above the carriage house where he could sleep. "The matters I must discuss with the count will take some time."

I smoothed my dress and went up the front steps. Lundt the major-domo appeared soon after I rang. He looked half asleep, but the sight of me shocked him awake.

"Countess Lejongård!" he exclaimed. "What brings you to us?"

"Good morning. I must speak with the count. It is quite urgent."

Lundt left me in the foyer and disappeared. Anna came down almost immediately.

"Good Lord, Agneta! What has happened?"

Plenty, I thought.

"I would very much like to speak to Lennard. Is he at home?"

"Yes, of course," she said. "Has something happened to your mother? Or the estate?"

I shook my head. "Nothing like that. I need to speak with him. That is all."

"Well, then, by all means, come in. We were about to have breakfast." She escorted me to the dining room. The food smelled delicious, but I doubted I'd be able to swallow a bite.

Anna gave me a searching look. "This is quite alarming, I must say."

"Please, Anna, I will explain everything, but first I must speak with Lennard."

"Of course."

Perhaps she was thinking of sending a telegram to my mother asking if I'd lost my mind.

Fortunately, Lennard arrived just then. "Agneta! Whatever is going on?" He looked to his mother, but Anna shook her head.

"I must speak with you," I said and took him by the arm. "Please, let us take a walk, and I will explain."

"As you wish," he said. "Gladly."

He allowed me to herd him out into the garden. I felt like a fugitive. Maybe I really had lost my mind, but I saw no alternative.

"Why are you here?" he asked once we'd gotten some distance from the manor.

I searched for words, wrestled with my conscience, and found myself still at a loss. I was feeling terribly ill and horribly anxious. "Are we still friends?"

He frowned. "Why would we not be? Of course!"

"Then please listen." I glanced back toward the mansion, fearing someone might overhear. "You offered to help me if I was ever in trouble. Well, now I am."

Lennard was perplexed. "In trouble? What has happened? Is it a financial matter?"

"Something quite different. And because of it, I have a request. You can agree or not, but please promise me you will keep it absolutely confidential."

"More and more mysterious," he replied. "For heaven's sake, Agneta, what is it?"

"Will you promise never to reveal what I am about to tell you?"

"Yes," he replied. "But please tell me what has happened!"

If only it hadn't been so hard to say!

"I—I wanted to ask . . . whether you still had any desire to marry me."

Lennard stared in amazement. "Have you changed your mind? Just a few months ago, you begged me to look for someone else."

"Yes, but things have changed."

I squeezed my eyes shut, wishing I lived someplace where it didn't matter if a woman had a husband or not. But was there such a place anywhere on this earth?

Speaking the three short words of confession was harder than any of the angry debates with my father.

"I am pregnant."

Lennard's jaw dropped. He was speechless for a moment. "You cannot be serious! How?"

I took a deep, shuddering breath. I was staking everything, win or lose, on his response. "There was a reason I could not entertain your proposal of marriage. I was in love with another. He was my estate manager, and—"

A strange, choked exclamation from Lennard interrupted me. Had he laughed? Did he find me ridiculous? Was he revolted?

"Your estate manager? That fellow too high and mighty to bother to attend the midsummer festival?"

"He is not from Sweden, and what does that matter anyway? I loved him. Now he has disappeared, and I am pregnant."

This time there wasn't a peep from Lennard. If looks could kill . . . "Do you have any idea of what you have done?" He threw his hands wide and gazed briefly up at the sky as if looking for divine guidance. When he turned back to me, he was incensed. "How could you give yourself to someone like that? How could you allow him to make you pregnant?"

I choked back tears. "It simply happened. I had a relationship in Stockholm, and because I was careful, everything went well, but this time—I know I was stupid, but even so, I beg you . . ."

Lennard turned away. His anger was palpable, and so was his disappointment. I'd probably have felt the same if I were he and the woman I loved rejected me, took another into her bed, got pregnant, and then came running to me for rescue.

I'd been an idiot to think he would help.

My shoulders sagged. I shouldn't have come. I should leave.

"So you turn up here with no notice to ask me to marry you, even though you do not love me. And the child you are carrying I am to claim as my own. That is all I am good for?"

My eyes filled with tears. I tried in vain to hold them back. "Forgive me!" Now I was the one who turned away. "I saw no other way out. And I refuse to lie to you. It is perfectly all right for you to turn me down. Just please say nothing to your mother."

I walked away. August was almost certainly asleep already, but . . .

Dizziness came at me out of nowhere. One moment I was sobbing, the next the world was turning in circles so rapidly, I lost my balance. The dew-soaked lawn flew up toward me, and I landed on my face. I couldn't breathe, but I felt neither pain nor fear. A white veil settled over my eyes. Then everything disappeared into the void.

55

I heard Lennard's voice through the gauzy nothingness.

"The rigors of the trip were too much."

Groggily, I understood I was being carried. I opened my eyes but still couldn't see. I was wrapped in a vague, black-and-white mist.

"I am sending for the doctor," I heard Anna declare, but Lennard asked his mother to wait. Then came the sound of footsteps on hard flooring.

My vision cleared at last as he carried me into one of the rooms and deposited me on the bed. I saw a pink canopy overhead, and then, immediately, Lennard's worried face loomed above me.

"Agneta?" he called and lightly patted my cheek. "Can you hear me?"

I wanted to say *yes*, but only a meaningless croak came out of my mouth. A door opened.

"How is she?" I heard Anna ask.

"She is regaining consciousness," Lennard answered. "Slowly." He ran a hand through my hair.

It took me a while to gather what had happened. Then I remembered I'd confessed to him. And that he was incredibly angry.

"Perhaps Frieda should prepare a tea for her."

"I suspect she actually needs a bit of broth. But more than that, she needs sleep."

The door closed. Anna was gone.

Lennard put his palm on my forehead. "Agneta," he called gently. "Can you hear me?"

I nodded. His kind face was clearly visible above mine, and I became aware of the sluggish pulse of blood through my limbs.

I tried to sit up. "Please forgive me for being such a bother."

Lennard pressed me gently back into the pillows. "You will not get up," he admonished me. "You need rest, for a couple of hours at least. This has all been too much for you."

He was right. And at that moment I didn't have the strength to discuss anything at all. I felt as if I were dissolving into the bed.

He caressed my forehead. "Please forgive my reaction," he said quietly. "I did not mean to be so insensitive."

"You had every reason. I will not importune you further."

"Shh. We will discuss this later, when you feel better. Sleep for now, and when you awake, you must have something to eat."

As he got up, I feebly clutched his arm. "Lennard," I said. "I am so sorry."

"Later," he said and again touched my hair. Then he vanished.

I slept deep and dreamlessly. When I awoke, I didn't know where I was for a moment. It took a few seconds for me to work out that I was at Ekberg Manor, in the guest room they'd always given me when we visited.

I sat up. I was still in my travel clothes. I looked around for Lennard. Had he told his mother everything while I slept? He'd never been one to betray confidences, but we were children back then and not involved in matters as serious as an illegitimate pregnancy.

Once I felt my legs would support me, I got out of bed. I unbuttoned the top of my dress and went to the washbasin next to the vanity table.

Sleep had done me good. But those dark circles under my eyes hadn't gone away. Perhaps they never would.

I washed up and saw that my valise had been brought in from the coach, which meant I could change my dress. I'd taken a second one to Stockholm, fortunately. It was fairly plain, for I hadn't wanted to stand out on the city streets. The fabric was a bit thin for the temperature inside a manor house at this time of year. Soft and delicate, it fit me like a glove. I studied myself in the mirror. It was time to make an appearance. I didn't want to tarry here until Lennard or his mother came to check on me.

I had to take matters in hand. I wasn't going to appeal to Lennard again. The only favor he could grant me now was to keep my secret while I sought help elsewhere. Some other solution would be found. I went downstairs to the dining room.

They were at the table when I entered, and they'd already started dinner. My stomach knotted at the heavy smell of a roast. I had the bizarre impression it was the child within me reacting, communicating its dislike for meat.

"Ah," said Lennard, "there you are!" He put down his napkin and came to me. "How are you feeling? We decided not to wake you, and we've already begun the evening meal. Hilda?"

The maid appeared immediately.

"A bit of the soup for our guest." Lennard guided me to my place, watching to make sure I wasn't going to collapse again.

I took my seat and looked warily toward Anna.

Her expression was solicitous and concerned. "Are you feeling better?"

"Yes, thank you. It was just a little too much."

Lennard gave me a warning look. "It appears Agneta was overwhelmed when I proposed to her again."

His declaration struck me like a whiplash. A proposal? But he'd turned me down! I stiffened with dread. I wanted to object, but a voice in my mind warned me to hear him out.

Anna's elegantly drawn eyebrows rose, and she went rigid. "You—"

She knew something wasn't quite right. I'd appeared without warning, unreasonably early in God's lovely morning, to talk to Lennard—yet he was claiming *he* had proposed to *me*?

I turned to him. Lennard wore a wide smile. He was completely transformed from the man I'd seen a few hours earlier.

I felt terribly ill at ease. Why was he smiling? In triumph at finally capturing me? Or was he planning to take his revenge on me for preferring another? For going so far as to sleep with another man?

"Indeed, I proposed to her," he said. "I did not wish to reveal it to you earlier, in Agneta's absence. But I did so. It seems to have succeeded . . ." He turned to me.

In my confusion I'd turned to stone, and I had the impression that at any moment a tempest would erupt over my head. The lightning bolt had just struck, but the thunder hadn't yet arrived.

"You will remember we spent some time alone while Agneta and her mother were visiting." He assumed a deeply contrite expression.

"Yes?" his mother replied in consternation. "And?"

"Well, the fact is, we were overcome by passion, and we—well, never mind the details, but the fact is that Agneta has come to tell me that she is now expecting a child. Hearing that, I proposed to her again. And to my great joy, she accepted."

My heart skipped a beat. The two of them turned to me, expecting confirmation.

"Yes," I responded faintly. "I did." I looked at Lennard. His face bore not the least trace of animosity; he was beaming!

Anna seemed not to notice my confusion, for she put a hand to her mouth and leaped to her feet. Now what? Was she appalled by our immorality? But no—she rushed to me and threw her arms around me before I knew what was happening.

"What marvelous news!" she cried and stifled a sob. "You will be part of our family at last!"

I hesitantly hugged her back. I hadn't expected such an enthusiastic reaction. I looked over Anna's shoulder and saw Lennard watching us. There was a glint in his eyes he hadn't shown his mother, and that worried me. It disappeared like a candle flame being blown out as soon as Anna released me and turned to her son. He was suddenly aglow once more. I'd never known he had such a talent for acting.

We hammered out wedding plans for the rest of the evening, and several times Anna broke into tears of joy. She shared memories of her own marriage to Gustav and came close to offering me her wedding veil and train, which she'd saved along with her bridal dress.

I felt awful and wondered at Lennard's motivation. I'd hoped for his help, but I'd been completely unprepared for such drama. I glanced at him repeatedly, hoping he'd give me a clue to what was going on, but his performance was flawless. I wanted to avoid arousing suspicions, so I smiled at Anna and pretended to be overjoyed, but what I really wanted to do was run away. Bedtime came at last.

Lennard escorted me to my room. With every step away from the salon, he became tenser and more taciturn. I sensed something was coming, but I was duty bound to thank him for rescuing me.

"Could you stay a moment?" I asked at the entrance to the guest room. "I would really like to have a word."

"Certainly," he said stiffly, then stepped into the room.

I shut the door behind to make sure no one could overhear. "I wish to thank you. You are doing a great deal for me, and I do not know how I can ever make it up to you."

His reply was cold. "I had already promised I would stand by you if you needed it."

"Yes, but even so. You were so angry, and I cannot forget that." Without thinking, I began to wring my hands.

"I am angry still," Lennard replied. "But that is beside the point. You are obliged to tell your mother the same story so I cannot be accused of lying."

"Of course," I said. "And what are your conditions? Given the circumstances, I can hardly expect you to do this without some sort of compensation. Must I live here? Or sign Lion Hall over to you?"

Lennard looked at me as if he'd been slapped. His eyes narrowed. "I do not want your estate. As far as I am concerned, you can draw up a prenuptial agreement, or whatever you and your women friends come up with. All I ever wanted was you! Considering what you have related to me, I frankly cannot congratulate myself that you are going to become my wife. You do not accept me out of love but because I have agreed to help a friend, respecting a vow we made as kindergarteners."

I was piqued. "And how do you intend to punish me?"

"I will not punish you," he answered. "That is not up to me. But you need not expect me to participate in all aspects of marriage. I will care for you, but otherwise I will tend to my own affairs. And if I find a woman who loves me, I will consider myself licensed to enter into a relationship. You will accept that without complaint, just as I am putting up with the fact that you willingly got pregnant by a despicable rascal."

His words shook me to the core. I was close to tears again, but I knew weeping would change nothing. I thought of Susanna and the emptiness she felt in her life because her husband was not truly hers. She too had seen the man she loved taken from her. But had she deserved that?

Not at all. Hendrik had sworn to marry her, while I, on the other hand, had given myself to a man who'd refused and abandoned me. I should consider myself lucky. Lion Hall would still be mine. My life would continue almost unchanged, except for the fact that I would have a child.

The only thing forever barred to me was the opportunity to marry a man who loved me.

"Agreed. If that is your wish," I said at last.

Lennard nodded. "And one more thing: I want never to hear of that bounder again. Do you understand? We will not discuss him, and if he should have the audacity to turn up at your estate, I will have him thrown out. He must never again come close to you. Do you hear?"

I stiffened, ready to declare I could speak with whomever I pleased, but the intensity of his anger intimidated me. "He will not come back," I said. "And if he does, I will not say a word to him."

"Good. Now go to sleep. You have a long journey to make tomorrow. And you must deliver the happy news to your mother." Lennard gave me one last grim look, then turned his back. "Good night."

"Good night," I echoed faintly. The door clicked shut.

I dropped onto the bed. The dark beyond the windows suddenly struck me as menacing. I still couldn't believe that Lennard was rescuing me. But I felt no relief, probably because of the conditions he'd imposed. Of course, I was the one who had commanded him to look for a woman to love, so what right did I have to feel hurt?

I shivered. Perhaps it was better just to abandon myself to sleep and wake to see what the morrow would bring.

56

I'd never thought I had any talent as an actress, but the next morning, we pretended to be in love, and Anna was completely taken in by our charade. As I was about to set off for home, she told me again how delighted she was to have me in the family at last. Lennard gave me a passionate kiss, and I tried my best to return it.

August set his team in motion. Both Ekbergs stood on the front steps and waved. I waved back but was relieved when the coach went around a bend and out of sight.

The night had brought me no solace. I was too keenly aware of my situation and the fact that I'd put myself entirely in the hands of Lennard and the Ekberg family. And now I was dreading the interrogation from my mother, who had certainly worried when I didn't return as planned.

Fear had me firmly in its grip when the coach rolled through Lion Hall's front gate late that afternoon. How would Mother react upon hearing I intended to marry Lennard? That news ordinarily would have been a reason for rejoicing, but the whole thing left a bitter aftertaste.

I pictured Lion Hall as a powder keg ready to explode. Mother would surely be pleased to hear of marriage plans, but she would want to know why I'd changed my mind. Should I tell her? No one else would much care when the child was born so soon after the wedding, but she would know something had been amiss.

August pulled up before the manor and helped me down. I was dismayed and disoriented, much as I'd felt the day I'd arrived after the fire.

I went inside and carried my valise upstairs. I could have left it for Lena, but I had no desire to speak to anyone. My mother appeared in the bedroom doorway as soon as I'd set it down.

"Where were you?" she demanded.

"You already know," I said. "Stockholm."

"I am perfectly aware of that. But where? And why did you have to ride off in such great haste?"

"I went to visit Marit," I responded. I didn't mention Susanna.

"Marit? Your friend who came here last year?"

I nodded.

"Then why did you tell everyone it was a business trip?"

"I told Bruns I was traveling on business. Nothing more. You are the one always reminding me there are things the servants do not need to know."

Mother sniffed impatiently. "Was it something to do with that estate manager? Were you looking for him in Stockholm?"

I shook my head. "No, Mother, I was not. I needed advice from Marit. And she provided it."

"What advice could your friend give that your own mother could not?" Stella was plainly offended. "A change has come over you since that fellow left. What is wrong? Were you in love with him?"

"No," I lied, looking down. I wasn't ready to have it out with her. "I will confess I found him extremely sympathetic. But that is over now in any case, because—"

That pause made my mother turn pale. "Because what?"

"I am pregnant."

There it was, but I felt no relief. Now the lying would begin in earnest.

My mother's eyes slowly widened. She opened her mouth, but not a sound came out. We stared at one another for a very long time. Stella sank down and sat on the edge of my bed. She stared at the carpet, as if seeking some sign this was a joke. Or a bad dream.

"I was alone with Lennard for a while, the last time we visited the Ekbergs. I don't remember much about it, but we found ourselves carried away. We . . ."

I couldn't put it into words. Not because I was a prude, but because it was a lie. "Later, I realized something was wrong, so I went to Dr. Bengtsen. He confirmed my suspicions. There was no one here to whom I could turn, so I traveled to Stockholm to see Marit."

"Why did you not come to me? To your mother? Why did you not seek my advice?"

"I did not know what your attitude would be. I wanted to find a solution to my problem, and only Marit could give it to me. After discussing this with her, I came to the conclusion it would be best to marry Lennard. That is why I told August to drive to the Ekberg estate."

I was shaking uncontrollably.

Mother stared at the pattern in the carpet as if trying to burn it into her memory. Finally, she looked at me. "I cannot claim to be pleased you gave yourself to a man before marriage. But you made the right decision afterward, and in my opinion, that is to your credit."

Was that all? Wasn't she going to say more? After all, I was expecting her grandchild!

Did she sense something was wrong? Had she noticed my secret visits to Max? Or how desolated I'd been by his disappearance?

"I assume you have already discussed this with Anna?" Her tone was unchanged.

I avoided her question. "Mother, I am very sorry I did not take you into my confidence."

"That is not the issue," she said crisply. "I am merely surprised you suddenly discovered this passion for Lennard. You were so adamantly against the idea of marrying him."

"Before . . . everything was different, before. But now I am expecting a child. Your grandchild! I thought that would make you happy."

"I am happy that after engaging in folly you have now made the correct decision," she responded. "We will need to hurry. In a matter of months, it will no longer be possible to hide your condition. I will give my seamstress instructions to procure the fabric for a wedding dress. You will marry in two months. What happens after that is no one else's business."

Having made that pronouncement, she got up, went to the door, and left.

I was miserable. I'd hoped the lie would make things easier, but I'd been wrong. Stella was not about to have the wool pulled over her eyes. My decision to go to Lennard and his generosity in granting my request had saved me from scandal, but my mother now looked at her daughter and saw her worst fears confirmed.

Those thoughts brought tears into my eyes for a moment, but then I balled up my fists and hammered the bed. Why was I still trying so desperately to win Mother's love? Perhaps I should just give up and not care what she thought. I was the mistress of this estate! Time would reduce the sting. I would get on with my life and take care of Lion Hall. All my other hopes had been dashed.

57

The following weeks passed in a blur. The welcome news that the mistress of Lion Hall would marry far overshadowed speculation about the rush to the altar. On the estate, at least. Fortunately, everyone at Lion Hall but my mother was convinced that Lennard was the father.

"These young folks nowadays!" Mrs. Bloomquist was said to have exclaimed when she heard. Lena, all giggles, recounted that to me. "Then she said, 'But at least our mistress picked the right man.'"

"We're so happy for you!" Lena added, her cheeks flushed. "It will be lovely to have the house filled with children's laughter."

I tried to smile. The others were overjoyed, so why wasn't I? My reputation was saved, and I was going to have a child.

But I'd betrayed myself. And there was always the problem of my mother. I saw and felt her suspicious looks.

At least she didn't bring up the subject. We scarcely said a word to one another outside of making wedding arrangements. I buried myself in estate work, kept the books, sold horses, and decided which mares should be bred. I attended births, named foals, and planned feed mixtures for upcoming months. Business as usual, except for the fact that I was bent and burdened by anxiety. I feared I might start fainting again. I feared Lennard would decide to withdraw from the agreement. I feared Max would return.

Yes, during all this time I was afraid of his return. Before, I'd walked the whole length of our usual promenade almost every morning, aching for him, but now I stayed home. Partly due to bouts of nausea and partly because I wanted to forget him.

I realized all this was deadly serious when Mother's seamstress arrived to take measurements for my wedding dress. I could always leave Lennard standing at the altar, but where could I go? To Germany, searching for Max? That was unthinkable. And I couldn't run to Marit, for she was finding her own happiness. So I let the preparations sweep me along. I worried that the woman measuring me would see why we were in such a rush, but fortunately, my belly was still flat.

I couldn't help asking myself on which of our nights together the child had been conceived, but I tried to put that out of mind, for it was a torment. I wondered if Max's father had received my letter. Why hadn't he answered? Had Max intervened? Did the head of the Von Bredestein family not know where his son was? Did he even care? Perhaps his reply had gone astray in the confusion of war. I brooded over those questions for hours on end.

But then came unexpected, distressing news: the palace informed us the crown prince and princess would not attend the wedding, for they would be traveling to Norway at that time.

That made Mother very unhappy. "They are afraid of another fire."

I shook my head. "You should not imagine such things, Mother. The arsonist was caught, and the fire is forgotten. Besides, one cannot expect the royal family to postpone a trip to attend a wedding."

"A wedding in the family of close friends!" Mother snapped. Then she sighed. "Perhaps after all this time, we've ruined our relations with them."

"But why do you say that?" I cried. "Can you not recall how pleased the crown prince and princess were when visiting us last summer? How their children squealed with delight while riding horses? I do not believe we are disgraced. There is war all across Europe, and the royal family is obliged to represent the nation and reassure our neighboring countries."

I thought back to the previous summer. Times had seemed difficult back then, but they were nothing compared to these. The royal couple had traveled often since the outbreak of war—to Denmark, to Finland, and now to Norway. King Gustav remained steadfast, forbidding any involvement in a war that by then had reached France and Belgium. Some newspapers published satirical articles and spread tasteless rumors, but I was convinced he would not waver. War could bring Sweden nothing but misery.

"You will see," I assured her. "They will attend the christening. They have plenty of time to put that on their schedule."

Mother gave me a dour look. "It would have been better to have more time to plan the wedding. Whatever were you thinking?"

Those words jolted me, for I didn't know what she meant. We'd never mentioned Max after the exchange in my room, but I still had the feeling Stella suspected. Or was that just my guilty conscience speaking?

"What's done is done," I said. "But I am going to be married, and that is the most important thing. Surely you agree?"

Mother looked tempted to contradict me, but she clamped her lips shut and went back to her preparations.

58

One month later, on an unusually warm and sunny morning in mid-November, the house was bustling with excitement. The maids whispered and giggled in the corridors, guessing who might be the lucky one to catch my bridal bouquet. Lennard had visited often in the preceding weeks and regularly spoken in private with Mother. He played the part of the supremely happy groom and expectant father and appeared above all suspicion.

Only when we were alone together did I sense the anger still brewing beneath his impenetrable mien. He might have loved me once but did no longer. He kept his promise, but he made it clear that was all I'd ever get from him. And now that I'd overcome my initial resentment toward Lennard's attitude, I'd decided this was best for both of us.

Mother's seamstress displayed the finished wedding gown on a mannequin. It was gorgeous, though a little old-fashioned. To her credit, she'd made an effort to incorporate touches from Stockholm fashions. White lace and cream-colored silk went together marvelously; an artful bouquet of pink roses accented the sash at the waist. The long, draped sleeves were bell-shaped. The skirt was ample enough to cover a crinoline, though I had no intention of wearing one. The veil was held in place by a narrow, jewel-studded tiara.

The feeling of unease I was experiencing had nothing to do with the ceremony itself. It was foreboding about the future, fear of what might become of me as well as unhappiness at what I had become. I could hardly remember the impetuous student who'd hurried to the Royal Academy of Fine Arts clutching a painter's kit under one arm. I had the impression I'd aged at least forty years. I felt like someone's grandmother disguised in a wedding dress.

Lena's knock at the door startled me out of my unhappy brooding. She'd arrived to dress me, surely with Linda's help. Stella must have confided her suspicions about paternity, for Linda's attitude toward me had bordered on disrespectful ever since the wedding announcement. She said nothing, of course; she didn't dare. Even so, I sensed her disapproval. She probably saw the mistress of the estate as an irresponsible little slattern. There was no telling what my mother had actually said to her.

Now the time had come for me to pretend to be overjoyed.

"Come in!" I called as cheerfully as I could manage. And in stepped Linda, with Lena close behind, toting a large wooden chest.

"Good morning, gracious miss," they chorused.

"Are the bridesmaids awake?" I asked.

Marit was one of them. She'd arrived by train the previous evening and looked completely exhausted. I desperately wanted to talk with her, but the rest of the bridesmaids were in the way. They were the daughters of other aristocratic families invited by my mother. Each hoped to catch a husband. The youngest had just turned seventeen.

"There is no better place to find a fiancé than at a wedding," my mother had commented, herding the bridesmaids into the salon. I had no idea what she'd said to them there. She'd probably lectured them on etiquette and warned against hopping into bed with their new swains.

"I sent Marie to wake Miss Andersson," Lena said, "but she was already up."

That was just like Marit, always ahead of the game.

"Once we have finished here, I would gladly have a private conversation with her. I do hope there are no difficulties with her bridesmaid's dress?"

"I assume not," Linda replied, somewhat miffed.

Marit was the only bridesmaid not from an aristocratic family. Worse, she'd arrived with her hair loose, which I knew had scandalized Linda. But Marit was my friend, and I couldn't have cared less about the other girls.

Lena and Linda got to work. They cinched me into my corset, a contraption I avoided whenever possible. Working together, they put me into the wedding dress and wrapped a voluminous sheet around me. Linda saw to my makeup. I followed the process of transformation in the mirror. Though her art was a complete mystery to me, I saw the dark circles disappear from under my eyes. My lips and cheeks bloomed in subtle tones of pink. Linda worked an even greater miracle with my hair. Her magic transformed my unruly locks into an artful arrangement topped by the tiara.

"We will wait to pin on the veil until just before setting out for the church," she declared as her nimble fingers shaped individual ringlets and set them in place.

In the mirror, I saw Lena, plainly captivated by the sight of Mother's maid at work. One day, Lena would surely achieve that level of artistry, but until then I'd have to rely on Linda.

"You have outdone yourself, Linda," I told her as I turned my head, examining the result from one side and then the other. "Thank you."

"Thank you very much, gracious miss," she replied, flattered. "May I offer a suggestion?"

"Yes, please do."

"It's best to keep to your room for now. It is bad luck if the groom sees you before the ceremony."

There was no danger whatsoever that Lennard would see me before the ceremony. I was certain Linda knew he and his mother were traveling directly from their estate to the church in Kristianstad. Besides, what worse luck could I possibly have?

"Thank you, Linda. I will remember that," I said anyway. "Would you please invite Miss Andersson in? She will help me pass the time."

Linda nodded and left the room. Lena stayed to tidy up.

I studied my image in the mirror again. I had to admit I liked both the hairstyle and the dress. I looked like a fairy-tale princess about to be whisked away by a prince.

But this was no fairy tale. Soon I would be a married woman, and that would shatter all links to my childhood and my youth. The dream of becoming a famous painter had faded as soon as I returned to Lion Hall. Now it seemed even further out of reach. Lion Hall and I were one and the same. Nothing was going to change that.

But what of my desires? And my dreams? Was there really anything other than barren duty in this new life of mine?

A knock at the door interrupted my thoughts. Assuming Linda had forgotten something, I forced a smile—but the face in the doorway was Marit's.

"You look fabulous!" she exclaimed and came to me. "I'd love to give you a hug, but you're a sugarplum fairy, and I don't want to ruin anything."

I got up. "No need to worry." I gave her a hug, heedless of my finery. I saw Lena quietly slip out of the room. "I am still flesh and blood. The rest is just decoration."

I drew her over to my bed, so we could stretch out together. "Did you ever think this day would come?"

Marit shook her head. "No. Or not like this, at least."

I glanced at the door to see if Lena was well and truly gone.

My friend saw that glance. "Don't worry. I know the walls have ears. I won't go into detail, but let me just say I would have wished for different circumstances for your wedding."

"I share your sentiment. Besides, if my father and brother were still alive, I probably would never have married at all."

"Perhaps sooner or later you would have married Michael."

"Yes," I said. "But fate obviously had something different in store."

How unimaginably far in the past was that day in bed with Michael when the telegram arrived. A scene from someone else's life.

Marit gave me a conspiratorial look. "And what about you-know-who?"

I sighed. "No news." I didn't want to think about Max, but he haunted me still. How could he not, considering his child was growing within me? "But forget all that. I am to be the wife of a respectable man."

"A respectable man who plans to take a lover."

I'd written Marit about the deal Lennard and I had made. She was livid at his condition, but I wrote back that it was only reasonable. Of course I'd rather he hadn't been so direct about it, but there was no denying it was exactly what I'd urged him to do: find a woman he loved, one who would love him in return.

"Everything is acceptable just as it is. I followed your advice and got a capable attorney to draw up the marriage contract. I will lead my life just as I have. Lennard consented to reside at Lion Hall and employ a manager for his own estate. All that is left for me to do is to try to be a good mother."

"What about your independence? You know that the law requires you to comply with Lennard's wishes as soon as you marry."

"I know, but he will never go so far as to make unreasonable demands. We will live in the same house, nothing more."

"You sound like you're on your way to your own funeral."

"Hardly a funeral. But I realize it is useless to resist. The day has not yet arrived when women are allowed to choose for themselves. Perhaps it never will."

"Don't say that! I'm sure things will change. We just need to get past this terrible war."

I'd paid very little attention to war news in recent weeks. I didn't want to know which army was rampaging where. It was too awful to imagine Max out there in it.

"We will wait it out. Perhaps I imagine things to be worse than they actually are." I huddled against Marit, and she stroked my arm.

"Change comes when you least expect it," she said. "Happiness is the same way. Maybe you'll find your own happiness soon. There may be some undiscovered way out. Or your redemption might come striding through some gorgeously carved front door. You mustn't lose hope. I'm sure you'll be happy someday. Especially since your husband promised to allow you to live your life as you wish."

"But I will be trapped in this marriage unless eventually I decide to let him renounce me before all the world."

"Perhaps he will ask for a divorce eventually, but he hasn't even raised the subject. All he said was that he'd take a lover if he got the chance. And what would stop you from doing the same thing?"

"I have had my fill of liaisons," I replied bitterly. "You see what came of them."

"But things could have turned out differently. Surely you won't swear off love forever?"

I shook my head. Carefully, so as not to disturb Linda's creation.

"All right, then," Marit said. "Maybe we should talk about something else. For example, these stuck-up little bridesmaids who're all speculating which handsome, well-born man will take an interest in them."

I laughed. "How fortunate I am you have nothing in common with them other than matching dresses!" I hugged her. Oh, if only I could have kept Marit with me there forever!

59

Two hours later, I emerged from the manor and climbed into the coach. Because I had no living male relatives to walk me to the altar, my mother would deliver me to my future husband.

Stella wore a lime-green dress printed with twisting tendrils and accented with cream-colored lace. It was almost too light for the unheated church, but it suited her wonderfully. Linda had fixed her hair in elegant waves. It was impossible to read Mother's thoughts, but she held herself with great dignity. A mother would normally encourage her daughter and wish her well, but Stella was just as silent as she'd been on our journey to arrange the funerals of my father and brother.

Our coach led the procession, followed by carriages with the bridesmaids and guests who had stayed with us overnight. Lennard, his mother, and their invitees would be waiting for us at the church.

We arrived at the square in front of the church, and I saw many of our villagers. They'd come to wish us well. I wasn't able to study the crowd because as Mother got out, she hissed that I must remain out of sight inside the coach. She told August to advise the priest the ceremony could get underway.

I peeked out at the carriage where Marit was seated between two other bridesmaids. Their names were Liv and Alva, if I remembered correctly. My friend was noticeably older than they were, and she rolled her eyes when she saw me looking.

My mother returned and opened the door to the coach. Most of our guests had gone into the church in the meantime. The crowds standing outside hadn't been invited to the ceremony.

The bridesmaids tripped up the steps, and I descended from the coach at last. Mother lifted my train for the few moments it took us to get to the red carpet on the steps.

The organist began the wedding march. My mother offered me her arm.

For an instant I thought I couldn't move. But Mother grasped my arm, and my legs obeyed her of their own volition, even though I had the sensation that at any moment my knees would buckle.

What would I tell my child someday? Would I lie and declare it had been a marvelous day? Would Lennard still be at my side, or would I be truthful because he'd left me long before? I could see nothing before me. The future was a dark, impenetrable wood.

The congregation rose as soon as I entered. I felt their eyes upon me, even though my own were fixed upon the altar where Lennard and his best men were waiting. They were his two best friends but strangers to me. They gazed at me, their heads close together as if they'd been exchanging confidences. Had Lennard told them our secret? Or were they just praising his resplendent bride?

And then we were already there. Mother handed me to Lennard. He wore an elegant dark-blue formal coat and a blue Ascot tie fastened with a silver stickpin. His lapel bore a sprig of pink roses like those I wore at my waist.

He gave me a brief glance and did not smile. He turned resolutely toward the altar.

I wanted to flee. That was the moment to break loose, race back down the aisle, spring into the coach, and make August take me far, far away.

I was imagining that scene as the minister began his address. What a scandal it would create! But of course I stood rooted to the spot. The words about marriage, duties, and even the joys this new life would bring made no impression on me. My marriage was a means of getting out of my difficulties. That was all. Lennard seemed to feel the same way.

When the time came to pronounce the vows, Lennard's voice sounded flat, even a bit unhappy, as if he too was realizing the life he once had known was now ending. Then it was my turn. Agitation fluttered inside me like a panicked sparrow.

"I, Agneta Sophie Lejongård, take you, Lennard Markus Ekberg, to be my lawful wedded spouse . . ."

I knew Mother was wiping tears from her eyes, feigning joy for the sake of the spectators. But Anna Ekberg's deep emotion was genuine. If she had only known what frauds we were . . .

"In sickness and in health. I pledge to love, honor, and obey, until death do us part." I shut my eyes for a moment. The priest probably thought I was elated.

I'd rejected the idea of obeying any man, but that was the vow I was now making to Lennard! The words echoed in my mind. I was marrying a man I didn't love, one who didn't care for me anymore. More than anything, I wanted to escape.

The ceremony concluded at last, and the moment came when Lennard and I were expected to kiss. I closed my eyes. As his lips brushed mine, I imagined Max was kissing me before the altar. The image was so vivid that I was almost surprised when I opened my eyes and saw Lennard's face. Applause filled the church. Lennard offered me his arm and beamed as if he had really just married the love of his life.

I was glad I could cling to him, for I had the sensation the floor was slipping out from under my feet.

Cheering villagers thronged before the church. I looked around. Almost all of our people were there. The Korvens hadn't come, of course, nor had two other families Father once took to court over water rights. Everyone else was present.

Lennard and I stepped up into the waiting coach with August stationed on the box in his best coat and with a top hat on his head. As we drove away, I waved mechanically, feeling nothing.

I welcomed the sudden numbness, for it would help me get through the day. The dances the bride and groom would have to open, all the feasting, the guests growing more and more tipsy, and my mother and Anna, united in the joy that their children had found one another.

We arrived at Lion Hall and entered the ballroom. Bruns and Miss Rosendahl had set out little sprays of pink roses everywhere. The roses were featured in the marvelous table settings; they were pinned to expanses of white lace that festooned the windows and mirrors. Women from the village had done the centerpieces, and Mrs. Bloomquist had even allowed them to contribute baked goods for the festivities. A generous spread was set out for the villagers in a heated tent in the garden. Fortunately, the weather was mild, and the tent walls would shelter people from the evening chill.

I took my place by Lennard and smiled as men congratulated us and women asked about our honeymoon plans.

I waved away their inquiries. "We will probably spend the first week in our house by the sea. We can always travel around the world, but for the time being, there is much to be done on the estates."

That answer seemed to satisfy them. In truth, we would probably take no honeymoon trip at all. Lennard had announced he had a business trip to make immediately after the wedding, which was perfectly fine with me. It would give me time to tend to my own business.

My only enjoyment was Marit's presence in the little crowd of bridesmaids across the room. They huddled together and ignored her, but she waved happily at me. Later, after she'd had a few drinks, she would probably try to enlist the daughters of the aristocracy in the women's movement. I very much hoped to be there to enjoy that spectacle.

Finally, the moment came for the bride and groom to open the dancing. The orchestra played a fanfare; Lennard and I left our table. My head was spinning with the din of all the voices, the congratulations, and the wine. We walked to the center of the dance floor. I put my hand into my husband's, and he put his other hand on my waist. I raised my right hand to his shoulder and had a vision of us as the figures atop a wedding cake: the fragile princess and her crumbling prince.

Lennard was anything but fragile. We'd danced together before at balls and celebrations, but this time he guided me forcefully, almost passionately, around the parquet space. I gazed up at him, but he only pretended to look at me. We flew across the dance floor, but my heart was heavy. I tried to pretend I was with Max, but I failed because Max and I had never danced.

Once the newlyweds' dance was over, the orchestra changed the tune, and I awoke to my surroundings as if from a trance. Lennard looked directly at me at last. He was probably trying to read my thoughts. He seemed about to say something, then changed his mind.

I was obliged to continue dancing for what seemed an eternity. At last I was allowed to rest. I knew people expected the bride to dance until her shoes came apart. A happy bride would do so, but I had more of a mind to lock myself in the office to review the previous month's accounts.

Eventually, Marit bounded up to me, tipsy and excited. She raised her champagne glass. "How's our newly married lady?" She plopped onto Lennard's chair, for he was still on the dance floor.

"As well as can be expected," I said. "I am wondering how long it is until midnight, when I can finally crawl away from here."

"This party isn't all bad," Marit replied. "Your bridesmaids are adorable. One of them thought 'suffragette' was some kind of medicine. I told her it was!" She made a sweeping gesture. "After all, we're the antidote to all this nonsense!"

In spite of everything that had changed, I still agreed with all my heart. This was just part of the paternalistic system of control. Marit always said the moral code that decreed women belonged to their fathers and then husbands was the male means of maintaining dominance.

"Your friend Peer would surely disagree if you told him weddings are utter nonsense."

Marit glanced at me, then at the floor. "Nope, no wedding for me. He broke it off."

"He left?" I exclaimed.

"His parents wouldn't hear of admitting a suffragette into the family. Peer finally gave in to them."

"I thought he loved you!"

Marit looked down. "Maybe he does. But he's not willing to rebel against his parents. So I plan to take secretarial classes. I intend to stand on my own two feet and forget about men."

I looked at her and didn't know what to say. Why hadn't she shared her heartbreak with me? Had she wanted not to burden me? And all this time, I'd thought she'd found her happiness.

"Don't worry about it," Marit said finally, seeming to emerge from a reverie. "I'll be all right. There was a time I thought he was the one, but I see now he wasn't. As for my dream of having a family—that's out of an orphan's reach."

Her words sounded so bitter, I had to take her into my arms. I hugged her tight, rocked her a bit, and wondered if she would remember this conversation the next day.

Lennard returned at last. He was surprised to find a tearful Marit in my arms. I'd mentioned her to him in the past, but he apparently hadn't made the connection.

"Why is she distressed?" he asked, perplexed.

"Nothing earthshaking." I released Marit and sat her up straight. Her eyes were glassy. She was more inebriated than I'd thought. "It seems the champagne went to her head. I will see that she gets some fresh air and a cup of coffee."

I rose and helped Marit up. She clung to me as we walked out of the great hall and onto the terrace. The air was chilly, but I preferred it to the equally cool attitude of my new husband.

From the terrace, we looked down at the boisterous villagers, now clad in their heavy coats. The newlyweds should have visited and celebrated with them, but Lennard preferred to keep to himself and communicate with his people only about business matters. Personal contact with villagers was not his way.

I pointed to three burly fellows warming themselves at the fire. "How about we go down there to hunt a husband for you?"

Marit leaned on me. "Never you mind. I'm doing fine. Everything will turn out all right, don't you think?"

"I do hope so," I said. As I watched the goings-on outside the manor, my thoughts turned to the tiny cottage where no one was waiting for me.

Long after midnight, when my feet were numb and drunken laughter echoed in the guest wing, it was time for Lennard and me to go to the matrimonial bedchamber.

Age-old tradition required that witnesses escort us to our first night together. Stella and Anna accompanied us, along with the gaggle of bridesmaids, every one of them tipsy and giggling. But I knew there was nothing to giggle about. We would lie beneath the chilly covers and try to still our overstimulated minds so we could finally sleep. This bride wasn't going to lose her virginity that night.

I felt acutely uncomfortable as we approached the door to the master bedroom. This was where Hendrik and I had been conceived, our parents' secret place up until the time they had taken separate bedrooms.

I'd protested, but my mother insisted. "You are the mistress of Lion Hall. Now that you have your husband, you will sleep in the master bedroom."

I knew Stella would not be moved. Nevertheless, I instructed Lena to keep my own bedroom tidy and warm, for I didn't yet feel ready to submit entirely to the requirements of tradition.

Mother said something ceremonial when she opened the bedroom door. Lost in my musings about the past, I didn't hear what it was.

The chamber was exactly as I'd remembered it, with a vast bed in a wooden frame, a canopy overhead. It dwarfed everything else in the room, even the capacious wardrobe, which I knew had been assembled from fifty handcrafted pieces of wood joined without a single nail to hold them in place.

Mother's vanity table was still there, as was Father's valet stand. Memories of my childhood ventures into this room were patchy and indistinct. No wonder, for more than twenty years had passed.

My mother had overseen preparation of the room by Miss Rosendahl and the chambermaids. It was magnificent. Two candelabra, each with five candles, spread warm light everywhere. Rose petals were scattered along the carpeted path to the bed and sprays of roses were fastened to the bedposts. They'd strewn rose petals across the bedcovers. Marie and Lena appeared and turned down the blankets, then disappeared, suppressing grins.

Fortunately, our escort didn't expect us to divest ourselves of our clothing in their presence. The assumption was that Lennard would help me out of my dress and we would waltz our way to a passionate encounter in bed.

They left, and relief broke over me. Finally, I could abandon the pretense of joy.

I kicked off my shoes and pulled the tiara out of my hair. I'd taken off the veil and train much earlier, at the beginning of the party, because I was afraid someone would step on them. At long last I removed my dress, loosened my corset, and took it off.

Standing at the other side of the bed, Lennard peeled off his clothes. Neither of us said a word. And neither made a move toward the other. I was exhausted, and because I was carrying the child of another, Lennard had no desire for me.

While I was pulling on my nightgown, Lennard turned discreetly away, as if wishing to avoid embarrassing me. That was thoughtful of him.

I slipped into bed, happy to be done at last with this grueling day. Lennard extinguished the candles on his side, and I did the same. I felt the mattress settle beneath his weight and the blanket move as he pulled it over him.

"Good night," I said into the darkness.

Lennard wished me the same. Within moments, his breathing became regular.

I closed my eyes and tried to fall asleep, but I couldn't. I'd never been apprehensive about sharing a bed with a man, but that night I was disturbed and wide awake. Would every night be like this? A dark time of silence and resentment? Why was I disappointed, anyway? I'd never wanted to have Lennard as my spouse! But my heart was aching, and I longed for sleep to come at last.

As my body warmed the covers, they felt heavier and heavier. I seemed to be sinking into the depths of the mattress. My eyelids fell shut, and the shadowy world around us disappeared.

In the middle of the night, I awoke from a disturbing dream. I'd seen Max waving at me from the edge of a dark forest. The vision had seemed so genuine that I cried out, believing for a moment I really was lost in the wood. I started in fright at the sight of Lennard sleeping beside me. My heart raced. I slowly recalled this was my wedding night, a night that soon would end and give way to a new day.

Still, the images from my dream were vivid and so confusing that they drove me out of bed. I had the feeling Max was somewhere close. My intuition told me he'd returned and wanted me to come to the cottage. Fear and desire overcame good sense.

I quickly pulled on clothes and slipped out of the master bedroom. The manor smelled of spilled wine and stale cigarette smoke, along with the faintest hints of food and flowers, and I could almost hear the laughter of the guests. I paid no attention.

I threw on a coat, left the mansion, and hurried past the festival tent that stood empty and abandoned. The staff would remove it in the course of the day, and the wedding celebrations would become memories. The outside chill crept under my coat, and my breath turned into clouds of white mist, but I paid no attention. I hurried to the place I hadn't visited for weeks. Hope still lived in my breast. Would he be there, by some miracle? Would he finally tell me why he'd disappeared? My heart pounded in anticipation, and the desire to throw myself into his arms spurred me on.

I was soon disappointed. The cottage came into view, but the windows were still dark. I was struck by the desolation of that uninhabited dwelling. I stopped, unable to take another step, as lost as a sleepwalker who'd just awakened. The realization that nothing had changed brought tears into my eyes. I felt Max had abandoned me a second time, again with no explanation. I wiped my cheeks and looked up at the heavens. Morning was slowly creeping up the sky beyond the woods.

I had to return to the manor before anyone noticed my absence. I'd promised Lennard I wouldn't mention Max.

I needed to try to forget him.

60

I gazed out the window and watched the wind shaking the bare branches of the trees. Early 1915 had brought an unusually rapid thaw. A gray sky hung over the estate as rain soaked the paths and garden. Snow was still piled at the waysides, but it would melt away entirely unless freezing weather returned quickly.

The weather affected me deeply. I'd felt better when the sun had gleamed across untouched surfaces of snow, but now I was almost always plunged in gloomy brooding. And worst of all, there was no escaping the mansion. I felt I'd been locked up like a mare in her stall who was kicking impatiently against the walls because she wanted to race proud and free across the pasture. I was no one's mare, but I had no escape. My belly had become so swollen that I could scarcely move. Dr. Bengtsen was convinced I was going to have twins.

I didn't know whether that prospect should please me or terrify me. Two babies! I was expecting a painful, extended delivery. Even though my physician and Marit had tried to reassure me, I knew all sorts of complications were possible. I might even die.

Why had Max left? Why had he abandoned me? I'd been able to suppress those thoughts for a while after my wedding, but recently they'd assailed me more often. Yearning visited me but so did anger. Anger at myself, and anger at him. I should have had some word from him, even if he were to vow we should never meet again. Why had we allowed ourselves to lose control? And why, for God's sake, did he vanish without leaving a word behind?

"Excuse me. Am I disturbing you?" asked Lennard. I hadn't noticed him entering the room.

"No," I said, rubbing my belly. "I was just lost in thought."

The lives developing within me were a daily reminder that my great passion was somewhere out there, and I'd betrayed him by marrying another. And not a day went by without Lennard making me feel he now regretted upholding his pledge. We ran our estates as best we could, and each of us was deeply involved in our entirely separate business affairs. We were intermittently in contact during the course of the day and treated one another with careful politeness, but in contrast to the past, we did so without enthusiasm. Marriage had turned dear friends into strangers.

"There's a letter here for you. Marie gave it to me, and I brought it immediately."

"A business letter?"

He shook his head. "Read it for yourself. I will leave you alone."

As you always do, I thought. I checked the return address, and my heart skipped a beat.

I'd given up expecting it, but finally I had in my hands a reply from Heinrich von Bredestein! No wonder Lennard had been so curt. I'd learned to tell the difference between my husband's indifferent silences and his offended ones.

I turned the letter over in my hands. In the worst of cases, Von Bredestein would write that his son had died at the front. That was a real possibility, especially given the long delay in answering.

I would find you, no matter how far I had to fly . . .

I heard again the words he'd whispered in my ear our first night together. Was he dead? Would he come back in the form of a butterfly? I felt a catch in my throat. I fumbled at the envelope and tore it open. It was in Swedish. The handwriting was that of someone scarcely able to control a pen. Was this letter from Max's mother?

Honored Countess Lejongård,

Please accept my thanks for your letter of last year. This reply was delayed by my poor health. I apologize.

My son Max has never been to Sweden, but I think I know what may have happened. Hans, his twin brother, left our estate some time ago, bound for Stockholm to purchase horses for our stables. He wrote he was living with a friend.

Twin brother? Were my eyes playing tricks on me? I shook my head to clear my vision.

It appears Hans represented himself to you as Max. No doubt you did not ask for proof of his identity.

We have no idea whether Hans is still in Sweden or has returned to Germany. You wrote that he may have joined the army, but unfortunately, I can neither confirm nor deny that. Nor can his wife.

His wife? Max—or rather, Hans—was married? Was this letter a practical joke? Or a fraud?

No, the voice of reason told me, *this is no joke.* Why would a mother invent such a thing about her son? She must miss him terribly.

Friederike was distraught when he disappeared. We have searched for him. We wrote to his friend but received no reply. I assume the gentleman just forwarded the letter to Hans.

Your letter brought her a glimmer of hope, but, sadly, that has now dimmed.

You write that he worked for your family as estate manager. Are there any personal effects you can send to us? And, if possible, a photograph? We would be very grateful to you for any help in locating Hans.

If we discover his whereabouts, we will advise you, no matter the circumstances.

With sincere respect,

Lotta von Bredestein

I stared at the letter in disbelief. Max wasn't Max? And, worse, he had a wife named Friederike?

My heart thundered, and my ears roared. The letter disappeared from my sight, not blurred by tears but because my vision dimmed, and I was about to faint. I reached out for something to lean on, but my knees buckled, and everything turned black.

When I came back to consciousness, a worried Lennard was leaning over me. "Agneta! Can you hear me?"

I nodded, confused. "What happened?"

"You fainted. Was it because of the letter?"

The letter! Should I tell Lennard? His searching gaze made my face flush and burn.

"I believe . . . this letter . . . falls under the terms of our agreement," I said weakly as I sat up.

"Is it from him?" He clenched his jaw.

"Do you really want to know?"

"Yes," he said, surprising me. "I do."

"His mother wrote."

"Is he dead?"

"No. He—his family does not know where he is."

I grabbed the letter and turned it over, so Lennard couldn't read it. He would be infuriated if he learned Max had masqueraded as his twin brother to escape his wife and family.

"You mean you were trying to locate him?" Lennard's voice was icy.

Suddenly I realized I was sitting on a powder keg.

"I wrote to his parents right after he disappeared. A long time before our agreement."

Lennard's hard look softened. "They took their time about it."

"The mother had health problems. Perhaps she was too ill to write earlier."

"You must let the matter drop," Lennard said. "That would be better for you and for all of us."

"You are entirely correct. It would be better just to forget about it." I crumpled the letter into a ball. A ball that proved Max's duplicity beyond all doubt.

I was deeply shocked by his double dealing, but my mind still clamored for an explanation. Why had he used a false identity? Why had he stayed at Lion Hall so long?

But I didn't want Lennard to see me struggling with my emotions. "Would you give me a moment?"

"Of course. Are you physically better now?"

"I probably will not be better until the children are born. I take no pleasure at all from these fainting spells, believe me."

I saw alarm and worry in his eyes. But why should he care about my health? If I died, he'd inherit the estate and regain his own freedom.

Lennard left the room. I brooded for a time, the letter still clutched in my fist. At last I threw it across the room with a scream of frustration. Why couldn't I just forget about him?

Because he never explained, a voice told me. *You won't find peace until you know why.*

Peace eluded me because I kept waiting and hoping. I hurried again and again to the cottage, hoping it could somehow magically summon him back.

I needed someone who knew how to locate him.

I had the coach team harnessed the following day on the pretext of having errands to do in Kristianstad.

"I can take care of those for you, surely," Lennard said when he learned I was going. "What if you faint in the street?"

"I am taking Lena." My maid stood behind me. She seemed much more mature now. "And besides, August will keep an eye on us. I feel fine."

Lennard didn't seem convinced, but I insisted.

We stopped at the Kristianstad telegraph office. I knew Marit and our sisterhood sometimes employed a detective. Perhaps she could persuade him to undertake a search. My wire said I wished to engage him and requested a speedy reply. The telegraphist sent it immediately and promised his messenger would immediately deliver any reply.

The boy arrived two days later with a telegram from the detective himself. He would be in our region on business and suggested we meet.

But how could I meet with the detective without Lennard knowing?

Fortunately, my husband had to visit his own estate for a couple of days. His mother's health was poor, and he wanted to make sure she had proper medical attention. Perhaps he was also motivated by Lotta von Bredestein's letter and the evidence that Max still haunted me. I didn't care. Perhaps Max could be located. I wired back that same day and suggested meeting at a Kristianstad café.

61

Hanno Boregard was a small, balding man easily overlooked in a crowd. His suit was slate gray and completely unadorned. He wore a bowler hat. Though his appearance was unremarkable, his eyes were vigilant. He was the best in his profession.

He offered me his hand. "Countess Lejongård, I am happy to see you again."

"I am grateful that you made time for me. I know you are very busy in Stockholm."

"That's true, but it's impossible to turn down a request from our mutual friend."

He and Marit knew each other well. At times I'd wondered if he was interested in her.

We ordered coffee. Dr. Bengtsen had advised me to avoid all stimulants in my current condition, but I felt this was overcautious.

"What can I do for you? Are you looking for information about a client or competitor?"

"Neither," I told him. "I want you to locate someone."

"Do you have a photograph of this person?"

"No, but I can describe him. He said his name was Max von Bredestein. He was employed as the manager of our estate. He disappeared shortly after Germany entered the war. I suspect he wanted to enlist. An inquiry to his family brought the news that his name is actually Hans von Bredestein, and he was pretending to be his twin brother. The family knows as little as I do about his whereabouts. I would like you to locate him for me."

I had trouble holding back tears as I spoke. I knew every inch of Max's body, but his interior life, his soul, was a complete mystery. And I hadn't realized it.

The detective absorbed all this in thoughtful silence. When he met my gaze, I feared he would immediately read in my eyes the reason I wanted to find Max.

"I gather he gave up his job with you?"

I nodded.

"Did he take valuables or prejudice the estate in some other way?"

"No, he did not."

"Are you closely involved?"

Of course he'd noted my protruding abdomen. That knowledge made me feel hot and uncomfortable under my dress. Boregard's inquiries for the sisterhood were often in connection with paternity cases, and it was natural for him to suspect something similar. He was right, but I absolutely could not confirm his suspicions.

"We are friends, and I am worried. He should have returned to his family or at least informed them, but he did not. There is also the question of his use of a false name."

"That is quite unusual, to be sure," the detective replied dutifully. "If his conscience is clear, why would he represent himself to you as his twin brother?"

"I really do not know." It occurred to me suddenly that twin births tended to run in a family. "The Von Bredesteins have ancestral lands in Pomerania. According to his own account, his relationship with his father was not particularly good. He evidently decided he could no longer put up with his life there."

Boregard was scribbling notes in a small notebook. "Is there anything else he kept secret from you, other than his name?"

"Yes. The fact that he had a wife named Friederike. According to the letter from his mother."

The detective noted that as well. "Did he promise to marry you? Or anything of the kind?"

That question shocked me. I understood why he needed to ask, but even so, it frightened me.

"No, he did not. As I already told you, I am simply worried about him."

"When I find him, what should I do? Should I pass a message to him or encourage him to return?"

I knew what "encourage" meant. From time to time, Boregard had strong-armed reluctant fathers into doing the right thing. I didn't want Max to be pressured into submission. I just wanted an explanation and the assurance he was still alive.

"No. Find out where he is. I myself will write to him."

The detective raised his eyebrows at that but nodded anyway. "As you wish."

"You will take the assignment?"

"Of course! I would not have come otherwise. You know my fee schedule, but I will also need additional funds to travel to Germany. As well as to the front, if that becomes necessary."

"You will receive everything you require."

"I will also need the address of the family of the missing man. I will make discreet inquiries to confirm that the account you've received is accurate."

I handed him the letter from Lotta von Bredestein, which I'd uncrumpled and smoothed out. I saw no reason to withhold it, for it contained nothing compromising.

"Lovely," the detective said. "If you have payment ready, then our business today is concluded."

I took an envelope from my purse. In our telegraphic exchanges, we'd agreed I would provide an advance of two hundred crowns. It was no trifling amount, but I knew Boregard's services were worth his fees. He accepted the envelope, and it vanished unopened into his pocket. His motto was "You trust me, and I'll trust you." Anything less would be an affront to his professional code of ethics.

"I will keep you apprised. If additional funds should be required, here is the address where you can send them. Please be patient; my research may take a while."

"I am well aware of that."

We sat, looking at one another for a moment, then the detective stood up and extended his hand. "Well, then! It's been a pleasure to see you again. I hope that next time we meet, I will be able to offer you my congratulations."

I nodded and gave him a firm handshake. "Best wishes for success, Mr. Boregard. I am counting on you."

"I will not disappoint you." He gave me a quick bow and left the café.

As I lifted the coffee cup for a sip, I saw him pass the window—the nondescript man nobody would notice. I was sure he would find Max.

Or rather, Hans.

62

I was exhausted by the time the coach got back to the manor. I went to my room and lay down but found it impossible to sleep.

I stared up at the ceiling. Two questions obsessed me. What was Max doing? And would this pregnancy ever end?

The light outside finally began to fail, so I got up and went downstairs to dinner. I knew what to expect. Mother would stare wordlessly at her plate, lost in thought throughout an uncommunicative meal.

Both of her children were disappointments. Our failings hadn't been published and our family hadn't been pilloried, but in her mind, the stain on the Lejongård escutcheon could never be washed away.

Mother seemed particularly gloomy that evening. She didn't look up from her plate. Once all the servants had left the room, she asked quietly, "Where were you all afternoon?"

"In Kristianstad." It would have been pointless to deny it, considering I'd taken the coach.

"That is the second time this week," she commented. "Were you in the city trolling for a lover?"

"Mother!" I exclaimed. "Do you think I would betray my husband?"

"Who knows? You treat one another like strangers. Anything is possible."

Was she goading me into a quarrel as a distraction from her dismal mood?

"I respect Lennard, and I like him. He was my friend. Now he is my husband. I made a wise decision."

"When you informed me of your wedding plans, you claimed that you two had been carried away by passion. Were you? Or are you hiding something?"

"I am hiding nothing from you."

"Then why take such an arduous trip in your condition? Is it about that fellow who ran off?"

I slammed my spoon down on the table. "I am hiding nothing! I contacted a detective to look for Max. Are you satisfied? I want to know what happened to him."

Mother stared at me, thunderstruck. "And why on earth do you want to know?"

"I want to know why he left. I want certainty!"

"Because he was a vagabond. Probably not noble at all, despite his pretensions. And you fell for him."

"I did not!" I protested.

"You think I am blind? I saw the way you looked at him, and he had eyes for you too. The way you kept sneaking out of the house at night and back early the next morning. Did you really think you were fooling me?"

I stared at her, speechless.

"Do you know what I thought when I heard you bolted off to the Ekbergs and came back to tell me you were marrying Lennard?" she berated me, trying to keep her voice low so the staff wouldn't overhear. "I told myself, 'That good-for-nothing seduced my daughter and left her pregnant!' You are fortunate Lennard is so generous. Does he know?"

Her words battered me like blows.

"Mother, how dare you!" I cried. "You cannot simply make up such a tale!"

Mother shook with anger. "Had I known, I would have thrown the man out. You have no idea how often I thought about obliging him to vanish and leave you in peace!"

"And did you?" I shrieked. "Were you behind this?"

I was seized with indignation. If she was the cause, I'd never forgive her. Her disloyalty was monstrous.

She stiffened. Her eyes opened wide, and her expression went rigid. "Agneta!"

My name was a strangled cry.

Her body lurched. She dropped her spoon and clutched the table-cloth. Her eyes were wide with terror.

My anger disappeared instantly. "Mother? What is it?"

"Terribly . . . dizzy," she said with great effort. And then she passed out.

"Mother!" I sprang up, rushed over, and caught her as she began to fall out of her chair.

"Help!" I screamed, as I tried to ease her to the floor. Had she had a heart attack?

Bruns appeared in the doorway but stood there, petrified.

"Call Dr. Bengtsen. Now!"

He turned and raced out of the room. Miss Rosendahl and Marie appeared.

"In heaven's name, what's happened?" cried our housekeeper as she rushed to me.

"My mother suddenly became dizzy. Then she fainted."

I rubbed Stella's cheeks, but she didn't respond. Her forehead was clammy. I leaned over and made sure she was breathing. I fumbled for her pulse and found it weak.

Fear washed over me. This was a heart attack. And I had caused it!

"Mama, wake up!" I whispered and stroked her cheeks. "You cannot leave me! Please!"

"Perhaps we should transport her to her room," Miss Rosendahl ventured. "She will be more comfortable there. Marie, see if Mr. Bruns has returned, and if not, get Linda." She turned back to me. "Gracious madame, your condition! You should not be sitting on the floor. It cannot be good for the baby."

At that moment I didn't care. My mother was only in her midfifties! She couldn't die!

Miss Rosendahl helped me up as Marie and Linda, who'd come running, carefully lifted my mother. We were in the entrance hall when Bruns appeared at the front door.

"Peter is on his way with our fastest horse."

"Good," I answered. Bruns took Stella in his arms. I felt my strength returning, clearing my head. "Let us take my mother to her bedroom. Miss Rosendahl, please let me know as soon as the doctor arrives."

"Shall I stay with her?" asked Linda, whose face was white as chalk.

"No, that is not necessary. I will watch over her."

"But—"

"Linda, please. I feel entirely capable of it. I may be pregnant, but I am not ill!"

"Very good, gracious mistress." Linda stood and watched as we left her behind. She probably felt slighted, but at that moment my mother had no need of her maid. I was her daughter, and even though our relationship was a rocky one, I wanted to do the right thing.

Bruns carried her upstairs in his arms. Together we settled her in bed. I took my place beside her. Her eyes remained closed. What was wrong?

"Can I do anything else?" Bruns asked.

I shook my head. "No, but stay close by. I will call if I need your help."

"As you wish." Bruns bowed and withdrew.

I stroked Mother's cheek. My heart raged, and the panic that possessed every part of my body made me forget my aching back and stiff joints.

"Mama," I whispered. "Mama, please wake up. I know what I did. But I was not trying to make your life difficult. I really did love him. I thought he was the one. There was no way for me to know I was making another mistake."

She lay motionless. I unbuttoned her dress, shifted her onto her side, and loosened her corset. As I rolled her onto her back again, she shuddered and gasped for air. She blinked up at me.

"Agneta? What happened? I thought it was dinnertime."

"Hush, Mama, and lie still," I told her gently. "We were downstairs, but you got dizzy and fainted. Dr. Bengtsen will be here soon."

"Dr. Bengtsen? But nothing is wrong with me."

"He will be the one to decide that." I pressed her gently back onto the pillow.

Mother seemed astonished to see me sitting with her. "Where is Linda?"

"Downstairs, probably. I told her I would take care of you."

"But in your condition . . ."

I reached for her hand and pressed it. "I am perfectly capable of sitting here and watching over you. Now rest. The important thing is for you to get better."

Mother stared as if she were seeing a ghost. Or perhaps a goblin that had assumed her daughter's form.

"I am so sorry we quarreled," I went on. "I did not want to upset you."

Mother didn't reply. She closed her eyes, and I was afraid she was about to lose consciousness again. But then she spoke. "Perhaps that is how it must be between mothers and daughters. Because mothers really do want the best for their children."

Someone knocked at the door.

"Yes! Come in!" I called.

Marie looked in. "Dr. Bengtsen has just arrived."

"Thank you! Please bring some water, soap, and a towel, so he can wash his hands."

"Right away, gracious mistress." Marie curtsied and disappeared from sight.

"Hear that?" I said to Mother. "The doctor is here. He will examine you, and we will see what the problem is."

I moved to get up, but she clung to my hand. "Stay here. Please. Do not leave me alone."

"Of course," I reassured her. "I will receive him and then be right back."

Dr. Bengtsen was already coming up the stairs when I stepped out of the room.

"Ah, Countess Lejongård."

"Good evening, Doctor." I offered him my hand. "Thank you for coming so quickly."

I led him into the room. Mother was now sitting up, and her face had regained some color. Maybe it had just been a moment of weakness . . . but Stella Lejongård had never been one to faint. She'd maintained her implacable fortitude even when Father died. And we'd often had similarly acrimonious disagreements without any visible effects upon her health.

"Good evening, Countess," the doctor said as he washed his hands in the basin of water Marie had brought in. "What happened?"

"You will have to ask my daughter. I cannot even recall what we were eating. All I remember is going downstairs to dinner."

Bengtsen glanced at me.

I was startled to find the attack had left a hole in her memory. Had her episode erased our dispute from her mind? Was that why she was being so restrained with me? Or was she hiding the subject of contention from the physician?

"Well, we were having dinner and a conversation." I thought it better not to mention our angry exchange, which was none of the doctor's business. "Suddenly she said she was feeling faint, then almost immediately collapsed. I tried to awaken her but without success. She regained consciousness only after we had carried her to her room."

"How long was she unconscious?" The doctor was taking Mother's pulse, his eyes intent upon his silver pocket watch.

"Ten minutes, perhaps."

The doctor nodded as he closed the watch.

"Madame, I would like to suggest that you divest yourself of clothing to the extent that you find it morally appropriate." He looked to me. "If that is acceptable, please help her remove the corset."

"Of course, Doctor."

He turned his back and searched through his medical bag. I helped Mother out of her dress and pulled off her corset. She sat there in her shift, looking more fragile than I'd ever seen her. She was still a handsome woman, but her body showed the ravages of age. Her shoulders and neck were undeniably scrawny, and her skin was no longer as firm as before. She was a vision of what I would probably look like in about thirty years.

After I'd folded her clothes, the doctor began his examination. He listened to her chest and gently tapped her back, checked her blood pressure, and verified her pulse. He looked into her eyes and mouth, then again used his stethoscope to listen to her breathing. His facial expressions gave nothing away—they could be signs of tension and concentration or reactions to some threat. He put away his instruments and asked to speak to me outside.

"Is it possible to discuss it in my mother's presence?"

Stella sat unusually still, as if she already knew what he was going to tell me.

"We will do so," Dr. Bengtsen said, "but first I need to speak to you alone."

We left the room. Anxiety raged within me. My belly cramped as apprehension burned in my chest.

"Well, Doctor? Please do not keep me in suspense."

"Your mother's pulse concerns me. It is irregular, and I found the same thing when I listened to her chest. It appears that her heart is having difficulty maintaining a regular rhythm. That would explain the sudden loss of consciousness."

"You mean she is afflicted with a weak heart?"

The doctor frowned. "Has your mother complained of anything recently? Episodes of weakness, perhaps? Difficulty moving?"

"My mother never complains," I said. "She is too disciplined for that."

"In that case, from now on you should regularly inquire about the state of her health. And insist on truthful answers. This is very important."

Truthful answers? Mother was sure to claim nothing was wrong, thereby forcing me to contradict her. Hardly an advisable routine, considering the diagnosis.

"I believe I hear water in her lungs. Not a great deal, but I detect a rattling sound when she breathes. I suspect that the right chamber of her heart is struggling, which places a strain on her breathing."

"So she is not getting enough oxygen? But wouldn't there be a blue cast to her appearance?"

"Not necessarily. Such shortness of breath comes on slowly and will diminish as soon as the strain is past. It will become apparent only if she is under stress for a sustained period."

Which was hardly ever the case with Mother, who was deliberate in everything she undertook. Except when we quarreled.

"The Kristianstad hospital has an X-ray machine," Bengtsen went on.

I nodded. "Yes, we arranged the purchase when Professor Lindström requested it."

"I would like for them to make an X-ray of her lungs and heart. That will help ascertain the cause of the problem."

I tried to suppress my shock. My mother, with a weak heart? "Yes, if you think that is wise. I do not think she will refuse."

"Good. I will contact Professor Lindström."

I was shaken. To what extent was I responsible for this? How long had she been hiding it from me? "What sort of therapy will be advisable if your suspicions are confirmed?"

"I will prescribe medication to strengthen and regulate the heartbeat. And she must avoid all stress. It would be a good idea for her to spend time at a spa or at the seashore. You have a beach house in Åhus, I believe."

"Yes, we do. Would a stay there help improve her condition?"

"Sea air will do her good. And it cannot hurt for her to get away from the estate, where she is constantly reminded of her husband and son."

"You are right, Doctor. But why didn't she say anything? She must have been aware that something was wrong."

"She probably blamed it on grief. Human beings are good at explaining away subtle symptoms. Until the day comes when that's no longer possible."

My mouth became a sharp, thin line. To think I'd caused her ever more worry . . .

"Very well. Shall we go back inside?" the doctor proposed. "I will explain this a bit more gently to your mother, provided that you consider it appropriate for her to know the truth."

"Do *you* know the whole truth?" I asked, eliciting an odd look from Bengtsen. "I mean, you want to have the X-ray done before you make your diagnosis. Or am I wrong?"

"That is correct, Countess."

"Good. Then tell her as much as you can say with certainty. She deserves to know. After all, she is neither a child nor feebleminded."

He nodded, and we reentered Mother's room. She had dressed in the meantime, though she hadn't put on the corset. Perhaps at last she would retire that horrible garment.

"Well, then, what did you discuss with my daughter?" she asked, herself once again. She was thin but strong, and her expression was stubborn.

"My desire to send you to the Kristianstad hospital for an X-ray of your chest." He explained his rationale and what he hoped to learn from the image. She listened closely, looking entirely serene.

"Very well. I agree," she said. "Make all the necessary arrangements!"

"Very good, gracious lady." The doctor seemed uncertain of himself. Had he been expecting her to object? "I will do everything within my power to restore your health."

"I thank you, Doctor." Hearing her tone of dismissal, Bengtsen glanced at me.

"Could you perhaps give my mother something to prevent another fainting spell?"

"Of course. I will prescribe some drops. If my suspicions are confirmed, I will add digitalis, which strengthens the heartbeat."

"Digitalis?"

"Foxglove," the doctor explained. "I am sure you are familiar with the plant. It strengthens the heart muscle. Until then, there are various other medications with similar effects. Heart irregularities are less dangerous than they once were. But we will start with a low dose at first. Once we have X-ray results, I can make the definitive diagnosis."

"We are very grateful, Doctor," I said as he wrote out the prescription. The name of the indicated drug looked unpronounceable, especially given the physician's poor handwriting, but the pharmacist would know what to do.

Dr. Bengtsen assured us he would inform us as soon as he had an appointment for the X-ray, then took his leave.

Mother and I sat for a while in silence. She gazed out the window at the woods in the distance, now shadowed in the evening light. It was a tranquil prospect, but I had the distinct impression Mother was feeling anything but at peace.

"A weak heart," she finally murmured to herself. "No one in my family ever had a weak heart."

"Perhaps it was never diagnosed. And besides, I believe trying circumstances can weaken a heart. These past years haven't been exactly kind to us."

Mother shot me a chilly look, and I was suddenly convinced she had only feigned her memory loss.

"I am very sorry, Mother." I looked at the floor. "I did not intend to quarrel. I should have told you I was trying to locate him."

"Would it change anything? You are headstrong, after all," Stella said, actually sounding a bit sad. "You should have stayed away from him from the first."

I slumped. She was right. But what should one do when the heart wants one thing only, and satisfying that desire gives such unalloyed pleasure?

"If I were to get some sort of news about Max, that would not change anything. It would just mean I could at last be at peace. I want to know why he left. When I do, that will be the end of it."

Mother made no comment. I imagined she was picturing how our lives would have been if things had gone differently.

"Tell me one thing," I continued. "Did you tell him he had to leave?"

"No," my mother said. "I wanted to summon the strength to do so, but I could not. For reasons I may someday reveal to you—but not now." She fell silent again and contemplated the hem of her dress.

"Should I tell them to bring you something to eat?"

"I am not hungry," Mother said. "But go and have something for yourself. You need the energy." She regarded my belly, and for a moment

I had the impression she wanted to reach out and stroke it. But her iron will kept her from doing so.

"I will check on you later." I stepped out of the room but lingered for a moment in the hall. Only then did I absorb what Dr. Bengtsen had avoided saying outright: that Mother could die if her heart condition wasn't treated properly.

Linda met me downstairs, wringing her hands. "How is the gracious mistress feeling?"

"She wishes to rest for a while," I answered. "She will ring for you if she needs something."

Linda nodded, curtsied, and went to the kitchen.

The meal in the dining room was stone cold. I seated myself anyway and pulled apart a roll. Then I consumed some vegetables and fruit. Not for me, but because of the baby—or babies. For the first time I felt their hunger, their desire to live, manifested less by their kicks inside my belly than by the acute hunger they caused me.

Max's children. If I only knew where he was and whether he was still alive! If only I could tell him how much happiness and good fortune he'd walked away from. If only I knew the reason why . . .

63

I accompanied Stella to the hospital for her X-ray. That morning my mother, always so composed, acted as if she was being taken to the scaffold.

"I do not understand why this is needed," she complained. "Dr. Bengtsen already listened to my heart. Does he not trust his own ears?"

"He simply wants to be sure of the measures to take. And besides, our family paid for the machine. It is entirely appropriate that we also benefit from it."

"Benefit by confirming my heart is ruined?" She shook her head. "What is the use of that? You cannot repair or replace a heart. What will he do when he has his certainty?"

"He can prescribe the right medication and give you a prognosis."

"Every illness leads to the grave, whether today or tomorrow." She stopped speaking and looked grimly through the coach window for the rest of the trip.

At the hospital, Professor Lindström escorted us personally to the room where the X-ray equipment had been installed. Peering through the door, I saw an immense, frightening machine.

"Am I allowed to enter as well?" I asked.

Professor Lindström shook his head. "It is not advisable, given your condition. Granted, we do not yet have any data concerning the effects of X-rays upon an expectant mother and her child, but we think it better for you to wait upstairs. I can examine you in the interim if you wish."

"That will not be necessary," I replied. "I am healthy and full of energy."

Stella kept her own feelings strictly hidden from the medical personnel, but she caught my eye before she entered the X-ray room. I saw the terror and pitied her.

The radiologist and his assistants busied themselves with their preparations. I went upstairs with Lindström.

"What is your due date?" the professor asked. Clearly he felt obliged to interest himself in my condition.

"Sometime in the spring. Dr. Bengtsen says that, if it's twins, they're often born before the due date. Frankly, that would please me."

"Have you decided where the delivery will take place?"

"At the manor, I suppose. To tell the truth, I have not given the question any thought."

"But you should. Twin births can be complicated. If your husband has no objection, I would recommend you give birth here in the hospital, where you can be in the care of our best physicians."

"Dr. Bengtsen can tend to me just as well at the manor."

A shiver ran up my spine as I remembered Hendrik lying in one of these very hospital beds, and I had difficulty hiding my agitation from Lindström. I hadn't the slightest desire to be admitted here.

"And what would Bengtsen do in the event of complications?" The doctor frowned. "It might become necessary to deliver by Cesarean section, for example, if one of the babies is in a dangerous position."

My belly quivered at the thought of being cut open. I really didn't want to hear this, but he was right.

"Would I survive such an operation?"

"Surgical techniques have improved greatly in recent years. Our surgeons have experience with successful Cesarean deliveries. I am not saying such a thing is inevitable, but I would be happier to have you in the care of doctors well versed in gynecology. A good deal is at stake for your family."

That was true. My brother was dead, and his daughter hadn't been acknowledged. Lennard was my husband, but he wasn't a Lejongård. Our family line would come to an abrupt end if I should die and take the babies with me. I felt an immense burden of responsibility.

"I will discuss it with my husband. What must I do if I decide to deliver here?"

"Simply let me know. I will make all the necessary arrangements."

Professor Lindström laid a reassuring hand over my own. "The Lejongårds have always been our greatest benefactors. Your annual donations have kept the hospital open. I will do everything I can to ensure a safe and healthy delivery."

I gave him a wry smile. "Only for the sake of the donations?"

"No, not only for those. I personally owe it to you. Your brother died in this hospital. I will never allow the last remaining heiress of Lion Hall to suffer the same fate as she brings new life into the world."

A knock interrupted our discussion. A nurse told us my mother's procedure was complete.

We went back downstairs. Mother seemed a bit confused. I saw that she was finding it difficult to disguise her dislike for the proceedings.

"I will take a look at the images before I give them to you," Professor Lindström said. "Could I ask you to give a few moments for that?"

The nurse guided us to chairs outside Lindström's consulting room. The sun had come out, and the air was becoming stuffy. As we seated ourselves, I noticed that Mother was again having trouble breathing. She was pale, and beads of perspiration stood out on her temples.

"How did it go down there?" I asked after a moment of silence. "Did you feel the X-rays?"

Mother shook her head. "No, not the rays. But the plate they pressed against me was as cold as a frozen lake. And it was quite uncomfortable to stand there for such a long time."

"It was the only way to determine whether Dr. Bengtsen's diagnosis was correct," I replied. "And we must identify your illness. I still need you very much."

Stella dismissed that with a snort. "You have no need of me. You will insist on your own way in life."

"That may be, but it does not mean I can do without your advice."

"You have never asked for advice," Mother snapped. "You have always done exactly what you wished."

"Not so! I do ask your opinion from time to time."

"And then you disregard it."

"That doesn't mean I don't listen." I took a deep breath. *Can we please, please not quarrel for once? Or has this become our inescapable routine?*

Luckily, Professor Lindström appeared just then. He held a large frame, which, at that distance, looked like a linoleum block printing plate.

"Ladies, I have examined the image with great care."

I was hoping against hope that he would take issue with Dr. Bengtsen's diagnosis.

"Unfortunately, I must inform you that my colleague's interpretation was correct. Look here."

He held the plate up to the light. Immediately, I could make out my mother's lungs. And her heart.

"Here you see the chambers of the heart," Lindström explained, outlining the corresponding area with his finger. "They may appear unexceptional to you, but there is a distinct enlargement of the muscle."

Unexceptional? I almost laughed. This was anything but unexceptional. The inside of my mother's body . . .

When I was young and Stella treated me with chilly indifference, I was convinced she had no heart at all. But here it was. And larger than it should be.

"I take it the enlargement is not a good sign," I said. Mother, sitting at my side, merely stared at the image.

"No, it definitely is not. It indicates a weakened heart; in this case, a weakening of the left chamber. Dr. Bengtsen did well to send you to me."

Mother remained wholly unresponsive. I would have given a great deal then for an X-ray that revealed the contents of her mind.

"And what medications would you suggest?"

"A compound of foxglove and lily of the valley. I will send Dr. Bengtsen my recommendation, but I believe he knows what needs to be done."

"Is this condition fatal?" Mother suddenly asked.

"No, not if properly treated. But you will need to modify your lifestyle somewhat."

"Is a stay at the seaside advisable?" I asked, since Dr. Bengtsen had raised that possibility.

"But of course! The sea air does the heart good. And long strolls along the beach will help strengthen the lady in any case."

"All right, Mother. Now we know what to do."

Stella stared straight in front of her for a long moment. Then she roused herself. "Thank you very much, Professor." She rose.

"I will have the image wrapped. You can take it with you," Lindström said and then left.

"So then, what do you say to a seaside vacation?"

Mother refused to meet my eyes. "You want to get rid of me."

"No, I want you to get well! A bit of exercise will do you good. And besides, I could use a breath of sea air as well."

"Traveling in your condition?" Mother shook her head. "Out of the question! We can travel after the children are born but not before! I do not wish to be trapped with you in the beach house when you go into labor."

I had a sharp retort on the tip of my tongue, but I held it back.

Lindström returned and handed me a neatly bound package. "Whenever you need additional advice, I am always here. For both of you. Please consider my recommendation about the delivery."

"Thank you. I will." I shook his hand.

We left the hospital and climbed into the coach. August set the horses in motion.

"What was the doctor recommending?"

"He suggested it might be better to deliver in the hospital."

"Every Lejongård has been born within the walls of Lion Hall!"

"I am perfectly aware of that," I said. "But no Lejongård has ever given birth to twins. I do not know if I am willing to take that risk. I want to be sure my children are not condemned to growing up without a mother."

Mother considered that. "You must discuss it with your husband," she said finally. "If he is in favor, I will not stand in your way. One's birthplace is not important; what counts is one's character. And you are still—always—a Lejongård."

Lennard returned the following Sunday.

Would Mother tell him I'd commissioned a search for Max? My worries about her health hadn't given me time to think about Boregard. I'd received no news from him, but the trip to Germany was a long one. And if he had to go to the front . . .

That evening after dinner, Lennard and I sat together in the bedroom. I held a book Lena had recommended, pretending to read. I was filled with misgivings. Mother had asked for time alone with Lennard to tell him about her illness. He'd appeared deeply concerned afterward, but there was no indication she'd mentioned Max.

Now he sat motionless at the desk, drafting a letter. I wondered what he was writing, but I dared not ask. He never inquired about my personal correspondence.

I hated the silence that persisted between us whenever we were alone, yet I had no idea what to say. With Max, I'd been able to discuss anything, freely and without constraint. Why was it so hard with Lennard?

Finally, I lowered the book. "Professor Lindström thinks it would be advisable for the children to be born in the hospital," I said. "So that any complications could be safely handled."

Lennard set down his pen and frowned. "Does the professor expect complications?"

"Not necessarily. But Dr. Bengtsen had also mentioned that leaving everything to nature when twins are delivered can entail considerable risk."

"Then we will take you to the hospital, if you believe that will be safer for you and the children."

I nodded. "But what if I do not know what to believe? If I cannot decide the right thing to do?"

Lennard barked a laugh. "You always know. Better than I do."

"And if I get it wrong again?"

He caught my meaning, and his body stiffened. He sat there, indecisive for a moment, then got up and came to me. He squatted down and took my hand, something he'd never done before. We usually avoided physical contact.

"Agneta," he said softly, "the decision to deliver in a hospital is entirely rational. It is the right thing to do."

"And if I die in childbirth? You would be free again, and you could live your life as you wish."

He recoiled as if I'd slapped him. "Enough nonsense! I want these children to come into the world hale and hearty. And for you to come through the ordeal unharmed. You must not think otherwise."

I didn't know what to say.

"In any case," Lennard said as he got up. "I will stay by your side, as I promised." He turned and went back to his desk.

64

I felt I was teetering on the lip of a volcano. I had the impression I was getting stouter and stouter, and my feet were often so swollen, my ankles simply disappeared.

In early March Dr. Bengtsen told me to make my preparations, for I could go into labor at any time. I wanted to stay at Lion Hall as long as possible, caring for Mother and tending to estate business, but eventually I realized that the risks increased with every additional day of delay. I made an appointment with Professor Lindström, who generously offered me a suite in the hospital guesthouse, used most of the time by affluent family members of the seriously ill.

I thanked him and told Lennard that evening. "We will have to go there soon. Do you think it might be possible?"

"Of course. Everything is running smoothly. Lasse is doing a good job of overseeing the stables. And I believe we have already taken care of the most important correspondence concerning our estates."

"Yes," I said. I'd written so many letters in recent days that my fingers had cramped.

"And in a moment like this, business is not so important." Lennard lost himself in musings.

We set out for Kristianstad with Lena a couple of days later. I felt an odd pulling sensation in my gut as the coach left the manor behind. Not from the babies; it was deep-seated panic, the fear of never seeing Lion Hall again. If something should go wrong during delivery . . .

I turned my gaze to Lennard. He'd promised to stay at my side, but I'd rather he took me into his arms and comforted me. He spoke of the upcoming births with detachment, like a physician wanting to reassure me but unable to do so because of the distance between us. Earlier, when we'd still been friends, he'd been far warmer. My confession in the Ekberg Manor garden had altered him.

The guesthouse was adjacent to the hospital, though fortunately it didn't have a view onto the hospital courtyard. There was a small garden in the back, and since the upper floor of the two-story building was empty, we had the place to ourselves. The garden wasn't particularly impressive in early spring, but traces of greenery were emerging here and there from the damp earth.

I positioned myself on the sofa most of the time, in a posture I'd worked out with lots of trial and error. Professor Lindström and Dr. Neumann, head of gynecology, visited to examine me every other day. They listened through their stethoscopes and agreed that there were unquestionably two heartbeats. What was more, both babies were strong and healthy. But I could see the physicians were concerned about me. I heard them conferring with Lennard in hushed voices, and not long afterward, he let me know that one of the babies was not positioned favorably.

"They say this is not unusual with twin births," my husband informed me. "And perhaps the child's position will change. We shall simply hope for the best. Right?"

He gave me an awkward, standoffish hug, making me want to scream in frustration. Why had he come at all? His presence was more of a punishment than a help. Lena was the only person with whom I felt at ease. She chatted about the books she'd borrowed from our library, and she shared her dreams of traveling around the world someday.

One evening I woke suddenly. I'd rarely been able to sleep through the night recently, because the twins pressed against me and kicked, making it difficult to breathe. I stared at the ceiling, my eyes open wide, but nothing seemed to have changed. I worked my way out of bed. My back ached, and I had to sit on the edge of the mattress for a moment, waiting for my dizziness to pass. I saw stars before my eyes, as if I'd been knocked in the head. But after a while the vertigo subsided.

Lennard lay deep asleep on the couch. Even here, living in close proximity, we hadn't made the time to discuss things. The phantom presence of Max made that impossible. I studied Lennard's face. In sleep he resembled the young man who'd wandered through the woods with Hendrik and me. But he was much more now, a grown man. And my husband. Would he have become my husband if things had been different? Why hadn't I recognized how good-hearted he was? What a good husband he would make?

I'd dreamed of love, a passionate, raging love at first sight. But now I saw that another type of love existed. One not based on passion but upon reliability, friendship, shared memories . . .

I reached out, longing to ruffle his hair, but suddenly a pain shot through me, as intense as if I'd just been stabbed. For a second, I thought someone had done just that, but I realized that the pain came from inside. I cried out at a second savage jab. Warm liquid trickled down my leg and wet the carpet. Was it blood? The next stab sent me to my knees.

Everything happened with blinding speed. Lena was with me an instant later, and Lennard was helping me up. I told him I was in labor. Lena was too upset to be of any use, so Lennard had to help me into my dress. He threw his own clothes on, draped a coat around my shoulders, and we left the guesthouse.

I was glad the hospital was right there. Lennard held me up as we crossed the paving stones. Every step was torture. Successive waves of pain overwhelmed me. Never before had I experienced anything like this. In the hospital at last, Lennard maneuvered me onto a bench and rang for the night nurse, who appeared moments later.

"My wife is in labor," he said. "Inform Dr. Neumann and Professor Lindström!"

The nurse started to protest, but when she saw her patient was Countess Lejongård, she rushed away.

The place smelled of carbolic acid and medication. It reminded me of when I was here to visit Hendrik. Was his ghost hovering over me? The thought of my brother's presence, the notion that he was watching, gave me some reassurance.

Lennard came and sat beside me. "They will be here right away." He was nervously rubbing his hands. "You can bear it, for soon it will be over."

I gave him a crooked smile but couldn't get a word out, for another wave of pain took my breath away.

I desperately longed for Lennard to hold me, but he sat, rigid and unbending, staring at his palms. And I was too proud to beg.

Dr. Neumann appeared. "Good evening. If you would please follow me? I will examine you once more before we go into the delivery room."

"May I accompany her?" Lennard's request astonished me. Why did he want to go into the delivery room?

"Very sorry! You must wait here."

I was glad to hear it, for I did not want him present for this. Lennard sank into his seat. I looked back; he was nervous and concerned.

In his consulting room, Dr. Neumann asked me how I was feeling and how frequent my contractions were. He ran his fingers lightly along the surface of my belly, then pressed firmly with both hands several times. He checked between my legs. His frown of concern didn't escape my notice.

I doubled up in pain again but eventually managed to speak. "Is something wrong?"

"One of the twins still seems misaligned. I would like to get Professor Lindström's advice." He rang, and the nurse appeared. "Is the professor here yet?"

"He arrived a second ago."

"I must consult him immediately."

Lindström appeared in the doorway, and the two physicians conferred outside. I didn't try to hide my fear. When they returned, Lindström looked just as worried as his colleague.

"Tell me, Countess, how do you feel?"

It was a moment for black humor. "Like a balloon about to burst?"

Lindström's smile wasn't convincing. "We must act quickly and accelerate delivery. As my colleague told you, it looks as if they are not correctly positioned. One is blocking the exit, if I may express it so crudely."

Now I was the one unable to smile.

"A natural childbirth would be extremely risky. I recommend a Cesarean delivery."

"An operation?" I asked in a panic.

"Nothing to worry about," Neumann said. "You will be under general anesthetic and will feel nothing."

"Anesthetic?" I repeated, even more terrified.

"That just means you'll be asleep during the operation. We will administer Veronal, a medication that will render you deeply unconscious for a time, so you will feel no pain."

"Is it dangerous?"

I saw the physicians exchange a glance. "If administered incorrectly. But we are experienced. I guarantee you we know what we are doing."

I took a deep, shuddering breath, then tried to continue breathing despite the heavy weight on my chest. "If I die, what then?"

The doctors made no effort to deny that possibility.

"We will do everything in our power to ensure that doesn't happen," Neumann said.

Lindström added, "But if it does, we will concentrate on saving the children."

A bitter laugh rose in my throat. I managed to stifle it, so that the physicians heard only a guttural moan. I tried to calm myself.

"You should speak with my husband," I said. "He has the right to know."

"Of course."

"Good," I said finally. "If he does not object, we will elect to do a Cesarean delivery." I knew Lennard would accept the doctors' recommendation. "In any case, I believe I am strong enough to withstand it. I place my full confidence in the two of you."

Both Lindström and Neumann looked relieved. They'd probably feared I would insist on delivering naturally. But I'd grown up on a horse farm. I knew how difficult it was to give birth and how many things could go wrong. I'd seen how horrible it was when a foal had to be turned, and I didn't want to submit myself to that agony.

Soon afterward I lay in the operating room in the strong glare of an overhead light. The physicians had summoned additional nurses. I felt terribly naked beneath the hospital gown and horrified by the thought of exposing my body to all these people. But the waves of pain were accelerating, and this was no time for modesty.

The professor leaned over me. I saw a large syringe waiting on a tray.

"I am about to have you inhale a little ether to dull the pain," Lindström said as he ejected air from the barrel of a syringe. "Then you will receive this medication. You will feel nothing, and when you awaken, you will be the mother of two healthy children."

"I wish you could guarantee me that," I said. "If I should die, tell my husband that I am sorry. He will understand."

The physician nodded and showed me a mask attached to a tube. At first sight, it was terrifying. It was emitting a strange odor. Almost as soon as it touched my face, my vision blurred, and all sensation faded away. I heard the professor saying something, but I couldn't make out the words. My world dissolved and became a void.

It's only a dream, but the eerie rocking seems undeniably real. I've been separated from my body, and I'm swimming toward the light, a harsh light, moving like a moth fluttering up into the operating lamp.

Just as the lamp is about to consume me, the world shifts and transforms, and I am standing in a deep-green meadow surrounded by dense underbrush. It looks like the meadow on my estate but somehow completely different. I turn in a complete circle. How did I get here? A figure emerges from the green depths and comes directly toward me. I know his gait, his hair, his smile.

Hendrik!

Am I dead? Is this how one encounters a loved one in the afterlife? Mesmerized, I observe the figure as it nears and then stops before me.

"Hendrik!" I say. But he doesn't move. With difficulty I get the words out: "I am so very sorry." I reach for his hand. "I wish you had known Father passed away. They wouldn't let me tell you. There was still hope for you then."

Hendrik smiles at me but says nothing.

"Does that mean you forgive me?"

Hendrik nods. Why won't he speak? Are the departed voiceless?

"You have a little daughter. Did you know?" I went on, bursting with news for him. "Susanna had your child. We could not take her into our family, but she is safe and healthy. And I will have children too. Two, in fact."

Even that news doesn't change my brother's expression.

I sob in desperation. "Hendrik! Are you angry? With me? With us? Please say something. Please!"

But my brother doesn't speak. Instead, he lifts a hand and pats my cheek. The last glimpse I have is his faint nod before something comes between us.

When I came to, everything around me was brilliantly lit. *Heaven has no hospital beds,* I told myself. I reached back into my memory, trying to sort things out. I recalled the doctors' decision to perform a Cesarean delivery. We'd entered the delivery room. I had no idea what happened after that. Darkness had swallowed up everything else.

And now I was lying here. As my vision gradually returned, I blinked, seeking details about the room. I saw a clock with the hands pointing to seven minutes after five. It was late afternoon. What had happened to my babies? Why weren't they here?

I spotted a cord lying on the bed. It was attached to a little bell. I wanted to reach for it, but at first I couldn't lift my hand. My heart filled with worry. Had neither survived? But the doctors had assured me their heartbeats were strong!

Panic gave me the strength to move my arm. After two failed attempts, I finally managed to grasp the cord. I didn't pull it; I just let my arm fall. But the bell rang. Just to be sure, I moved the cord once more before my arm sagged and rested limp on the covers.

The door opened, and a young nurse with a starched cap came in. She beamed at me. "Good day, Countess, I am Nurse Hilda. I will inform the professor you are awake."

"Wait!" I called. My tongue felt dreadfully heavy. Was this because of the anesthesia? Perhaps the chemical was still in my bloodstream.

The nurse turned back. "Yes?"

"My babies. Where are they?" I felt my heart flutter. She wouldn't tell me if the news was bad.

"Oh, they haven't told you yet?" Her eyes lit up. "You've brought two healthy young boys into the world. Your husband says he won't choose their names until he can consult you."

Their names! We hadn't even thought of that yet! Lennard's icy distance had so depressed me and memories of Max so obsessed me that we hadn't discussed names. Not once.

I pushed that bitter thought away and made room for joy. Two healthy sons! The continuation of the house of Lejongård was assured. No one but Lennard and my mother would know about the boys' paternity. A feeling of warmth streamed through me. Tears rose in my eyes. "May I see them?" I asked.

"The professor will be with you shortly." She disappeared.

I sank back against the pillows, unable to grasp the enormity of it all. I'd given birth to two sons. Without even choosing their names. I was seized with shame. Why hadn't I thought to choose names?

Echoing footsteps broke into my thoughts, and Professor Lindström appeared. "Greetings to you, Countess. How are you feeling?"

"Good, as far as I can tell. But very weak."

"Hardly surprising, for you lost a good deal of blood. I will give you medication to enhance and rebuild your blood supply over the coming days. But we can discuss that later, for congratulations are in order." He smiled broadly. "You have given two healthy sons the gift of life. Each weighs almost six pounds, quite exceptional for twins."

"But is that normal?"

"Normal, and very good, in fact. I am sure the two of them will give you much joy."

"When may I see them?"

"Right away. The nurses are wrapping them now to bring to you. You missed their first mealtime because you were asleep, but the next and all succeeding ones will be entirely your affair."

I had two healthy sons, and I had survived as well! Could I ask for more?

"Your husband was with you earlier. He wanted to see you as soon as possible," Lindström told me. "Unfortunately, you were only half conscious. I assume you do not remember."

I didn't.

"He was very relieved, in any case. As are we. We took the liberty of sending your lady mother a telegram. I am sure she was worried as well."

"Thank you, Professor." I was relieved the telegram hadn't been a death announcement.

Someone knocked.

"Aha! Those must be the nursery assistants." The professor opened the door. Two women entered, one middle-aged and the other young. Each was pushing a crib.

"Allow me to present the future of the Lejongård family."

An unimaginable wave of warmth swept through my heart. Aching and wounded as it was, that heart was still capable of experiencing a love nothing like all previous imagined loves. It shone like the sun and drove away every trace of bitterness.

The nurses carefully placed the children in my arms, two tiny bundles with dark-blond locks plastered to their skulls. They had tiny snub noses and were struggling feebly to wiggle free of their wraps. They had big, watery blue eyes, the color of springtime skies. Two little caterpillars that one day would turn into resplendent butterflies. Tears filled my eyes when I remembered Max's words. He had indeed come back to me in the forms of these two small creatures.

I pushed away that thought. Max's absence shouldn't poison this moment. These were my sons, two genuine Lejongårds! As I carefully caressed them, my breasts began tingling almost painfully.

"We can put them to your breasts if you wish," the senior nurse told me. "We gave them a wet nurse's milk while you were unconscious. But I see no reason for you not to give it a try."

She looked for the professor's assent. He nodded and went to the door. "I will look in on you later."

"Thank you!" I said in a faint voice and then went back to contemplating the miracles in my arms.

Later that evening, an older nurse came to check on me. The pain medication was gradually losing its effect, and I ached as if someone had cut me in half. But my legs were still there, and I could move them, even if I was reluctant to do so. Nurse Krista cared for me like a mother hen. She administered more pain medication and urged me to take some vegetable broth.

"Oh, you should've seen your husband," she said, trying to comfort me. "He was quite sick with worry. He paced back and forth and interrogated every nurse he saw. Some said they found him downright intimidating. When he heard you and the babies had survived, he collapsed in a heap, crying his heart out. The doctors sent him away to get some rest, for the poor dear was beyond exhaustion."

Was she really describing Lennard? The man I'd left in the waiting room, grim and controlled, the man who hadn't made a move to comfort me? That man had made a spectacle of himself outside the delivery room?

"Everybody could see how madly he loves you," the nurse prattled on innocently.

I had the feeling she must have witnessed a completely different man. Max, perhaps. *No,* I told myself. *Max isn't here. Forget him! He's been gone for half a year, with no sign, no explanation. He doesn't deserve you!*

That conviction gave me an unusual feeling of serenity.

65

Lennard came to me the following morning. He held a little bouquet of pink roses. He was composed, but his face couldn't hide the agony he'd gone through. His cheeks were hollow, and he had dark circles under his eyes. There was a gray sheen to his skin.

"Hello," he said with a faint smile.

"Hello," I replied, sounding not much more animated. I was still weak from loss of blood, and the medication didn't entirely eliminate the ache and tenderness in my lower abdomen.

"How are you?" Lennard offered me the flowers. "I found them in a shop two streets from here," he explained. "They're nothing special."

"They are the most beautiful I have ever seen." I put them to my nose. Their perfume reminded me of a warm summer evening suffused with the sweet smells of roses and fresh-ground wheat, fragrances that filled the garden and wafted through the windows of the manor.

I sat that way for a time, then handed him the flowers so he could have them put into a vase.

"The nurse told me you behaved like a wild beast," I teased him. "And they say you wept with happiness. Is that true? Or was she just making it up?"

Lennard took my hand. "It's true," he said. "When I heard how much blood you lost, I was about to take the doctor by the throat. But then he told me you survived, and I completely lost control."

"You wept. For me."

"I did." He lifted a hand and touched my hair; then he pulled it back as if he'd burned himself. He put his hand over mine again.

"Lennard?" I said.

"Yes?"

"Please, if you want to touch me, do not hold back. This awful distance between us drives me mad!"

His brows shot up in surprise. "I thought—" He blushed. "I thought you had no desire for such things."

"Oh yes! I do desire them. You have no idea how often in these last months I have longed for you to hold me. To comfort me. And kiss me."

I framed his face with my hands. "But I know I do not deserve you."

"Why not?" he asked. "I am here. I always have been. You never knew it, but I have loved you since you were just fourteen. I would lie awake, thinking only of you. I always knew you were meant to be my wife."

He pressed my hand, and his expression became woeful. "We were so close, your brother, you, and I. But I did not realize you could never feel the same way about me."

His words squeezed my heart to the breaking point. I suddenly recognized his yearning and my selfishness. Lennard had married me when others would have abandoned me. *Had* abandoned me. Michael hadn't been ready to share the burden of my inheritance. Max had preferred to go to war instead of stay with me. The men I'd thought I loved trampled my heart underfoot. And Lennard, the friend of my youth whom I'd never wanted as a lover, unhesitatingly placed his heart at my feet.

I was bad, so terribly bad. And even though he would have insisted otherwise, I hadn't deserved him. I would never deserve him. But now

I felt something else. Something I'd overlooked in my longing to hear from Max.

"Perhaps, just perhaps, I am beginning to feel the same way. It is such a torment that things between us have been so cold. I want them to be different."

Lennard couldn't believe it. "Truly?"

I nodded. "Yes, truly. All these months—your attitude hasn't encouraged me to fall in love with you, but now, when I look at you, I realize something within me has changed, nonetheless. Or, rather, I see those feelings have always been in me. I just did not recognize them."

Lennard was transfixed. Then he bent and kissed me properly for the first time since we stood before the altar. And I felt the change within, real and genuine. The wedding kiss had seemed false, but this one was warm and tingling, and it made me feel a bit tipsy.

"There is a problem," I said after we released one another.

"A problem?" he asked in alarm.

"We have not discussed names for our children."

"Good Lord, we forgot that!"

"We were so wrapped up in mutual unhappiness, in pointless brooding, that we forgot the most important thing."

"Their names," answered Lennard, painfully moved.

I reached out and did what I'd wanted to do the night before giving birth, before the contractions had overtaken me. I gently stroked his hair.

He almost flinched but then allowed it. An uncertain smile flickered over his face.

"How would it be if we named them after our fathers?" I proposed. "Thure and Gustav?"

Lennard thought for a moment, then shook his head. "We should not burden them with the fates of their grandfathers. Those could be middle names, though."

I reflected. What names would be right for these children? I knew nothing about them!

"How about Magnus and Frederik?" Lennard asked.

Frederik sounded too much like *Friederike*, and I wanted Max's wife to have nothing to do with my life. "Perhaps Magnus and Hendrik?" I replied. If not Father's name, then why not that of my brother?

I saw Lennard wasn't enthusiastic.

"I think of my departed friend often, but I'd prefer not to be reminded of him every time I look at my son."

My son. My eyes filled with tears. All the pain, all the exasperation I had put him through, and yet he spoke so naturally of his son, confirming that love meant more to him than blood. My heart almost overflowed. "Do you remember our game? About your ancestor Ingmar the Viking?"

Lennard pondered, and then his face lit up. "Yes, that time in the woods, by the big boulder."

"What do you say to Ingmar? Ingmar Gustav and Magnus Thure?"

"Those are splendid names," he replied. "I will inform the nurses immediately."

"We can tell them together when they bring the children. Will you stay with me until then?"

Lennard gave me a smile and settled onto the chair. He kept my hand in his, kissing it from time to time, and he seemed very happy.

66

I was discharged from the hospital with instructions to have Dr. Bengtsen visit regularly to monitor my healing. August was waiting with the coach. His hair was as tousled as always, and his coat hung loose as if he'd lost weight. The sight of the two baby boys in our arms brought tears to his eyes.

"'Tis a shame your sainted father can't be here to see them. He'd have been right proud of ye."

"Thank you, August. You're very kind. How is my mother?"

"Ah, she's filled with joy as well. She's looking to give a little reception in your honor, Marie tells me. But don't let on I told ye."

"My lips are sealed," I replied. I managed to climb into the coach with difficulty. Lennard handed me Ingmar. My tiny one squirmed and shrieked mightily, but everyone had assured me his colic would pass with time. Magnus was in Lennard's arms and chose to sleep through his first trip in a coach. He'd been the calmer of them from the very first. August shut the door for us and climbed up onto his box.

As we left Kristianstad behind, I turned to Lennard. "What do you really think about these automobiles?"

He grinned. "My mother calls them 'stinking coaches from hell'!"

I laughed aloud. "Yet another subject your mother and mine agree upon. But what is your opinion? It seems to me it could be lovely to cover the distance to Kristianstad or to your estate in far less time. Perhaps we two could even learn to drive!"

I'd read in the newspaper that, in other countries, women were being trained to drive motorcars. That was part of the war effort, allowing them to provide for their families at home as well as supporting their husbands and sons at the front.

"I suspect you would be quicker to learn than I," Lennard said with a smile. "But to tell the truth, Chamberlain von Bergen's coupé really has impressed me."

"Well, let us review our finances, and if circumstances permit, we can get one," I replied, my eyes twinkling.

"But what of August? Do you intend to encourage him to drive a thing like that?"

"Hmm . . . I expect he would not care for it."

"Nor would he be pleased to find himself replaced," Lennard pointed out.

"But surely he has earned his rest after all these years?"

Lennard nodded. "You are right about that." He wrapped an arm around me and kissed me.

The sun shone brightly as we approached Lion Hall, as if reassuring us our home was now safe forever. Ingmar waved one hand as Magnus woke briefly and squinted to shut out the bright light. Whenever the coach rolled through a shaded area, he opened those eyes and looked at me. Ingmar was cooing. I knew humans changed over the course of their lives, but one could already see that Ingmar was the livelier of the two. Magnus seemed more disposed to contemplation. I studied them, thankful there was little of Max to be seen in them, at least not yet.

The coach passed through the looming gateway and up the drive. There were still no leaves on the trees, but green had begun sprouting on the ground. Snowdrops had pushed their little heads up through last year's growth alongside the first crocus flowers, still closed as yet. When we came to a stop, the entire staff was arranged on the front steps. Miss Rosendahl and Mrs. Bloomquist pressed handkerchiefs to their eyes. Even Bruns seemed choked up.

We descended from the coach. A murmur ran through the assembly, and the group broke into loud applause. My mother was nowhere to be seen.

It was thoughtful of her to be planning a reception to celebrate the births, but that wasn't necessarily a sign she was delighted with the turn of events. Would she be as unmoved by my sons as she'd been by Hendrik's daughter?

Miss Rosendahl and Bruns came to us with congratulations. I looked around and saw Lena's eyes were red with weeping. I felt close to tears myself, for the staff's enthusiasm touched me deeply.

Mother appeared at the front door. She wore a beige dress, and her hair was pinned up as if she were on her way to a formal reception. Our eyes met. She came down the steps.

"Welcome back," she said and gave me a kiss on the cheek.

"Look, Mother!" I said. "This is Ingmar Gustav, and Lennard is carrying Magnus Thure."

She didn't deign to glance at them. "Enchanting. Really," she said. "But come in. I have already arranged for their cradles." She turned and walked ahead of us.

I looked at Lennard, who furrowed his brow.

Together we followed my mother, and I found it hard to hide my disappointment. Any other grandmother would have swept the children into her arms or at least given them a good look. My mother was treating them as one more task to be gotten out of the way.

I'd arranged the nursery before our departure for Kristianstad. I'd decided to use my father's former room, for it was adjacent to ours.

The maids had bedecked both cradles with lace-covered pillows and cute little blankets. A bureau and changing table stood next to them.

Delicate curtains of white and blue hung from the windows. The dark-blue carpet muffled our steps. A hint of lavender hung in the air, for Marie and Lena had gathered lavender flowers the previous summer and sewn them into sachets. As we surveyed these arrangements, it nonetheless seemed to me this room would keep my little ones too far away.

"Perhaps we should let the children sleep in our bedroom at first," I said to Lennard, "so I can respond quickly when they are hungry."

"I already told you to get a nursemaid!" my mother cried.

"Bruns, please have the cradles brought into the master bedroom," I said, overruling her. I already knew I didn't want someone else taking care of my children. Though the doctors had insisted I rest over the upcoming weeks, I believed I was capable of fulfilling my maternal duties.

Bruns bowed and left the room. He returned a couple of minutes later with two young men. The distinct smell of soap told me he'd insisted they wash their hands thoroughly before being allowed to approach the cradles.

They carried the baby beds into our room, one after another, and we settled the infants there. Magnus slept on, and Ingmar was too tired after the trip to resist.

"I assume you both would like to rest." Mother turned away. "We will have time to discuss things at dinner." She left.

Lennard turned to me, his face a mask of surprise at her behavior.

"I hope your mother will be more pleased than mine," I said and hugged him.

"Mother is on her way here, certainly beside herself with joy. But surely your mother must be pleased. Perhaps she feels somewhat over-taxed at the moment."

No, she considers these babies the bastards of an adulterous father, a voice said in my head. *That may be true,* I thought, *but it is equally true they are Mother's grandchildren, just as I am her daughter.*

"I hope you are right," I said. "It will be unbearable if my children's grandmother cannot stand them. My father's mother was like that, grim and gloomy. I believe you met her once, not long before she died."

"Not that I can remember." Lennard pulled me close and kissed me.

"You can thank your lucky stars for that. She was the most joyless human being I ever knew. Severe, a stickler for the Bible, never seen to smile. Hendrik and I were afraid of her."

"Who knows what miseries she may have had to endure? My grandmother was quite warmhearted. She was forever spoiling me."

"Well, your mother is sure to spoil them, at least." I felt a pang of guilt every time we spoke of his mother, who had no idea these boys were not her own flesh and blood. "Thank you," I said. "For everything."

"No, it is I who should thank you," Lennard said. "You have given me two wonderful boys. Nothing else should matter. Ever again."

I nodded, despite my doubts.

"We actually should rest for a bit," I said, checking the twins again. They would wake me if they needed something, so I sank down on the bed, glad to be able to put my mother's disappointing reaction out of my mind, if only for a moment.

After a somewhat awkward coffee hour that afternoon, during which Mother's thoughts seemed to be elsewhere, I went into the office. Lennard was in the kitchen, consulting with Mrs. Bloomquist and giving her details about his mother's favorite dish.

Letters were stacked on the desk, and files stood in tidy rows on the shelves behind. The sunshine threw glimmers of light across the carpet. One day I would show all this to my sons and teach them how to run Lion Hall. Of course, if they took after me, they'd probably want nothing to do with it. And if they took after Max . . .

No! I refused to think of him. He'd forfeited every right to my heart, and now I'd found other kinds of love. Perhaps he was no longer even alive. Boregard would have notified me if he'd located him.

I took a deep breath. The office had reminded me of Max, and I didn't want that. And besides, I felt strongly drawn back to my children. I wanted to be with them, to thrill at every breath they took. Work could wait. I left the office and went to the bedroom.

I'd left the door slightly ajar, but now it stood wide open. I heard gurgling. The boys were awake again. Was Lennard with them?

I pushed the door open and couldn't believe my eyes. Mother was seated on the edge of the bed with both babies in her arms. She was whispering to them and rocking them, fully focused on their little faces. She smiled and didn't notice I was there.

I stood rooted to the spot, my hand to my mouth. My eyes grew moist.

She sensed my presence and looked up. To my amazement, her smile didn't disappear. "I just wanted to take a look at them," she said almost apologetically. She made no move to get up.

"You cannot imagine how much I wished for that," I replied. "Before, when we arrived, why did you not show some sign of excitement?"

Stella's face filled with pain. "I'm sorry. All I could think of was your father and Hendrik. I heard Thure's name, and—do you know what day this is?"

I searched my memory and then it clicked. Two years! The following morning, two years would have passed since the flaming roof of the horse barn collapsed onto my father and brother. In the excitement and joy of homecoming, I'd completely forgotten the date.

"All day long I've been haunted by the fact that tomorrow marks the anniversary of the fire that caused their deaths," Stella said. "It is such a blessing the children were not born on that unholy day."

I took Magnus and sat beside her. "It seems so long ago now." I ran a finger across Magnus's tiny cheek. Ingmar had his hand wrapped tightly around Mother's finger, as if he'd never let her go.

"And for me it seems like just yesterday," my mother responded. "My heart broke when I saw these babies and realized Thure will never see his grandchildren. He will never know his family and estate are safe and secure. And Hendrik would surely have been delighted to know his nephews."

"Two men were taken from us," I said. "But now we have received the gift of two others. Someday we will tell them about their grandfather and their uncle."

Mother nodded, doing her best to hold back tears. "Lennard told me how you almost died. He said you lost a great deal of blood."

"Perhaps so; I wasn't aware of it. But under the anesthetic, I had a dream. I saw Hendrik in a meadow. He came to me and looked at me. I asked him to forgive me for not telling him Father was dead, and he nodded. Then he patted my cheek and—then I woke up."

"Your brother was watching over you. And so was your father, even if he did not appear."

I nodded. I was more than willing to believe Father and Hendrik knew what was happening in our lives. Of course, that meant they'd witnessed all the dark times as well, but now they saw that life at Lion Hall continued through good times and bad. I studied my boys' faces for a while, then looked at Stella. "No one can change what's happened, but what if you and I seek a new beginning?"

Mother gave me a searching look. "Would you be ready to start over? You know that life on this estate means responsibility, not freedom."

"Perhaps responsibility is a different form of freedom and happiness. How about you, Mother? Can you overlook the fact that your daughter is not perfect?"

"I thought you were the perfect child when you were born," she said, gently rocking Ingmar in her arms. His little eyelids slid slowly shut. "You were so incredibly beautiful, and I put all my hopes on you. But then you grew up and became a woman. My hopes never went away, but I must admit that they were not realized. Perhaps it is wrong to expect so much from a creature who is still so tiny." She looked from one grandson to the other. Her smile was pained. "You are my daughter, and you will always be my daughter. And these are my grandchildren. I will learn to put up with your obstinacy."

She looked directly at me. "In any case, I am very proud of you. So, yes. Let us make a new beginning."

67

"Don't forget to tell Lena to bring your sunbonnet. Otherwise you'll be brown as a peasant by the time we get back."

I almost sighed in exasperation. "Mother, our trip to Åhus is a week away. Lena will have everything packed by then. Including the sunbonnet."

After the royal couple's brief visit in August, we'd taken some time and then decided to get away to our summer house in Åhus. Mother wasn't happy with this because she thought the estate needed our full attention. But she eventually gave in. Her heartbeat was sometimes irregular despite the digitalis, and the sea air was sure to do her good.

"One must always let the maids know what to pack well in advance," she insisted, standing in her dressing room as she selected clothing for the trip.

I noticed garment bags in the back of the wardrobe. Several months earlier Mother had instructed the maids to pack our mourning clothes with mothballs. They hung there, dark and grim, and I hoped they would remain in that obscurity as long as possible.

"I promise to give them a detailed list. Do you need me for anything else?" I'd always hated being surrounded by piles of unpacked clothing. "I would like to look in on Magnus and Ingmar," I added. "They probably do not remember me."

"Fine, just go. Your elderly mother will handle this all by herself."

By herself was something of an exaggeration, for Linda was stationed somewhere in this abundance of batiste, silk, and brocade, waiting to tend to her mistress's whims.

I left the dressing room and hurried upstairs. The boys had learned to crawl entirely too quickly. No tablecloth was safe from them, so I'd instructed Bruns to tie the edges to the table legs. It didn't look at all elegant, but it meant we didn't have to worry that our tots might yank a bowl of steaming sauce down on their heads. I stopped where the door stood slightly open and peeked in at the nanny and the two boys.

Rosalie had been with us for several weeks. She got along splendidly with the twins, playing with them as if they were her own. In moments of infantile crisis, she sang to calm them. I'd had my misgivings at first because of her youth, but those had proven unfounded. I was eager to join their activities.

Magnus and Ingmar were puzzled by the wooden building blocks Lennard had fetched for them from the Ekberg nursery. His mother had kept them as souvenirs of Lennard's childhood, and it delighted us all to see they'd be put in use again.

Much had changed over the previous six months, including the relationship between Lennard and me. We had come no closer physically, but that was due to Dr. Bengtsen's warning of the dangers of another pregnancy while my uterus was healing from the Cesarean delivery. He'd advised me to avoid becoming pregnant for at least two years.

After that, I was determined to give Lennard his own child. There was absolutely no doubt he regarded Magnus and Ingmar as his own, but I saw he wanted more. A little girl, perhaps, to restrain her two brothers. But that was all to come, imagined future music I heard only faintly as I opened the nursery door at last.

"Oh, gracious mistress, I didn't hear you at all!" Rosalie scrambled to her feet and gave me a proper little curtsey.

"I just wanted to look in on those two. It looks as if they are not ready for their midday nap."

"No, they've been too busy playing. But Magnus is starting to look tired. I'll put them to bed right away."

"Excellent. Be careful not to let these little charmers take you in!"

"Truly, they're hard to resist. But it's for their own good."

I took Magnus into my arms. He really did look tired. Their characters hadn't changed over the last half a year. His brother had all the energy, while Magnus was the snuggler.

"Perhaps you should give a thought to what you would like to pack," I said as I put Magnus down and picked up Ingmar. He gurgled happily and grabbed a lock of my hair. I had to be careful to keep him from yanking it.

Rosalie would accompany us to the seaside, as would Lena and Linda. Mrs. Bloomquist would have gladly come, but she was needed at the estate to feed the staff and the stable boys. We'd make do with a replacement cook. Lennard had already threatened to do the cooking himself, but we weren't quite ready to trust him to that extent.

"I won't take much. Three dresses and my books. I don't need anything else."

That genuine smile, framed by dark-blonde hair—the men in Åhus wouldn't be able to keep their eyes off her.

"If you wish for anything else, tell me. Miss Rosendahl is going to Kristianstad tomorrow to take care of the last arrangements."

Rosalie gave me another of her sunny smiles. "Thank you very much, gracious mistress! I have all I need."

I was impressed by her simple self-sufficiency.

Together we put the twins to bed. Rosalie seated herself between the cradles to keep watch. I gave each of my little boys a kiss and continued upstairs to the bedroom I'd occupied as a girl. I stretched out on the bed.

At that moment my eyes fell on something I hadn't thought of for a very long time.

My old easel leaned forgotten against the wall, almost hidden by the curtains. The smears of paint had darkened, and the wood was now dry and drained of color. I got up and pulled it out. The hinges squeaked as I set it up. It looked a bit unsteady, but it would still serve. My fingertips began to tingle. How long it'd been since I'd held a brush! Recently, I'd caught myself staring at outdoor scenes and trying to pick the colors that would suit them on canvas.

I stroked the wood and felt a strange excitement. The sea was certain to offer wonderful views. Even though I'd given up my studies, I couldn't have lost all my talent. What if I just gave it a try? If I let the images take hold of me and set them free again with my paintbrush?

"Well, now, what is this?" Lennard asked several days later when I carried the easel into our bedroom, where the trunks waited, already packed.

"An easel!" I responded with a laugh. He'd often seen me seated in front of one when we were young, especially on his last visit before my abrupt departure to Stockholm.

"And what do you plan to do with it?"

"Use it as a clothes hanger."

"Now, now, teasing is not polite."

"You deserve it, with a question like that. I plan to paint, of course."

"But I thought you had given that up for good?"

"Perhaps I was a bit hasty. The sea awaits us, along with its splendid sunrises. I admit that recently I have been tempted to dabble again." I set the easel down by the trunks. "Do you think we can find canvas somewhere in Åhus?"

"Certainly. And no doubt they have paints available for ambitious young artists." Lennard pulled me onto his lap. "Have you often regretted giving up your art?"

"Yes, I have. But I swore never to paint again. I already told you what happened with Michael."

Lennard nodded. We'd had many long discussions over recent months. We'd finally become a true couple. Granted, the fiery passion of young love wasn't part of our experience, and perhaps it never would be. But we had one another, we trusted one another, and we supported each other. I'd learned that marriage was more than just love and passion; it was also trust, confidence, and friendship.

"I have not missed the paintings I destroyed in Stockholm. But now that everything is falling into place, I have begun to feel attracted once again to paints and the smell of linseed oil and turpentine." I looked at him. "I could do annual portraits of our children. Every year until they're grown."

Lennard was amused. "No doubt they would be delighted to show off such a picture gallery when they give their guests the tour of Lion Hall."

"You forget that paintings do not have to be large. They can be small; a mother can keep miniatures in her desk drawer. Our sons might come across them and find them terribly funny." I leaned against his chest. "I would so much like to paint again."

"Then indeed you must. I will see you get everything necessary."

"You are a darling. Thank you." I kissed him and looked back at the easel with a smile.

The notion of a little portrait gallery had settled firmly in my heart.

68

I went into the office one last time the next day before forcing myself to deal with travel arrangements. The incessant stream of mail would continue, but I could bring the most important items with me. One of these items was from a man in Stockholm who'd seen a photograph of Evening Star published in a breeders' magazine; he was inquiring whether I might be interested in helping organize a horse racing circuit. Our stallion had completely recovered from his illness, and the veterinarian saw no reason not to clear him for breeding.

I was reluctant to devote attention to horse racing, considering that this never-ending war was raging its horrible, bloody way across Europe. I intended to reply that Lion Hall would participate only after peace was restored. I didn't know if Evening Star would be up to it, in any case. And I didn't want to race the horse born on the same day my brother died. The animal deserved a pleasant, quiet, and—above all—long life.

The lead article in the daily newspaper was about the ebbing enthusiasm of the German people for the war. I pushed it aside. The euphoria of August 1914 had resulted in the loss of hundreds of thousands of lives. How many more would die? How long could this madness continue?

I looked around the room, and my gaze settled on the landscape I'd carried home as the only souvenir of my days in Stockholm. The tempest threatening Lion Hall had not entirely disappeared, but I was glad that after these turbulent years we'd come to a period of relative calm.

I turned my attention to the pile of correspondence and found an envelope I'd almost overlooked. I froze at the sight of the return address. It had been half a year since I'd dispatched Hanno Boregard to search for Max. With everything that had happened since then, I'd almost forgotten.

I stared at the envelope in my hands for a while and then threw it down on the desk. Did I really want to know what had become of Max?

I had a very pleasant life now. Lennard's devotion to the boys was total, and my mother was calmer and more approachable than ever before. I still felt responsible for her illness, but her loving expression when she regarded the twins warmed my heart. The frozen shell around Stella the Ice Queen had shattered to reveal a kindhearted woman. I had no idea how my sons had brought about that transformation.

And now Max threatened to intrude. I hoped Mr. Boregard had sent nothing more than an invoice, but I had the feeling there was more. I hesitated, tempted to open it, but then decided against it. Max had hidden so much from me, and who could guess what might come out now? Did I really want to blight my stay at the seaside with the contents of that letter? No, I certainly did not. If Boregard had taken this long, his letter could wait. I would open it when we returned. I placed it in the same drawer where I'd discovered Father's promissory note. Then I turned to the rest of the mail.

That afternoon Mother sent Linda to summon me to her bedroom. In recent months, she'd gotten into the habit of sleeping for a while in the early afternoon and then having coffee in bed. The drops had strengthened her heart sufficiently to allow her to resume her daily routine, but she found herself slow to revive after rest.

I walked in to find Mother presiding over the room from her bed like a queen on a throne. A gold-rimmed coffee service stood on the small wooden tray across her lap. The coffeepot was only half full, and a few crumbs and a dab of fruit jam were all that remained of the croissants Mrs. Bloomquist had baked that morning.

"Hello, Mother." I pulled up the small chair and seated myself by her bed. She wouldn't tolerate it if I tried simply to perch upon the edge. "How are you feeling?"

There was a rattling sound as she took a deep breath. She'd had that worrisome rattle for three months now, and the medication had done little for it. Perhaps the dose should be increased? I would consult the doctor as soon as we got back.

"I wish I could tell you I feel like a young filly, but that unfortunately is not the case." She studied her hands for a while, then looked up at me. "I would like for you to do something for me. You alone."

My eyebrows rose. She'd made several little requests of me in recent weeks, but her tone suggested this was something particularly significant.

"And what is that, Mother?"

She reached out and opened the drawer of the nightstand. She took out something with a metallic glint. "Here."

"A key?" I accepted it, but my expression must have been puzzled.

"To a safety deposit box at the bank in Kristianstad. Not at Commerce Bank but at a private institution. I will give you the address. I would like for you to bring me the metal box you will find there."

"What's in it?" I asked, surprised. My mother had a secret locked away in a bank vault? I'd always thought her heart was the place where she kept her secrets.

"I will show you when the time comes," she answered. "Please bring it to me. Today or early tomorrow, if you can. This is important."

Her gaze was so earnest and insistent that I could do nothing but nod in agreement.

An hour later I climbed into our new motorcar with the address of the Arnulf & Wenders Bank in hand. Like the one Count Bergen had driven on his visit to us, it was a Packard Touring car but a newer model that one could drive either as a covered vehicle or a roofless convertible. Neither Lennard nor I had taken the time yet to obtain a driver's license, but our chauffeur, Tjorven, knew all about the vehicle.

This acquisition was made in conjunction with August's retirement. Not that he departed without complaint, but he was now living contentedly in the village with a widow and received a monthly stipend from me.

The vehicle was capable of a good thirty miles an hour, so I was in Kristianstad in only half an hour—a great relief considering the coach had always taken at least twice as long. Mother still considered the vehicle a devilish contraption, but I was sure she would soon get used to it. I enjoyed the trip, in any case, especially the way the wind blew my hair as we roared through the countryside. I often let Tjorven take a longer route, just to prolong the sensation. During that day's ride, I took out the little key and turned it over in my palm. Why did my mother want that little box? Why now? It seemed unlikely there was only a piece of jewelry or some such object inside. But the contents must be extremely valuable, for otherwise she wouldn't have kept them hidden under lock and key.

The bank was on a nondescript side street and looked nothing like a financial institution. I had to ring for admittance. Things were clearly set up so that not just anyone could enter. An elderly gentleman soon peered through the half-open door. I held up the key for him to see.

"My name is Agneta Lejongård. I have been sent by my mother, Stella, to fetch something."

The man scrutinized me and then took the key. He inspected the number engraved upon it, and then he opened the door. "Come inside." He returned the key to me.

I stepped through the doorway onto a carpet that looked as if thousands of feet had shuffled over it.

"I am Arvid Wenders, one of the proprietors," he introduced himself. "What is it your mother wishes you to collect?"

"A metal container. She says that it is in a deposit box."

Wenders nodded. "Fine. Let us take a look." He beckoned.

We entered a small room with a counter. It was completely deserted, and there was no sign of ordinary banking activity.

"Tell me, please," I asked Wenders as we walked down a corridor, "what kind of bank is this?"

"You are surprised to see the counter room so bare, I suppose."

I nodded.

"Well, we used to be an ordinary bank. But the time came when my father saw we had no future as such an institution. He had to decide whether to close the business or change it fundamentally. He decided to lease space in the vault where clients could store whatever they wished."

He smiled conspiratorially. "We safeguard not only objects of value and documents but other things as well. Our clients lock up whatever they wish to keep safe."

"Are you aware of the contents?"

Wenders shook his head. "No. Our policy is that the contents do not concern us."

"Suppose someone were to store the confession to a murder?"

"Then the world would learn of it only when the owner so desired."

"And what happens with deposit boxes that have been abandoned? If no one is paying the rent for them anymore?"

"They are destroyed. Along with the contents. No one ever looks inside."

A massive reinforced steel door blocked the end of the corridor. Wenders opened it with a special code, turning the dial several times and alternating directions too quickly for me to make out the numbers. The vault door swung open with a quiet click. The walls of the room behind it were inset with many small rectangular doors. They reached all the way to the ceiling.

"If you will be so kind as to lend me the key?"

I gave it to him.

He went inside and looked around. After a moment, he stepped to the left and opened a door all the way at the bottom of the installation.

I wondered how long the box had been stored there. Were the oldest deposits located lower or higher in that imposing steel wall? A lock clicked open. Seconds later Wenders turned to me with a metal container in his hands. It struck me that destroying such a contraption would be quite a challenge.

"You open this inner receptacle with a key," the man said, handing me a pair of keys similar to my mother's, though considerably smaller. "We retain your key until you return the container. If you retire the contents and wish to give up the deposit box, simply deliver the container with appropriate instructions." He placed the box in my hands.

It was heavy, but that might be because it was made of steel. Or maybe there was something heavy inside it.

"I thank you very much," I said and allowed him to escort me out.

It was already dusk by the time we got back. I shed the touring coat I always wore in the automobile, and I carried the container to my mother. She was tucked away in the salon, for our custom was never to have the evening meal until every family member not traveling elsewhere was seated. I'd gotten quite hungry, as evidenced by my growling stomach.

"You sound like a bear," Mother said without looking up from her solitaire game.

"I have the appetite of one. But first, here is your box." I stepped forward and placed it next to her cards.

"Thank you," Mother said without affording it a look.

"What now?" I was consumed by curiosity. "You are not going to open it?"

"No," she answered. "Not yet. First I have to prepare myself."

"Prepare? Is there something terrible inside?"

"Terrible? No. But there are things I need to consider while we're at the seaside."

"And will you tell me about them someday?"

"When the time comes." My mother put away her deck of cards. "But now we should have something to eat." She got up and led me to the dining room.

I wondered why she hadn't opened the container. But then I remembered Boregard's letter. I hadn't opened that either.

Should I wait until we returned from the seaside? Or take it there? If I decided I didn't want to know, I could throw it into the sea. Or into the fire on the hearth.

69

The fresh Baltic breeze met us as we climbed out of the motorcar. Tjorven dutifully held the door for us. Mother was a bit green around the gills.

"Are you all right?" I asked as Lennard helped her out of the vehicle.

"I will never accustom myself to this dreadful speed!"

"Of course you will. Besides, a little bit of excitement stimulates the heart. You heard what Dr. Bengtsen said."

"That doctor talks just to hear himself talking."

I followed and took my babies from their bassinets in the back seat. Lena and Linda were waiting for us. They'd left for Åhus by train early the previous day, accompanied by Rosalie, who now already had Magnus and Ingmar in her arms.

The house had changed little since our last stay. The paint was flaking a bit in places, but otherwise, the caretakers, a married couple, had everything well in hand. The rooms were airy and smelled gloriously of the sea, which was a stone's throw from the terrace. Our villa stood on a gentle hillock with a splendid view of the Baltic. Vacationers strolled along the sandy beach as fishing boats sailed past. Crowds were thin, for we were toward the end of the bathing season.

"This place is gorgeous," Lennard said. "We should have come much earlier."

"Yes, it would have been a fine place for a honeymoon," I said, watching Mother intently instructing Linda. "Perhaps someday we'll make up for that."

He smiled. "Once the boys have grown up a bit, we can travel, just the two of us. Here or somewhere else."

"That would be lovely."

We devoted the next two days to soaking up sunshine.

Lennard procured paper and a painter's kit for me, just as he'd promised. Paints and linseed oil were in just as short supply here, as was painter's canvas, but I didn't mind. I used watercolors, which I considered perfectly appropriate for the seaside. On my sketch paper I evoked the waves, tracks in the sand, washed-up mussels, and the red- and green-colored pebbles of the beach. I didn't take a formal approach; I simply followed my instinct and watched the images emerge. I was expressing my feelings rather than trying to capture reality.

And I spent lots of time with my little boys, sweet, calm hours feeling their warmth and taking in the precious smell of their bodies.

On the third evening, after a wonderful dinner of fish fresh from the sea, Mother took me aside. "Would you care to have an after-dinner schnapps with me?"

"Certainly! Though you know you ought not be drinking late in the evening."

"I myself am not interested. But you will probably need some when you hear what I have to say."

We waited until everyone had gone to bed, even Linda, Lena, and Rosalie. I'd told Lennard I needed to discuss some things with Mother and there was no need for him to wait up. Mother seated herself with me in the small salon, a pale imitation of the one at Lion Hall. The fresh scent of the sea streamed through the slightly open kitchen window, making candle flames flicker, and we wrapped ourselves in woolen blankets. She'd placed the container from the bank on the table. Like a reliquary.

We sat without speaking for a long time. Stella was musing; I was expectant. She seemed to be questioning her decision to reveal her secrets to me, but at last she leaned over, unlocked the box, and lifted the lid. As far as I could see, it contained only a small packet of letters and a locket. I shivered.

"I stored these things in Wenders' vault many years ago to keep them from prying eyes. I could have burned them, of course, but I did not want to lose what I once had. And now at the end of life I want to make a clean breast of it."

"You are not going to die," I protested, throbbing with anxiety. Why was she saying such a thing? "The doctor said—"

"The doctor is simply trying to reassure us. His medicinal drops are palliative, but I sense my heart is not healing. It will fail one day, and I will be gone. I will probably pass away in my sleep. Rather than just leave you a key, a deposit box, and a puzzle, I have decided to explain."

"And what is the explanation?" The thought that she might die raised a storm in my breast. I couldn't bear the thought that she might leave me. Not now!

"Love!"

Her declaration broke through my haze of alarm. "Excuse me?"

"Love," she repeated. "A short-lived, passionate love, one I could not resist."

An affair? Mother? When? Surely before she'd married Father . . .

"I know what you are thinking," she went on. "Or at least I have an inkling of it." She paused briefly as if inviting comment, but I had nothing to say. "When I heard you were with child, it reminded me so much of my own situation. Everything I once experienced came back to me." She stroked the package of letters with a strange, nostalgic expression. She picked up the locket.

"Your own situation?"

"Your father had a serious riding accident the year after Hendrik was born. A horse threw him and trampled him, nearly crushing his pelvis. His life was on a knife's edge for a very long time. Thure was in a coma, and gangrene set in. He did recover, but he was bedridden for six months. I was overjoyed he had survived, and I had no thought of any consequences. All I wanted was a second child, a brother or a sister for Hendrik. Preferably a sister, for I wanted no competition for the firstborn. But no matter how we tried, I did not become pregnant."

A sudden intuition took my breath away. My face flushed and stung, even though the schnapps stood untouched before me.

"The physicians suggested that I was to blame, of course, wanting to spare Thure. They speculated that something had gone wrong at Hendrik's birth but found nothing to substantiate that theory. So they declared that Thure's accident had so traumatized me psychologically that my fertility was affected. But I knew the real reason."

She opened the locket and pondered the portrait of a young man with blond locks and a dainty mustache.

"The king visited us, and Alexander was part of his entourage, an adjutant to the chamberlain. They were there for our fall hunt, that rowdy, confused event you know so well. During that stay—well, we fell head over heels in love. Alexander was younger than I, but he had eyes only for me. We threw ourselves into bed together while Thure was away in the village with some of the guests. We even managed to have a second assignation before Alexander had to leave. He promised to write." Mother gazed directly at me. "Perhaps it is time now for a drink?"

I shook my head. My heart struggled in my breast like a captive sparrow, and my gut knotted in apprehension, but I paid them no mind. I was trying to imagine the breathtakingly beautiful young Stella of that distant day.

"Tell me more," I begged.

"A few weeks later I noticed I was not menstruating. I had already borne a child, so of course I recognized the signs. I was panicked to discover I was pregnant. I had slept with Thure in the meantime, even though I was tormented by guilt and thoughts of Alexander. I suspected the child was not Thure's."

I stared at Mother as if she'd just slapped me. For a moment, I couldn't move, and my voice failed me. The shock transformed me into a pillar of salt.

I couldn't believe it. Father and I resembled each other so much, and our preferences were so much alike!

"Are you sure?" I asked. "Father could just as well have—"

"I am absolutely sure that it was not his seed that made me pregnant. A doctor finally tested your father's fertility when you were five years old. After that we took separate bedrooms."

"Did Father know?" I asked in a strangled voice. My pulse pounded in my throat.

"Perhaps he had his suspicions, but he never voiced them. In any case, he idolized you. You were his last child, and you and Hendrik were his hopes for the future. Perhaps now you see why he was so dismayed when you insisted on going to the university and breaking with Lion Hall. He had expected you to become Lennard's wife, even then."

Without realizing it, I had blundered my way into fulfilling Father's wishes.

I needed a few minutes to absorb Mother's revelation. I pushed myself to my feet and paced back and forth. My surging blood roared in my ears. The parquet floor creaked underfoot, and outside the sea wind howled.

My father was not Father but instead a man named Alexander. And Mother had hidden it from him! At least with Lennard I'd laid all my cards on the table. I did so precisely because so much was at stake: my life, my mother's, the reputation of Lion Hall, and more. If Father had indeed suspected, wasn't it that much more significant that he chose to take that knowledge to his grave? This new information filtered fitfully through my consciousness, presenting itself to me again and again. Father was not my father. Mother had had an affair. Stella, the perfect dowager countess, above all reproach? My mother, cold as a fish, had thrown herself after a wild passion?

Neither of us found anything to say for a long time.

My mother wasn't the same woman I'd known a couple of hours before. Suddenly I had a glimpse of her as a wild creature, as passionate in bed as I'd been with Michael and Max. The old proverbs couldn't be denied. The apple never falls far from the tree; like mother, like daughter.

Why hadn't she told me long before? Why hadn't she been more understanding? Had I aroused painful memories? Had she wanted to shield me from a guilty conscience?

Was I now obliged to see Father differently? Maybe not, for I could never call anyone else my father. Father had taught me to ride and had comforted me when I'd fallen, and the battles of my youth were waged with him. I'd had only him. I had not loved any other man as I had Father.

"What happened afterward?" I finally asked, returning to my chair and sitting absolutely still. My voice seemed to come from somewhere far away. My heart still raced, and my hands trembled.

"We corresponded for quite a long time. He sent me a locket with his portrait and pledged he would return. I no longer remember if that promise thrilled or terrified me. But if my emotion was terror, it soon eased, for there was no threat; Alexander was assigned to the far north. He married the daughter of a landowner, a man with a huge estate. He wrote me one last time simply to say we would probably never see one another again. That was the end of it."

Mother was finding this very hard to say. She lifted her chin and looked me straight in the eye. I saw glistening tears, tears of guilt and tears of loss.

"When you obviously fell in love with that man, I saw myself in you. I knew what you were feeling, but even so I wanted to rip him out of your life. More than once I told myself to go confront him and order him to leave Lion Hall."

My eyes widened. She'd denied it before, but had she in fact caused Max to flee?

She answered my question before I dared to ask. "No. I had nothing to do with his disappearance, and I have no idea where he is. Things did not improve even after he finally left. Oh, I was relieved—until you told me about the pregnancy and the wedding plans. When you said you were hiring someone to search for him, I was beside myself. I was angry at both of you, but, really, I was still angry at Alexander. For months I had dreamed of escaping with him, but then there was the woman he married . . ." A tear trickled from her eye, trembled on her left cheek, dropped, and broke on the back of her hand. "I thanked God every day that rascal had left you in peace. Believe me. I did not want you to go through the torment of learning he loved another."

I grabbed Mother's trembling hand. It was ice-cold. A deep shudder passed through me.

"I know he has another," I said. "His mother wrote. He gave me a false name and hid the fact that his wife was waiting for him in Pomerania."

"I am not surprised in the least."

I grimaced and shook my head as if trying to dislodge my thoughts. "It is over. No one can change anything now. I wanted an explanation, but I do not want it anymore. I know where I am and who I am."

Mother pressed my hand. "I am very glad to hear that. But I know human hearts are fickle."

"Perhaps, but you stayed with Father, after all."

"I did. And in the years that followed, I learned to love him anew. His death devastated me far more than the news of Alexander's marriage."

I clasped Mother's hand, put it to my cheek, and held it there. "And what about the contents of the deposit box? Are you going to put them back in the vault?"

"I have not decided." She stroked my hair with her free hand. "Perhaps I will take them with me to the grave. Or I might burn them all. Now you know the truth, and my conscience is clear. That is what I wanted, more than anything."

After that we each drank an aquavit, mostly to ward off the chill. We sat in silent contemplation for a while, but eventually gave in to our fatigue.

We rose and left the salon together. Mother carried the small steel box under her arm. Would she deal with the contents right away or was that decision too difficult just then?

I hadn't yet come to terms with the knowledge that I was the daughter of another man. What did it mean? Did it come down to the fact that a true father is the man who takes care of the child and loves that offspring unconditionally, regardless of parentage? Did I have any desire to meet my biological father? Did he even know I existed? Probably not, considering how Mother had kept her secret. Would I tell Lennard? Or would it be better not to burden him with this?

"Good night, Mother," I said at the door of her bedroom.

I sensed Mother was relieved and in a new state of peace. If death should come to claim her, she could yield with an unburdened heart. I hoped that would not be soon, not now that we'd finally reached one another.

"Good night, Agneta. Until tomorrow morning." She disappeared into her room.

I waited a moment longer before the door, then turned and walked the length of the corridor.

In our room I found Lennard dozing in the armchair next to the cribs.

My men, I thought with great affection. I undressed and went to bed, where I stared at the beams overhead for a long time.

70

A strange dream woke me early the next morning. I'd imagined the ceiling overhead as a great weight laid across my soul. I slipped out of bed, put on my morning robe, quickly checked Magnus and Ingmar, and left the bedroom. I stumbled a bit, like a sleepwalker, but I knew exactly what I was going to do. I'd prepared myself, just as Mother had prepared to open her box of secrets.

I'd slipped Boregard's letter into my trunk's secret compartment shortly after my return from the bank. I took it out and went to the kitchen. I lit an oil lamp, found a knife in a drawer, and settled onto the clean-scrubbed bench that smelled faintly of lemon.

The night without moon or stars was black beyond the windows. I saw nothing in the panes except my own indistinct reflection. The image of my morning robe reminded me of the ragged robe of Max's great-grandfather. Had Max made up that story?

I picked up the knife with an unsteady hand and took a deep breath to calm my pounding pulse, with little effect. I felt a twinge deep in my abdomen, and the roaring in my ears left me almost deaf. I imagined myself perched on the edge of a precipice as howling winds threatened to hurl me into the void. I slid the blade under the flap and slit the envelope open.

Nothing happened. I was still there, seated at the table, the lamp flickering beside me. My ice-cold fingers extracted the typewritten sheets.

Most esteemed Countess Lejongård,

No doubt you have been expecting my report for some time. I regret that I have not been able to write before now. The search for Hans von Bredestein turned out to be an extremely challenging task. I believe he used various identities to make his way to the German coast. When I did finally discover a trace of him, he was long gone.

I suspected he had called upon Count von Kranitz. When I enquired further, I learned that the count had been brought back from the front because he was severely wounded. It was not possible to interview him because his injuries had left him confused and unable to speak.

An enquiry to his regiment brought no results. No Max or Hans von Bredestein was known. No Von Bredestein had been on the count's command staff.

Next I called on the Von Bredestein family. His wife, Friederike von Bredestein; his father; and his twin brother had no idea where the subject might have gone. The family reported him missing in early summer of 1913, and the police found no trace of him despite their best efforts. The family's last contact with him was before a trip to Stockholm undertaken on his father's behalf. The only other information provided by the family was a letter from you, the contents of which you will certainly recall.

I then sought information in various other locations, including all the ports in the Stockholm region. None of this being successful, I turned again to the military authorities. There also I encountered various obstacles. I was referred from one regimental office to another, none of them able to suggest who might help.

I came across one ambiguous clue about three weeks ago. It seems a man giving his name as Max Breden volunteered for an Austrian infantry unit more than a year ago. His description was not unlike that of the subject. I made further enquiries.

I eventually located the unit and was able to interview soldiers who had carried out a bloody attack at the Stelvio Pass in northern Italy. They were greatly affected by the experience. They told me Max Breden was among the fallen. He was shot through the head and died instantly.

I gasped and put one hand to my mouth.

I cannot establish with absolute certainty that this individual was Max or Hans von Bredestein. These given names are common in Germany.

I will continue my efforts if you wish. If I have no further instructions from you upon my return to Stockholm, I will send my invoice in the coming weeks.

Wishing you the best in the meantime,
With great respect,
Hanno Boregard
Vienna, July 28, 1915

Bewildered, I stared at the report. So had Max really gone into the army? I recalled reluctantly his increasing enthusiasm for the war. His comments had been off-putting, but at the time I was too blind and too much in love to challenge him. It was entirely possible he'd thrown himself into the tumult of war. And plausible he'd have given a false name.

I'd told my mother I no longer wanted an explanation. But the truth was that I wished Boregard had been able to confirm what had happened. I sensed that, without the certainty of closure, Max would haunt me for a very long time.

I will continue my efforts if you wish.

Did I want him to continue? Would it lead to anything? Hans von Bredestein was obviously a master of disguise, capable of eluding any effort to capture him. In some ways, his thirst for freedom reminded me of my younger self. But I was wiser now.

No, I would tell Boregard to desist, and I'd leave it to fate. I knew who I was: Agneta Lejongård, the mistress of Lion Hall.

After staring at the typewritten sheet for a while, I rose and left the house.

The sea breeze was sharp that morning. Waves crashed on the beach. I walked out to the end of the nearby pier where the wind whipped around me. I pulled the letter from my pocket and regarded it for a time. With an ache in my heart, I ripped the report and the envelope into the tiniest pieces I could and flung them into the wind. They disappeared into the air and the waves.

Lennard was waiting for me when I got back to the broad porch. He'd noticed I was missing but had the discretion not to pursue me. He'd simply waited patiently, once again. I climbed the steps, went to him, and embraced him. Should I tell him about the letter?

No. It was better for everything to remain as it was. Max was gone, probably forever. He would never learn of his children; he would never make any claim upon me or them. Our secret, the one I shared with Lennard and Mother, would be safe.

We looked out at the sea for a quiet moment, at the vast, dark, moving surface that had swallowed up the letter.

"You took a stroll?" my husband prompted.

"Yes, I had to put my thoughts in order."

Lennard's gaze was indecipherable.

I looked back at him. "You know, I really love you!"

Lennard was puzzled for a moment, but then he smiled. "Six months ago, I would never have dared to dream such a thing. But I must confess I see it now."

"Well, that makes me very happy," I said with all my heart, threw my arms around him, and gave him a passionate kiss. When I leaned back, he appeared astonished.

"We still have a little time before Mother and the children wake up," I said.

"Are you sure? But the doctor told us—"

"No need to worry. There are things we can do that pose no risk." I smiled at him.

Our hands intertwined, then I pulled him with me to the bedroom. Our lips found each other again, and I knew in that moment that nothing in the world could be more marvelous than Lennard's body close to mine.

About the Author

Photo © Hans Scherhaufer

Corina Bomann is the bestselling author of *Butterfly Island* and *The Moonlit Garden* as well as a number of successful young adult novels. Her books have been translated into many languages and have been on bestseller lists in Germany, Italy, and the Netherlands. All the books in her Lion Hall trilogy went straight to the top of the bestseller list in Germany upon release. Bomann was born in Parchim, in northeastern Germany, and now lives with her family in Berlin.